First Winter Count

Jerry A. Sayre

For information contact :
Jerry A. Sayre
184 Snapp Bridge Road
Limestone, Tennessee 37681
www.jerrysayrebooks.com

Book and Cover design by Jeff DeHut
ISBN: 9798286803323

First Edition: May 2025

This novel is dedicated to the memory of my maternal grandfather, Owen Lester Clark. He encouraged my love of wild places, adventure, reading, and the American West.

Thanks, Pop.

Transitions

"For everything there is a season, and a time for every purpose under heaven."
Ecclesiastes 3:1

CHAPTER ONE
1500 Hours Local-Friday 25 September 1987
Southeast of Eagle, Alaska

Tragedy and death often arrive at the end of a long train of poor choices rather than following a single decision. When Jimmy took off from the fourth cache site and turned the De Havilland DHC-2 Beaver floatplane northwest, he saw a reflection at his right front as it passed along the top of the cockpit. Dropping the right wing a bit, he saw the source of the reflection. There was broken glass and crumpled metal in the trees below. The source of the reflection wasn't far off his course and wouldn't take more than a few minutes to investigate. He knew of several cases of downed bush pilots rescued because another pilot noticed their signal and came to help. He had time. Boone was probably having the time of his life, so he decided to investigate the source of the reflection.

He flew to the sight and put it off his left wing for an optimal view. He dropped altitude to two hundred feet and circled the area and saw dull, silver, crumpled metal, and another reflection of glass but no movement. If it was a crash site, it was new. Jimmy had flown around 1this area all summer and knew where the old crashes were. The closest landing site was an unnamed lake one half mile northwest of the wreckage.

He could land, walk over, and confirm what he saw in just a few minutes. He couldn't say beyond a doubt that what he saw was a downed aircraft, but he couldn't say it wasn't either. The trees obscured it enough to prevent a complete view from any angle. He couldn't confirm what he was looking at from the air. He tuned his radio to 121.5, the universal emergency frequency for aviation, known in military circles as the "Guard" frequency. He listened for a verbal

1

mayday call or the distinctive tone of an Emergency Locator Transmitter (ELT) beacon. Jimmy circled the site for several minutes, listening for a call or beacon but heard nothing. He decided if he were lying down there, injured in a crash, he'd want another pilot to investigate.

Jimmy set up on the lake for his approach. Once the pontoons momentarily slid across the water, he chopped the power and came to rest in under two hundred feet. He pushed the right rudder pedal to the stops and added power, taxied, killed the engine fifty feet from the shoreline, and coasted to the small beach. Jimmy stepped from the cockpit, walked along the pontoon, opened the cargo door, and retrieved the crash ax and the trauma kit. He stepped into the water and secured the floatplane with the pontoon bowline.

Sixteen minutes after landing, he stood next to the crash, except it wasn't a crash. It was what was left of an old trapper's cabin. The logs were completely deteriorated. The roof's metal was twisted in the middle of the pile, and glass that had once served as windows was strewn throughout the old cabin. Until that moment, Jimmy didn't know the cabin even existed. He was thoroughly embarrassed—it was a rookie mistake he'd keep secret from his fellow bush pilots.

He returned to the beach, secured the gear, untied the bowline, and pushed the big floatplane back from the shoreline. Once in the cockpit, he ran through a quick check, started the engine, taxied to the opposite end of the lake, turned the aircraft, did his final checks, and applied full power. As the aircraft started to come up on plane and skim the lake's surface, Jimmy glanced at the airspeed indicator just before rotation. His sight diverted from the water. He failed to see the obstacle that would kill him and put Boone Taggart in a fight for his life.

Jimmy was shocked when he felt the entire aircraft shudder hard as both pontoons contacted the granite rock three inches beneath the surface, instantly opening the right float its full length. The immediate introduction of hundreds of gallons of water and thousands of pounds of weight into what was left of the pontoon caused the plane to sit deeper in the water, and Jimmy instinctively pulled the yoke into his torso. His airspeed was too low, and the immediate weight of the water in the pontoon destabilized his take-off. The plane broke contact with the water, but for all the left yoke input Jimmy put in, he couldn't overcome the weight that pulled his right wing down.

The right wingtip dug into the lake's surface, cracked at the wing root, but stayed connected to the fuselage, causing four thousand pounds of plane and cargo to cartwheel. Jimmy's head snapped into the control yoke, knocking him unconscious. As the Beaver continued its death throes, the fuselage snapped off just behind the cockpit and sunk into twenty feet of water while the remainder of the fuselage and wings came to rest partly out of the water at the end of the lake.

James "Jimmy" Regan was crushed as the left side of the cockpit hit a large spruce tree at the water's edge. Two considerable failures had nagged him for the final fifteen minutes of his life. First, in his haste to investigate what he thought was a crash site, he failed to circle the lake he landed on to look for obstacles, and second, he failed to notify anyone where he dropped Boone Taggart.

CHAPTER TWO
1730 Hours Local-21 June 1958
Double A Ranch-Sheridan County, Wyoming

Luther One Knife was a man comfortable in his skin, a master of his environment, but he was unsuited for the present age. He entered the wood-paneled study where fourteen-year-old Boone Taggart sat in a leather chair, reading Bernard DeVoto's *Across the Wide Missouri*. If Boone couldn't be outdoors, his father's study was his favorite place on earth. His second favorite place was a similar study at his grandfather's home. He looked up from his book, pushing his chestnut hair out of his eyes, when Luther walked through the door, holding a cup of coffee and his meerschaum pipe shaped like an eagle claw.

"Pack your gear tonight and have it at the tack room before daylight. We leave at sunrise."

"Where are we going?" Boone said. Luther stepped to the porch for his evening smoke, ignoring the boy. Boone knew better than to push for too many details, and besides, he trusted Luther enough to know details weren't necessary. He trusted Luther in the same way he trusted his father and grandfathers.

Boone put the book in the chair, headed to his room, and prepared his bedroll, a large rectangular piece of canvas with a Hudson's Bay three-point blanket, a cotton sheet sown like a sleeping bag, and an old pillowcase that he stuffed his jacket into to form a pillow. He laid a single change of clothes and an old Army wool sweater on top of the blanket, then rolled it inside the canvas cover and tied it with a woven strap.

He took a small green canvas haversack from the bottom of his closet. He packed it with a small metal tin that included a fire-starting kit, his fly box, the binoculars Luther gave him on his previous

4

birthday, a flashlight with spare batteries, a brass Marble's compass, a small pair of pliers, and a sewing kit to make needed repairs. He sat at his desk, took his hunting knife and Boy Scout pocketknife from the center drawer, and honed each on an oiled whetstone. Once satisfied with the edge on both, he laid them next to the haversack. He tied his fly rod case to his bedroll and headed downstairs.

He walked back through his father's study, took his Winchester Model 94, .30-30 lever action rifle from the cedar gun cabinet in the corner, checked to ensure it was unloaded, then sat at the table in the center of the room, cleaned the rifle and returned it to the cabinet. Boone's last stop was the barn to check his tack. He rolled his oilskin coat and tied it behind the cantle of his saddle and checked the contents of his saddlebags, a roll of baling wire, fencing pliers and staples, a spare horseshoe with a few nails and hammer, first aid kit and a quart metal canteen that he filled at the spigot and returned to the bags. He finished his inspection as his father, Wade Taggart, walked through the tack room door with his saddle.

"Where you headed?" Wade said.

"I was hoping you could tell me," Boone said.

Wade smiled. "What're you talking about?"

"Luther told me to pack and check my gear. We're going somewhere in the morning, but he didn't say where."

"Well, I'm sure he's got a good reason," Wade said.

"You all are up to something," Boone said. "What is it?"

"Don't worry about it." Wade patted his son on the shoulder. "You'll have the time of your life, and if you're smart enough to stay quiet, listen, and pay attention, you'll learn a lot." Then he turned and left. Boone's gaze followed him.

The following day, in the pre-dawn darkness, Boone curried and saddled his favorite bay horse, Rebel. He tied him in the barn hall and helped Luther pack the mule with a canvas fly, bedrolls, lantern, and kitchen box. They made final checks, mounted their horses, and walked into the yard between the barn and the house, leading the pack mule. Wade stood on the porch watching the familiar scene with his father, John Marion Taggart.

"Wait here," Luther said, handing Boone the pack mule's lead rope. Luther touched his heels to the sorrel's ribs and rode up to the edge of the covered porch. Staying in the saddle, he talked with the two Taggart men, but Boone couldn't hear the conversation no matter how hard he tried.

Luther One Knife was an Ogallala Lakota. He was born sixty-one years earlier and grew up on the Standing Rock Reservation. His father was a child when the Lakota and Cheyenne fought the Seventh Cavalry at the Battle of the Greasy Grass in 1876, and his grandfather fought the battle with Sitting Bull and Crazy Horse. Luther transitioned the passing of his people's time by adjusting as best he could, in fact, better than many. He and Boone's grandfather, John Marion, became close friends in their late teens and had remained so over the years, although the details of their friendship were obscure. The elder Taggart treated Luther with unusual respect compared to how most of Luther's people were accustomed. One of Boone's earliest memories was his grandfather and Luther trouncing a gang of Sheridan street toughs for insulting Luther's mother.

Luther was the manager of the TF Ranch, John Marion's place, and the de facto manager of the Double-A Ranch, Wade Taggart's operation. He managed the cattle herd, developed a first-class ranch remuda, and took care of daily operations. He was the best horseman, hunter, angler, and woodsman that any of the Taggarts, all superb outdoorsmen in their own right, had ever known. The three men on the porch wielded immense influence over Boone. He loved and respected them.

When the secret conversation ended, Luther turned the sorrel, signaled Boone to follow, and they rode out of the barnyard. His father and grandfather waved, big smiles on their faces.

"They're all up to something," Boone said as he spurred Rebel, led the mule, and followed Luther.

By mid-afternoon, Luther and Boone set up camp deep in the Bighorn Mountains in the pine trees along a mountain stream. They strung a small canvas fly across a pole lashed between two trees, spread bedrolls, and collected water and firewood to last for several days. They spent the late afternoon fishing, catching an ample supply of trout to last the next two days. Luther watched Boone wield the

6

seven-foot fly rod like an expert, and he took great pride in how comfortable the boy was in the mountains.

When night fell, Boone built up the fire and sat against a tree, reading Zane Grey's *The Thundering Herd*. Every other page he glanced up to watch Luther cooking the two large trout.

"You're here for the same reason your father was at the same age," Luther said. "It's time to add to your education, the kind of training you won't get in school." He paused, stoked the fire and then continued.

"You're fortunate to have these opportunities. You have a family and friends who love you, your family is respected, and you can spend your time working in the mountains." Luther flipped the fish in the pan and then looked at Boone.

"Yes, you're a fortunate young man. You've learned things that most will never know, and the knowledge will serve you well, no matter what you decide to do. You're a good horseman and woodsman, a well-behaved, respectful young man. You're intelligent, and this week, if you chose, you'll transition to the next phase of life."

Luther turned his attention back to the fish. Boone didn't know what to say. When Luther looked at him, Boone gave a slight nod. Luther served the fish and the two ate in silence.

"After supper, get some sleep," Luther said. "It'll be a busy time."

The following morning, Luther shook Boone from a deep sleep. They brewed coffee, cooked fish, ate, and did the dishes. When they finished their camp chores, Boone's education took on a new flavor. Over the next fourteen days, the education and training Luther gave him was akin to drinking water from a fire hose. The days were long, as Luther led him through the mountains, educating him about flora and fauna, teaching him hunting and survival skills. The nights were equally long, sitting around the campfire listening to Luther's view of life and completing tasks he assigned.

Over the two weeks, Boone learned to build various shelters, each for distinct purposes and seasons, and fire lays for heat, cooking, and the Dakota fire hole—the fire below ground. He learned to set snares for small and large game, which plants were safe to eat, which were suitable for medicine, how to build a bow and arrows, how to chip flint into knives and arrowheads, the difference in a deer's track when running and walking, what high wispy clouds meant for tomorrow's weather, how to brain-tan hide into clothing and moccasins, how to make rawhide for cordage and repairing material, how to use camouflage and stealth to move through the woods unseen and unheard, and hundreds of other essential skills.

The passing of nineteenth-century skills to a twentieth-century boy was a matter of course in the Taggart family. Boone knew this. His dad told him his grandfather had chosen this tradition when he felt modernity pushed upon them as old ways began to fade. It was clear to Boone that Grandpa John Marion held to an ethos rapidly becoming antiquated in the post-war years of the United States. The pace of life quickened, technology increased, and traditions died. Boone knew the elder Taggart was trying to do more than pass a skill set to his grandson. He was attempting to ground him in an older culture.

His granddad was an old soul, so was his father, and he felt himself following the same path. They hunted for solace in an older, more traditional time and place—they were almost tribal. Boone's education was more than learning to hunt and survive in the open. It began the transition from boy to man. It was a display of reverence for millennia-long traditions. It was a means to teach respect, honor, and courage, traits treated as obsolete but traits that John Marion, Wade, and Luther still held in high regard. Boone knew they'd pass these time-honored traits to him, and hopefully, he'd pass them to his children.

On the morning of the fourteenth day, Luther walked into camp after cleaning the breakfast dishes.

"Pack your gear and saddle your horse," Luther said. "We're moving."

Boone did as he was instructed and four hours later, they rode into a high mountain meadow covered in wildflowers. Luther dismounted without saying a word and gestured for Boone to do likewise. Boone stepped to the ground.

The horses, trained to ground tie, stood in place munching meadow grass. Luther proceeded to explain the final test. Holding

8

Boone's canvas haversack open, Luther said, "Empty your pockets."

Boone pulled everything from his pockets: his journal and pencil, a brass compass, a pocketknife, his Marble's match container, and a pocketful of rifle cartridges. He placed them in his canvas haversack.

"Your wristwatch, too," Luther said.

He patted the boy down to ensure he wasn't holding anything back.

"Do you still have your hunting knife on your belt?" Luther asked.

"Yes, sir," Boone said as he put his hand on the knife his grandfather had given him the previous Christmas. Luther nodded and handed him a small tin container.

"Put this in your pocket," he said.

Boone put the small tin in the back pocket of his jeans.

Luther placed the canvas bag on the pack mule and retrieved a small piece of brain-tanned antelope hide. On the back of the buckskin was a hand-drawn map of the northern section of the Bighorn Mountains. He spread it on the ground between him and Boone.

"You're here," he said, pointing at the map. "Don't move from this meadow today. Camp here tonight and start moving in the morning."

Boone watched as Luther traced the route north with his finger.

"Be at the confluence of these streams, in three days," Luther said pointing to another place on the map. "If you aren't there by sunset, walk home."

Before Boone could speak, Luther tied Rebel's lead rope to the pack mule, mounted, and rode away. Boone stood alone in the wilderness for the first time in his life.

One mile south of the alpine meadow where Boone prepared his overnight camp, Wade and John Marion met Luther.

"Well, how did he take it?" John Marion said.

Luther laughed. "About like his father," he said. "Confused. I think he thought I was going to come back and get him. He just stood there and watched me ride away."

Wade smiled. "There's no better family tradition than

9

harassing teenage boys," he said. "What's the plan from here?"

"You two take the pack mule and Boone's pony and go make camp," Luther said. "I'll shadow him until he's within a few miles of the rendezvous and then meet you at camp."

Wade took the lead of the pack string and turned back down the trail.

"See you in three days," John said.

Luther turned back up the trail and rode to within one hundred yards of Boone's camp. He dismounted and watched the boy from the shadow of the trees.

***

Boone watched Luther and the pack string disappear into the tree line.

"He left me here alone," Boone said out loud.

He stood for another minute, hoping that Luther would return. Realizing this wasn't a terrible joke, he searched for a place to spend the night. It didn't take him long. One hundred yards from where they dismounted, Boone found a perfect spot to build a shelter. Satisfied with the location of his overnight home, he sat next to the alpine lake on the north side of the meadow and inventoried the contents of the tin Luther had given him.

It included three fishing hooks, fifty feet of fishing line, a small flint, a steel striker, and three pieces of charred cotton cloth. He set three lines in the water and walked around the lake looking for anything he could use. He found two old beer cans and a quart-size beer bottle, which he washed and used to boil water. By sundown, he caught a few small trout, started a fire with the flint, steel, and char cloth, built a debris shelter, and was ready to sleep. It had been a long day, and he was exhausted. He cut a strip from the bottom of his flannel shirt and made six new pieces of char cloth for later. He sat at the fire and studied the map as the darkness crept down the mountainside.

He was familiar with this area. He'd hunted many times in this country. He was sure he knew the stream confluence where he was supposed to rendezvous, and it would take most of the three days to traverse. He'd be up and moving as soon as it was light enough to travel. He drank a quart of water before going to sleep. His dad used the same technique on hunting trips. He'd often said, "You don't need an alarm clock. Just drink water before bed, and you'll have to pee before daylight." Boone filled the bottle again, set it in the coals to boil, and nestled into his shelter.

His dad's technique worked like a charm. He woke up in the pre-dawn twilight and barely made it out of his shelter. After relieving himself, he stoked the fire, drank more water, and checked his fishing lines. There was one trout that he cooked and ate. After a breakfast of broiled trout and lake water, he retrieved his fishing lines and poured water on his fire. He checked the coals with the back of his hand, ensuring it was cold and no coals would come to life in the wind. He rechecked his few survival items and moved south as soon as it was light enough to walk.

When Luther saw him put out his fire, he moved deeper into the trees.

Luther shadowed Boone from a respectful and safe distance. It was sneaky to do to the boy, but it was a time-honored technique that allowed him independence with assistance nearby, even though the victim didn't know it. Luther's father and grandfather had done this for him, and he'd passed it on to Wade and now Boone. The young man would figure out many years later that Luther was watching him all along, but for now, the ruse was complete. The experience would give Boone confidence without more risk than he could handle. Boone was doing well, and Luther felt pride in the young man he'd helped to train and mold. He was honored that Wade and John allowed him this opportunity with another generation, probably the last.

On the evening of the second day, Boone was three miles from the rendezvous, moving down a ridge toward the stream that led to camp. Watching, Luther could tell Boone had decided that he'd traveled far enough for the day and would camp near the stream. He positioned himself in the trees downstream on the opposite side of the creek.

Boone walked out of the trees into the clearing beside the stream and it was clear to Luther that he couldn't see the large boar bear walking upstream behind a snag of flood-washed trees one

11

hundred yards away. Luther pulled the Winchester Model 1886 from his saddle scabbard, chambered the 45-70 cartridge, placed the fore stock over a limb, and followed the bear's movement.

Boone and the bear saw one another at the same time and stopped. Several seconds passed as they eyed each other, then Boone moved first. He put his hands above his head, started talking to the bear in a clear, strong voice, and slowly stepped back up the ridge. Luther smiled with pride when he saw that Boone had judged correctly. The bear was just walking beside the stream. No recent kill was nearby, no cubs, just a bear moving from one place to another. Luther kept the sights of his rifle on the bear, watching Boone wisely give the bruin the right of way. The bear backed away from Boone twenty feet, crossed the creek, and trotted upstream. Luther took a deep breath, cleared his rifle, and placed it back in its scabbard. Boone moved another fifty yards downstream and set camp for the night. Luther watched him until he laid down in his shelter and slept.

At the end of Boone's journey, the three most influential men in young Boone Taggart's life watched from the edge of the camp as the young man walked the last two hundred yards.

"Would you call that a walk or a strut?" John Marion asked.

"Yeah, we may have created a monster," Wade replied.

"It's okay," Luther said. "We'll teach him humility, too. It's all part of the process."

The three men met Boone at the stream's edge, embracing and congratulating him on a well-done job. That evening, they sat shoulder to shoulder around the fire while Boone regaled his mentors with stories of his quest. As he started the bear story a second time, his grandfather interrupted.

"The bear's a little bigger this time, son."

"Wait to see how big it is when he tells his mother," Wade said.

Boone took the teasing in stride, and when he finished, he listened to their stories until he faded into sleep. It was a night that Boone would never forget, nor would the three men who shared camp with him. The older men passed on their wisdom about honor, courage, duty, and manhood. They were leading Boone from boyhood into the ranks of men. He wasn't a man yet, but he had the essential underpinnings to becoming a good man.

CHAPTER THREE
1600 Hours Local-28 December 1958
TF Ranch-Sheridan County, Wyoming

Boone stood in the kitchen and watched Luther walk from his cabin to the tipi lodge in his backyard. He lived in the contemporary world but maintained the trappings of his history and culture close at hand. Once Boone saw the smoke waft from the opening at the lodge's top, he filled the thermos with hot chocolate, pulled on his wool coat and hat, and walked across the yard. He stopped at the lodge's entrance.

"Luther, can I come in?" Boone asked.

"Yes."

Boone pulled back the canvas flap that served as the lodge's door and entered the growing warmth. He paused and allowed his vision to adjust from the sun's glare on the snow to the relative darkness inside the lodge. He was amazed at how efficient this lodge was during the depths of the Wyoming winter. Luther had tied a second canvas layer on the inside of the lodge from the ground to about five feet height and packed straw between the outer and inner layers. Boone removed his jacket and boots.

"It's amazing how comfortable this lodge stays," Boone said, looking around.

"They were even better when they were made of buffalo instead of canvas," Luther said, shrugging and adjusting the hide he held in his lap.

"What's in the thermos?" Luther said.

"Hot cocoa. Want some?"

Luther held out his mug. "That's a silly question, son. Just pour."

With his newly charged mug in hand, he returned to his task,

14

painting small pictures on the soft hide of a tanned steer skin. Luther One Knife was putting the finishing touches on the annual Winter Count.

"Did I make the cut this year?" Boone asked.

Luther smiled without looking up.

"Yes." He shifted the hide in his lap and pointed to the picture of a young boy facing a bear beside a stream.

Boone smiled.

"Thanks, Luther. That means a lot. The last time I made the cut was when I was born."

"That day with the bear was a sort of birth, too, don't you think?"

Boone was pleased that Luther, his father, and his grandfather viewed him differently since the summer trip, particularly the bear encounter. They treated him less like a boy, they expected more out of him, showed him greater respect, and he carried himself in such a way that allowed for more responsibility and duty. He was handling it well, without complaint or failure. He was happy with the new arrangement, and they displayed their pride in him. That pride, earned, not given, was essential to Boone. More than anything, he wanted to be like these men.

Luther had prepared a Winter Count as long as Boone could remember. This annual ritual was just one of the many ways Luther honored his people's history and culture. Boone thought it sad that the count had to be painted on cowhide instead of buffalo. It was just another reminder of the transition that the Lakota people endured, but Boone was thankful to be exposed to the tradition and was honored to be memorialized in this Winter Count.

Luther taught Boone that every great civilization records its history in some fashion. Many First Nations of the North American Great Plains did so in the annual Winter Count, which were long-standing cultural practices among all the bands of Lakota, Dakota, Blackfeet, Mandan, Kiowa, Hidatsa, and Absaroka people. Shamans and elders decided which of the year's events would be recorded. A single artist would then record the events in pictographs on bison hide. The Winter Count recorded the year's significant events: war and peace, drought and flood, planting and harvest, pandemics, and birth. The Winter Count wasn't an interpreted history. It was a narrative story of the events, good and bad, that impacted the people. It was the personal history of a band or even a family, and it was revered.

Boone watched Luther paint silently, but when he extended his coffee mug for more cocoa, Boone took the opportunity to ask a question.

"Why do you paint it in a circle?"

"The Whites think time moves along a line," Luther said. "The Lakota believe it moves in circles. What has happened will happen again. Not in individual terms, we won't have this exact conversation again, but life has cycles, and those cycles rest on a large wheel. We'll all grow old and die, and we'll all have health and sickness. Civilizations will rise and fall, war and peace, and so on. Unfortunately, we seem not to learn much from our past." Luther paused a moment and smiled. "Especially Americans."

"You're lucky, Boone. You were born into a family that values their past, and they wanted me to teach you mine. You'll benefit from both educations but understand that you'll transition through many periods of your own life. It won't go exactly like you plan, making it interesting. Understanding your people's history will help you transition from one time to another."

They sat shoulder to shoulder, Boone watching the fire silently, Luther painting on the hide. Boone stood to leave.

"Thank you, Luther."

"You're welcome, son."

CHAPTER FOUR
1053 Hours Local-Sunday 30 April 1975
Saigon, South Vietnam

The commander of the Russian-made T-54 tank in the column's lead saw the ornamental gates of Doc Lap, the Presidential Palace.

"Don't stop," he told his driver through the tank's intercom system.

The tank's mass and speed collapsed the gate. The commander glanced to his right and saw several ARVN soldiers standing under a small stand of trees, but he knew instantly, just from their demeanor, they weren't a threat. They were waiting to surrender. He ordered the driver to stop, disconnected the intercom connection from his helmet, reached below the commander's seat, and retrieved something. He jumped from the commander's turret, then to the ground, and ran to the entrance of the Presidential Palace, waving the yellow and red flag of National Liberation. Within moments, he stood on the palace roof, cut down the flag of South Vietnam, and raised the flag of the Democratic Republic of Vietnam. It was just after 1100 hours.

The tank commander walked down the palace's steps to guide his crew through the compound's security and nodded to the colonel walking up the stairs toward the entrance.

The colonel had an unlikely role in the war. Due to the strange circumstances common to all wars, he was the highest-ranking military officer in the Presidential compound.

He stepped into the second-floor conference room and stopped in front of General Minh, the most recent and last president of South Vietnam. The General extended his hand.

"I've been waiting since early this morning to transfer power to you," he said.

17

"There is no question of your transferring power," the colonel said. "Your power has crumbled. You cannot give up what you do not have."

A burst of automatic weapons fire startled Minh's staff.

"Our men are merely celebrating," the colonel said. "You have nothing to fear. Between the Vietnamese, there are no victors or vanquished. Only the Americans are defeated. If you are a patriot, consider this a moment of joy. The war for our country is over."

The colonel turned, left the room, walked down the hallway to the presidential suite, sat at the desk, and composed a short dispatch to his higher headquarters, reporting the fall of the Presidential Palace and the surrender of the apostate government. As his pen scratched across the paper, he reflected on his thirty years of fighting—he remembered the Japanese occupation of his youth, the French occupation, and his first taste of combat. He recalled his unit's victory at Dien Bien Phu in 1954 and the defeat of French colonialism. He considered the Geneva Accords of 1954, when Western influence forced a divided Vietnam. He reflected on the arrival of the Americans and the continued struggle that led to this moment. He handed the dispatch to an aide, walked from the building, strolled to a nearby park, found a small grassy spot in the shade, lay down, and closed his eyes. He wondered if this was his final war.

1635 Hours Local - Saturday 29 April 1975
Walden Lake-Fort Richardson, Alaska

He set the hook as lightly as he could but missed the fish. She felt the canoe shift slightly, quickly retrieved her lure, and cast the half-ounce white Rooster Tail into the growing concentric rings. Within three revolutions of the Zebco 33 reel, she connected with the two-pound trout her dad had missed just seconds before.

"Got him," she screamed.

She fought the trout for a couple of minutes, maybe to make her dad think it was bigger than it was.

"Is it a grayling, Dad?" A trophy grayling was on her Alaska fishing bucket list, and she'd yet to connect.

"Nope, sorry, it's a rainbow," Boone said as he netted the fish from the back seat of the canoe. The battle was over. Boone was exceedingly proud of his daughter's angling prowess. He constantly bragged to his soldiers about her uncanny outdoor skills, often to the point that she'd attained minor celebrity status among the paratroopers of Charlie (Airborne) Company, 4th Battalion, 23rd Infantry Regiment, 172nd Separate Infantry Brigade (Alaska).

"You're the most competitive angler I've ever known," Boone said to his middle child. "Are you sure you're not cheating?"

Rachel smiled.

"Remember, Dad, if you're not cheating, you're not trying," repeating the phrase she'd heard him use many times.

He had to remember to give her some context when using that phrase. He'd eventually hear from a teacher.

Boone turned the canoe with his paddle and Rachel took the trout from the net, removed the hook, and dispatched the fish with the small club they carried for this purpose. She was a dedicated angler, trained to stop suffering quickly.

"What do you think?" Boone said. "Three apiece should feed the family. How about we head in?"

"I guess if you can't take the competition," she said.

Boone paddled across the small lake while Rachel leaned back, her hands interlaced behind her head, watching him do the work.

"You not going to help paddle?" he asked.

"It pays to be a winner, Pop," she said giggling.

It was a perfect spring day. The reflection of the Chugach Mountains was interrupted only by the ripple of the canoe and the small island of slushy ice in the middle of the lake. The loons had been calling all afternoon, the sun was warm for this time of year, and the mosquitoes weren't too bad on the water.

The canoe scraped to a stop on the sandy beach at the lake's edge. They stepped out of the canoe and pulled it out of the water. They put their gear in the back of Boone's new 1974 International Scout II, which he loved. He had an affinity for American-made four-wheel drive trucks, and this one was proving invaluable to his life in the wild.

19

"We better clean the fish at home, Dad," Rachel said. "We're running out of time, and the last time we were late, Mom called the MPs, and you made the blotter."

Boone glanced at his scratched Rolex Submariner and wanted to agree with her. Still, it was safer to clean the fish at the lake rather than put the guts and skins in the housing area dumpsters, where a bear could visit for a quick meal, but he also knew the consequences of being late. The previous summer, he and Rachel fished the same lake and lost track of time. They arrived home an hour late to an MP jeep sitting outside the Taggart's quarters, MP's interviewing his bride, Abigal. The next day, the incident was in the MP report, known as the blotter, that went to all commanders on the post. He got ahead of it by calling his boss and telling him the details, knowing he would get a call from the general in the morning. *The things we worry about in the peacetime Army.*

"There's only six. Let's clean them and then head home," Boone said.

They finished cleaning the trout, strapped the canoe to the top of the truck, and turned down the dirt road, past Malamute Drop Zone and south toward the main post and their family quarters.

He pulled the Scout into his assigned parking spot in front of Company Grade Officer housing. When the truck came to a full stop he looked at his seven-year-old sidekick.

"No MP's, mom's getting more patient with us," Boone said.

Rachel ran through the door to report that she'd caught the biggest trout. Boone set the cooler at the front door, took the steps to the basement, opened the gun safe, and put the Ruger Super Blackhawk, his preferred bear gun, on the top shelf. He took the steps two at a time, grabbed the cooler, ascended the steps to the living room, kissed Caroline in her bassinet, and put his nine-year-old son, Roan, in a headlock.

"Get your chores finished?" he asked.

"Yes, sir. I learned my lesson," Roan said. "Next time, chores on Friday afternoon and fishing the rest of the weekend."

Boone smiled at the boy and whispered, "It wouldn't have done you much good anyway. She out-fished me again."

Walking into the kitchen, he kissed Abby, set the cooler on the table, and stepped out to light the grill. As he lit the charcoal, he heard the phone. Roan stepped through the back door, "Dad, it's Major Hardy."

"Colonel Hardy since Friday," Boone corrected.

"Sorry, it'll take me a while," Roan said.

Boone stepped through the door and picked up the receiver. "Lieutenant Colonel Hardy, that's going to take a while to get used to," Boone said. "Are you calling just to hear the new title?"

Recently promoted Lieutenant Colonel Daniel Beckwourth Hardy was one of Boone's oldest friends dating back to their first tour in Vietnam, Boone a young communications sergeant on a Special Forces A Detachment, and Dan a new Army aviator supporting their operations among the Montagnard's of the Central Highlands. Their other tours overlapped. Now they were posted together again, Boone a senior captain and Dan a newly promoted Lieutenant Colonel.

"Are you watching the news?" Dan asked. His tone was somber for a man with a reputation as a laid-back, calm professional.

"No, Rachel and I just walked in from the lake," Boone said. "What's going on?"

"Turn on the news and call me after you get up to speed." Dan hung up.

"What's going on?" Abby asked.

He stepped into the living room and turned on the television without answering.

Boone saw it, recognized the place and equipment immediately, and understood what was happening. The lead tank hit the gate of the Presidential Palace. It stopped in the courtyard, the vehicles behind it moving throughout the compound, a small group of weaponless South Vietnamese soldiers standing to the right of the tank waiting for the inevitable. The commander of the T-54 that crashed through the gate jumped from his position with a yellow and red flag in his hands and ran to the steps of the building.

"It's over," Boone said. "We lost."

CHAPTER FIVE
0930 Hours Local-Monday 7 July 1975
Post Headquarters-Fort Richardson, Alaska

Boone walked into the outer foyer of Lieutenant Colonel Dan Hardy's office and greeted the young Sergeant controlling access to the inner office.

"Good morning, sir. How's life in Airborne Country?" she asked.

"Every day's a holiday, and every meal's a feast, Sergeant Lee. How's your boss this morning? He's not treating you poorly, is he?"

"No, sir. He's in a pretty good mood this morning," she said, smiling.

"Are his leave papers in proper order? I don't want to miss the fish because he can't manage his affairs."

"He's good to go, sir. You all will be on the river on time. I promise. How's Mrs. Taggart?"

Fort Richardson was a small post, and Sergeant Lee was always in the know, regarding the latest gossip. She knew Boone's wife, Abigail, had delivered their third child in March.

"Do you have pictures yet?"

"Abby's doing great, so is Caroline, and no, I don't have pictures. Sorry."

"Sir, that's unacceptable. I want pictures of that cutie."

"Next time, I promise."

Dan opened the door and entered the outer office with an empty coffee mug.

"I would've filled that for you, sir," Sergeant Lee said.

"You're not a coffee getter, Lee, you're an Administrative Specialist—so administrate," Hardy said.

22

The young Non-Commissioned Officer shook her head, pushed her glasses up her nose, and returned to work.

Dan reached under the counter of the office coffee bar and pulled out a white China mug with Master Parachutist wings on the front and "Captain Boone Taggart" in gold lettering on the back. He handed it to Boone.

"Merry Christmas—early. You're here enough to earn your own. By the way, the coffee club is $5 a month. Pay Sergeant Lee on your way out," Dan ordered.

"I knew this would cost me, but thanks. I appreciate it."

Boone filled his mug, followed Dan into his office, and closed the door.

Dan Hardy's office was like most offices on Fort Richardson or, for that matter, on all Army posts. The walls were covered with framed photos of Dan with fellow warriors in Vietnam, Alaska, Germany, and dozens of stateside locations. Boone was in three of the pictures. Several miniature versions of Battalion colors were framed on the wall: 2-502 Infantry, 5-39 Infantry, 1st Aviation, and two others plus various unit flags and school certificates. Directly behind Dan's chair was a sky-blue guidon with crossed rifles in the middle. It was a gift to then Captain Dan Hardy from the officers and soldiers of A Company, 5-39 (Mech) Infantry, 9th Infantry Division, upon his change of command in June 1968. The small brass plaque at the bottom of the framed guidon read:

Captain Dan Hardy, Infantry, Commander
A CO. 5-39 Infantry (Mech), 9th Infantry Division
Old Reliables
Firebase Cougar, Bien Hoa, Republic of South Vietnam
November 1967 - June 1968
With great appreciation for outstanding leadership under
challenging circumstances.

What was conspicuously absent from the walls of Dan's office, compared to many other officers, was any framed medals, citations, or awards, of which Dan had plenty: two Silver Stars, three Bronze Stars, two with "V" Device, a Soldier's Medal, Distinguished Flying Cross, four Air Medals, three Purple Hearts and a dozen other awards and campaign medals. Dan didn't have an "*I love me wall*" but a memory wall. He was one of the humblest leaders Boone had ever known. More than that, in Boone's eyes, he was the best soldier he knew, his mentor, advisor, and his best friend.

"I notice that you're never associated with unattractive women," Boone whispered after closing the door.

"Young Captain," Dan said. "Sergeant Lee was assigned here by personnel, and I haven't noticed her gender or looks. She's an American Soldier."

"Yeah, right," Boone said.

"You're going to have to change that knuckle-dragger mentality. The world will change, and you, my friend, must deal with female soldiers, not just the boys.

"Now to the charge of beautiful women," Dan said. "You, sir, are simply jealous. You've only attracted one beautiful woman, who subsequently made the grievous error of marrying you and, worse, allowed you to abuse her attractive figure through childbirth three times. You should be ashamed."

"You're right, at least about her being hot, and for the record, three children haven't taken that away. She might be better looking. The fact that she married down is her problem, not mine. I did well for myself," Boone said, smiling.

"Surely you didn't risk coming to the head shed to talk about good-looking women." He wanted to move Boone to the point of his visit so he could get back to work.

"Nope, I just wanted to talk about the trip," Boone said. "The First Sergeant will drop us off at the Denali Highway bridge, crossing the Susitna River. We'll float down to Talkeetna, where Abby will pick us up seven days later. Chip in some money, and I'll pick up the food. I've got the rest of the camp gear. You bring your ruck, fishing gear, and bear gun. First Sergeant and I will pick you up at your quarters on Thursday morning at 0500."

"I'll be ready," Dan said.

Boone stood up, took the money, and drained the coffee from

his new mug.

"Thanks again, buddy," he said.

"No problems," Dan said. "See you on Thursday. By the way, I saw the Major's list came out, and you're on it with a low number. As soon as you get promoted, I'm pulling you up here to the staff. Congratulations."

"Thanks, sir. It looks like they're going to promote me beyond my capability again. We can talk about the transfer later."

Boone dropped a five-dollar bill on Sergeant Lee's desk and turned to leave the office. "Do your best to keep him in line, Sergeant Lee."

"Thanks, sir. have a great day," she said. Boone turned down the hallway, pulling his hat from his cargo pocket, and looked for the closest exit from the headquarters building.

As Boone turned his International Scout II out of the parking lot of the Brigade Headquarters, he hoped the float trip would help him accept his planned course of action.

CHAPTER SIX
0430 Hours Local-Thursday 11 July 1975
Company Grade Officer's Quarters-Fort Richardson, Alaska

Boone shifted the truck into reverse as Abigail leaned through the window and kissed him. "What do you think Dan will say when you tell him you've decided to resign your commission?" she said.

"Well, if he comes back from this trip with some made-up story about how a grizzly bear ate me and he survived unscathed, don't believe the suicide note," Boone chuckled. "I think he'll be mad and maybe take it personally, but there's no way I can do this without telling him face-to-face. I owe him that."

Six hours later, First Sergeant Eldridge Courtney stood along the highway, watching the two men pull heavily into the river's current. The two argued the virtues of their particular commissioning source for the previous six hours. The battle of quips, barbs, and insults continued as their voices faded down the river. Dan Hardy, a West Pointer, and Boone, a former enlisted man and Officer's Candidate School graduate, had engaged in this battle for the eleven years of their friendship. The First Sergeant shook his head as he turned the truck around and drove back to post. He knew this, though—having served with both men, they were superb soldiers and leaders. Regardless of the source of their commissions, he was thankful there were officers like them in his Army.

They'd planned this trip several weeks earlier because they were both having trouble processing the events of the last few years that culminated the previous April when Saigon fell to the North Vietnamese Army. They'd invested almost a decade of their lives in the war and believed in the stated national strategy of the time: Communist containment. They believed national leaders, civilians,

26

and military were doing their best to win a war against communist aggression in Southeast Asia. At least, they believed that up to their last tour in 1970. By that point, political revelations were public. It was obvious that the government was no longer trying to win. It was running out the clock.

They'd shared the loss of close friends in combat, their soldiers, men they were responsible for. Their families carried a burden. They witnessed violence and tragedy on a large scale, but they were willing to bear the responsibility because they believed in the cause, but now, they weren't sure what to think. Dan believed time in the wilderness might provide some clarity.

The publication of *The Pentagon Papers* cast a long, painful shadow on the relationship and trust between military and political leaders. Worse, it cast a similar and novel shadow of mistrust of senior military leadership amongst rank-and-file soldiers. The report brought the execution of the war into sharp focus by exposing the failures of senior leaders. With the leaked Pentagon report, it was clear that senior leaders in the Department of Defense and the White House lied and misled Congress, the citizens of the Republic, and, worse, the military personnel who answered their country's call. Key members of the Johnson Administration, including the President, Secretary of Defense, and the Commander of all forces in South Vietnam, knew the United States was losing the war. Yet, they generally continued to execute a failed strategy and sent additional troops motivated only by political expediency. It was grotesque.

After his fourth and final combat tour in 1970, Boone pored over the recently published *The Pentagon Papers* to try and make sense of the first American war loss in history. After Vietnam, he was assigned as a Ranger Instructor at the Mountain Ranger Camp in Dahlonega, Georgia. Now commanding a company of paratroopers in Alaska, meant that he continued to serve with the best soldiers in the Army, but something had changed. There was a keen distrust of senior leaders, both civilian and military, and morale was at its lowest in Boone's experience. Both issues were directly connected to the senior-level leadership's mishandling of the war.

27

He studied the report for several years, talked to analysts and other leaders, and concluded that the critics of the war's execution, Daniel Ellsberg, John Paul Vann, Colonel David Hackworth, and others were right. He seriously questioned the time, effort, blood, and treasure expended in a war the nation wasn't committed to winning.

Boone Taggart wasn't a pacifist—he was a warrior and didn't object to sacrifice for a worthy cause. He was a soldier, and he fought his nation's wars. He and his brothers-in-arms understood the arrangement. Boone objected to how the war was mishandled and prosecuted with more consideration of political consequences for a few than the real-life consequences for many.

The warriors were restricted to the point that victory was beyond reach. He objected to the military tradition of service and honor being used to extend the careers of bureaucrats and politicians. He mourned the loss of his soldiers and the sacrifice of their families. He regretted the mistreatment of America's sons when they returned home to an ungrateful citizenry, most of whom couldn't comprehend what they'd experienced in the jungles of Southeast Asia.

Boone also mourned the tragedy brought on the Vietnamese. Over a century of French colonialism, Japanese occupation, a corrupt government in the south, and now, the tyranny of communism. The fall of Saigon brought all these questions into sharper focus.

His generation of combat veterans faced a different situation than their fathers in World War Two—a clear national objective, a distinct and identifiable enemy, and a measurable end state. Additionally, the fascist regimes of Japan and Europe were a clear threat to American and global security. The Allies secured a decisive victory, and the entire nation was invested in the overall effort.

General George Catlett Marshall's brilliance during World War II was evident as he groomed the most outstanding group of senior military leaders in history. He was unafraid to fire a general officer who failed to lead and perform at the highest levels. Still caring for them as soldiers, he sought positions where their talents and skills could be used most effectively to win the war. He replaced those failing generals with tactically sound commanders who could win. The nation changed in the twenty intervening years between the end of the war and the beginning of broad US involvement in Vietnam and so did the military. There were no General Marshall's in Saigon.

Boone looked forward to time on the river with his friend and mentor for all the usual reasons, but there was another more significant reason for the journey. Dan believed this trip would give them time to discuss recent events and how they affected them. He hoped to find some peace for both of them in the shadow of a lost war. He didn't know Boone was planning on leaving the Army and that his resignation was an act of protest.

Boone and Dan had spent much time in the field together, enough to function without speaking. The Taggart Family ranches, and adjacent Big Horn Mountains, became a second home for many men Boone served with over the years. Dan and others enjoyed many decompression trips with Boone and his family. After each tour, they hunted, fished, camped, and rode through the backcountry to put themselves back together.

Boone stepped from the canoe as it scraped to a halt on the gravel bar, pulled it onto the beach, and secured the bowline on a large driftwood trunk. Dan stepped ashore and helped Boone remove their gear and set up camp. As they pulled the gear from the canoe, Dan began to recognize much of the ancient kit and took the opportunity to needle his closest friend.

"You sir are a Luddite," Dan said, as he threw a canvas fly on the beach.

"What do you mean?"

"Are we really going to use this old crap? You can go to any sporting goods store in America and find gear twice as good for half the cost of this Oregon Trail outfit." Dan lifted the wooden kitchen box from the bottom of the canoe.

"This gear is better," Boone said.

"In what world is a forty-year-old, twenty-five-pound tent better than a brand-new lightweight nylon tent?"

"Right here in the nineteenth century," Boone pointed to his head and laughed.

"Can't you occasionally live in the modern world?" Dan asked.

"Not if I can help it."

Dan started on the canvas wall tent, Yukon stove, and field kitchen. Boone pulled the canoe from the river, tipped it on its side, supported it with the paddles, threw a canvas tarp over the canoe, and secured the edge of the tarp behind the canoe and about six feet in front of the long edge. He put the rest of their gear under the shelter of the canoe and tarp. He collected firewood and water for the night and morning. The camp was set. The two long-time friends had adjusted to the daily life cycle in the open. Stress was on the way out, but Boone was about to change the mood.

An hour after landing, Dan was thigh-deep in the swift, cold water, working a red and white spoon down the river's rocky bottom. He'd already connected twice with nice Rainbow Trout, but they were still ahead of the salmon run. Boone sat on the sand bar with a map in his lap, holding a compass in one hand, a notebook and pencil in the other, and a protractor between his teeth. He watched his friend masterfully work the rod and reel while he worked out their exact location.

Dan wore his standard issue, permanent Alaska resident uniform—faded blue Carhartt logger pants, red and black plaid wool shirt, canvas fishing vest, Filson tin cloth wading jacket, and chest waders, all topped off by the faded OD green "boonie" hat that showed up for all his outdoor activities. When Dan wasn't in uniform, he looked like a mountain man. He held the trademark cigar clenched between his teeth. It was an accessory he was no longer smoking, just chewing.

Dan retrieved his line, placed the treble hook into the rod guide, and waded back to the sandbar, pulling two trout on a stringer attached to his chest waders. He stopped at the river's edge and cleaned the fish, threw the guts and heads into the river, and cleaned the body cavity of each. Walking across the sandbar with their supper, he shouted to Boone.

"Alright, Magellan. Where are we?"

"We're about ninety-five miles in, just short of halfway," Boone said. "Take a look. I calculate us here." Boone used a small twig, pointing to the spot on the map on the north side of the river as Dan sat next to him.

"I think we're in good shape, maybe stay here for a couple of days if the salmon run begins in the morning. If not, we press on until we connect and then stay put while we fill the cooler and our bellies. What'd you think?" Boone said.

"I concur, my friend. Lieutenant Colonel Daniel Beckwourth Hardy, the great fisherman of the Far North, declares the salmon will appear in the next twelve hours."

"Where'd you get a ten-dollar middle name like Beckwourth?" Boone asked.

"James Peirson Beckwourth," Dan replied proudly.

"The mountain man?"

"That's right, *the* mountain man, or at least my dad thought so," Dan said. "You know about him?"

"Yeah, a little," Boone said. "He was born in Virginia, his mother was a slave, and his father was a white plantation owner. He escaped slavery, traveled west, and apprenticed to a blacksmith in Missouri, then went up the Missouri with Ashley's fur brigade. The Crow adopted him and he became a war chief, right?"

"That's right," Dan said. "Beckwourth was also an inveterate liar and storyteller. There were several African American trappers and mountain men, but he was the only one who left a journal. Many of the events actually happened, but a lot was embellished or just outright made up. Most old-timers were probably stretching their exploits a little to make good press."

"Sounds like us, you know, the way every war story starts," Boone said.

"There I was," Dan said. "Up to my knees in grenade pins, no ammo, an entrenching tool in one hand, and a K-Bar in the other." They both smiled at the memory.

Dan wrapped the fish in foil, placed them in the coals of the fire, and then sat against the driftwood log beside his closest friend.

"You going to stay up here after you retire?" Boone was trying to ease his way into an uncomfortable conversation.

"I think so. At least that's the plan now, but you know what they say. *If you want to hear God laugh, tell Him your plans*," Dan said, his face breaking into a wide grin.

31

After a short pause, Dan continued. "Being in the wilderness has kept me sane over the years, and I'm in love with Alaska. I can relax out here and decompress. I've finally found some peace. I grew up hunting and fishing in Mississippi and always loved the outdoors, but I would've never thought about coming to Alaska until I served with a couple of guys on my first tour who were stationed up here. The way they described it, I had to see for myself, so I went after my tour in '64 and again after my tour ended in '68. I was so happy when the Army sent me up here. Since I met Linda, we've thought we might stay after I retire. I might get a civilian job on post and become a semi-professional outdoor adventurer.

"You think about retiring much?" Boone asked.

"Not much, but I know it'll eventually happen," Dan said. "It's just part of life. The Army doesn't need old people in the ranks. So, I think about it occasionally but don't plan anything beyond returning here.

"Listen, brother, we're carrying a lot, and it's probably not a good idea to ignore it. The wilderness can heal what gets broken. At least, it has for me. Being out in the open, living in a tent, hunting, or fishing for my food has been a godsend to me, and the Lord knows you're a better woodsman than me by orders of magnitude. It seems to come easy to you. It's natural, so let me give you some friendly advice: Get out more. You're carrying the same stress as every combat veteran, but you seem to be struggling with something since our last tour. It's been worse since April. I can feel it. Other people can see it. I think Abby's a little worried. Don't let it get away from you. The wilderness is therapeutic if you let it be."

Boone sat quietly, watching the willows on the far side of the river gently shaking in the wind.

In a minute, Dan stood and said, "I need to check the fish."

He walked to the field kitchen beneath the faded white canvas rainfly, checked the fish and started the rest of the meal. Boone folded his map, stored the gear in his green canvas map bag, and threw it under the tarp over the canoe. He helped Dan with the meal of trout, fried potatoes, onions, cornbread, and coffee. After they ate, Boone did the dishes by the river. Dan put two large kettles of water over the

32

fire to boil and cool overnight so they would have fresh drinking water come morning. They sat shoulder to shoulder next to the fire.

"What're you reading?" Boone said.

"*Once an Eagle* by Anton Myrer."

"A wise man once told me that's the best book in print about leadership," Boone said. In another moment, he continued. "Dan, I need to talk to you about something."

"Go, brother."

"I've given this a lot of thought and talked it over with Abby," Boone paused, dreading the next moment, "and I've decided to resign my commission. I'm leaving the Army." Boone thought this was like telling your older brother you're changing your last name. Dan's demeanor shifted. He put the book down, pulled his boonie hat lower, reached into his jacket pocket, retrieved a Zippo lighter emblazoned with the 9th Infantry Division patch, and lit his cigar. It was evident to Boone that he'd shifted from buddy on a fishing trip to a mentor and counselor. He'd witnessed the mental shift many times and knew Dan wouldn't fail him.

"Why?" Dan asked as he stoked the cigar.

"Well, several reasons, I guess," Boone said.

Dan stepped to the canoe, reached inside his kit bag, and retrieved a bottle of Jack Daniels. He poured a healthy amount into two canteen cups and sat beside Boone, handing him a cup.

"We don't have anywhere to be for four days. Explain your reasons to me, please," Dan said.

Boone sat the canteen cup on the sand beside him, dug a tin of Copenhagen snuff from his jacket pocket, and packed a dip into his lower lip. He spit once, picked up the cup, took a sip, and began the well-rehearsed explanation.

"I've spent more than half my marriage away from Abby, either in Vietnam, the field, or school. Travel is constant, and we've moved more than half a dozen times in the same period. I regularly work fourteen to sixteen-hour days when we're in garrison. I'm in command, which is a time-consuming assignment even with a top-rate First Sergeant like First Sergeant Courtney. When I end up back on a staff, depending on the Commander, that will require more time and return less satisfaction.

"The kids are at the age that they'll need me more. I don't think it was such a big deal when they were babies, but Roan is nine, Rachel is seven, and Caroline will never remember any of this. Not to mention that this profession can get you killed. I've done my time, served my country, and got hurt a few times but survived four tours. Maybe it's time to stop rolling the dice."

"So, you're leaving the Army for your family's sake? That's noble and selfless. I'm impressed," Dan said sipping whiskey from the metal cup.

"This is no time for your smart-ass sense of humor, you know?" Boone said.

Dan smiled, "Other reasons?" he asked.

"Dad could use the help back home. The kids would have a more stable life, and I could probably make more money on the outside, too."

"What does Abby think?"

"She supports me, one hundred percent."

"She supports you or thinks it's the right decision? There's a difference. Abby's the kind of woman who'll back you even when you do something stupid. That's loyalty, but does she think this is a wise decision for everyone involved? You, her, the kids?"

Boone shot the remainder of the whiskey and held out the metal cup for another.

"You need a little more liquid courage to tell me the truth?" Dan laughed.

"Liquid courage is still courage," Boone shot back. "To be fair, her exact words were, 'I'll support you one hundred percent in whatever decision you make, but I think you're making a dreadful mistake.' Then she elaborated that, for all the frustrations, I was doing what gave me the most meaning and fulfillment. That I'd be miserable as a civilian and, in turn, make her and the kids miserable. She thinks I'm doing what I'm made for."

"Wise woman," Dan said.

"I put off talking to you earlier because I knew we were coming on this trip and would have more time to talk out here. What do you think?" Boone asked.

"Have you already dropped your resignation paperwork?" Dan asked.

"Not yet, and I haven't mentioned this to anyone but Abby and you."

Dan poured more whiskey into his own cup.

"Liquid courage?" Boone asked.

"Still courage," Dan said. "Boone, I could give you all the seemingly logical reasons to stay. You have thirteen years of service, so you can retire in seven years with a pension. If you've not noticed, the national economy is crap right now. You're guaranteed a monthly paycheck, free housing and medical care, access to the commissary and exchange, thirty days paid annual leave, and that pension I mentioned would start when you're thirty-eight. Plenty of time for maybe two more careers.

"Along with the economy, the state of the union isn't perfect right now. But frankly, I always thought that trying to convince a man to become or continue to be a soldier for economic reasons was wrong. If a man wants to do this, it needs to be for something greater than a pension. It needs to be a calling, and you have that calling."

Boone held out his cup again.

We aren't going to catch any fish in the morning. Dan poured Boone's third whiskey, swallowed what was left in his cup, and poured again.

"I believe the reasons that you've stated so far are things that you've thought about from time to time," Dan said. "We all have, but I think they're convenient things you're telling yourself, Abby, and me. They sound noble, but they're supporting arguments, not a main argument. What's the real reason?"

Boone removed his battered cowboy hat, ran his fingers through his hair, paused momentarily, and carefully put his words together.

"Dan, for the first time in our history, we lost a war. It happened on our watch, and worse, it was avoidable, and too many people knew it and didn't do anything about it."

And there's the real reason, Dan got it.

35

"What about the blood, American and Vietnamese, the wounded, the sacrifice of the families?" Boone said. "Why'd we do this if we weren't going to try to win and give the South Vietnamese a shot? I know why they said we did it, but it's not true."

Boone stood up and started pacing the sandbar. He kept venting. As he talked, his speech became louder, more animated and passionate. He wasn't just upset. He was fiercely angry, a terrible cocktail of emotions started to rise—frustration, sadness, fear for the next generation of men, his son included, soldiers that'd be exposed to the same mistakes by politicians and careerists with no skin in the game.

"I've been thinking about all of this since our last tour in '70 because it was obvious that no one, except the warriors, was interested in even trying to win the war," Boone said. "We were running out the clock. They just wanted out, not because people were dying, but to try to save political face and set up their legacy. It's sickening."

Dan let him go on.

"But even earlier than that, man, we made a mess of the whole thing. We were totally unprepared and untrained to fight the war we needed to fight. There were a few who advocated for a shift to counterinsurgency and winning hearts and minds, but we never made that adjustment. We fought the conventional war we were trained and organized for instead of the war we were engaged in and could've won.

"We looked at everything through the lens of our experience in Europe, tried to make the situation fit the training and tactics, instead of the other way around. We tried to fight a guerilla war like we fought the Wehrmacht on the plains of Europe. We used artillery and airstrikes when we should've used rifles and knives. We made as many enemies as we killed.

"And then, when the conventional war started, and the NVA showed up with tanks, armored personnel carriers, and air defense artillery, we were disengaging from a style of war that we're good at. They wouldn't let us chase the bad guys into their sanctuaries. We're inflexible at the top of the organization. They see everything through the wrong lens. Over half a million soldiers were deployed to Vietnam, and the Puzzle Palace was still worried about the Soviets invading

Western Europe. They mismanaged a war we were engaged in because they worried about a war that'll likely never happen."

"I know, brother," Dan said. "The voices in my head say the same thing every day."

"No one was held accountable or responsible for the failures, at least not those who should've paid a price," Boone said. "The generals who bungled the whole thing got promoted and then retired and went to work on the boards of defense companies. The egghead systems analysts thought they could run a war from D.C. because they were smarter, went to the right schools, and ran in the right circles. Instead of being canned they just kept moving through the government bureaucracy. The United States government is the only institution where you can so galactically screw things up and get promoted. The only people who got fired in all this were the people who told the truth and tried to change the system.

"The people trusted and charged with an accurate analysis of the situation, and then the development of a cogent strategy supported by the right tactics, were dismal failures and their error didn't cost them anything, personally. But it sure cost us and our friends. The politicians lied to or marginalized the military advisors and they eventually went along with the whole mess. Even after McNamara's report came out in '67 the system never adjusted. We just kept moving forward with a broken strategy. The politicians and national security apparatus are almost always wrong about everything and rarely have the country's best interest at heart. They never pay the price for their sins."

Boone took a deep breath, faced the river, and, in a more controlled voice, finished.

"So if that's the way they're going to approach things, I'm out," he said. "They don't want to listen to a Captain or, no offense, to Lieutenant Colonel's either. Our view is irrelevant, but we're the ones that they send to do the dirty work and then cluck their tongues about 'peace with honor' and 'noble causes.' I'll have more opportunities outside the Army to speak my mind than I ever will in uniform. So I'm done."

Dan splashed another round in both cups and walked to where

Boone stood, looking out at the river. He handed Boone his cup. They stood shoulder to shoulder, in silence, under the long Alaskan midnight sun.

Dan addressed his thoughts. "Brother, everything you said is true, and I've thought the same things a thousand times," he said. "The higher-ups bungled that war, no doubt. There were experienced people telling them we were making mistakes, and it was ignored. But if you think you're going to make a difference on the outside, you're wrong. There's a long and distinguished line of men who resigned in protest and didn't accomplish anything about changing the policy.

"Quitting in protest is a dicey affair. No doubt there comes a time when a man has to draw a line he refuses to cross. There are times when resigning is a moral act even if it doesn't produce any change but, in most cases, you go from having some influence to zero, which is especially true at our level. We're small fish, and nobody's listening to us.

"Resignation in protest only carries weight when practiced by those at the very top and then en masse and then only if they're diligently vocal. And it still might not work. If the entire Joint Chiefs of Staff resigned, maybe. But one or two resignations get a couple days of press and then die. The resignation of a Captain or a Lieutenant Colonel means absolutely nothing. The Big Green Machine keeps grinding."

Dan's voice was metered and controlled. "You ever hear of Smedley Butler?" he asked.

Boone was confused but he answered. "Yeah, Marine, right? Medal of Honor recipient back in the early 1900s."

"Major General Smedley Butler, USMC. Two Medals of Honor," Dan said. "He participated in every combat engagement from the Spanish-American War through World War I, the Philippines, Central America, and the Banana Wars. The guy was a warrior. When he retired, he was a candidate for Commandant of the Marine Corps. He was known to be outspoken during his career, and that probably had something to do with him not getting the Commandant slot. After he left the Corps in the early 30s, he wrote a book, *War is a Racket.* He used his own experience to highlight the problem with war profiteering. In his view, profit, in some form, was the motive for all wars the US had ever fought. He didn't resign in protest, but the result was similar. He wasn't in a position to change anything and the system ground on.

"More recently, Colonel David Hackworth. He went on ABC in uniform while on active duty. Man, he was crazy enough to do the interview while he was in country, and I believe he told the truth, but the system came after him with a vengeance. He finally retired, but there was talk of courts martial, and do you know what he accomplished? Absolutely nothing. The establishment closed ranks and painted a much different picture than Hackworth's version of the war.

"Boone, if you think you can go home to the ranch, write your congressman, or run for office and change any of this, you're sadly mistaken. Teaching in the right environment, maybe you'd have some influence over a few. But if you stay, you can influence the next generation of leaders, officers, and NCOs. That has an exponential effect, because those leaders pass the lessons they learned from you to their soldiers and so on. Those at the top are almost always disconnected or wrong, but we can help manage the damage. That's a legacy that will help them navigate what we've experienced, and they'll have to. Mark my word, if you and I live long enough, we'll see something like Vietnam happen again. The revolving door of generals and national security experts never seems to learn the history lessons they should, and the politicians are either clueless or don't care.

"Have you thought about what happens if soldiers like you leave? I'll answer that for you: Those nineteen-year-olds who stand in your formation every morning are left with no one as a buffer between them and the bureaucrats in uniform at the Pentagon and the politicians in Congress or the careerists in our units. Your position gets filled by someone, and instead of a warrior, maybe it's one of those careerists who cares more about his future than his soldier's welfare and training. Commanding soldiers is a ticket punch for him.

You have to make your own decision about this, but Abby is right: You'll be miserable as a civilian. If you're asking my opinion, and I think you are, you should soldier on and influence young soldiers who'll have to endure this madness again. We can do some good inside a broken system and the dire circumstances they keep putting us in."

Boone slapped Dan lightly on the shoulder as he returned to camp, "I'll take that under advisement, Colonel. Do we have more of this?" Boone turned his empty cup upside down.

"Sure do, sonny."

The next several days were spent talking, reminiscing, and trying to solve the world's problems. All fueled by copious amounts of Tennessee whiskey and Silver Salmon. The run started within six hours of Dan's prediction, a fact that he would never allow Boone to forget. They were behind schedule and had to move to link up with Abby. The two hungover friends packed up camp, loaded the canoe, and made the final adjustments before they hit the river. As Dan started to push the canoe off the sandbar in a drizzling, cold rain, he asked Boone the question he'd pondered all night.

"If you knew what you know now about Vietnam, would you do it again?" Dan said.

After a moment, Boone answered. "I've always said that the whole thing was one of those million-dollar experiences I wouldn't give a nickel to relive, but yeah. I'd do it again. I think I did some good in a terrible situation."

"Seems like that's the answer to your problem," Dan said. "Most people are content to get a job, have a house and a car, raise their family, and go to work and church. Have a few weeks' vacation each year, go fishing on the weekends, attend their kids ball games, and so on. They're happy and content with that life, the American Dream, and I don't say that as a criticism. In some ways, I'm jealous, but the mold never fit me. It doesn't make me better, just different. That mold does describe my dad though—he's content being a farmer. He loves it."

Really?" Boone said. "It's amazing to think a black man enjoys being a farmer in Mississippi in 1975."

"He does," Dan said. "He owns his place now and would've experienced terrible racism no matter what he did for a living. He could've been a store clerk or a preacher and would still have to deal with bigots. The fact is my dad loves farming, the land, the animals, and the seasonal routine. He's well respected by most of the other farmers around the county because he's a master at what he does. It's not a job with him. It's his calling. He believes that God put him on earth to be a steward of the land he stands on every day. But that wasn't for me, and it's not for you or most of the guys we serve with.

"They're here for something else. Maybe they don't even realize it. I didn't at first, but I see it now. The stated reason for a guy joining, and the reason that keeps him here, is different. We're looking for something: Adventure, excitement, service, whatever it is. Nature breeds outliers in every generation that seem to swim upstream. Whether they're artists, cowboys, mountain men, or soldiers, they're looking for something they can't find in the suburbs. You and I are outliers, my friend. We have to have something to fill that void in our souls."

"That was beautiful, man," Boone laughed sarcastically.

"Kiss my black ass, you inbred hillbilly." Dan pushed the canoe into the current and picked up his paddle as he and Boone pulled hard for the pickup point with Abby.

As the two approached Talkeetna, they witnessed more "civilization," at least by Alaskan standards. They passed numerous islands at the confluence of the Chulitna River and then the confluence of the Talkeetna River in a few more miles. From then on, the three rivers flowed to Cook Inlet as the Susitna. They passed a handful of cabins and other structures on the outskirts of town, followed by the little village itself, a jumping-off point for trips into the interior for hunters, anglers, and climbers on their way to Denali. The river widened, and the volume of water and, thus, the current increased for the final fifteen miles of the trip. It was a long day of paddling with a few stops to grab a bite and cast for a few minutes in hopes of another fish. As the Parks Highway bridge came into view, Boone broke the silence for the first time in hours.

"I'm staying in," Boone said. "I'm not going to resign. You and Abby are right. I wouldn't change anything if I left, and I'd be miserable and make the people around me miserable. If I stay, I still have a seat at the table, and I can influence and train as many leaders

41

as possible. This is where I belong."

"Seems like I heard someone say that recently," Dan said, slapping the paddle against the water's surface, soaking his friend's back.

They passed beneath the bridge and deftly pulled the canoe to the gray sand beach where Abby was parked. As she started walking to meet the two, Boone grabbed his rucksack, kit bag, and gun case and walked to meet her. He stopped long enough for a kiss and then continued to the truck.

"How'd he take it?" Abby said. Boone looked over his shoulder.

"We're staying in the Army. Dan said I had to."

Within a few minutes, Boone and Dan had the canoe on top of the Scout and all the gear loaded. Dan jumped in the back seat, crushed his jacket into a pillow, and stretched out as best he could for a nap. Boone sat in the passenger's seat as Abby put the truck in gear and eased onto the highway for the two-hour drive back to post. It was chilly, overcast, and drizzling, but Abby couldn't take it any longer. She cracked the driver's window for fresh air.

"What's the matter?" Boone asked.

"You two smell like a mix of sweat, tobacco, fish, and whiskey. With an emphasis on whiskey. What happened out there? Was this whole trip just an excuse for a seven-day drunk?"

"No, just three days," Boone said. He could tell Abby wasn't amused by his sarcasm. They would talk of this again in private.

"Not our finest hour, but we resolved some things or at least put them in perspective. The wilderness is a good place to do that for a man," Dan said without opening his eyes.

The three drove silently for a few minutes.

"Abby, if your man ever gets out of whack again, just call me," Dan said, "and I'll take him back out in the woods for a counseling session."

"Agreed." She reached over and touched Boone's thigh and smiled. Boone took the advance in the wrong context.

"So, the usual post-deployment shenanigans tonight, dear?"

Abby laughed. "It depends on what you smell like after a

shower, hot shot."

Brothers

"There is no sound I like better than adult male laughter."
C.S. Lewis

CHAPTER SEVEN
1830 Hours Local-Thursday 13 February 1987
Taggart Home-Washington County, Tennessee

Abby Taggart hung up the phone and stepped through the back door to the deck. Boone sat in the wooden Adirondack chair and spat a stream of brown tobacco juice into an open beer can.

"I thought you were going to quit," she said.

"I'll tell you what, I will when I retire."

"Maybe I should stop kissing you. Would that motivate you to quit?"

He smiled at her. "We both know you're not gonna' do that," he said, pinching her on the side.

"I really will quit when I retire. The doctor said it's easier to quit during a transition."

"It's such a nasty habit," Abby said.

"And yet, you can't keep your hands off me."

He set his book, *On Strategy* by Colonel Harry Summers, on the table beside his chair, picked up his binoculars, and scanned the field behind their house.

"Right there," he said. "Three does and a buck feeding in the clover I planted."

"That's nice, but you're avoiding talking to me about something," Abby said.

"I am not."

"Something's bothering you, and you aren't talking about it, so you sit out here every day pretending to read, spitting Copenhagen into a beer can, and watching the deer. I'm concerned. What's going on?"

"I'm good," he said.

"You're not well, though."

45

She's precise with her words, Boone thought, *the challenges of being married to an English major.*

"You've not been right for a while," Abby said, "and I'm a little worried. You haven't been like this since Alaska."

"This isn't that," Boone said.

"I know, honey, but it's like it and maybe connected to it. You need to talk about this. It isn't going to get better with age." She kissed him on the forehead and returned to the kitchen.

Three days earlier, Boone came home in a mood.

"According to my jackass assignments, officer, I won't be returning to a tactical unit, and you want to know why?" Boone said. "Because, according to said jackass, 'it's time to pay my dues.' Yeah, that's right, pay my dues, as if four tours in Vietnam, one as a Ranger instructor, an entire career in light infantry units, and getting a bachelor's and master's degree on my own time isn't payment. He said I was due for a joint assignment or worse." Boone paused for a moment. He whispered. "The Pentagon. He also said I probably won't make the next Battalion Command list. I'll bet you that turd's on it, though, and finally, I'm not making full Colonel. So, we're going to retire."

"Did you call him a jackass?" Abby said.

Boone looked at her and shrugged.

"Lord honey. What do you expect? This is why you're not making Colonel. What do you always tell the kids, 'Don't crap in your own mess kit?' Rest assured, though, if you decide to take a Pentagon assignment, someone will pay their dues."

Secretly, she'd been hoping for this for a long time. Abby was relieved and thankful. Roan, their oldest child and only son, had already left home, joined the Army, and loved it. Rachel was living with Boone's parents in Wyoming to finish her senior year of high school and meet the residency requirements to attend the University of Wyoming in the fall. That left only Caroline at home, her at twelve years old, for only a few more years. Abby was ready to settle down and enjoy some alone time with her high school sweetheart. She and Boone had spent more than half their married life separated by the tyranny of time and distance.

46

She knew that short of returning to an infantry unit, preferably an airborne infantry unit, Boone wouldn't be happy because he wouldn't be training soldiers. Unfortunately, there's only one Lieutenant Colonel per battalion, the commander. Boone's chance at selection was slim. If he decided to stay, he'd be desk-bound until he was forced to retire.

"Let's work on this, please," she said. "Go take a shower, change, and cool off. Caroline's at a ball game and won't be home for a while. We can talk this over calmly."

"OK, I'll be back in a minute," Boone said.

Abby put dinner on hold and poured herself a glass of wine, and a splash of Jack Daniels with Coke and two ice cubes for Boone. She walked into the den, turned the gas fire logs on, set the drinks on the table between two leather chairs, and waited for her husband. She knew he was struggling with the prospects of retirement. It was the pinnacle of his career to command an Airborne Infantry Battalion, but even if that happened, he would still retire someday, and now his hope of command was gone.

Boone entered the room wearing his favorite jeans and Screaming Eagle sweatshirt. He sat in the reading chair. Picking up the drink, he thanked her and blew her a kiss. His hair was still wet from the shower, and she noticed the gray around his temples was more pronounced than a few months ago.

As long as there are chemicals, that won't happen to me. Abby thought.

"OK, my rant is over. I want to know what you think," Boone said. "We knew this day was going to come, one way or another. I didn't think it would come today or even at the end of this assignment."

"First, as always, I love you more than anything, and you have my complete support no matter your choice," Abby said. "If you retire at the end of this tour, you'll have served for twenty-five years. As you've so eloquently and humbly stated," she smiled, "four tours in Vietnam, an assignment as a Ranger Instructor, almost your entire career was in light infantry, airborne or air assault units. It doesn't look like you'll get a command—I was hoping you could look at this from

47

another perspective. As much as you and your buddies complain about ROTC assignments as a backwater, your assignment here as the PMS will have a great impact on the Army for a generation or more.

"Your students idolize you. They hold you up as a standard to live and soldier by. There are a few of them that even try to copy your speech. I heard one of them call another one a rookie the other day. Where'd he hear that? You commission an average of twenty-four Second Lieutenants annually, most of which are molded in your image. If you decide to retire at the end of this tour, that's four years, ninety-six Second Lieutenants that you've molded and trained to be the kind of officer that will make a difference. You've not done it alone, but you led the effort. What'll those ninety-six young men and women do with your example? They'll go out and emulate it. Some of them will serve where you are right now, and they'll pass what you taught them on to another generation. You've prepared them to endure what you, Dan, and so many others did, and they'll do the same. If you commanded a battalion, you'd influence 20 or 25 officers. Honey, your service here casts a longer shadow on the Army than anything you would've done as a Battalion Commander."

Boone took a sip from the glass and glanced at Abby. *Is this weak drink meant to send me a message?* He thought. He took another sip and looked out the window.

After a short pause, Abby continued. "You aren't well right now, Boone. You spend too much time on the back deck, drinking, spitting into a beer can, watching the deer, and acting like you're reading—it's just the thousand-yard stare. You had the same look when you came home from your last tour in Vietnam and had it again when we were in Alaska after Saigon fell. We need to try to make some peace, honey. We need to plan a healthy transition to whatever is next. You're always telling me and the kids to get ahead of problems. We need to get ahead of this one."

"You're using my own words against me?" Boone said.

She smiled and touched his hand. "Absolutely. I have a suggestion. Plan a hunt with a few of your friends, maybe go back to Alaska. It's been a few years since you did something like that, and you probably need the challenge and the time. Go out in the wilderness and live like savages, eat nothing but meat, don't bathe, etcetera. Go in the fall after you retire. It'd be a good transition. Call Dan, he has contacts and can help you set it up, but if he's going on the trip, no alcohol is allowed. Take a breath and accept that this part of your life has ended, but more is left to live. Put some of the demons to rest. Figure out what's next. Come home to me happy. I miss your smile."

After a minute of silence, looking into the fire, turning his glass in his hand, Boone sighed. "Darling, you're right. We're retiring and doing something else. I don't know what it'll be but it's time to go."

"We'll figure it out, Boone. We always do." She sat her glass on the table, stood, and kissed him on the cheek. "In the meantime. Caroline won't be home for a while. You want to play escaped prisoner and the warden's wife?" she said, winking.

"As long as I can be the prisoner this time," Boone said.

He took her by the hand and walked down the hallway to their bedroom. "I love you, Abigail." He closed and locked the door.

Two days later, Boone sat in his office going over the packets of twenty-six lieutenants he would commission in just a few months. He glanced at the Rolex Submariner, did some quick calculations between local time and Alaska time, reached into his battered helmet bag, and retrieved a standard Army-issue green Memorandum pocket notebook. He flipped through the pages, found the number he was looking for, and picked up the phone on his desk. He dialed and glanced at a framed photograph of two young men in jungle fatigues and boonie hats. They were smiling with their arms around one another in front of a sandbagged bunker. The date was penciled on the bottom of the photo: 14 May 1970, Camp Eagle, SVN. It was hard to believe it was that long ago.

On the third ring, he answered. "What?"

Boone held the phone away from his ear for a second. "Man, your personality just gets better with age. Are you out of bed yet?"

"Ranger, I don't sleep. I just idle," Dan said.

"How are you doing, old buddy?" Boone asked.

"It's great to hear from you, brother. I thought maybe I'd fallen from grace with the Taggart clan. Did you forget how to write a letter or dial a phone? Been a while."

49

Feeling guilty about the candid confrontation, Boone glanced back at the photo. "Guilty as charged man. I should've called a long time ago."

After a few minutes of their usual banter, Boone came to the reason for the call. "Hey, I have an idea that I want to run by you."

"Sure, what do you got on your mind?"

"I want to plan an Alaskan hunt this fall," Boone said. "You and me, maybe Roan, if he can get leave. Possibly one or two others. What do you think?"

"I thought you'd never ask," Dan said. "Put together a basic concept and send me your ideas. I can work on the major pieces of the logistics from up here. I'll send you a copy of this year's hunting and fishing regulations, so you'll have general ideas of hunting areas and seasons."

"Great but mail it to me here at the office," Boone said. "This was all Abby's idea, and it's a bad precedent for her to start thinking she's right about everything. I'll ease her into it."

"Man, you married up more than anyone I know," Dan said.

"Check. Speaking of Abby, she said no alcohol."

"Well, that's understandable, considering the last time we did something like this."

"All right, my friend, I'll be in touch. I can't wait. Talk soon." Boone hung up the phone.

CHAPTER EIGHT
1300 Local-Friday 1 May 1987
Overmountain College-East Tennessee

"All right, let's go through it one more time." Sergeant Major Thomas Rutherford, the ROTC Detachment Senior Enlisted Adviser, was at the end of his first academic year in a world entirely different from the balance of his career. It still boiled down to training soldiers and upholding standards. For the first time in his long career, he was training officer candidates. He took pride that his final assignment before retirement offered the opportunity to influence the training of a new generation of leaders—brand new Second Lieutenants. His influence would cast a long shadow on the Army for years to come by giving them a perspective that few possessed.

"The colonel deserves better than this," Rutherford said. "You people are a soup sandwich, and we aren't leaving this room until we get this perfect. Again, from the beginning."

As the cadets comprising the honor guard, escorts, and narrator moved back to their original positions, Lieutenant Colonel Boone Taggart walked into the room, stood against the back wall, and watched the rehearsal. Rutherford walked to the back of the room and stopped next to the man whom he'd come to respect over the previous eight months. If these young men and women turned out like Taggart, his Army would be fine.

"Sergeant Major, it sounds like progress is slow. How's it going?"

"They're doing alright, sir. I don't want them to get too cocky. We'll run through it again and smooth a couple of rough spots, then we'll be set." Rutherford's pale blue eyes almost closed as he smiled.

Boone was fortunate to have Sergeant Major Rutherford as the detachment's senior non-commissioned officer. The tall NCO with wavy red hair was one of a kind. A personal tragedy for Sergeant Major brought Boone a tremendous professional blessing. Rutherford recently lost his father and discovered his mother had advanced cancer. The Army authorized a compassionate reassignment so his family could be as close as possible to his mother. Although not what the Sergeant Major wanted, the ROTC assignment was only forty-five miles from the farm where he grew up, and where his mother lay dying.

Tom Rutherford enlisted in the Army in 1960, serving as an infantryman his entire career. He didn't serve in the units perceived by many as the "high-speed" units. He spent a career in what paratroopers called "leg" units. Still, he had more combat experience than almost anyone in the Army. Boone knew the value of his experience, leadership, and example for these soon-to-be officers who'd never served as enlisted soldiers. Soldiers like Sergeant Major Rutherford, and younger versions of him, were crucial to an officer's future success. Although Boone started his career as an enlisted soldier, he'd been commissioned now for twenty-two years. During his tenure as the Professor of Military Science, he emphasized to his cadets the importance of the relationship between officers, NCOs, and enlisted soldiers.

In two years, Sergeant Major Rutherford would experience what Boone would in 24 hours—retirement. Both men had been in the Army since they were eighteen. It was the only life they knew, at least as adult men. Boone's transition was proving tenuous at best, and the Sergeant Major didn't even like thinking about what was next.

"Sergeant Major, I've got a few small changes to the ceremony," Boone said. "The University President has decided that he can fit it into his schedule, and the Brigade Commander's calendar changed, so he'll attend both ceremonies."

The Sergeant Major made some notes on his itinerary. "Roger, sir, I'll take care of it," Rutherford said.

"Thanks, Sergeant Major." Boone turned and left the room.

The following morning, Boone finished his run, stopped at the gym for a quick shower, and changed into his dress green uniform for the commissioning and retirement ceremony. It occurred to him the previous day this was the last time he would wear the uniform as an active-duty soldier. The next time he put it on, if he ever wore it again, would be for a ceremony of some type and then, as a retiree. The previous week was a flurry of administrative stress and frustration. The bureaucratic grindings, common to all large organizations, had occupied so much time he hadn't thought much about the implications of retirement. But the moment had arrived.

He completed Officer and NCO Efficiency Reports for the active-duty personnel assigned to the detachment and reviewed and signed the packets for twenty-five newly commissioned officers. Fourteen were headed for active-duty assignments, five for duty in the Army Reserves, and six to the Tennessee Army National Guard. He completed the last few tasks of his retirement packet. This chore had taken up much of the previous year. Boone and Abby were working on the details of selling a house, moving their family and all their possessions twelve hundred miles to a new home, a new piece of property, a new community, and sending a daughter to college in the fall. In short, almost everything in his world was changing. *No sweat!*

They were accustomed to some of those changes, such as frequent moves. Since their wedding in 1964, they'd moved almost a dozen times, but it was always to the same community, the insular world of the United States Army. Regardless of the post—Fort Campbell, Fort Bragg, Benning, Richardson, and all the rest—the routines were familiar. At every post, there were soldiers and families with whom they'd previously served. The Taggart Family had experienced the same life for the previous twenty years, but it played out at different locations. Retirement was the most dramatic change Boone had experienced. They were moving to a place that, even though he and Abby grew up there, they'd only visited a few times over the past two decades. The Army was home.

Boone stood in front of the mirror and glanced at his uniform to ensure it was right. If it wasn't, the Sergeant Major would notice and say something. To avoid that embarrassment, he took one more look and, approvingly, headed to his office. Major Deborah Strand, his executive officer, met him walking down the hall.

"Good morning, sir. Are you ready for your big day?" she asked.

Strand was a solid officer and leader and would be in charge through the summer until the new PMS showed up in August, just before the start of the academic year. Boone was at least comfortable with that transition.

"Morning, Deb, I'm *not* ready for my big day," he said.

She turned and followed him into the suite that included his office and an executive assistant in the outer foyer. Mary Williams was one of only two civilians in the detachment. Still, she'd been in this job for the past 28 years. She ran the place and wasn't reluctant to let Boone know that long after any military personnel were gone, she would still be here making things happen.

"Good morning, Mary," Boone said.

"Good morning, sir. The Brigade Commander will arrive here at 0930, and the commissioning ceremony begins at 1000 in the Student Center main conference room. The Sergeant Major reports that they finally got their head out of their asses, and he has high confidence that they won't screw this up too bad, his words, not mine. Your family will meet you here before the ceremony. Lunch with the Brigade Commander is at 1200 in the main dining facility. You have a private room. Do you want anyone else attending?"

Boone thought momentarily about asking Abby, but she'd suffered through enough of these in her life. The kids would prefer McDonald's. He thought about his parents, but his mother wouldn't say three words, and his dad, well...

"No, I think I'll take that one alone."

"Your retirement ceremony is at 1400," Mary said, "also at the Student Center Conference Room, with a reception to follow in the same room. You're free to go after that."

Deborah noticed that the walls of his office were still filled with framed photographs, certificates, and memorabilia from twenty-five years of soldiering. It didn't look like the vacant space it should be.

"Sir, you retire in a matter of hours. When are you cleaning out the office?"

"I'll get to it over the weekend. Abby said she'd give me a hand."

Quickly changing the subject, Boone said, "Major Strand, how about putting someone up front watching the door for the Brigade Commander."

"Already done, sir."

Deborah and Mary stood and left the office. Within a few moments, he heard a cadet near the door call the building to attention, letting him know that a higher-ranking officer had entered the area. Boone stepped around his desk and walked down the hallway to see Colonel Stewart McCoy, Brigade Commander, round the corner of the foyer.

"Good morning, sir. Welcome," Boone greeted his boss.

"Morning, Boone. How are you doing?"

"I'm well, sir. We can discuss today's itinerary if you want to join me in my office. Need a cup of coffee?"

"Sure, sugar and cream, please," the Colonel said.

Mary delivered the coffee in standard military ceramic mugs. One emblazoned with Master Parachutist wings on the front, "*Captain Boone Taggart*" in gold lettering on the back. The other with the Fourth Infantry Division patch.

"Sir, sugar and cream," Mary said, handing the Colonel the mug with the 4th Infantry Division patch, and to Boone, "Black."

"Strong enough to float a horseshoe nail?" Boone said.

"Yes, sir, it'll take the hide off your mouth."

Colonel McCoy took a sip from his mug and noticed the patch of the unit he served with in Vietnam.

"Custom mugs for all visitors, or are you brown-nosing for something?"

"No, sir, custom mugs just for the Brigade Commander," Boone said. "You can take it with you since I'm retiring and you're PCSing. By the way, sir, the line of people I've brown-nosed is long and distinguished."

The Colonel chuckled—he knew the last statement was a lie. Taggart was generally an outspoken critic of senior officers, blunt to the point that he might've advanced his career beyond teaching ROTC at a small, public liberal arts college in the Appalachian Highlands.

McCoy had heard several legendary stories about Taggart's last tour in Vietnam. Rumor had it that he and some of his Green Beret friends liberated an American POW from a camp in Laos. There was some major political fallout over the incident, but McCoy didn't know why. It was just a war story though. It probably wasn't true.

They'd never had a serious disagreement, but Taggart differed from the other PMSs in the Brigade. Many were on their last Army assignment and saw teaching ROTC as a 3–4-year break to prepare for retirement. Several Lieutenant Colonels in the Brigade used whatever influence they had to be assigned to schools close to their retirement homes. Taggart was different even in that way. He was moving over twelve hundred miles back to Wyoming and a ranch even farther in the middle of nowhere than East Tennessee. Also, unlike most other PMSs, Taggart ran the ROTC Detachment like an active-duty Army unit, at least as much as he could. He took the task of training the next crop of Second Lieutenants more seriously than the other officers in the Brigade. To his credit, he'd produced some exemplary young leaders in the previous four years.

"Thanks for the mug. I figured you were trying to highlight that your boss is a leg," McCoy said.

"Happy side effect, sir."

The two career officers reviewed the day's events, coordinated times, and made notes. As their meeting ended, Colonel McCoy gave Boone a more serious directive.

"Boone, I recently attended a friend's retirement ceremony at Fort Knox, and his boss asked him an interesting question just before the ceremony. He requested that he share the answer during his farewell speech."

"What's the question, sir?"

McCoy took the last sip of his coffee, placed the gifted mug in his briefcase, and looked back at Boone. "What was your best day in uniform?"

McCoy could tell Boone was taken back a bit. He figured Boone had expected the question to be something more philosophical, more profound, even spiritual. The answer to the question would highlight what a soldier held dear, and what aspect of the service meant the most to him.

"I'll have to think about that, sir," Boone said. "Do I have to answer you now, or can I think about it and add it to my comments?"

"Add it to the ceremony. I'm interested in hearing it, and I think it'll be helpful for your cadets to hear what was so meaningful for you at the end of your career as they start the beginning of theirs."

"Yes, sir."

Boone shook hands with his commander and escorted him to the front door. "Sir, this is Cadet Brookings, soon to be in about an hour, Second Lieutenant Brookings. He'll escort you to the Student Center."

"Good morning, Brookings. Lead the way," McCoy said.

Boone watched the two walk down the steps. Then his attention was drawn to his family parked and pouring out of the Chevy Suburban. He was thankful his parents were able to attend. Rachel and Caroline stepped out of the car. Abby had picked up Rachel at the airport the day before, but the surprise came when the young man in dress greens, bloused jump boots, and an overseas cap with a glider patch stepped from the passenger's seat. The young man exchanged salutes with Colonel McCoy as they passed in the parking lot.

The young man sounded off with his unit motto. "Strike and kill, sir." McCoy returned his salute.

Boone bounded down the stairs. The young man repeated the salute for his dad but was swallowed in a bear hug.

"What're you doing here? I thought your unit was on gold cycle, and you couldn't get a pass," Boone said.

"My Battalion Commander heard you were retiring," Roan said. "I guess you two served together in Korea, and he thought it was important that I be here for the ceremony—so he gave me a three-day pass. I think either Mom or Colonel McCoy had something to do with it."

"Well, either way, I'm thankful you're here."

57

Abby walked up and kissed her husband. Boone kissed Rachel and Caroline on the cheek, hugged his mom, and shook hands with his dad.

"There's one more surprise," Abby said. "I asked Colonel McCoy if Roan could read your retirement orders during the ceremony, and he agreed."

Boone fought back his rising emotions.

"He didn't say anything this morning when we talked," Boone said.

Abby touched his chest, "That's how surprises work, dear. You don't get to control every aspect of everything you know? Mary and Deb Strand were in on it, too."

"Thanks, honey, this means the world."

***

When the last note of the National Anthem played, the color guard posted the colors and marched to the back of the room. Boone had noticed one small mistake, which most of the audience wouldn't see, but the Sergeant Major did, along with four additional errors. The crowd was seated as the newest Second Lieutenant in the United States Army began the narration. He welcomed guests and distinguished visitors and read Colonel McCoy's and Boone's biographies.

Colonel McCoy mounted the podium, gave the standard retirement ceremony speech, welcomed the guests, congratulated the newly commissioned officers, highlighted the sacrifices of Army families, and ended with Boone's decades of service to the country. It was Boone's turn. He did the same, welcomed the guests, expressed his pride for the new officers, profusely thanked Abby, the children, and his parents, conveyed his pride for Roan's service, and then answered the Colonel's odd question.

"Earlier this morning in my office. Colonel McCoy asked me an interesting question, 'What was your best day in uniform?' I thought about my answer long and hard and want to share it with you. It was a beautiful, sunny January day in 1975 at Fort Richardson, Alaska. I was commander of C Co/4-23 Infantry. I was the primary

58

jumpmaster standing on the tailgate of the last C-130 in the lift. When we turned onto final approach to Malamute Drop Zone, Mount McKinley, Denali, or the Great One, was right there in view. The mountain is only visible for about forty-five days a year, and it's spectacular, especially during the winter months. Although two hundred miles away, it looked as though I could reach out and touch it. It seemed so close. I commanded an airborne infantry company in the most beautiful place on earth. I was with men I respected, experts in their skills, tough men serving their country, in a place that filled my soul. That was my best day. If it were possible, and the Army allowed me to do that for the rest of my service and pass the promotions and advancements, I'd have agreed without reservation."

The ceremony ended with Colonel McCoy decorating Boone for the last time in his career, and his son, Specialist Roan Boone, 20 years old, infantryman assigned to A Co, 3-502 Infantry, 101st Airborne Division (Air Assault), read his father's retirement orders, something that didn't happen very often. It was over.

The ceremony was followed by cake, punch, and small talk, the social function of military life. This was a part of his career Boone never adjusted to. It was Abby's department, and she was good at it, thus alleviating him from the perils of human interaction. Roan and Caroline were like their mother. They worked the crowd, while he and Rachel found a wall to back against, and talk about hunting, fishing, horses, or dogs, waiting for the end.

As the reception wrapped up and the guests faded away, Boone said goodbye to his family.

"I need to go by the office, but I'll be home in a while," he told Abby.

They kissed and he walked across campus, entered the ROTC Department, and headed for his office. Walking past the day room, he heard the familiar voices of his cadets and decided to step in for one more war story, ping-pong, pool table session.

The day room was like so many others around the Army. One wall covered with a bookshelf containing field manuals, the basics of military history, tactics and strategy, military thought and theory, biographies, and a handful of military and geo-political thrillers. The other walls displayed recruiting posters and photographs of alumni in Germany, the Pacific Islands, Korea, and Vietnam. Two sofas dominated the central open space in front of a large TV and VCR. The cadets in the room were watching *A Bridge Too Far* for the thousandth time. Behind the sofa was a ping-pong table, pool table, and a worktable with chairs there for study but most often littered with maps and field manuals instead of textbooks. The refrigerator held sodas, lunch bags, and occasionally a few cases of cheap beer, even though they inhabited a dry campus. It smelled like a combination of weapons cleaning fluid, beer, sweat, and tobacco. A small cargo parachute was tacked to the ceiling in clear violation of fire codes, giving the room a uniquely military ambiance. Boone loved this space.

Four cadets, now promoted to their senior year, and two newly commissioned lieutenants, saying goodbye to their friends and planning for the evening's festivities, all stood as Boone walked into the room.

"At ease," Boone said. He hung his dress green jacket on the back of a chair and loosened his tie. "Which one of you rookies has the next game of ping-pong?"

"You sure you want that kind of challenge, sir?" a young, bald cadet said.

"Let's see what you got, Airborne." The game was on.

Boone beat the young man 15-12. Laughing, he sat on the couch next to Second Lieutenant David Farmer. Dave was a solid performer in the detachment and was commissioned a Field Artillery officer that morning. He was leaving on Sunday for Fort Sill, Oklahoma, where he would attend the Field Artillery Officers Basic Course. Every officer attended their basic branch Officer Basic Course or OBC as the first of many career-enhancing courses. OBC was designed to prepare them for life as a lieutenant in an infantry or armor division, in Dave's case, to serve as a Fire Support Officer.

"You ready to go to Sill, Dave?" Boone asked the young man.

"Yes, sir, the truck's serviced, and I'm leaving on Sunday morning but don't have to report until Thursday. I thought I'd go out and get the lay of the land."

"You'll enjoy your time at Sill. There's good fishing, plus upland bird, and duck hunting north of Fort Sill at Wichita Mountains Wildlife Refuge. Work hard but get outside and decompress now and then."

"Check, sir."

The young lieutenant paused momentarily and seemed reluctant to say what was on his mind. Boone felt the pause, and although they had many professional and personal conversations over the previous three years, he detected the young man's reluctance to say what he had on his mind. Dave had talked to him earlier in the week about some final professional questions—they'd talked twice earlier in the year about a personal issue, and Dave had already expressed his gratitude for Boone's leadership and counsel.

"What're you thinking about Dave?"

"Colonel Taggart, I have a question for you, and maybe it's painful, and you don't want to answer me, and I understand. I thought about this after your comments at the retirement ceremony, though. You described your best day in uniform, and what you said only confirmed what most of us already knew about you. But what was your worst day?"

CHAPTER NINE
1500 Hours Local-Wednesday 10 June 1987
Double A Ranch-Sheridan County, Wyoming

The two-vehicle convoy pulled off the county road onto the gravel driveway of the Double A Ranch. Boone was leading in his new Dodge truck, pulling the trailered International Scout behind. Caroline sat next to him, chatting excitedly. Now she'd be living near both sets of grandparents. It was every parent's nightmare. Her grandparents would spoil her beyond repair. Abby followed in her Chevy Suburban, pulling a U-Haul trailer with the basics for living during their transition.

The trip from Tennessee to Wyoming was uneventful. There were no accidents, breakdowns, or other roadside calamities. In every fashion, it was a typical Taggart Family road trip. They visited Badlands National Park, Mount Rushmore, Devil's Tower, every possible museum and battlefield along the way, and the greatest attraction on the northern Plains, Wall Drug. They camped at different locations every night, ate sandwiches at roadside pull-offs for lunch, Abby made breakfast on the Coleman stove, and they ate supper at greasy spoon diners on back roads. Caroline repeatedly reminded her dad that "there are interstate highways, hotels, and nice restaurants in every state," but he wouldn't be swayed.

"We're making memories," he reminded her.

Boone insisted on following the back roads as much as possible, believing that this was the "real" America. He wanted to immerse his kids in the country's history. It hadn't been easy for the children of a historian and soldier wrapped in one package. He regularly gave reading assignments before family trips, so they'd better understand what they saw and experienced. On long weekends throughout his career, Boone took the family to museums and battlefields, not once to an amusement park. His plan had created some enduring memories. They hiked long sections of the Appalachian Trail through Virginia's Shenandoah National Park, witnessed battle reenactments at Antietam battlefield, drank boiled river water in the Missouri River Breaks country, and hiked over Lolo Pass in the shadow of the Corps of Discovery. His only concession was an occasional weekend at a secluded beach, but he agreed only because Abby still looked great in a bikini.

He accomplished his mission. All the children were dedicated readers, and he even turned Abby into an amateur historian. He expressed his take on it one day in a museum.

"You're a woman from a southern Appalachian family," he said. "You're nosy, you like knowing what people in other times were up to."

He was confident that she didn't appreciate his conclusion, but he knew she loved their family road trips and mealtime discussions of books, history, and culture. She would often admit to him that they made some great memories.

This move was the Taggart's twelfth. Moving and traveling were inherent parts of military life, and they were experts. The contents of the U-Haul and two vehicles would sustain them while they remodeled the house that Abby hoped would be their forever home. They'd get organized for a few days, see family members, and settle into a temporary life in the guest house at the Double-A. A small three-bedroom house, it housed family members in transition and occasional workers at the ranch.

Boone backed the Scout off the trailer and parked it and the U-Haul next to the guest house and, with his father's help, unloaded the contents of the U-Haul into the house while Abby, Caroline, and Boone's mother unpacked the boxes and established their temporary home.

The first morning in the guest house, Boone sat on the front porch watching his father walk across the driveway with two cups of coffee, pipe clenched between his teeth. He handed Boone one of the coffee mugs and sat in the cane-bottomed chair beside his son.

"New pipe in the collection?" Boone asked.

"Yes, sir. I was on a hunting trip down in New Mexico last fall, and one of the guys in the lodge ran a pipe shop in Pennsylvania. We talked about pipes and tobacco, and he sent me this in the mail a couple of weeks after the trip."

Wade handed Boone the pipe. The meerschaum had the face of a Scottish soldier carved into the bowl and was beginning to develop a light brown patina. Boone turned it in his hand, admired the work of art, and handed it back to his father. The face carved in the pipe reminded Boone of the man beside him—bushy hair, thick beard, and deep lines on his face.

Wade put the pipe between his teeth, retrieved a matchbox from his vest pocket, lit a single match, held it over the bowl, moving it in a circular motion until the tobacco burned. He lay the expended match on the table between the chairs and packed the tobacco lightly with his tamper. The smoke lingered around his head. It was clear he was enjoying his morning ritual.

"Mm, Mm, that's mighty fine."

Lighting a pipe is quite a process. Boone thought. *It's more than the pipe and the tobacco.*

"How does it feel to be a civilian?" Wade said.

"Technically, I'm not a civilian yet. I had sixty days of leave stored up, so I'm still in the Army until 1 August."

"I got news for you, son. You might as well adjust now as later."

"I know," Boone said. "How did you do it when you came home?"

"Our situations aren't parallel, son. I served for eight years and came home. I didn't make it a career."

"Yeah, but your entire military experience was combat, in two theaters during the war, and then you went back in during Korea."

"Son, you've been in uniform for twenty-five years. You've dedicated your entire adult life to this. There's no reason to think this will be easy, but it's not impossible either. You loved what you did, you're better at it than most, and if you were honest with me, it didn't end the way you thought it would. I know you wanted a command, and

I know you wanted to make full colonel. Having said all that, you have to do it. You might as well think about how to be productive, figure out what you can do with your skills, or learn new ones. You've got to have a new mission, a reason to get up every morning and put your pants on."

Boone leaned the cane-bottomed chair back against the porch wall and looked down at his coffee mug.

Wade paused for a moment. "A lot of people have trouble making this transition. I did, your grandfather did, and even your mom missed the Army when she left. To answer your question, we came home, bought land, and worked. We've always lived close to the land. It seemed to fit all of us. It was our therapy. It may be something else for you, but it has to be something. It was raising you and your sisters for your mom. She was back here after she left the Army and made a home while I finished out my time. You were her new mission.

"You'll be busy remodeling the house this summer and preparing for our trip this fall, but then you'll have to figure something out. Use this time to think about what's next. I don't want to see you make the mistakes a lot of guys make. I saw too many of my friends and my dad's friends drink themselves to death or ruin their marriages and reputations, because they couldn't put it all behind them and figure out what was next. It'd kill me to see that happen to my son."

"I know, Dad. I promise I'll figure it out, but I may need help occasionally."

"At supper last night, you said you're looking forward to some peace and quiet," Wade said. "I've discovered that quiet is easy to find. It's right up there in those shining mountains." He pointed to the Bighorns with his pipe stem. "Or out in that hay field, but you'll have to create your own peace. It doesn't come automatically and is harder to find than quiet."

After a moment, Wade said, "You work on your house, work on our trip, and work the ranch as much or as little as you want. If you need anything, you know where to find me."

"Thanks, Dad. I appreciate everything." His dad stood and limped toward the barn to start the day's work.

Wade Taggart and his bride, Rebecca Crabtree Taggart, bought the Double A Ranch in 1946, two months after Wade returned from service in the China-Burma-India Theater of Operations. The Double A, named in honor of the 82nd Airborne Division, the All Americans, was where Wade served in North Africa, Sicily, and Italy. Where he cut his teeth as a young soldier, and later Infantry officer, before being recruited by the Office of Strategic Services, posted in Burma for the remainder of the war. The Double A was directly across a dirt road from the TF Ranch where Wade grew up, and it was part of the original TF Ranch homesteaded by his great-grandfather following the Civil War. For a few years, three generations of Taggarts ranched in Sheridan County.

Rebecca was an Army nurse in England when she met Wade in 1943. By the end of a long weekend, they were in love and married one month later. A pregnant Rebecca was discharged and sent back to the US to live with her mother and father-in-law. She'd never met them. Far from her southern Appalachian home, she fell in love with her new in-laws and the Wyoming prairie and mountains. Once Wade came home, she never imagined living elsewhere and dedicated herself to her family and the ranch.

For the first ten years of their marriage, they lived in a small two-bedroom house that was nice but tight for a growing family. A few minor additions made it more comfortable, but the family eventually outgrew the tiny house. Wade built a larger western-style log home as the main ranch house. It's where they raised their children and now looked forward to having grandchildren around. The old house became the guest house, and the addition of barns, sheds, workshops, corrals, and sorting pens completed the working ranch. The Double A wasn't large enough to make them cattle barons, but they made a living, raised their family, and were content to raise grandchildren on the same piece of land.

Boone walked into his mother's kitchen. Rachel and Abby were cutting the pie and pouring coffee for dessert. He spread out three

66

maps on the large harvest table. Wade sat beside him.

"You want to see the plan?" Boone asked his father.

Boone walked him through it from start to finish. He showed Wade the flight routes and where they would camp and hunt. They talked about logistics, meal menus, camp chores, and specific tools they would need. They discussed firearms and equipment.

"Did you send everyone a gear checklist? I don't want anyone up there without the proper equipment. This is an Alaskan hunt, not the typical back forty deer hunts," Wade said.

"Yes, sir, I did. Roan gave me his gear the last time I saw him. I quizzed him to make sure he was properly packed. He's the junior member of the expedition and the least experienced. Bobby is an accomplished outdoorsman. He's hunted in Africa a few times. Dan has years of Alaska experience. You've hunted all over the world, including Alaska and Canada, so I think everyone is properly equipped, regarding personal gear. I'm taking care of the expedition gear, tents, stoves, coolers, and so on. I'll get you to look at everything as I pack to ensure I'm not missing anything."

Boone smiled. "Now, what're your questions?" He asked his father.

"Well, first, don't you want me to drive up with you?"

"Nope. Truthfully, Dad, I could use some time alone."

"I understand," Wade said. "We'll have plenty of time to catch up on the drive back."

"Check."

"Emergency contingencies, break in contact, lost hunter," Wade said. "Do you think we should develop an E&E plan?"

"There are probably a few emergency contingencies that we'll need to discuss, like a lost hunter or what we do if someone doesn't return to camp at the end of the day. We'll always be working in buddy teams, but an E&E plan, Dad? You know we aren't at war with the Japanese anymore," Boone said, laughing.

"I know that smart ass. What I mean is having a plan if something happens when someone has to walk out, a lane they should follow so we know where to search. I know it's farfetched, but it's within the realm of possibility. Alaska is a big, unforgiving place."

Boone had always known his father as a meticulous planner. A contingency guy, thinking about what could happen and then developing a response plan. When Boone was a kid, Wade quoted Eisenhower. "In war, plans are nothing, but planning is everything."

And now a generation and another war later, Boone knew the importance of planning, even though both had experienced the age-old military axiom, "no plan survives first contact with the enemy."

The detailed planning process guided them through the possibilities of the fog of war or hunting, in this case.

"We'll look at an E&E plan, Dad."

CHAPTER TEN
2115 Hours-Monday 31 August 1987
Double A Ranch-Sheridan County, Wyoming

Abigail took the last of the coffee mugs to the kitchen sink. Boone followed her with a tray of plates and silverware, the remnants of dessert. What a ranch family could do to a beautifully decorated cake was impressive and marginally violent. Family gatherings were an innovation for his branch of the Taggart's. Boone, Abigail, and their children had rarely been at the ranch to participate in these rituals. The last time Boone lived at home was in 1962 when he left for the Army. They married in 1964, and Abigail didn't return except when they visited on leave. She hadn't moved home during Boone's tours in Vietnam and Korea. She preferred to stay in their quarters at various Army posts. She believed the continuity of school, friends, and church was necessary for the children's well-being and her sanity. Living full-time around both branches of the family was an adjustment.

"This is a mess," Boone said. "That's the last time we're having company...ever."

"Really, we're never having our parents over again?"

"Check. This is ridiculous. We didn't have send-offs like this when I went to Vietnam. We're just going on a hunting trip. We're not landing on Normandy. Never again. Did you hear what my sister said? She wants to have everyone together for a birthday party for a two-year-old, and I'm telling you something. That kid's not smart enough to know it's his party."

"Boone, that's terrible to say about that baby."

He smiled. "Mark my word, no Harvard for that kid."

"Yeah, well, there was no Harvard for you either," Abby said.

"OK, fair enough, but still never again...never."

69

"Listen, I think our mothers are enjoying this. It's the first time in their lives this many children and grandchildren have lived at home. They've missed out and are just trying to catch up."

Boone knew he was fighting a futile battle against logic and motherly instinct. As much as he missed the Army, he'd enjoyed preparing for the trip and working the ranch with his dad the previous summer. He'd lost some of his skill as a cowboy, but Wade was surprisingly patient as Boone smoothed things out.

Abby stood behind him and wrapped her arms around his waist. "I'm going to miss you."

"I'll miss you too, but I'll only be gone a month or so, six weeks at most, and we're old hands at being apart." Boone placed his hands on top of hers.

"I know, but you didn't have to travel that much in your last assignment," Abby said. "I'm spoiled. I'm used to having you around. I'll miss you." After a short pause she said, "If we're planning on the night before deployment ritual, I need to get Caroline squared away and in bed, and I need a shower. I stink."

"OK. I'll get the dishes taken care of."

Abby disappeared down the hall. A few minutes later, Caroline walked up next to Boone as he worked on the dirty dishes. "I've never seen you do that," she said.

"I'm pretty sure I've done this several times."

"Well, I've never seen you do it. I'm going to miss you, Dad."

"I'm going to miss you too, honey."

"Will you bring me something back from your trip?"

"I always do, don't I?"

"Yes, sir," Caroline smiled.

Boone dried his hands, pulled his youngest daughter close to him, and kissed her cheek. "I love you, sweetheart, and I'll miss you."

"Love you too, Daddy. Goodnight."

"Goodnight, baby."

Boone finished the dishes, dried them, and put them back in the cabinet, except for a couple of pots and pans. He had no idea where Abby stored them. Maybe Caroline was right. He didn't do this enough.

Boone checked the locks on all the doors and flipped off the lights in the kitchen. When he passed Caroline's room, he peeked through the door. Seeing she was asleep, he sneaked in and kissed her once more. He closed her door and then quietly knocked on Rachel's bedroom door.

"Come in," she said.

"I just came in to say goodbye. I'm leaving early in the morning," Boone said.

"I'll be up. I want to see you off."

"Honey, I'm leaving early. Are you sure?"

"Yes, sir, I'll see you in the morning."

"Okay. Love you, goodnight," Boone said.

"Goodnight, Dad."

Boone closed the door, walked down the hallway into the master bedroom, closed and locked the door behind him. Abby was out of the shower and in the walk-in closet, getting ready for bed. He stepped to the stereo and pushed the play button on the cassette player. Momentarily, the smooth sounds of Sam Cooke softly filled the room.

If Sam can't make it happen, nobody can. Boone thought.

He stepped into the bathroom and took a shower. He couldn't help but laugh about the night before deployment and post-deployment rituals. They made love the night before any trip lasting five days or longer, and on the night he returned, regardless of the length of absence. When they were first married, Abby laughed at him for even thinking of such a thing.

"Only a soldier would have a standing policy about his sex life," she said. He always defended it as sound. It was now a codified tradition.

Stepping out of the shower, he dried and wrapped the towel around his waist, wiped the mirror off, brushed his teeth, combed his hair, and splashed on some Old Spice. *I'm ancient. I'm still using the same cologne as my old man.*

He looked in the mirror and decided that was the best he could do. He winked at himself and turned toward the bedroom.

"Alright, baby, prepare to experience erotic pleasures that most women dare not dream of," he said.

His smile was broken by the vision of his beautiful wife lying on her back in bed wearing his favorite short, black teddy, sound asleep, arm over her head, mouth wide open, snoring like a grizzly bear.

"Well crap."

He dressed, set his alarm clock for 0400, kissed her on the forehead, and went to sleep. So much for tradition.

***

Boone put the last of his gear on the truck seat. He quietly closed the driver's door, walked toward the horse corral, and took two apples out of his jacket pocket. He pulled the small buckaroo knife from the sheath on his left hip, cut the apples into slices, and fed them to the four horses standing at the paddock fence.

"You boys, behave yourselves while I'm gone. Mom doesn't need any trouble from you all. I'll see you guys in a month or so."

He patted each animal on the forehead and walked back to his truck.

He reached for the door handle but stopped when Rachel stepped down from the porch, dressed in her usual sleeping attire— long john bottoms and a faded black sweatshirt with a black and gold "Ranger" tab on the front, a souvenir absconded from Boone. She carried a cup of coffee in one hand and a package in the other, walked up to Boone, set the coffee on the truck's bumper, and wrapped her arms around him.

"You be careful, please," she said.

"You know it, kiddo."

She handed him the package. "Here I got you a present. Don't open it now, but I know you'll love it."

Boone placed the package in his helmet bag on the passenger's seat. "Thanks, honey, but aren't you a starving college student? You shouldn't be spending money on your old man."

"You're not old, and I had some money saved from working for Grandpa this summer. Like I said, you'll love it. I couldn't pass it up when I saw it."

"Truthfully, I was a little surprised when you came home yesterday," Boone said. "You're not laying out of class, are you? We've spent a lot of time apart. You aren't getting sentimental in your old age, are you?"

"No, sir. But I'll admit I wish I was going too. It's been a while since we've been on an expedition together, but Roan, that little turd, would've complained about hunting with his little sister. I think he's just afraid I can outshoot him."

Boone and Abby marveled at how competitive their children were with one another but how loyal they were when outsiders intervened.

"I'll tell you what, you and I will take the same trip when you graduate," Boone said.

"Okay. I'd like that. I'll hold you to it."

Rachel hugged him again, kissed him on the cheek, retrieved her coffee, and walked back up the steps. She turned to him. "I love you daddy. Please be careful."

"I love you too, darling," Boone said.

He started the engine, put the truck in gear, and started down the drive toward the county road. Rachel stood on the porch, watching the truck turn onto the pavement, and felt her mother standing beside her. "I thought it was family policy that you didn't get out of bed if his trip was less than six months," Rachel said, referring to another of her parent's traditions.

"It is, and he didn't wake me up. I woke up on my own, but I didn't want to interrupt your goodbye. Besides, we violated another family policy last night."

Rachel thought for a moment about what her mother was referring to, then it hit her.

"O Lord, momma, that's gross."

CHAPTER ELEVEN
0830 Hours Local-Sunday 6 September 1987
Fairbanks International Airport, Alaska

Boone lay in the camper wrapped in a poncho liner when Bart "Yeti" Chapman stepped to the door announcing that coffee was on. Boone backed the truck and trailer into the Chapman Aviation hanger just after midnight the night before and slept.

"I thought you Airborne Ranger types didn't require sleep," Bart said.

Boone threw back the poncho liner and stepped to the camper's floor. Bart handed him a cup of hot coffee and sat across from him in the dinette seat. Boone removed the black wool watch cap and scratched his head,

"I didn't a few years ago, but now I need an occasional nap," Boone said, squinting through partially opened and bloodshot eyes.

"Yeah, me too."

"What're you talking about?" Boone said. "You aviators were always complaining about crew rest. You all require at least eighteen hours of sleep a day just to function."

"Good point. How was the trip? More important, how are Abby and the kids?"

"The trip was good. Thankfully, uneventful. Going home might be more challenging after eighteen days in the field and winter coming. If I don't miss the last ferry out of Whittier, I might see if they have an open slot or a cancellation."

Boone held the mug in both hands and blew across the top, cooling the coffee as he and Bart caught up on family and friends' gossip.

"How about you? How do you like working for your old man

74

in the far north?" Boone said.

"A dream come true," Bart said. "No kidding. I love it and wouldn't do anything else. When I left the Air Force, the last thing I wanted to do was work for my dad, but we've both changed, and it's great. He's mellowed a little over the years, and I've grown up. He's built a great business, life is good."

Bart topped off both mugs. "What do we need to get done in the next couple of days?"

"I have a few small tasks to complete before the guys show up, but what I really need is space," Boone said. "Is it OK if we set up a small base in the hangar to prep?"

"Absolutely. Just use this one. It's our maintenance hangar, generally, we only use half."

"What do we need to do on your end of things?"

"The Otter will come in on Wednesday afternoon," Bart said. "We'll do a maintenance check, top off fuel, and park it in front of the hangar. I'll be here around 1700 and supervise loading the gear. Make sure you all are ready to load by then. Dad's already out in Eagle with the other pilots who'll support you guys. I'll fly you to Eagle in the Otter. Dad and one of the other pilots will fly you into the hunt area in Super-Cubs. Have the boys ready to fly on Thursday morning. We take off at 0800."

"We'll be ready," Boone said.

"Until then, if you need me, just leave a message in the office or at the FBO, and they can find me," Bart said. "I'll check in with you when I'm back here at the airfield and help you out if I can, but I've got other clients we're picking up, dropping off, and resupplying. So you and your merry band aren't the only show in town, but you'll get priority."

"Thanks for everything, man. We'll be fine. Go run your business, brother. I've got work to do, too."

The Chapman Family held a special place in Taggart clan lore. Bart's father, Colonel Donald "Chappie" Chapman, United States Air Force, retired, was an extraordinary fighter pilot who flew multiple aircraft platforms in three wars over more than three decades. Chappie first came into the Taggart's orbit in the jungles of Burma in late 1944.

He flew with Boone's father-in-law, Herman "Hoot" Clark. Boone's father, Wade, an OSS Captain, was somehow involved in Chappie's rescue from behind Japanese lines. The three men never revealed the entire story to the rest of the family. It was reserved for them. It must've been quite a story—Boone would love to know it in detail.

Chappie was an occasional guest at the Taggart ranches and Wade's constant hunting companion for hunting trips worldwide. Boone was eight when he first met Chappie and saw him a few times again as he passed through Sheridan County. He'd never met Chappie's son, Bart, until Boone stood in the cargo compartment of Bart's HH-53 Jolly Green Giant, just west of the Laotian-South Vietnamese border. Bart's crew pulled Boone from the jungle and spared him from capture by the North Vietnamese Army. Fate allowed Bart to level the debt of honor between the two families. Wade Taggart rescued Chappie Chapman in Burma in 1944, and Bart Chapman rescued Boone Taggart from the jungle in another war in 1970.

Bart was given the callsign "Yeti" by his squadron mates in Vietnam because of his size—six feet three inches and two hundred twenty pounds of muscle, blond hair, blue eyes, and the fact that he was born and raised Alaskan. Father and son Chapman ran a successful bush flying service.

Boone set the bacon and eggs, sourdough bread with jam, and four large slices of caribou summer sausage on the camper's dinette table, poured his fourth cup of coffee, and started on breakfast. He propped *The Hunt for Red October* against another stack of books he carried as emergency reading provisions in the camper. Over the years, Boone amassed an impressive library, and there was very little of what he called "mind candy." He was a student of warfare, which was reflected in his library and other collections. He ate breakfast as he read, finished the dishes, and brewed another pot of coffee.

He sipped the hot, black coffee and continued Clancy's book when he remembered the package Rachel gave him. He put the book down, reached into the helmet bag, and pulled out the package. It was wrapped in brown grocery bag paper. He untied the coarse string that held the package together and pulled away the paper. It was two hardback books. The first, a western, *Lonesome Dove* by Larry

McMurtry.

Good girl, Rach. I love a good Western.

And the second, *The Last of the Breed*, Louis L'Amour's latest novel. Growing up on a Wyoming ranch, L'Amour and Zane Grey were mandatory reading. Boone appreciated both but leaned toward L'Amour's writing.

A leather marker sat on page 150 in *The Last of the Breed*. Boone opened it and looked at the marker. It was a piece of latigo strap from the tack room at the ranch. She'd stamped "Daddy" down the front and in black marker, "I love you - Rachel" on the back, a Father's Day gift many years ago. There was a handwritten note.

Daddy,

I saw these in a bookstore in Laramie and couldn't resist. I hope you don't mind, but I read them before I wrapped them up for you. You're going to love both, I know it. Sitting next to a campfire in the Alaskan wilderness, they'll take you away to another time and place. Before long, you'll follow a herd north to Montana and survive in the Siberian Arctic, seeking revenge for the men who tortured you. There's one passage in L'Amour's book that reminded me of you. I underlined it in pencil on the page I marked. I'm looking forward to talking to you about both. Have a great trip.

I love you.
Rachel.

Boone opened the book again to the marked page and read the underlined passage, *"I walk in the shoes of the men of today. I fly their planes, I eat their food, but my heart is in the wilderness with feathers in my hair."*

Boone rewrapped the two books and put them in his rucksack.

Over the next several days, the hangar of Chapman Aviation, not surprisingly, took on the flavor of an Army camp. The five men, three retired and two still serving, hovered over their gear, inspecting, preparing, and re-packing. The hangar was a sea of packs, gun cases, lanterns, stoves, tents, axes, saws, and various other camping and hunting gear. A table against the back wall was a command post with several maps and notebooks. Boone's camper served as the kitchen. Bobby Doyle sat on a cot, showing Roan a more efficient technique to stow and carry essential gear. Roan had a new hero.

Boone met Master Sergeant Robert "Bobby" Doyle in 1962 during Basic Infantry Training at Fort Benning, Georgia. They attended the same Airborne and Ranger classes and the Special Forces Qualification or "Q" Course. The two young sergeants then deployed to the Central Highlands of South Vietnam on the same A Detachment, Boone, the junior communications specialist, and Bobby, the junior weapons specialist. They were the junior men and only replacements on a well-established, experienced team. They grew close during their time in Vietnam. Although the careers of the two warriors had parted not long after their tour, they remained close friends through the years, occasionally seeing one another on subsequent tours and sharing many hunting and fishing camps on the Taggart ranches and around the globe.

When their tour ended in early 1965, Boone attended Officer's Candidate School. Although more talented and cerebral, even by Boone's admission, Bobby remained a Special Forces NCO, serving multiple tours in Vietnam, including time with MACV-SOG and the Delta Project. Then came post-war tours covertly battling Soviet communism in Europe, Iran, and Pakistan in the first, but not last, stumbling steps of American involvement in the Middle East. He participated in Operation Eagle Claw, the failed attempt to rescue American hostages from Iran. He earned a bachelor's degree in history while on active duty and, since his retirement in 1986, had been working on a Ph.D. in International Relations. He took a "sabbatical" semester to come on the hunt. He was one of the most solid soldiers and thinkers that Boone had known in his long service, and his son Roan had taken to the auburn haired, freckled, warrior-scholar the same way Boone had in 1964 in the piney forests of Camp Mackall, North Carolina.

Bart supervised the loading of the aircraft. He weighed each item and then each man. Boone and Dan, under Bart's supervision, handed each piece of equipment to Roan in the cargo bay behind the seats of the forty-year-old aircraft. When the loading was complete, Bart threw a cargo net over it and ratcheted it into place on cargo hooks on the floor. Satisfied with the placement and security of the cargo, he jumped to the tarmac and briefed everyone on the flight to Eagle.

"Welcome to Chapman Aviation," Bart said. "We'll load tomorrow morning at 0745 for a 0800 departure. The flight from here to Eagle is approximately one hour and seventeen minutes. When we land at Eagle, we'll taxi to our hangar and offload the gear.

"In an emergency, please exit the aircraft, pull out any wounded, put out fires, and remove the survival bag under the back row of seating. Roan, that will be your responsibility. If he's incapacitated, Dan, you bring it out. We'll assemble at the six o'clock position and determine our next move. If I'm out of action, there's a survival radio with extra batteries in the survival bag and, beyond that, you're a bunch of grunts and Green Berets. I'll leave the details to you. Any questions?"

"Any stewardesses on this flight?" Bobby said.

Bart smiled a wide grin, "Just me," he said.

"That's disappointing," Bobby said, winking at Roan.

The six men migrated to the field kitchen Wade had established between the camper and a fifty-five-gallon drum grill he "secured" from an adjacent hangar. Wade started moose steaks on the grill, baked potatoes, and corn on the cob while Dan worked on a couple loaves of sourdough bread in the camper. Roan and Bobby sat in folding chairs beside the coolers and worked on their beers. Roan was engrossed in whatever Bobby was pontificating upon. With two beers in hand, Bart stood beside Boone while he taped two maps to the wall. He handed Boone one of the bottles.

"Are they getting the rest of the briefing after chow?" Bart said.

"Check," Boone said. "You can stay and listen if you want. It might help when something goes wrong."

"No plan survives first contact, huh?"

"That's right," Boone said. "Dad thinks I might be a little light on contingencies."

"Considering his background, he may have good reason to be cynical"

79

"Yeah, I guess."

"No worries," Bart said. "I'll stick around after supper, get the brief, and then hit the sack. Crew rest, you know." He winked at Boone and walked away to join Roan and Bobby.

Supper was consumed with true soldierly gusto, inhaled rather than savored. It was just fuel. A blackberry cobbler with vanilla ice cream followed the main course. Bachelor life, recently ended, had turned Dan Hardy into an excellent cook. The men grabbed their favorite beverage and joined Boone around the table, serving as the temporary command post for their operation. Boone stood behind the table with two maps taped to the wall. One was six sections of USGS 1:24,000 quadrangles; the other was a larger scale, 1:250,000 Joint Operational Graphic. The five men sat in folding chairs around the table. Out of habit, all pulled notebooks and pens from their pockets and placed them on the table to take notes.

"Gentlemen, this is your final briefing," Boone said. "Please hold all questions to the end."

"First, thanks to all of you for coming on this trip, although I didn't have to twist anyone's arm. It's good to be here with you. I also want to thank my bride—this was her idea. She thought it'd be a good way to transition to retired life."

"Wise woman," Bobby said.

"Who deserves better," Dan piled on.

"Steady men," Boone said.

Laughing along with his family and closest friends, Boone continued attempting to regain some semblance of control.

"Reveille tomorrow is 0500. Dad has agreed to cook breakfast, which will be served at 0530. We'll clean the place up, secure any gear that's staying behind, and be mustered at the aircraft at 0730. Yeti will give us a weather update and brief us on any changes to the air plan. We'll load at 0745 for an 0800 departure. We'll arrive at Eagle at approximately 0920. We'll unload gear into the hangar. Dan and I will be on the first Super Cub lift."

Looking at Dan, he said, "Rucks and gun cases only."

Dan nodded.

"The first lift should be off the ground by 0945. It's about

80

twenty-five minutes one way to our base camp. So, each lift is about a one-hour round trip, at least if we keep it quick and nimble on landing. The second lift is Dad and his gear in one bird and the expedition gear in another. They leave Eagle at 1045. Dan and I will receive that lift at the landing zone. Third lift, Bobby and Roan, and their gear leave Eagle at 1145. By 1230 latest, everyone should be on the ground at the landing zone. A fourth flight can bring in any overflow gear. We can take all afternoon setting up, as Alaska state hunting regulations prohibit hunting on the same day you fly. After we land, Dan and I will recon a base camp site. I've done a map recon and think we'll put it here on the high ground north of the creek, about three hundred yards from the sandbar we'll use for a landing strip." Boone pointed at the 1:24,000 map.

Bobby opened his map, found the landing zone and pointed it out to Roan. The men, all accustomed to dangerous conditions in dangerous places, paid close attention. They all knew that the plan would inevitably change as challenges emerged. But the plan was important to guide them when things got western.

"Once the gear arrives on the second lift," he said, "we'll start transporting and set up camp. We can glass and scout on the day we fly in, but remember, don't kill anything on the first day. We can, however, fish as much as we want after the work is done. The next day, we'll go out in pairs, always in pairs, when traveling. Nobody goes off on their own—fishing, scouting, nothing. We travel as Ranger buddies, not individuals. We can mix the groups up each day, though.

"Dad has graciously agreed to serve as camp keeper and head cook until someone tags out, and then he'll go out. Our daily routine will be to eat before sunrise, move to the high ground and glass, cloverleaf around our hunting area, have lunch in the field, walk back to camp around sunset, and eat. We'll compare notes and adjust the plan for the following day. What're your questions?"

Initially, there were no questions. They'd been discussing the trip for the past year and were well-versed in the plan. Additionally, all these men were top-rate woodsmen. All of them, except for Roan and then only because of his youth, had hunted over much of the globe, including Alaska. Wade was the only one to ask a question or make a statement. Boone couldn't be sure.

"Contingencies," Wade said.

Boone winked at Yeti and continued, "Yeti and his crew will pick up, drop off, and resupply other parties around us regularly. He's agreed to have his guys fly over the camp. If we put out a signal panel, they'll land, and we can tell them what we need, and they'll bring it on the next trip out."

Bart chimed in, handing Boone a handheld radio and extra battery wrapped in a large plastic bag. "That's a handheld aircraft radio," he said. "There's a frequency card taped to the back and a spare battery. If you run into trouble, wait until you hear any aircraft and then transmit your traffic. If you put out a panel, try to tell us what you need so we don't have to land. But as you guys tag out, it'll be easier to bring the meat out a little at a time instead of all at once on the last day."

"Keeps us from having raw meat in bear country, too," Wade said.

"Stay together in your pairs and be prepared to live away from camp overnight," Boone said. "If a pair doesn't return to camp, stay put; the rest of us will find you the next morning. This means we must be clear on where everyone is hunting daily. I've got maps to issue if you don't have one. If more than one pair comes up missing, the radio will be at camp. Dad, you bring in the cavalry. Anything else?"

Everyone was silent. They were ready to go.

"On my mark, the time is 2015 local." Ten seconds later, "Mark."

Everyone corrected or confirmed the time on his wristwatch.

Bart shook hands and headed to his office for a few hours of sleep. Wade said goodnight to all and left for the camper, Dan to his truck, sleeping on an air mattress in the bed. Roan and Bobby were now close friends and were taking cots set up next to vehicles in the hangar. Boone crashed on the bench seat of his truck.

Planning was over. Time to execute, Boone thought as he dozed off.

CHAPTER TWELVE
0745 Hours Local-Thursday 10 September 1987
Fairbanks International Airport, Alaska

The de Havilland DHC-3 Otter was a staple Alaskan bush aircraft, the one that'd carry the men into the heart of the Alaskan bush was manufactured in 1954. A bigger version of de Havilland's DHC-2 Beaver. Although the company ended production in 1967, the Otter continued to fly in the bush and for a dozen or more military organizations around the globe. It was part of the US Army's inventory in Vietnam as the U-1A. Boone, Dan, and Bobby all had time in the back of that version. It was a rugged, capable airplane that thrived in the Alaskan bush. It also reflected Yeti Chapman's love for aviation and "old" Alaska, a love passed down from his father.

The Otter that began their adventure was on wheels instead of floats, although it had that capability plus skis in the winter. The fuselage was yellow, highlighted by a blue cowling, wing leading edges, and a broad strip down the body. The white oval of "Chapman Aviation - Fairbanks, Alaska" was emblazoned on both sides. It was like many of the Otter's that operated in this part of Alaska except for the two green footprints painted just forward of the pilot's door.

The Otter was a beast of an airplane and could easily carry the five hunters and all their gear for eighteen days in the field. The men strapped into their seats as Yeti began his preflight checklist. Wade was in the right seat. Although not a pilot, he was no stranger to flight in general and bush flight in particular and assisted Bart where asked. With the checklist completed, Bart tossed it on the dashboard, set the initial fuel settings, opened the window on the pilot's door, and shouted. "Clear."

On the opposite side of the cockpit, Wade repeated the

procedures.

"Clear, Clear."

The next moment, the single Pratt and Whitney R-1340 Wasp-9 radial engine roared to life, belching a stream of blue exhaust smoke.

In an age of jets, the sound of the radial engine sent all the occupants back in time, except Roan, who at twenty-two wasn't old enough to be taken back in time. For the others, Bart included, the sound resulted in ear-to-ear grins. He never tired of hearing the old radial chug to life. Even though he was an experienced aviator, he still looked skyward whenever he heard a radial engine aircraft overhead. It was a reminder of a beautiful time in aviation. Something about these bush planes invoked thoughts and memories of campfires, dog teams, and epic landscapes, at least to those prone to such sentimental thoughts.

Yeti turned to his passengers, put his thumb up, and yelled over the big Pratt and Whitney engine rumble. "Everyone ready to go?"

Five thumbs shot up. Bart turned the radio to the Ground Control frequency and keyed it.

"Fairbanks ground, this is Otter November 7531 at Chapman Aviation, ready for taxi with information Sierra for eastbound departure."

"Otter 7531, runway two zero left taxi."

"Otter 7531 will taxi to runway two zero left," Yeti said.

Following the taxiway into position, Yeti completed the run-up. "Fairbanks tower, Otter 7531, ready two zero left."

"Otter 7531, Fairbanks Tower, hold short runway two zero left."

"Holding short, two zero left, 7531."

"Otter 7531 runway two zero left clear for takeoff, make a left downwind departure to the east."

"Cleared for takeoff on two zero left, left downwind departure for 7531."

Cleared for departure, he turned the thirty-year-old taildragger onto runway two zero left. "Here we go, gentlemen."

Bart added power. Six hundred horsepower of air-cooled radial pushed the almost four-ton plane down the runway. Yeti added forward pressure to the yoke as speed began to build and the tail began to fly. He pulled on the yoke, taking flight after using 1,800 feet of runway. As he adjusted and gained altitude, he banked left and crossed the Tanana River away from Fairbanks International Airport. Once over Tanana Flats and clear of airport traffic, he took up a heading of zero nine two degrees for the one hour and seventeen-minute flight to the airfield east of Eagle, Alaska.

Boone was perpetually enamored with Alaska's natural beauty, especially in late August and September. He'd flown over the interior tundra hundreds of times in the past two decades, but Alaska continued to deliver. Each time he started a new adventure in the Great Land, it was like discovering this gem for the first time. For Boone, this handful of weeks that constituted autumn in Alaska was heaven on earth. He took in the beautiful golds and reds of the leaves, highlighted in the growing light of the sun. It was like coming home after a long journey.

They cruised in relatively smooth air at one hundred twelve knots at three thousand feet. In a few minutes, Boone could see the small town of North Pole and Eielson Air Force Base as they crossed the Chena River. Once beyond the Chena, Boone was reminded how big Alaska is. It was incredible that this wilderness still existed in a modern world that seemed to be going out of its way to destroy or control nature. He hoped this wilderness never suffered that fate. Maybe its proximity and remoteness would be its saving feature.

Forty-five minutes into the flight, Yeti yelled. "Everyone look out the left side of the aircraft, and you can see the area we're going to put you down. I'll circle once and then in the other direction so the right side can see."

Dan, Yeti, and Roan looked out the left-side windows at the sandbars along the creek where they would land in the next couple of hours.

"Look at this long sandbar next to the lone tree on the north side of the creek," Yeti said. "We're going to try to put you guys in there. It's the best place to land near the spot where Boone wants to put the base camp. If you'll notice to the northwest of the campsite, that hill is about five thousand feet and is probably a great glassing site. We put hunters in here last year, and they tagged out in a couple of days. They connected with a couple of real trophies, too."

Yeti turned the aircraft one hundred eighty degrees to fly a circle over the area in the opposite direction so Boone, Bobby, and Wade, on the other side of the aircraft, could look.

There's no substitute for personal reconnaissance. Boone thought. He saw the sandbar that Yeti talked about. There was a good spot for the base camp closer to the landing site than he originally thought. He marked the position on the map, sitting on his knee. Plenty of trees for a wind break and fuel, and the creek would provide water. It was also close to the sandbar landing strip, which would make hauling gear easier. He looked for a route from the campsite to the glassing knob but was distracted by the small caribou herd grazing across an opening two hundred yards from where they would set up their base camp.

"Caribou," Boone yelled.

"Got them," Wade said. "There are a couple of nice bulls in that group. There's a double shovel in the middle of the herd."

Twenty minutes later, the Otter touched down at the Eagle Airport and taxied to the Chapman Aviation Hangar, where Donald "Chappie" Chapman, CEO, and senior pilot, stood with his hands on his hips in front of the hangar. Inside and around the hangar was an assortment of bush planes with similar paint schemes as Bart's Otter. Chappie was dressed in his typical Alaskan uniform, faded brown Carhartt double-faced logger pants, green and black plaid wool shirt, canvas vest, hip boots, and a faded khaki ball cap with the blue Army Air Corps patch sewn on the front. The most unique item was the well-worn leather flight jacket.

Don was about an inch shorter than his son but now outweighed him by fifteen pounds. *Why would these two gargantuans decide to spend their entire lives crammed in a cockpit?* Boone wondered. Yeti pushed the left rudder pedal and applied power as the aircraft spun its tail wheel to face the hangar door and killed the engine. Bart and his passengers deplaned as a Chapman employee pushed an equipment cart to the cargo door. Bart removed the cargo net securing the gear. While Roan supervised the unloading of their gear with

Bobby's assistance, Chappie walked around the tail of the plane and reacquainted himself with old friends.

"Welcome to Eagle," he said. He reached Wade first and hugged his old friend.

"Thanks, Chappie. I've been looking forward to this."

Chappie hugged Boone and then Dan, "Is that Roan?"

"Yes, sir, he's a grown man now," Boone said. "It's been a while since I had him up here."

Don hugged Roan. "I heard you're at Campbell with the 101st. Couldn't grandpa pull any strings to get you assigned to the 82nd at Bragg?" He laughed and slapped Wade on the shoulder.

Smiling, Wade returned fire. "At least he didn't join the Air Force."

As the banter continued, and an occasional war story kicked off, Boone lost control of his timeline and recruited Bart to help him get the expedition back on track.

"Boone, grab your gear," Bart said. "You're with Jimmy in tail number zero-two. Dan, you're in the other bird with Dad. Let's start moving."

Boone and Dan headed toward their aircraft with their gear as the two pilots began their final checks and stowed their passengers' gear. Jimmy Regan stowed Boone's gear behind the backseat.

While he was busy Boone stepped over to Bart. "Does he drive yet? How old is this kid? Twelve?"

Bart laughed. "Nope, he's twenty-one. He just looks twelve. I know for a fact he shaves at least once a week."

"I'm not questioning your judgment, brother, but how long has this youngun' been flying?" Boone asked.

"He got his private license at sixteen, he's flown with us for a year, and he's a good pilot. All his flying experience is here in Alaska. Besides, if my memory serves, I was about one year older than him, with twenty fewer flying hours, when I was plucking guys off the ground under fire."

"That was different," Boone said. He stepped back to the plane as Jimmy finished with the gear and final checks.

"Ready to go, young man?" Boone said.

"Yes, sir, climb in."

Boone climbed into the Super Cub's backseat and yelled to Dan in the other aircraft. "See you on the ground."

Dan shot him a thumbs up and smiled, tapping Chappie on the shoulder. "Let's go."

Chappie gave him a thumbs up and applied power. Jimmy and Boone were in the lead in a few minutes, with Don and Dan trailing off their right wing on a two-hundred seventy-two-degree azimuth. On the ground, Roan, Wade, and Bobby began organizing the gear for the second lift with the assistance of Bart and another Chapman employee.

Once the gear was ready for loading, the three hunters sat leaning against their packs, reading, or talking. Bart supervised the ground crew loading the DHC-3 Otter with another hunting party's gear.

"Why does Bart have two green feet painted on the cowling of his bird? None of the rest of them have that," Roan said.

"Jolly Green Giants," Wade said.

"What?"

"The rescue squadrons in Vietnam flew the HH-53," Bobby said. "They were called the Jolly Green Giant, because it's a big aircraft, especially for a helicopter which is technically not supposed to be able to fly anyway. They started with the smaller HH-3. In the early days, they flew the Husky, this crazy-looking bird with the rotor blades side by side but transitioned to the 53's in 1968. They were called Super Jollys. Because of the nickname, their mascot was the Giant on the vegetable commercials, you know, 'ho-ho-ho-green giant.' The green feet go back to the HH-3 pilots in the rescue squadrons. Legend has it they took the feet as a symbol because the footprint of the bird landing in the mud left big fat footprints. Thus, the green feet."

"So why does Bart have them painted on the cowling?" Roan asked.

"He doesn't know the story?" Bobby said, looking at Wade.

"Nope," Wade said.

"What story?"

"I'll let your old man tell the whole story," Wade said. "But

Bart pulled your dad and others out of the jungle under challenging circumstances."

"So, Bart was a rescue pilot when you guys were in Vietnam?"

"Yep, he graduated from the Air Force Academy in '67," Bobby said. "Requested helicopters and Vietnam. After flight school and all the other training those dudes go through, he flew the HH-3 in 68-69, took six months back home as an instructor, and then went back for a second tour in 70-71, flying the HH-53. He said Vietnam was safer than training new pilots."

"After he left the Air Force, he crop dusted for a while and then stayed at the ranch and flew with your Grandpa Clark doing fire suppression. Alaska's pull was pretty strong, so he moved back up and flew for his dad," Wade said.

"No kidding?" Roan said.

"There's a lot of men alive today, your old man included, that wouldn't be here if it wasn't for Yeti and men like him," Bobby said.

Bart closed the cargo doors of the Otter and started his walk around. Satisfied with the plane's condition, he jumped into the cockpit and waved at the three relaxing hunters. "See you guys in a couple of weeks."

The three waved in return.

CHAPTER THIRTEEN
0600 Hours Local-Saturday 12 September 1987
Two miles north of basecamp

Boone and Roan leaned against their rucksacks beneath the lightweight poncho tarp strung between two small bushes. Boone set up the spotting scope, and Roan prepared his binoculars. Sunrise was in thirty-five minutes, and they could glass the dark valley below them. This was Boone's favorite part of the day. The east was coming alive, this morning slightly pink because of low clouds and drizzling rain. He loved being afield as the sun came up. Boone especially loved sharing this experience with one of his children. The opportunities were few when they were young because of the pace and nature of his chosen profession, and now that he had more time, they were busy. *Cats in the Cradle* played in his head.

He and Abby had done well making memories with their children, despite his frequent and long absences. They'd made a conscious decision when Roan was born that, even though Boone planned to stay in the Army, their priority when he was home was the family. He lived up to that promise. He was with his family when he wasn't in the field, deployed overseas, or working late. Abby kept the wheels on the wagon while he was away. She was the glue that held them all together.

He and Abby didn't have much of a social life outside the three little people who brought them such joy. They spent every free weekend making inexpensive memories by camping, fishing, hunting, canoeing, and hiking. They'd raised their children outdoors, and they were all good woodsmen. Every evening was spent reading and talking and occasionally watching a good movie. Over the last twenty-six years, five closely-knit people loved one another dearly and would do

90

anything for each other. They were a team and a good one. If there was an accomplishment that Boone was proud of, it was the close-knit, capable family that he and Abigail had nurtured.

Like many, his priorities and source of pride evolved throughout his life. It wasn't just a sense of service and duty to country that drew him to military service, although he certainly felt those intensely. Rather it was a sense of adventure. Boone was an adrenaline junkie, and he knew it. He reveled in his life of soldiering. He enjoyed the rush, the excitement, and the constant movement. It suited him better than anything else he could imagine, but he realized that his purpose for service wasn't wholly altruistic. He loved being a soldier. In his mind, it wasn't much of a sacrifice. But he was changing with age, maturity, and experience.

His idealism had died slowly, and cynicism had grown over the past decade. Though the seeds went back even further, he now had more profound questions. He was committed to duty, but he was disturbed by the spirit of careerism in his Army, the connection between money and the national security apparatus, and what felt like a growing gulf between the highest echelons of the profession of arms and the young men and women who died at their bidding. He was bothered by the lack of historical understanding and analysis at the highest levels of government. He was thankful that Dan had convinced him to stay, and as much as he wanted his career to go further, he was grateful for the opportunity to spend his last few years in uniform, training the next generation of leaders. Other than his family, those soldiers were his legacy. Now, he sat in the pre-dawn rain next to the one young paratrooper he wanted most to influence and prepare.

Boone pulled his Stanley thermos from his rucksack, filled two cups, and handed one to Roan. They sipped the steaming coffee, held the cups to warm, cold fingers, and talked quietly. It was the first time they'd been alone in the field since they hiked and fished in the Cloud Peak Wilderness of Bighorn National Forest the summer before Boone started his last assignment four years previous.

"Where are Dan and Bobby hunting this morning?" Roan said.

Pointing down the ridgeline to his right. "They're a mile down this ridge to the north. They should have a good view of the valley back that way."

"Okay, Dad, what's the plan for the day?"

"You get the first choice," Boone said. "No matter who sees a caribou first, you can decide whether to take it or pass. If you want to pass, I get to make the same decision. If we decide to go after an animal, we stay together until the final stalk."

"Now, to get the caribou to cooperate," Roan said, looking through his binoculars.

The two glassed the valley and hills to their west for the next two hours and enjoyed the spectacle. They watched a small black bear bolt when the wind carried the scent of a large grizzly sow with two cubs. They watched a handful of remaining ducks land and feed on three small ponds and saw a red fox stalk some grouse. Roan broke the long silence.

"Dad, tell me about Bart pulling you out of the jungle."

Boone was intentionally cautious about which parts of his service he shared with his family. The war stories he told them were the funny ones, not the worst moments. He kept those to himself, and if he ever talked of them, it was only with the people who shared the experience. Even Abby didn't know all the details, just that he was rescued by Yeti's crew. But Roan was twenty-two and now in the same profession. Maybe it was time to open up to him about some things.

"How did you know about that?" Boone said.

"Bobby and Grandpa were explaining the green footprints on Bart's plane, and they told me Bart picked you up in Vietnam. They said you should tell me the whole story. Am I getting someone in trouble?"

"No, you aren't," Boone said. "They're probably right. You ought to hear some of these stories."

He continued to glass the valley and drink coffee and then began the most serious war story he'd shared with his son. "During my fourth and last tour, I commanded an A Detachment in I Corps near the DMZ and the Laotian border, near the A Shau Valley," Boone said. "Dan was a Battalion S3 in the 101st Airborne. It was one of your sister battalions. We were planning an operation where Dan's battalion had conducted a big push, and I wanted some intelligence, so I met

Dan at Camp Eagle, the division firebase. He was getting ready to DEROS but gave me some good intel and put me in touch with some guys who could answer my questions. I took off for an aerial recon of the area we would insert into.

"I was flying right seat in a 0-2 Skymaster with an Air Force FAC pilot, Captain Lee Christian. He was a great American. It was his third tour and he volunteered to fly Forward Air Controller in an O-2, a twin-engine Cessna with no guns.

"We flew out and found the area I wanted to look at and started our low and slow runs. We never used the same approach twice, and he was great about varying speed and heading. We got shot at a lot, but no hits. As we were leaving a forward refuel point, we got a radio call from a MACV-SOG team led by one Sergeant First Class Robert Doyle."

"Bobby?" Roan said.

"The one and only. They were in the heat of it, and their FAC got hit hard by ground fire and had to pull off station, so Lee called in close air support to keep the NVA off them. I helped coordinate an extraction and call artillery between the close air support missions. The CAS and arty pushed the NVA off Bobby's patrol, and they extracted when we got hit hard. Lee thought he could get the bird home, but it started falling apart, so he found a small, narrow stream bed he thought he could get into. While he was concentrating on flying the plane, I got out the mayday call and planned our E&E based on what I knew about the local area. About thirty feet above the creek, we got hit again by small arms fire. Lee was killed in the first salvo. Even before we hit the ground, I knew it.

"The plane quit flying and hit the ground. I worked my way out and hit the tree line. A rescue operation had already started, and a few days later, after E&Eing around NVA units and some other high adventure, Bart's crew picked me up, under fire, and carried me home. Lee's buried in Arlington. He was thirty-two years old and never married, no children. The Air Force was his whole world. I'll feel guilty about his death for the rest of my life."

The two sat in complete silence for the next hour. Roan tried to process this new view of his father. Roan's respect for him only grew.

"I got one," Boone said.

"Where?" Roan raised his binoculars to his eyes.

"Look due west to the opening of that valley," Boone said. "I see eight so far just to the right of that rock outcropping and two fingers up from the stream intersection. They're moving slow, grazing straight toward us."

Roan looked for a moment. "I see them."

The two men watched for several minutes, evaluating, and finally, Roan decided. "I'm going after that biggest bull in the middle of the herd. The one with the double shovels."

"Good enough," Boone smiled. "Get your gear ready and let me watch him for a few more minutes and see where they might be headed."

Boone watched the small herd graze out of the opening of the smaller valley, and into the edge of the main valley in front of them, as Roan prepared their gear to move. Boone pulled his map from the inside of his shirt, placed his compass along the grid lines, and oriented the map north. He used a small twig to trace their route for Roan.

"We'll dip behind the east edge of the ridge and move quickly to this saddle, cross the ridge, and get into the valley here," Boone said. "I'll stay up higher, just below the crest of the hill, and watch your stalk. You keep looking back at me, and I'll give you hand and arm signals to guide you. I recommend working your way into this stream bed, which will mask your movement. If you work downstream, you'll be paralleling their current direction and close the distance. Right now, the wind is on our side for a stalk. You'll have to decide when to start your final stalk. What's your cutoff range for an ethical shot?"

"Three hundred yards," Roan said.

"Don't get excited and bust that distance," Boone said. "Make a good shot. We don't have much wind right now, so that shouldn't be a factor, but pay attention for it to pick up. Let's go."

They shouldered their rucksacks, grabbed their rifles and slipped off the back side of the hill. Once they were screened from sight, they moved south for a speedy mile then Boone, in the lead, moved up the ridge line to the saddle he selected and stopped at the

94

crest. He raised his binoculars to locate the herd. Roan settled in next to him and did likewise. Shortly, Roan spotted them. So far, the plan was still intact.

"Drop your ruck with me," Boone said. "I'll watch from here and give you hand and arm signals."

Roan dropped his ruck, rechecked his rifle, and started down the ridge line toward the creek bed that'd mask his movement from the herd. Boone moved a few yards below the ridge's crest and set up the spotting scope to watch Roan's stalk. Ten minutes later, Roan slipped into the creek bed undetected by the caribou. Boone watched them graze slowly down the main valley on a course that'd intercept the creek in about six hundred yards. Roan looked back at Boone through his binoculars, and Boone flashed a thumbs up. *You're on track.* Roan moved downstream quickly and silently. The terrain hid his movement, and the stream masked any slight noise. In another ten minutes, he looked back at his father. Boone gave him the signal to start his final stalk.

Roan climbed out of the creek and started to move slowly in the direction the herd was grazing. After a couple of short course corrections from Boone, he could see two of the caribou cows. He stopped, scanned behind the two cows, and saw the bull through the brush. He moved slowly forward. He needed to cover another seventy yards to make a good shot. He looked back at his father, and Boone flashed another thumbs up. He was still on track. Roan moved slowly forward through the brush as the small herd continued to graze down the valley toward the stream. Roan saw a gap, a shooting lane, through the brush. The bull would walk into the gap in about two minutes.

He lowered himself to the ground, extended the bipods mounted on the bottom of the Ruger M77 rifle, and took up a solid prone firing position. He flipped the scope covers up, pulled the butt of the rifle into his shoulder, placed his cheek on the stock, and checked his scope. Roan saw the bull in the trees through his binoculars, sat them aside, and took up his final firing position. He dialed his DOPE into the scope, pulled a small sock partially filled with sand from his pants cargo pocket, slid it beneath the buttstock, and held it with his left hand. He settled the scope's crosshairs at the center of the opening at about the same height as the caribou's vital organs and worked to control his breathing. Ten seconds later, the bull walked into the opening.

A little high, Roan added slight pressure to the sand sock beneath the stock, and the crosshairs moved down slightly. He pressed the initial slack from the two-stage trigger as the scope's crosshairs rested just behind the point of the bull's shoulder. He continued the consistent press on the trigger until the shot broke. He absorbed the recoil and racked another .300 Magnum cartridge into the chamber to reacquire the target and mentally called his shot with trained smoothness. *It's a bit back and high, but it's a kill shot.* It was a complete miss.

Boone watched the entire stalk through the spotting scope and gave his son direction changes by hand signal. He was focused on the caribou herd, the bull, specifically when the report of the rifle came. All eight caribou heads came up at once as they picked up their pace but they didn't yet break into a run. However, they were moving quickly out of the trees and into the open. A second shot report came, and the animals began trotting down the valley. The speed and agility of the caribou crossing the tundra was amazing.

Boone moved his scope back to the left and found his son in the open, rifle in hand, looking back at Boone, shaking his head, and shrugging his shoulders. The younger Taggart started walking up the ridge to meet his dad while Boone broke down the spotting scope, grabbed both rucks, and walked out to meet him.

"What happened?" Boone said dropping their gear.

"I'm stupid. That's what happened," Roan said without smiling. "I made a rookie mistake. When I got in the prone for my first shot, my scope cleared a log ten feet in front of me, but the bullet didn't. When I pulled the trigger, the bullet hit the log. When they started moving, I got up and stumbled into another clear shooting lane, but by that time, my whole body was jackhammering with adrenaline, and I missed the second shot."

Boone slapped him on the shoulder and tried to console him. "A hunter who says he never missed is a liar. Everyone screws up a shot occasionally. Just learn from it. You could've rushed another shot, wounded him, and never recovered him."

They spent the rest of the day glassing the valley. They ate jerky and drank coffee while Boone regaled Roan with his many failures in the field in an effort to heal his son's spirit. Later in the afternoon, after Boone caught a nap, they split up by a couple hundred yards to view the valleys on both sides of the ridge. As twilight fell, Boone walked to Roan's side of the ridge, and they started the hike back to camp.

"Cheer up, it's early in the hunt. They call it hunting, not killing for a reason," Boone said.

"I know. Tomorrow will be better."

"At least say it like you mean it. Let's go see what your grandpa has for supper."

Boone and Roan walked down the ridge from their afternoon position until they came to the creek, then turned northeast and followed it downstream. As they approached camp, they heard laughing voices, then saw the light of the Coleman lantern. In minutes, Boone could smell his dad's cooking, and his mouth started to water. He didn't know what was on the menu and didn't care. He was hungry, and hunger makes a good sauce.

"Hello in the camp," Boone said as they got close enough to be heard.

"Come on in," A voice said.

Wade was at the Yukon stove stirring supper in a frying pan, and Dan was kneeling at the grate over the fire, turning meat in a pan. Using a second lantern hung from a tree limb, Bobby was salting a hide. Boone and Roan cleared their rifles, dropped their packs next to the tent, went to the fire, and poured two large cups of coffee.

"Did you guys get something?" Boone said.

"Bobby got a nice bull this morning," Dan said. "It's got nice double shovels, an older bull, but nice."

"Double shovels?" Roan said.

"Yeah, why?" Dan asked.

Roan and Boone walked to where Bobby was salting a hide and looked at the caribou's rack.

"That's the bull I missed." Roan said.

"You gotta be kidding me?" Bobby said, looking over his shoulder with a smile.

"Nope, we put a stalk on him this morning, and I missed twice. What time did you shoot him?"

"About 11:30 this morning."

"That makes sense," Roan said. "They must've kept going down the valley, and you all spotted them."

Bobby stood up and put his arm around Roan's shoulder. "There's plenty of caribou in these valleys, kid. You're going to get one. I was just in the right place at the right time."

"Supper's ready," Wade yelled from the kitchen tent.

"What's for supper, Pop?" Boone asked as he walked into the tent.

"Black beans and rice with mallard breasts, peach cobbler for dessert, plenty of coffee to wash it down, and a dram of whiskey with a bowl of tobacco just because we're civilized men. I hope you boys enjoy."

"How'd you get ducks, dad?"

"I brought a half-dozen inflatable decoys with me. This morning, while I was getting water and firewood, I found a slough downstream about a half mile. I set up there and killed supper,"

The men sat on stools under the pale light of the Coleman lantern and ate supper together, reminiscing, telling stories, and laughing. After they finished, they worked on gear for the next day, cleaned and checked rifles, and completed the evening's chores. They all migrated to the sleep tent, and in moments four exhausted men snored almost in unison. Boone lay in the dark, trying to stay awake for another minute to enjoy the peace. This was the happiest he'd been in a long time. He hadn't thought about retirement, and he'd so enjoyed the time spent on the side of the ridge with Roan. It was a good day. He needed to work harder to make more of these.

CHAPTER FOURTEEN
2030 Hours Local-Thursday 17 September 1987
Base Camp

Days began to run into one another like a well-rehearsed routine. Each night before bed, they studied the map, determined the next day's locations and partners, prepared gear, slept, ate breakfast in the dark, walked out to their glassing points, hunted, napped, returned to camp, ate supper, sat around the fire, told lies, repeat. It was a familiar routine to all of them as they were experienced in the field through their military service, and the life they shared outdoors, when not soldiering.

There was comfort in life in the open. It's counterintuitive that the absence of convenience produces comfort, familiarity, contentment, and joy for some. But they were happier hauling water, cutting firewood, cooking plain meals over a fire or on a wood-burning stove, and hunting for their sustenance than they were in the modern world of convenience and complacency. They reveled in brotherhood with men of kindred spirits.

The day after Roan missed the double shovel bull, he killed an even larger bull in the same valley. Boone was with him to share the experience and the pack out to camp. After they secured the meat bags in their packs, they sliced and cooked the caribou heart on willow sticks over a fire next to a small stream. Dan and Boone killed caribou two days later in the valley south of their camp. Bobby and Roan spent the day glassing a valley for black bear farther to the north and came up dry. Wade killed a small caribou not a half mile from camp that provided them with camp meat for the rest of the trip. They'd hunted for the previous week, had another week to go, and had all punched caribou tags.

"What's the plan for tomorrow?" Dan asked the group.

After a pause with no suggestions, Bobby spoke. "We've all tagged caribou, and we've still got a week and change to go. How about we spend a few days fishing some of the drainages around camp? We use the same plan we've used so far. We go in teams, someone can stay in camp, and we debrief at the end of each day and adjust the next day's plan. I think we can afford a day or three to fish. I know Boone wants a trophy grayling to mount."

"I like it," Boone said. "Anybody else got any ideas?"

"I concur," Dan said. "Wade, why don't you go out tomorrow and let me stay in camp, cook, and do the chores? I can work on salting the hides and prepping skulls."

"I'd like that," Wade said. "Thanks, Dan. I think I'll go out with my grandson."

"I'm not sure I can keep up with you, Grandpa," Roan said, not joking, considering Wade was the most well-rested of the party and still in excellent shape.

"I'll take it easy on you, son."

"We got our first resupply scheduled for tomorrow," Boone said. "Bobby, why don't you go with Roan and Dad, and I'll stay in camp to help Dan with the resupply. We're sending out the meat, hides, and trash. Chappie said he would be here mid-morning for the first lift. If we get finished early, I'll fish close to camp."

"Alright, that's the plan," Dan said.

They did their evening chores and prepared their gear for the next day. They would drop their packs and carry rifles or shotguns for bear protection, some essential survival gear, lunch, and fishing gear. Most brought small packable fishing kits with just the basics: Four-piece fly or spinning rods with reels and a small box of lures or flies. Wade carried his two-piece bamboo rod in an aluminum tube and flies he'd tied during the previous winter. Roan brought the latest spinning reel and a packable four-piece rod with small spinners and spoons. Bobby carried an old two-piece fly rod and flies.

After helping with the chores, Boone stepped beyond the firelight and the trees to an open meadow between camp and the creek. The full moon rose in the southeast, giving off enough light to read. The valley was awash in the moonlight, casting long shadows as far as he could see. He pulled a tin of Copenhagen from his Filson hunting coat, packed it down, and put a pinch of snuff in his bottom lip.

Dan walked up beside Boone carrying two canteen cups. He handed one to Boone and said, "I thought you were going to quit when you retired."

"You sound like Abby, Rachel, Caroline, my mom, basically all the women in my life."

"That puts me in good company."

"Man, I love this place," Boone said.

"So do I, brother. I don't ever plan on leaving."

"Of all the places we've lived or traveled, Alaska is the only place I miss when I'm not here," Boone said. "I love Wyoming, and have seen some other spectacular places, but nothing fills my soul like this place."

"Why don't you move up here?" Dan said. "Get a job on post or teach or maybe be a fishing and hunting bum. I'm retiring in a couple of years. Maybe we could figure out how to make some side money running a fishing service or something."

"Abby and I've talked about maybe buying a summer cabin up here," Boone said. "Maybe stay from June until hunting is over and head back to Wyoming. I don't know. I'm in one of those weird transition periods. I owe Abby. She's lived all over the place and now has a chance to be close to her parents. Rachel's in school a few hours down the road, and Caroline loves being close to both sets of grandparents. She's in love with the ranch. He wouldn't admit it, but my mom says Dad's happy to have me back around. He knows I'm not the one to take over the ranch, but Rachel might, or Caroline, and I can help him until one of them is ready. I guess we'll stay there for now."

"You know, you're in a pretty good situation when you can 'settle' for Wyoming," Dan said. "It's a special place in its own right. I love it there, and if I didn't love Alaska so much, I'd probably be your neighbor."

"I'll have the time to come up here and hunt and fish more now that I'm retired," Boone said. "Thanks for the coffee." Turning his gaze to Dan, he said. "I thought we were saving the good stuff for the last night."

Dan laughed and rubbed his back. "It's just a nip. It's cold tonight. My rheumatism is acting up."

The other men filtered to the meadow. They stood shoulder to shoulder, watched the moon illuminate the valley, and enjoyed the absolute silence of the wilderness and their spiked coffee.

CHAPTER FIFTEEN
1245 Hours Local-Friday 18 September 1987
Base Camp

Bobby stayed in camp to cook and finish the daily camp chores. Roan and Wade walked upstream to duck hunt the sloughs south of camp. Dan and Boone hiked north downstream, looking for a trophy grayling. Bobby caught a four-pound grayling the previous day and gave Boone a description of the pool. Dan and Boone hiked three miles, stopped, and watched the pool where Bobby caught his grayling and then hiked another mile before turning back upstream and starting to fish their way back to camp.

They caught and released several nice rainbows and some smaller graylings. As they arrived at the tail of the grayling pool, they spread out and worked the exit methodically. Dan connected almost immediately with a nice three-pounder and then a second and a third. In frustration, Boone yelled to Dan. "What're you throwing?"

"Purple egg-sucking leech," Dan said.

Boone tied on one of the flies his dad tied and started casting. Finally, he connected, and although it was a nice fish, it wasn't the one he was looking to mount. After two hours of fishing, catching several nice graylings, they waded to an island and started a driftwood fire. Boone pulled his thermos from his vest and filled their cups with coffee. He packed his lower lip with Copenhagen, and Dan lit a new cigar. They ate two trout a piece and leaned back against a log, enjoying the day. Fifteen minutes later, Dan kicked Boone's waders, disturbing his nap.

"You ready to go?" Dan said.

He slung the Mossberg 500 twelve gauge over his shoulder, checked the placement of the Smith and Wesson Model 29 .44

magnum in a nylon shoulder holster under his left arm, and picked up his fly rod.

"I guess," Boone said.

He threw the last drink of cold coffee on the fire and scattered the remaining coals. Dan lit his cigar and started moving back into the stream. Boone slung his Remington 870 twelve gauge over his shoulder and checked the placement of his Ruger Super Blackhawk .44 magnum in the leather holster on his right hip. He passed his hand over the hunting knife resting behind the pistol, picked up his fly rod, and started moving.

"I'm going to work around the other side of the island," Boone said over the sound of the stream and an increasing wind.

Dan raised a thumbs up and continued casting upstream. Boone waded into the right fork of the stream with the island between him and Dan and slowly worked the riffles and pools under the overhanging diamond willows on the right bank of the stream. As he continued upstream, he noticed a beautiful pool on the backside of the willows. It was a picture-perfect fly-casting pool. He had to get past the twenty-yard thicket of willows that separated the stream and the pool.

He positioned his fly rod in his left hand with the length of the rod behind him and the reel facing forward. He slowly worked through the willow and alders lining the stream, methodically moving branches, and stepping over fallen logs. He moved deliberately and quietly through the brush. He could see a small sandbar ten feet ahead where the brush cleared, and the pool began. As he reached the edge of the stream, a fallen alder caused him to stoop low to get under. As he cleared the tree, he glanced down at the beach directly in front of him and saw the clear print of the right front paw of a large grizzly bear.

An experienced woodsman, Boone realized several things almost simultaneously—the wind was increasing and quartering from his right front, there was running water, both of which impeded hearing, both his and the bears, and he was in a position that the shotgun slung on his back would do no good in the next few seconds. He prayed that it wasn't a sow with cubs. As these things burst through

Boone's mind, water began to seep through the sand and fill the print cavity. The bear stepped there seconds ago.

Boone dropped the fly rod as his right hand touched the leather holster on his right hip. He indexed the holster bringing his hand straight up, his thumb disconnected the leather safety strap over the hammer, and he gripped the pistol's handle. He cleared the holster and cocked the .44 magnum, bringing his left hand up to a two-hand grip. He took two giant steps onto the sandbar, scanned left, and then heard a splash to his right thirty feet downstream. A giant boar stood in a foot of water along the willows. The grizzly was now surprised by the strange sight of this creature, considerably smaller than him. *Don't miss Boone.*

The bear's ears laid back, and the hair on the hump at the base of its neck stood on end. He started to move toward Boone quickly, but not at full speed.

Boone screamed at the top of his lungs. "Dan, Bear," and the pistol came up.

Dan understood the situation from Boone's tone more than his words. They'd spent much time together in dangerous places, doing dangerous things, and he knew that whatever situation Boone was in was deadly. Dan high-stepped through the stream toward the tip of the island. At the edge of the stream, he threw his fly rod on the beach, pulled the Mossberg over his head, put it to his shoulder, and ran twenty feet down the beach toward the end of the island. He heard the Ruger's report.

The bear charged. Dan thought.

When he cleared the trees at the end of the island, he saw Boone standing on the beach with his pistol in both hands extended. Dan slid the safety off with his right hand, but he, Boone, and the bear were perfectly aligned. He didn't have a shot if the bear continued the charge. He maneuvered left back into the stream, trying to maintain his balance and get an angle on the bear.

"I'm on your left flank, Boone. Don't move left."

As Boone was screaming to warn Dan, the bear stopped and began to paw at the water and make a horrible popping or grinding sound with its jaws and teeth. Boone worked two primary problems

105

simultaneously, first, to keep the front sight post of the large revolver on the spot between the bear's eyes. The bear was now at twenty feet, no more, and if charged now, Boone would start shooting. *If he charges, keep hammering him until he stops, or you expend your ammo, then curl up and wait for impact. Dan will have to fight it from there.*

The second problem was that all the liquids in his body were trying to get out simultaneously. He'd felt this before, in his first firefight. Now it returned. The bear swatted the water again, and Boone thought to put a round in the water right in front of the bear. He fired and cocked the hammer again—*No more warning shots. You're down to five rounds.* Boone knew that in twenty feet, he would be lucky to get off two shots, if that.

He heard Dan's voice at his seven o'clock and immediately felt more confident. Dan was solid in a crisis. Boone slowly began to back up toward Dan and talked to the bear in a firm but not panicked voice.

"Come on, bear, go on your way," Boone said. "I don't want to kill you. You don't want to be dead, and I sure don't want to be dead."

As Boone started to back away and talk to the bruin, Dan remembered bears had terrible eyesight. Someone had once told him to try to make himself as big as possible when confronted.

"Keep it up, buddy. I'm moving toward your left shoulder," Dan said.

He started moving toward Boone. There was now forty feet between Boone and the bear. *This might work.* The bear began to pace a bit left and right, almost like it was confused or unsure of what it saw. Boone and Dan stood shoulder to shoulder and continued back toward the island with sixty feet between them and the bear. The wind paused and then swirled. Catching a whiff of the humans, the animal turned around and disappeared into the willows and up the ridge west of the stream.

They backed out of the water and watched the bear run effortlessly up the ridge. *What a magnificent animal.* Dan slid the safety back into position on the Mossberg.

"You alright, brother?" Dan said to his friend.

106

"I think I might of crapped my britches," Boone said.

Dan started laughing, and then, because of the adrenaline, he couldn't stop laughing.

Boone took a couple of deep breaths. His hands shook so violently that it took three attempts to reload the expended cartridge and holster the revolver. He sat down on a log while Dan retrieved their fly rods. They trained their binoculars on the bear as it continued up the ridge and back to the north. Occasionally, the grizzly stopped and looked back at them as if he wasn't quite sure what had just happened.

Dan produced a small silver flask and handed it to Boone. "Here, it's medicinal," Dan said. "You didn't really crap your pants, did you?"

"No, but it was close there for a second," Boone admitted.

0815 – Wednesday 23 September 1987
Spike Camp

The previous several days were a mix of snow, wind, rain, and sunshine, but when they left their tent just before dawn, there were six inches of new snow on the ground, and it was still snowing hard. They sat quietly under the tarp, preparing oatmeal and coffee on the packable stove.

"Tell me about the mission in Laos," Roan said.

"Did your dad tell you the story?" Bobby said.

"He did, but just the major points. He said your team extracted, his bird got hit, and Yeti picked him up. That's about the extent of his account."

Bobby pulled his watch cap lower and pulled up the collar on his wool hunting coat. "Roan, there's a lot more to this story than that, and I'd love nothing more than to tell you the gritty details, but what happened in Laos is still classified, and I'd guess always will be. I'll tell you this, your dad deserved the Medal of Honor for what he did, but it almost ended his career and landed him in jail. His actions, between getting shot down and picked up by Yeti, caused political problems for the US. The politicians in Washington were desperately trying to get out of Vietnam, and what your dad did made that more difficult. It was all swept under the rug for political purposes, and they tried to blame him. I wish I could tell you more." *It's not my place to tell him more.*

"Thanks, Bobby. I appreciate it and won't tell Dad you gave me any more information."

Looking at the snow accumulate, Bobby knew it was time to decide. He killed a nice black bear on their second morning, and Roan shot the rarest of northern animals, a large wolverine, on their first day in the valley.

"Alright, young man, you know the situation. What's your recommendation?" Bob said.

"Chappie's not coming in this morning," Roan said. "The ceiling can't be more than a hundred feet, and it's snowing hard. I can't see a reason to wait until tomorrow. I say we head back now. We may get slowed down to the point we have to stop for the night and finish tomorrow, but Dad and the rest of the crew won't come looking for us until Saturday morning. We have time if we need two days."

"Good call," Bobby said.

With that, the two quickly packed camp and moved up and over the ridge to the valley that'd take them back to base camp.

108

CHAPTER SIXTEEN
0920 Hours Local-Thursday 24 September 1987
Base Camp

Dan read the message Chappie dropped in a low pass over camp.

"A big weather front is due to hit in a few days. Chappie wants to get everyone out over the next twenty-four hours. He's coming back for half of us this afternoon, and the rest go out tomorrow morning. What do you think?"

"We can do that, easy. We've all tagged out," Boone said. "We'd be hanging out fishing or in the tents."

Over the next two hours, the camp came down except for one tent and the rucksacks belonging to the three men staying behind. They carried the gear to the landing strip and waited on their ride.

The men had one last toast before they separated. In the distance, they heard the two Super Cubs that'd pull them out of the wilderness over the next two days. The sun was bright and warm, with only a light breeze. The snow from the night before melted from the rocks and sand on the landing strip. The late morning sun filtered through the aspen and diamond willows on the far side of the creek and dappled the water. They were frozen in time for a moment before movement separated them again. It was one of those moments that Boone had learned to slow down and pay attention to. He forced it into his memory. He wanted to hold this in his heart forever.

They hugged and shook hands in a rush as the first Cub lined up on the sandbar.

"I love you, son. Be safe getting back to Campbell," Boone said.

"I love you too, Dad," Roan said.

"Tell your sister thanks for the books. I love them."

109

"I will."

"And tell your mom and sisters I love them."

"Yes, sir. See you at Christmas," Roan said.

Boone nodded and waved goodbye as Roan put his gear in the plane and took his place in the backseat. Jimmy waved, turned the plane, and, in a few feet, it was in the air headed east.

As Jimmy's bird cleared the creek bed, Chappie started his approach. In another minute, he was on the ground. Bobby put Wade's gear in the back of the plane, and Boone hugged his dad.

"I love you, Pop," Boone said. "Thanks for coming on this trip. It means the world to me."

"Thanks for having me. Love you too, son. You three, be safe. See you tomorrow."

The remaining men stood on the sandbar, waved as the Cub took off, and turned east in a perfectly clear September sky. They watched the plane until it was a speck.

"I'm hungry," Bobby said.

"Yeah, me too," Dan said.

Boone agreed. "Let's go fix some lunch and then go fishing." He watched the planes fly east.

CHAPTER SEVENTEEN
1920 Local-Thursday 24 September 1987
Base Camp

The camp was oddly quiet, considering that it had only lost two members of the party, and the three remaining hunters were longtime friends. In many camps, the hunters spent the last night looking forward to a meal without dirt or ashes, a hot shower, clean sheets, and female companionship. But these men were different. They were throwbacks, outliers. As much as they appreciated those comforts and longed for the companionship of family, this was a form of home, even though they arrived in the valley for the first time only days before. Other hunters may have hoped for the sound of airplane engines, but these three heard it with some regret. There was a kind of sadness that it was coming to an end.

They fished most of the afternoon upstream and caught more than enough for a robust last night supper over the fire—rainbow trout, black beans and rice, and the last loaf of Dan's Dutch oven sourdough bread. After the early supper, just before sunset, they grabbed their rifles and binoculars and walked north to sit on the ridge, glass for wildlife, and watch the sunset on what they claimed as their valley.

As they sat side by side on the ridge overlooking their valley, the breeze died, and silence returned. The last of the sun dissected the horizon in the southwest, and twilight began. Dan pulled a bottle of whiskey from his hunting coat pocket. Boone and Bob pulled their tin cups from their coats, and Dan poured.

"What're we drinking to?" Bobby said.

"Here's to those who can't share this with us," Dan said. "The ones that didn't make it home."

The three warriors lifted their cups in honor of the fallen, many

111

of their faces familiar. They were men with whom they shared the most difficult and rewarding events of their lives.

"You think we'll ever be back here again?" Bobby said.

"I sure hope so," Dan said.

"Let's just decide to be back," Boone said. "I'm retired, Dan will be retired soon enough, and I don't know what you'll do with an International Relations Ph.D., but you'd better keep September clear on your calendar. We can do this every other year or so. It's therapeutic on a lot of levels."

They agreed, right then, they would continue to hunt the valley as a tradition. They drained the last of their cups and returned to camp in the growing darkness.

The following day broke cold and clear with no wind. The weather wouldn't prevent them from extracting today, barring mechanical issues, they would be back in Fairbanks by sundown. They stood next to their gear on the sandbar landing strip, looking to the northeast. Boone placed the Pentax camera he bought at the Saigon PX on a log, set the timer, and the three men were frozen forever on the creek's bank. As Boone retrieved his camera, the two aircraft came into view.

"Who's going out first?" Dan said.

"You two," Boone said. "I'm going to try for a grayling one more time."

Jimmy brought the Super Cub in like an old pro, Dan loaded, and they were back in the air in moments. Chappie landed his Piper, Bobby loaded, and Chappie yelled to Boone.

"Don't go anywhere. One of us will be back in an hour. Hope you get your grayling."

Boone waved as Chappie spun the Cub, added power, jumped into the air, and headed east to Eagle. Boone was alone in the wilderness.

***

Jimmy was walking to the hangar as Chappie parked his Cub and Bobby unloaded. Chappie caught up with Jimmy.

"How about you go back out and pick up Boone," Chappie said.

"Be happy too, boss."

"Here's what I want you to do," Chappie said. "Pick up Boone and fly down to the Fortymile cache. Park the Cub, get in the Beaver floatplane, resupply the other three caches, numbers one, two, and four, and then fly back here in the Beaver. I need it here. I'll take you back in the morning and pick up the Cub. We'll have all the birds home before the storm and the caches will be reloaded for any emergencies. Any questions?"

"No, sir."

***

Boone fished for the next hour within a few hundred yards of the landing strip and caught several nice rainbow trout and some smaller graylings but no trophy. He glanced at his watch and did some quick math. The plane would return in minutes, so he broke down his rod and reel and stowed them in his rucksack. He sat against his ruck, took off his hat, and leaned back to enjoy the last few moments. It was cold but clear, winter was coming, but at the moment, it was perfect. He would enjoy it, because waiting for him in the modern world were challenges and issues that he could no longer avoid.

Jimmy was getting better on this landing strip. He landed right on the waterline touchdown point, stopped with thirty feet of the sandbar remaining, spun the plane, and idled the engine for Boone to load. Boone ran around the tail of the small plane and packed his rifle case and rucksack behind the rear seat, climbed aboard, strapped in, and placed the headphones on his head. Jimmy keyed the intercom.

"Hey man, I'm going to give you a chance to get a trophy grayling if you want."

"Go ahead," Boone said.

"I have a few errands south of here and thought I could drop you at a lake to the west, known for huge grayling. I guided some guys in there last summer. When I finish my chores, I'll pick you up along with your giant fish and head back to Eagle."

"Sounds good. Just one request. Let someone know where you're dropping me."

"Can do. Here we go," Jimmy said.

He checked his control surfaces and pushed the throttle forward. In fifty feet, the airplane was flying. He gained air speed and turned south.

"There's a lake to the south where we keep a cache of fuel and survival gear in case one of us needs something in an emergency," Jimmy said. "We've got a few sprinkled throughout the area. It's a good floatplane lake with a good beach landing strip. About a week ago, one of our guys landed a floatplane to drop some fuel and somehow broke his leg, bad break. He got back to the plane and radioed a passing aircraft. The State Police came in and got him, but we haven't been back to get the airplane. I'll drop you off at the lake in this bird and get the floatplane, finish resupplying our emergency caches, and then return to get you. I'll land on the lake that you'll fish in."

Twenty minutes later, Jimmy circled the spot where he would drop Boone near a small lake in the Charley River valley. Like many lakes in the north country, it was formed when a river changed course and was cut off from the primary current by sediment. The fish in these lakes were thus trapped and grew to prestigious size if not fished out. Jimmy circled again, giving Boone a view of the surrounding terrain, details he put to memory through long practice.

Charley River drained the Mertie Mountains, southeast of Boone's Lake. On the west side of the river was a series of five-to-six-thousand-foot mountains. The mountain tops were void of trees, but most valleys and lower ridges were covered by tamarack and spruce, common to the boreal forest.

Jimmy flew a short length of the Charley River drainage and landed on a small sandbar. "About a quarter mile east is that lake," he said. "You saw it from the air. If you can't catch a trophy grayling there, I can't help you. You can leave your pack and just take your fishing gear if you want. I don't need the space."

"Were you ever in the infantry, young man?"

"No, sir."

"Never get separated from your rucksack," Boone said, smiling at the young pilot.

"I'll be back in two or three hours."

"See you then. Don't forget to call it in."

Boone stepped back from the plane as Jimmy turned, applied power, and took off. He turned southeast toward the first cache. Boone was alone in the wilderness again. He grabbed his gear and started moving toward the small lake, searching for a wall-hanger grayling.

Jimmy flew off the sandbar. Looking down, he saw Boone walking through the brush to the lake. He keyed the radio.

"Eagle Tower, this is November seven, niner zero two over."

His headphones were silent. He attempted a second call, and there was still no response. He tinkered with the radio as much as he could while in flight, checking the headphone connections, frequency, and volume, but no response. He pulled the handheld aviation radio that he carried in his flight bag and transmitted again, but the smaller radio didn't have the power to reach back to Eagle. He could look at the radio when he landed and then transmit Boone's position once he took off in the Beaver.

He flew twenty-five miles to a crescent-shaped lake where the Chapman Aviation Beaver floatplane was beached, landing the Super Cub just down the beach from the Beaver. After tying it down, he finished resupplying the cache, then pre-flighted the Beaver for the remainder of his flight. In ten minutes, he was in the air heading further southeast to resupply three additional emergency caches. The furthest was ninety-six miles southeast of Boone.

As he finished resupplying the last cache, he pushed the Beaver back into deeper water, jumped into the pilot's seat, and started the engine. As he taxied to the opposite end of the lake for takeoff, he looked at his aeronautical chart and made some quick calculations. It was about a forty-five-minute flight to pick up Boone, then another forty minutes to the airport. They would be back in Eagle well before sunset.

***

Boone stood almost thigh-deep in the cold water. Holding his fly rod under his left arm, he tied the purple egg-sucking leach to the tippet. Satisfied with the knot, he fan cast into the slight breeze, on the third cast the water exploded, the line went tight, and his fly rod bent double. With his right forefinger, he put pressure on the floating line and palmed the bottom of the reel with his left hand to slow the fish's run. The line sliced through the water to the left. The fish broke the water's surface, a beautiful, iridescent grayling. He thought it would be pushing five pounds or more.

"Alright, Boone, don't mount this sucker just yet."

For the next three minutes, he enjoyed the moment. The exhausted grayling finally gave up its fight. Boone scooped him into the small net attached to his vest. He tucked the fly rod under his arm, took the fish from the net, and removed the hook from its jaw. He hefted the fish momentarily and was confident it was at least five pounds. This is the one he would mount. He set up his Pentax on a nearby log, set the timer, and stood alone, holding the fish until the shutter snapped. He killed the grayling at the edge of the lake and placed a small, forked willow branch through its gills. Laying the fish in the water, he pushed the willow into the mud to secure his trophy.

Satisfied, Boone sat down against a rock, pulled his thermos from his rucksack, and poured coffee. He put a dip of Copenhagen in his lower lip and stretched back to enjoy the afternoon. The nights had grown colder since they arrived, and the snow was coming more often. It had stayed on some of the higher peaks, but the sun was shining right now, there was no wind, and he'd just landed the fish he was looking for. He knew this would only last a moment, but he enjoyed it immensely.

CHAPTER EIGHTEEN
1500 Hours Local-Friday 25 September 1987
Ninety-seven miles southeast of Boone's Lake

Jimmy took off from the final cache site and turned northwest to pick up Boone when he saw a reflection at his right front. He first noticed it as it passed along the top of the cockpit but now saw the source. It was along his course and wouldn't take more than a few minutes to investigate. He'd heard many accounts of downed bush pilots rescued because another pilot noticed their signal and came to help. Boone was having the time of his life. He would check out the source of the reflection.

He flew to the sight and put it off his left wing for an optimal view. He dropped altitude to two hundred feet and circled the area. He saw crumpled metal and reflection of glass but no movement. If it was a crash site, it was new. Jimmy had flown this area all summer and knew where all the old crashes were. There was a lake just about a half mile northwest of the site. He could land, walk over, and confirm what he was looking at. He didn't know if it was a downed aircraft, but he couldn't say it wasn't either. The trees obscured it enough to prevent a complete view from any angle. He couldn't confirm what he was looking at from the air. He would want another pilot to investigate if he were lying down there injured in a crash.

Jimmy set up on the lake for his approach. When the pontoons slid across the water momentarily, he chopped the power and came to rest in under two hundred feet. He pushed full right rudder and added power, taxied, killed the engine fifty feet from the shoreline, and coasted to the small beach. Jimmy stepped from the cockpit, walked along the pontoon, and opened the cargo door to retrieve the crash ax and medical aid kit. He stepped into the water and secured the Beaver

117

with the pontoon bowline. Eighteen minutes later, he stood beside the crash, except it wasn't a crash. It was what was left of an old fishing or trapper's cabin. The logs were completely deteriorated. The roof's metal was twisted in the middle of the pile, and glass was strewn throughout the pile.

He returned to the Beaver, secured the gear, untied the plane, and pushed it back from the shoreline. Once in the cockpit, he ran through a quick check, started the engine, taxied to the opposite end of the lake, turned the aircraft, did his final checks, and applied full power. As the Beaver started to come up on plane and skim the water, Jimmy glanced at the airspeed indicator. His sight was diverted from the water. He failed to see the obstacle that would take his life and put Boone in a fight for his own life.

Jimmy was shocked when the entire aircraft shuddered hard as both pontoons contacted the granite rock three inches beneath the surface, instantly opening the right float its entire length. The immediate introduction of hundreds of gallons of water and thousands of pounds of weight into what was left of the pontoons caused the plane to sit too deep in the water, and Jimmy instinctively pulled the yoke into his torso. His airspeed was too low, and the right pontoon had taken much more water than the left. The plane broke contact with the water, but for all the left yoke input Jimmy put in, he couldn't overcome the weight that pulled his right wing down.

The right wingtip dug into the lake's surface, cracked at the wing root, but stayed connected to the fuselage, causing four thousand pounds of plane and cargo to cartwheel. Jimmy's head snapped into the control yoke, knocking him unconscious. As the Beaver continued its death throes, the fuselage snapped off just behind the cockpit and sunk into twenty feet of water. The remaining fuselage and wings rested partly out of the water at the end of the lake.

James "Jimmy" Regan was crushed as the pilot's side of the cockpit came into contact with a large spruce tree at the water's edge. Two considerable failures had nagged him for the final fifteen minutes of his life. First, in his haste to investigate what he thought was a crash site, he failed to circle the lake he landed on to look for obstacles. Second, he'd failed to notify anyone where he dropped Boone Taggart.

118

Isolation

"It ought to have been different, but oftimes you will find,
That the story doesn't always go the way you had in mind."

The Ballad of Jeremiah Johnson
Tim McIntire and John Rubinstein, Songwriters

CHAPTER NINETEEN
1815 Hours Local-Friday 25 September 1987
Boone's Lake-Day 1

Boone looked at his watch and then held his hand, fingers extended and joined, horizontal, parallel to the southwestern horizon. The sun was just above his index finger. A little more than an hour until sunset and then another forty-five minutes to complete darkness. *Fifteen minutes per finger width,* there was a fifty percent moon, and the sky was clear, so there'd be plenty of illumination tonight. He turned his attention to the trout and grayling skewered on a split willow branch, sizzling against a rock. Jimmy was late, and Boone was hungry, so he caught two more fish and cooked them on an alder fire.

Boone Taggart was an experienced woodsman before he became a professional soldier. Add twenty-five years of military experience all over the world, both in combat and peacetime, and he knew there were a million reasons why an aircraft would be a day or more late for a scheduled extraction. He could've had a maintenance issue or a bird strike that bent a propeller. It was unlikely that it was weather—it was beautiful, and Boone had heard the most recent weather forecast from Chappie and knew it was clear from now until late Monday night or early Tuesday morning. Jimmy might be involved in a rescue. Another pilot needed assistance, which takes priority over picking him up. Nothing to worry about. He had the gear to spend a night in the field. Thankfully, he had enough gear to stay here indefinitely. Jimmy would be here in the morning if he wasn't back before sunset.

Boone inhaled the two freshly caught fish, packed his gear, and walked three hundred yards to the tree line overlooking a tributary of the Charley River. He would hunker down for the night in the trees, pack up in the morning, and return to the lake for pickup. Something happened that kept Jimmy from picking him up tonight, but he knew someone would be here shortly after sunrise to take him back to Eagle.

He dropped his gear, pulled the Granfors-Bruk hunter's ax from the side of his rucksack, and removed limbs from several spruce trees to make room for his shelter. He trimmed the limbs that were head high or lower from several trees, stacked the limbs up under one tree, and cleared a few rocks and roots from where he'd put his sleeping bag. He piled spruce boughs almost knee high. At waist level, he attached a 550 para-cord ridgeline to two trees fifteen feet apart. He threw his poncho across the ridgeline and secured it in place. He used his hunting knife to sharpen four stakes, two, twice as long as the others, and in combination with four bungees, Boone secured the corners of his poncho twelve inches above the ground in the back, twenty-four inches in the front—home was built. He glanced at his watch-six minutes from start to finish. *You're getting old and slow, Ranger.*

He put his sleeping bag on the spruce boughs under the poncho, took his rucksack one hundred yards away, pulled the pack twenty feet into a spruce tree, and then walked back to camp. He built a small fire, cut several downed trees to four-foot lengths, and fashioned a reflective wall so the fire would be between the wall and his shelter. He put three-to-four-foot sections of limbs on the fire to create a long fire that'd provide some heat the length of his shelter. He'd be plenty warm once he was wrapped in his sleeping bag.

He drank a bottle of water, re-filled it and heated the water on the fire. A bottle of hot water at the bottom of his sleeping bag would help keep his feet warm overnight. He added more water to a pot and placed it over the fire. It would boil, then cool overnight, and he would have plenty of clean drinking water in the morning.

He press-checked his shotgun, pulling the action of the Remington 870 back far enough to feel and see the shell in the chamber, returned it forward, checked the safety, and lay it on his right side in the shelter. He removed his gun belt and placed it by his head on his left side, pulled the Ruger from the holster, checked all six chambers, returned the pistol to the holster, and then crawled into his sleeping bag. It was only one of countless nights that he'd slept on the ground under a poncho. It was cold, but it wasn't raining or snowing, and there was no wind. He was fine. In two minutes, he was snoring.

Wade and Chappie stood side by side on the tarmac outside the Chapman Aviation hangar, scanning the darkening southwest sky. It was too dark to see a plane at this point. They were looking for navigation lights. Chappie made some quick calculations based on the location of the caches. He determined if they'd departed the farthest point from Eagle at last light, they would've landed an hour earlier.

From long experience, both men understood the countless factors that could require a bush plane to overnight at a remote site. Attempting to get home had killed more than one hunter or pilot over the years. Chappie was a big believer in the adage home is where you are, and he'd always instructed his pilots to choose to sleep in the plane instead of pushing their luck to get back to the field. Pushing the envelope too much just to get home, so you can sleep in a soft bed, get a warm shower, and eat hot chow can kill you. Dan and Bobby approached the two older men and handed each a hot coffee.

"We need to devise a plan for first light," Wade said.

"I agree," Chappie said. "We can do initial planning and get a few assets in place overnight. A search is easier to turn off than on."

The four men turned and walked to Chappie's office and forward command post of Chapman Aviation. They were all experienced with emergencies and contingencies. Within a few minutes, they'd considered possible actions that'd cause Boone and Jimmy to sit down for the night, and then they developed a contingency plan for first light. Chappie walked to the aeronautical chart that covered most of one wall, depicting almost all of Alaska from Fairbanks to the Canadian border and well north of the Yukon River to almost Valdez.

He pulled a clear acetate overlay that showed the locations of the Chapman Aviation emergency re-supply caches. They needed to focus on four, one where the Beaver was left and the three southeast of that location that Chappie instructed Jimmy to resupply. Chappie drew a black grease pencil line with a long straight edge between Eagle and the lake where the Beaver put down the three caches to the

123

southeast, and then back to Eagle, creating an oddly shaped triangle that bounded more than 2.4 million acres of wilderness.

"I'll call Bart and get him back here tonight with the Otter," Chappie said. "Tomorrow, at first light, we'll fly to your hunting camp and then to the Fortymile cache. Dan, you go ride along as my observer. Simultaneously, I'll send two of my pilots to the other caches to see if they're there and if the caches were resupplied. Bart can fly Highway Five in the Otter, Bobby you go as his observer. A lot of guys land out there if they get in trouble. Wade, would you run command and control back here?"

"Absolutely," he said.

"They're in either a Super Cub, which can land virtually anywhere, or a Beaver on floats, so pay attention to any lakes near your flight routes," Chappie said. "We'll check out those sites and then fly the same course home for a second look. We'll meet back here, debrief, and decide what to do next."

"I'll walk over to the FBO and tower and let them know we've got an overdue bird. I'll ask them to contact us if they get any radio traffic," Bobby said.

"I'll call Bart and brief my other pilots, we'll get the birds checked out tonight," Chappie said.

"Bob, while you're at the tower, ask if there's any report of an ELT signal," Dan said.

"What time is daylight tomorrow?" Wade asked.

Dan looked at his notebook, "Civil twilight is 0630, and sunrise is 0719."

"Let's plan on being in the air at 0800. That should give us enough daylight to ensure we don't miss anything."

"Are you going to call Abby?" Dan asked Wade.

"Not yet. Those guys could be sitting somewhere safe for many reasons, and there's no reason to get her spun up. She doesn't expect to hear from us until tomorrow night anyway."

"If we don't know anything when we meet back here tomorrow," Chappie said. "I'll notify the State Troopers. We have three days to figure this out, or it gets serious. The weather due in here Monday night or Tuesday morning will shut us down for at least

124

seventy-two to ninety-six hours. Lots of snow, wind, and dropping temperatures. Lakes will freeze during this one. Any questions?"

The men remained silent.

"Let's get our coordination done, check gear, and get some sleep. Tomorrow could be a long day," Chappie said.

With that, the four men went in different directions to coordinate the initial search for Boone and Jimmy.

CHAPTER TWENTY
0712 Hours Local-Saturday 26 September 1987
Boone's Lake - Day 2

Boone collected the wood prepared the night before and rekindled the fire with birch bark. As water heated, he took down his shelter, retrieved and packed his rucksack. By the time he got back to his fire, the water was boiling. He poured it into his canteen cup and added a tablespoon of instant coffee. He walked out from under the trees and looked back toward the lake. Frost crunched beneath each step, and the valley was silent and windless. It was beautiful, but he would be thankful when the sun was higher in the sky. The lake had ice at the edges this morning, but it would melt off quickly.

He finished his coffee and caribou jerky, brushed his teeth, packed his lower lip with a dip of Copenhagen, shouldered his rucksack, grabbed his gun case, and headed for the lake. He just had to wait now. Jimmy or one of the other pilots would be here in the next hour or so.

***

Chappie circled the lake where Jimmy retrieved the Beaver. The Beaver was gone, but the Super Cub was still there. *They made it this far.* Chappie started his approach, dropped his flaps, and almost hovered the Piper as the tundra tires met the beach. He stopped the plane in fifty feet. He released the brakes, added power, taxied to the end of the beach, pushed the left rudder to the floor, applied power, turned the plane into takeoff position, and killed the engine. Chappie went to the cache while Dan looked at the parked Super Cub.

Ten minutes later, Chappie was back at the beach.

126

"The cache is resupplied, so whatever happened didn't happen here," Chappie said. "They were still inside the plan at this point. There must've been a problem at one of the other sites."

"The Cub's tied down properly, no sign of any emergency," Dan said.

"Let's get back in the air and head back. Maybe the others found something," Chappie said.

All four aircraft returned to Eagle and reported to Wade. Nothing. John Abbot and Howard Shefler, the Chapman pilots who flew to the other caches, said they were resupplied, there was evidence Jimmy had been there, and there was no sign of any emergency. Chappie put both pilots in one Cub and sent them to return Jimmy's Cub from the Fortymile cache.

"Fly a straight course to the cache, but on the way back, fly the search box perimeter again," Chappie said.

The two pilots turned for the flight line and Chappie walked to the hangar. He stood next to Wade looking at the wall sized map.

"I think it's time to report an overdue aircraft to the State Troopers," Chappie said.

"And call Abby."

Wade left Chappie in charge of the Chapman Aviation ad hoc Command Post and walked to the FBO, putting his thoughts together, *facts only*, he thought. He sat at the phone and made the call.

"Hello." Twelve-year-old Caroline had answered.

"Hey honey, it's Grandpa. Can I talk to your mom, please?"

"Sure Grandpa." He heard Caroline call for Abby in the background. "Mom, it's Grandpa Wade."

Wade knew Abby was surprised by this call. She'd heard from Roan since he flew out, and instead of Boone, it was him. She already knew something was wrong.

"Wade?" She said, anxiety in her voice.

"Honey, Boone's plane is overdue getting back to Eagle."

"Okay."

"I'm going to tell you exactly what we know right now," Wade said. "Boone was on the last lift out of our hunting camp. One of Chappie's pilots, Jimmy Regan, went back for Boone. After the pickup, they were to fly south, transfer to a floatplane, resupply three caches, and then fly back to Eagle. Based on the flight time of that mission, they should've been back here by mid-afternoon, yesterday at the latest. This morning, at first light, four aircraft flew to the resupply sites and the hunting camp. The floatplane was gone, Jimmy's plane was where we expected, and the other three caches were resupplied, so we know they made it that far.

"We've called other airports in the immediate area, and they haven't landed at any of those fields. No mayday calls have been heard on the emergency frequency, and no emergency beacon is active. Chappie is talking to the State Troopers, and I think a search will be initiated immediately. The weather is great here until sunset on Monday. Then we're expecting a big storm. That's what we know right now."

Abby's mind rushed through a dozen scenarios, sorting through hundreds of tasks and details she had to accomplish and running through courses of action. She'd never served in uniform, but she'd undoubtedly served. The wife of a career soldier, she'd watched other families go through great tragedy. She'd experienced consoling a widow on more than one occasion in the past quarter century. She thought she'd lost Boone several times, but he always came through unscathed. *Don't panic. The first report is always wrong,* she thought. *That's what Boone would tell me.*

"Wade, what do you think?"

"I can't say for certain, but my experience is there are many reasons for a bush plane to set down somewhere and wait for help. Communication's dicey out here, so getting a message to headquarters can be tough. It's a good sign there are no mayday calls or locator beacons. Boone and Jimmy are probably sitting on a lake somewhere due to a mechanical issue or bird strike, just waiting for us to find them and pick them up. But for now, let's stick to what we know. I'll give you several phone numbers to Chapman Aviation hangar here and in Fairbanks and the FBO here at Eagle. I'll call you twice daily with updates, around noon your time, and after we suspend searches at night or when there's any news."

Wade read off the numbers and asked Abby to repeat them.

"Honey, hang in there and say a prayer," Wade said. "Do you want me to call his mom, or do you want to talk to her?"

"I'll walk over and tell her right now. Then I'll call the kids. Thanks, Wade. Please bring him home."

"I'll do my best, honey. So help me God."

Abby hung up the phone and paused with her eyes closed, silently praying for her husband's safety and strength to lead her family through another ordeal. Then she went to work. "Caroline, get your jacket," Abby said. "We need to go talk to Grandma."

Rebecca Crabtree Taggart was the family matriarch, a position she would've held, even if there was another woman older than she in the family lineage, simply because she was a force of nature. Tough and resilient and loving all at the same time. The first time Boone introduced Abby to his mother, he eloquently described her as "tougher than Chinese arithmetic," and she was. Still, she was also kind and compassionate and cared for her family more than anything. From long experience, Rebecca was good in a crisis. Abby needed that now.

Rebecca volunteered as an Army nurse on December 8th, 1941. She served in Europe until a four-day date with a cocky young paratrooper from Wyoming resulted in a wartime wedding, followed by her discharge shortly after due to pregnancy from their wedding night. She witnessed first-hand the cost of the battles in North Africa, Sicily, and Italy before returning to Wyoming to live with her in-laws and raise newborn Boone until Wade's return in 1946. She had to deal with Wade's return to combat in Korea four years later, Boone's four tours in Vietnam, and now a grandson in the family profession. Abby loved her like a second mother. It pained her now to have to break her heart.

Rebecca was standing at the sink finishing the morning dishes. She saw Abby and Caroline walking the twenty yards separating the guest house from the main ranch house. Halfway across the space, Rebecca recognized something peculiar—a woman with bad news had a particular look. She dried her hands, threw her faded denim work jacket over her shoulders, and stepped onto the porch.

"What happened?" she said, as Abby and Caroline reached the

steps.

Tears welled in Abby's eyes. Rebecca put her arms around her daughter-in-law's shoulders and led her into the house. Three minutes later, she had the whole story.

Rebecca put her arm around Caroline, consoled her, and reached for Abby's hand.

"Listen to me, both of you," Rebecca said. "We don't know enough yet to mourn, so let's take this one step at a time. Boone has experienced plenty of danger in his life and seems to thrive once it shows up. This isn't the first time he's come up missing, and he made it home each time. He knows more about living in the wild than anyone I know. Until we learn otherwise, let's picture him sitting next to a lake, cooking his lunch over a fire."

"You're right," Abby said. "That's what we're going to do until we know otherwise."

"Do you want me to call the other children?"

"No, I'll take care of that, and I need to call my parents. Can Caroline stay here with you for a while?"

"She can help me make the cake I'm serving for dessert tonight."

Abby walked to the door, turned, and motioned Rebecca to follow her to the porch.

"I think I'll fly up there if we don't know something soon," Abby said. "Can Caroline stay with you until I get back?"

"Of course," Rebecca said. "I don't blame you, dear. I'd want to be there if it was Wade. Be strong. If Boone's heart is still beating, he'll find a way home."

***

Abby was amazed at how different children raised by the same two people responded to life. Roan was confident in the outcome.

"Don't worry, Mom, Dad's fine."

He was just like his father. Rachel, their middle child, didn't let her finish the phone conversation. "I'm on my way," and she hung up.

Rachel couldn't sit still. She had to move, do something, be actively engaged in what was happening. She, too, was just like her father.

CHAPTER TWENTY-ONE
1630 Hours Local-Saturday 26 September 1987
Flight Base Operations-Eagle, Alaska-Day 2

Two Cessna 182s landed within minutes of one another, taxied to the FBO tarmac, and shut down. One bore the paint scheme of the Alaska State Troopers and the other of the Alaska Wing, Civil Air Patrol (CAP). The passengers deplaned, and Chappie and Wade walked to intercept them on their way to the FBO office. Chappie recognized them both. He'd worked with them on several searches.

"Good afternoon, Chappie," Trooper Bill Larsen said, shaking his hand.

"Wish it was better circumstances. Bill, this is Wade Taggart, one of my clients and the father of the missing hunter."

"Good to meet you, Mr. Taggart. We'll do everything we can to get your son back safely."

"Thank you. I know you will."

Chappie continued the introductions, "Wade, this is Captain Diana Brown, a rescue pilot with the CAP wing. We've worked together on a couple of SAR missions."

"Good to meet you, sir," Diana said, shaking hands with Wade.

"If you both want to get caught up, I can brief you on what we know and where we've looked so far," Chappie said.

"We'll do that," Larsen said. "Let me talk to the FBO first. They're going to provide us with command post space. I'll be over once we figure that out, and I get my folks to work."

Chappie and Wade walked back to the hangar. Twenty minutes later, Trooper Larsen and Captain Brown stepped up to the map on the wall of the Chapman Aviation hangar. Chappie briefed both on the instructions he gave Jimmy the day before, the routes they flew that morning, and their search results. He provided tail numbers, aircraft descriptions, and the survival equipment he knew was packed in all his aircraft. He finished with a weather update.

"Questions?" Chappie said.

"Tell me about the pilot, please?" Trooper Larsen asked.

"James Regan. He's twenty-one, a good pilot, and has a few years of Alaska flying. I've been training him since we hired him earlier in the summer. Seems like a mature kid."

"And the hunter, what's his experience?" Captain Brown asked.

"Lifelong outdoorsman, twenty-four years in the Army, infantryman, Ranger, Green Beret. He was stationed in Alaska 75-79, has hunted here a couple of times since, hunted all over the northern Rocky Mountains, and made one trip to Africa. If he's not severely injured, he'll be fine," Wade said.

"Chappie, what assets can we get from you?" Trooper Larsen asked.

"My hunters all in, at least in this unit," Chappie said. "I've got two Super-Cubs and a Caribou if we need cargo or personnel moved. I've got to keep my Otter flying people and cargo out to other sites. I have a total of three crews, which include a pilot and an observer. If you need the Caribou, that will require two of my pilots. I also have survival packs we can drop by parachute from the Caribou if we can't extract them immediately."

"Chappie, this is your pilot, and you talked to him last. What's your view on an approach to the search?" Captain Brown asked.

"I'd suggest concentrating the search in the area bounded by the route out to the caches and back and then expand that area to the south and east to the Canadian border. There wasn't any reason for them to fly north or west."

"Makes sense."

"We established the Command Post in the conference room in the FBO," Larsen said. "The CAP is providing two more aircraft and crews as well as Diana's bird. We have two full days to search, and then, unless the forecast changes dramatically, we'll be shut down for four days. If you can have your pilots and observers at the FBO command post at 0600, we'll brief the plan and get them in the air."

"We'll be there," Wade said.

CHAPTER TWENTY-TWO
1130 Hours Local-Saturday 26 September 1987
Boone's Lake-Day 2

Boone worked through possible scenarios while waiting for the two fourteen-inch trout to cook. He considered two primary questions—what could've happened to Jimmy, and what was going on at Eagle. The first possibility was Jimmy experienced a mechanical issue or a bird strike that put the Beaver down to wait for Chappie to show up. In that case, the guys in Eagle would have to find Jimmy first, fix the bird, and come get him. The second possibility is that Jimmy is down hard somewhere, injured, or worse, dead. In that scenario, a search and rescue operation is going on. *But why haven't they picked me up yet? They don't know where he crashed, and they're searching, although they would've done a cursory, initial search with Chapman Aviation assets before they called in the heavies.* He glanced at his watch. *They're just now getting a search organized.*

As Boone went through the various scenarios, one horrible possibility kept pushing to the front. *What if Jimmy didn't report where he left me?* He started working through that possibility. *If Jimmy is down and injured, they'll eventually find him. The ELT is going off right now. He may have even gotten off a mayday call. When they find him, he'll tell them where I am. If he crashed and didn't survive, the ELT would be going off, and they would find the aircraft and see I'm not with him and come get me. That could take a couple of days.*

What if Jimmy didn't report where he left me? If they don't know I'm here, find the aircraft crashed, Jimmy dead, and me not there, then they'll start a search for me. But what if they don't know where to look?

Boone decided he was going to hunker down. He couldn't just

135

wait beside the lake. If they didn't come, the weather on Tuesday would kill him.

I'm digging in. A plan is easier to turn off than on. If they show up, I jump on the bird and leave. If they don't, I need to be ready to survive for a while on my own.

He wolfed down the two fish in a few bites, took out his notepad, and began planning. *Write it down, Boone. You might get tired or freaked out and need a reference. Commit the plan to paper. You can adjust as the situation develops.*

On one page of the notebook, he wrote the acronym S-U-R-V-I-V-A-L down one edge of the page. He thought back to Survival School at Camp Mackall and Jungle School in Panama before deploying to Vietnam for the first time. The Army couldn't communicate or train soldiers without the use of acronyms. Next to each letter, he wrote out the phrase that went with the letter.

Size up the situation
Undue haste makes waste
Remember where you are
Vanquish fear and panic
Improvise
Value living
Act like the natives
Learn basic skills

There were other basic principles they taught him, or he learned from real-world experience outside the schoolhouse. Mitigate the risk that will kill you first. Accept the situation for what it is. Keep mind and body busy with productive work, not just busy work. Solve one problem at a time. Prioritize your work. The mind is the final weapon—all else is supplemental. Semper Gumby—*Always Flexible.*

Boone made some initial notes about the priority of work. He had the remainder of the afternoon and two full days to prepare for a major snowstorm, plunging temperatures, lots of snow, and high wind. *What'll kill you first? Environment. Priority is shelter and fire. He had to maintain his core body temperature. Most people in a survival scenario die from exposure to the elements. Shelter first. Second: Signal. Be able to draw attention. They're looking for you. Third: food and water were covered. Even if the lake froze over, he could use it as a source of water and food in the short term. What if this goes on longer? I'll need more food. Cold weather gobbles calories. Solve that problem later. You have food and water for now.*

Size up the situation. Time was limited to prepare for the changing weather. He was in good physical and mental condition and wasn't injured. *Keep it that way. You can't afford an injury. No dustoff out here.* He had stronger-than-average outdoor skills. He was an excellent woodsman with a lot of time in the boonies.

Undue haste makes waste. *Reduce false starts, plan. Get it right the first time. Slow is smooth, and smooth is fast. Slow down. Be deliberate.*

Remember where you are. Boone did some quick calculations and determined that he was seventy or eighty miles from Eagle and forty miles to the lake where Jimmy was headed. He pulled the books from Rachel, out of his rucksack and used the brown paper to draw a rudimentary map. *I can't walk out before the weather hits, and I don't know if they know I'm here. I'll stay for now and decide to go later.*

Value living. *No problem. I have dozens of reasons to make it out of here.*

Improvise. *Again, no problem. I've been a soldier all my life. Improvising is what I do. Think unconventionally and consider alternatives others wouldn't.*

Vanquish fear and panic. *Fear is normal but conquer it. Panic kills—so don't. Logic—not emotion. Remember—it can always get worse.* Boone remembered Master Sergeant Sobolewski, the primary survival instructor at Camp Mackall when he and Bobby went through the Q Course. Sobolewski fought the Nazis in World War II in Poland as part of a partisan group. Under the Lodge Act, he became an American citizen and eventually a Green Beret. He knew more about wilderness survival and mountaineering than anyone Boone knew. During training, he reiterated the importance of controlling your mental state.

"You can fall apart and cry all you want when it's over, but when you're fighting for your life, put your emotions in a box and put them away. Be a robot."

Act like the natives. *People have lived in this environment for centuries with only stone-age tools. Leverage those skills.*

Learn basic skills. *I'm good at this. I have the skills needed.*

1648 Local - Saturday 26 September 1987
Double A Ranch - Sheridan County, Wyoming

A cloud of brown dust hit the side of the house as the 1975 Ford pickup slid to a stop in front of the main ranch house. Boone and Abigail's middle child, Rachel, threw the door open and headed for the front door, taking the porch steps two at a time.

Standing at the kitchen sink, Rebecca watched the spectacle of Rachel's entry off the county road, down the ranch road at top speed, at least top speed for her old truck, and the stunning gravel slide in front of the porch. Wearing her usual, too tight for grandma's taste Wrangler jeans and pearl snap shirt, and a denim jacket, her *King Ropes* ball cap was pulled low over her red, bloodshot eyes. Her boots stomped across the porch. Rebecca looked over her shoulder at Abby.

"Hurricane Rachel is coming through the door."

"Have you heard anything yet?" Rachel asked.

"It's good to see you too, dear," Grandma said, hugging her.

Abby met her halfway across the kitchen and held her in her arms. Rachel started crying again.

"Nothing yet, honey. Grandpa will call with an update:" Abby did some time zone calculations in her head. "In an hour or so."

Abby finished telling Rachel the whole story. In her haste to get home, she hung up the phone on her mother, packed a bag, jumped in her truck, and drove four and a half hours from campus.

"Mom, I'm going to fly to Alaska and help them find Daddy," Rachel said.

"Let's slow down a little. I know you're worried, and so am I, but you have school."

"School will be there later, Mom. I can go to school whenever I want. I'm only eighteen. One year isn't a big deal at my age. I can start next year. Are you flying up?”

"I don't know yet. I'll wait to see what your grandfather says tonight before I decide,”

"So, you're going up, but you don't think I should?" Rachel said.

"Rachel, think about this. If you go up and miss a week of school, and your father walks out of the woods, you've set your education back by one year, not one week. You can't afford to miss a week of class.”

"I don't care. School will always be there. I need to be close to Dad.”

CHAPTER TWENTY-THREE
1200 Hours Local-Saturday 26 September 1987
Boone's Lake-Day 2

Boone stowed the notebook, remembering another piece of advice from Master Sergeant Sobolewski. He inventoried his equipment. *Size up the situation. What gear do I have, and what can I do with it?* He pulled his poncho out of the center pocket of his rucksack, laid it on the ground, and then organized his equipment by category, signal, food, tools, and so on. It made him feel better. He had enough gear to last indefinitely. *Let's hope this doesn't last that long.*

Weapons first. He had his rifle, a Winchester Model Seventy in 30-06, with a scope and two boxes of cartridges, forty rounds. He also had a Remington 870 shotgun, twelve gauge with a box of twenty-five sabot slugs, good for bear protection or large game, and a box of twenty-five shells in number six bird shot. He touched the gun belt around his waist. Ruger Super Blackhawk in .44 magnum, fifty cartridges of hard cast bullets for bear protection, and twenty rounds of shot. A hunting knife with elk antler scales in a beaded buckskin sheath sat on his right hip, a gift from Luther One Knife. He'd given it to Boone when he left for the Army. He could hunt and protect himself.

Clothing. He had what he was wearing. Wool Filson hunting coat, Carhartt pants, wool shirt, wool vest, canvas fishing vest, two pairs of wool socks, one pair of polypropylene long underwear, an Army issue green five-button wool sweater, rubber hip boots, Danner insulated hunting boots, a pair of insulated leather gloves, wool watch cap and his cowboy hat. Around his neck was his drive on rag, technically a green triangular bandage, or cravat, but popular among soldiers worn as a bandanna around the neck. It had hundreds of uses. He also had a heavy sleeping bag in a waterproof bag.

140

Cooking and sustenance. A stainless-steel water bottle, canteen cup, fishing gear, small roll of wire for snares, three dehydrated camp meals, spoon, and a cooking pot. He had a fly rod and fishing vest with tackle.

Fire kit with a ferro rod, small striker, and cotton balls in Vaseline.

A robust trauma kit. Several tubes of antiseptic cream, gauze, various bandages, suture kits, hemostats, antibiotics, a mix of painkillers and pain relief pills, antiseptic wipes, and water purification tablets.

Tools. He had the Leatherman Pocket Survival Tool that Rachel got him the previous Christmas. A Granfors-Bruk hunter's ax, breakdown bow saw.

Signal. Whistle and small signal mirror.

Navigation. Compass but no map.

Other. Notebook and pencils. Binoculars. Headlamp and a mini-mag flashlight, one set of extra batteries for each.

Comfort items. A jar of instant coffee, one unopened pint of Jack Daniels that Dan gave him their last night in camp, and four more tins of Copenhagen.

He gave his map to Dan and the spotting scope to Bobby. Unfortunately, he also gave Bobby the handheld radio. He dumped the contents of his pockets on the poncho as well. Zippo lighter that Abby bought him before his third tour in Vietnam. He picked it up and ran his thumb over the Widowmaker crest of the 502nd Infantry on the front. He turned it over and looked at the engraving on the back. "1LT Boone Taggart" Rolex Submariner watch, a gift from his dad when he graduated from the Special Forces Q Course. It was inscribed on the back, "Congratulations. SGT Boone Taggart, Green Beret." He had his wallet in a Ziploc bag and a Swiss Army Knife. On his belt was his grandfather's small buckaroo knife.

He was in good shape. People had survived for a long time with much less gear. There's no reason a trained professional soldier can't survive indefinitely with this gear.

You're lucky, Boone. At least you were smart enough to keep your rucksack with you.

Priority of work. The clock's ticking. Mitigate what'll kill you first. Shelter and fire. Get ready for a three- or four-day snowstorm.

Boone packed his rucksack, strapped the gun case to the outside of his ruck, and walked to the small knoll west of the lake. He scanned three hundred and sixty degrees for a likely place to hunker down. *How long?* On the west side of the Valley, three quarters of a mile west, was a large stand of timber, spruce, birch, alder, and tamarack. Some were standing dead, suitable for shelter construction and fuel.

The area was slightly elevated from the river, protected from prevailing winds by the trees and a ridge line. He was close enough to water and a food source—he was also close to where they would look for him. That's where he would dig in. He walked back to the lake, grabbed his fly rod, and caught another rainbow trout and grayling in fifteen minutes. He'd eaten his trophy for breakfast. These two would be supper. He shouldered his rucksack, picked up the Remington 870 shotgun, and headed west to his new home and mission.

***

Rebecca, Abigail, and Rachel sat at the kitchen table in the main ranch house, picking at leftovers on their plates. Caroline finished eating, returned to the leather chair in the corner, and was now lost in the pages of her book. Rachel paced the kitchen floor, Rebecca worked on the dishes, and Abby dried and put them in the cabinets.

Abby answered the phone after one ring. "Wade?" she asked.

"Hi honey, I wanted to call and update you."

"Go ahead."

"The State Troopers and CAP are on site in Eagle and have set up a command post. They'll start the search tomorrow morning at first light. There's still no evidence of an active beacon. That may be a good sign. It would indicate there was no crash. They haven't been reported at other airports, and word has gone out to all the bush pilots flying in the area to be on the lookout for their aircraft. We have two solid days of good weather, and then we'll likely be shut down for three to four days. That's what I know right now."

"So, no change."

"No, Abigail, not yet," Wade said. "I'll call again tomorrow at noon and give you another update."

"That's fine, Wade, thank you. Rachel and I are flying up. I'm going crazy here. I have to move," Abby said.

Rachel glanced at her mom. She'd evidently conceded and wouldn't fight about school.

"We'll take care of everything here, and then drive to Denver tomorrow," Abby said. "I don't know when but expect to see us sometime on Monday. Are there regular flights out to Eagle?"

"No, but I can have Chappie arrange to get you both out here," Wade said. "I'll find you accommodations here at the airfield. You've got the numbers here. Update me on your arrival time into Fairbanks, and I'll take care of the rest."

"Thanks, Wade. We'll talk soon."

She and her daughter made plans.

CHAPTER TWENTY-FOUR
1230 Hours Local-Saturday 26 September 1987
Boone's Camp-Day 2

Boone finished the debris shelter framework. Four spruce poles were locked into the fork of a larger tree about four feet above the ground, with smaller poles added parallel and perpendicular to the main beams. Once finished, it would look like a green igloo. He spent the rest of the afternoon covering it in spruce boughs two feet thick, except for a small hole that allowed smoke to escape the shelter and a small door opening to the east. He dug a fire pit and lined it with rocks, built a rock reflector around the fire hole, and collected enough firewood to last at least five days. It was basic but would keep him alive in the upcoming storm. He knew that if he wasn't rescued soon and had to stay here long term, he would need a better shelter, but this shelter would suffice through the first storm.

Just after sunset, Boone tested his shelter. He could easily sit upright in the middle, next to the fire. He managed the fire carefully to ensure he didn't burn down the shelter. He cooked another trout and settled into his sleeping bag for the first night in his new wilderness home. The firelight danced in odd shapes on the spruce boughs, and Boone thought about what was happening in the world beyond his valley. The world that was diligently working to find him, the world that was worried about him beyond description. He couldn't control any of that. He had to focus on what he could manage. His family would have to worry. They'd worried before and would likely do so again in the future. *Put your emotions in a box, Boone.*

First thing tomorrow morning, he'd prepare a signal in the open area, north of the shelter. He'd also find and prepare the makings of a pair of snowshoes. Building a pair of snowshoes would keep him busy during the storm, and he'd need them to move around in the snow after the storm, at least until it melted off. If it melted. He dosed off into a tired sleep.

Herman "Hoot" Clark was among the first people to deplane at the arrival gate. He made his way to baggage claim. There was no wasted movement. He was on a mission. He retrieved the well-used, standard-issue military OD green A-3 and B-4 bags from the baggage carousel, walked to the nearest pay phone and dropped them beside him, pulled a small notebook from his worn leather flight jacket, and dialed the number for Chapman Aviation. He talked for under thirty seconds, hung up, and made a collect call to Sheridan County, Wyoming to let his wife, daughter, and granddaughters know he'd arrived safe. In another ten minutes, he was waiting at the curb when a Chevy Suburban, with "Chapman Aviation-Fairbanks, Alaska" painted on the doors, pulled up. Clark threw his bags in the back and climbed into the passenger's seat.

Clark interrogated the Chapman driver as they made their way to the hangar on the far side of the airport. At least, it felt like an interrogation from the driver's perspective. Bart would be back at Fairbanks in the Otter around 1700 and make the last run of the day to Eagle. Clark could take that flight. He spent the time until the flight, grabbing a bite to eat, checking his equipment, and scrounging aeronautical charts from Chappie's office. At 1650, when Bart taxied the DHC-3 Otter to the Chapman Hangar, Clark met him with his bags in hand.

"Hoot Clark," Bart said. "I figured you'd be here shortly." He stopped long enough to shake hands.

"How are you, son?" Hoot said.

"I wish we were all together under better circumstances."

"Me too. But Boone will be fine."

"My guys radioed ahead and let me know you were here," Bart

145

said. "Let me grab a sandwich from the cooler, top off my thermos, and I'll get you to Eagle. I can brief you on the latest enroute. We'll take off in ten."

He walked back to the hangar as Clark stowed his gear in the cargo bay of the Otter and took a seat in the right-seat cockpit.

Bart came out of the latrine and walked to the coffee pot to fill his thermos, and the Chapman driver walked through the door from the hangar. He glanced around to make sure Clark wasn't in the room.

"Who's the intimidating hillbilly?" he asked.

Bart chuckled. "That's Hoot Clark. He is a hillbilly, and he is intimidating. That's true, but there's no better friend to have, good times or bad. He, my dad, and Wade worked together during the war in Burma. I don't have all the details, but they're tight, so it must've been a wild ride. He's also Boone's father-in-law, and there's no way he was going to watch this one from the sidelines."

"Man, he interrogated me with no mercy on the drive from the terminal. I'd hate to get locked in a small room with that guy," the driver said.

"He's a teddy bear," Bart said. "Once you get to know him. Of course, not many get to know him."

Bart laughed as he walked out of the office and across the tarmac.

Bart and Hoot exchanged information on the flight to Eagle. Bart updated him on the day's search, which produced nothing. Hoot gave Bart the time of Rachel and Abby's arrival Monday. Bart would meet them and take them to Eagle before sundown.

When they landed the DHC-3 Otter, Bart taxied to the hangar, turned, and before the radial engine completely shut down, both cockpit doors were opened with Bart and Hoot deplaning. They retrieved their gear from the cargo area of the Otter and walked to the hangar, where Chappie and Wade waited. The three old friends shook hands and then got to work.

"Any change?" Hoot asked.

"None," Chappie said. "The last aircraft are returning now, but we didn't find anything. No one detected an active beacon, so today, we focused on the route they should've taken to each cache and then back here, but nothing."

"When's the weather supposed to hit?"

"Tomorrow night after sundown, so we have another full day to search," Wade said.

"Can you work me into the pilot rotation tomorrow?"

"Absolutely," Chappie said. "We're rotating pilots and observers every few hours, so I'll put you on the schedule. The incident commander will brief tomorrow's plan at 1900 in the command post."

"Come with me," Wade said. "I'll get you settled in a living space in the hangar."

Chappie walked back to the command post as Wade and Hoot headed for the Chapman Aviation maintenance area, now turned into a barracks and ready room for the employees involved in the search operation.

"There's an empty cot next to mine," Wade said. "The latrine is through the doors there, and we're using the office for planning. Chow is available over at the FBO. Let me know if you need anything specific, and I'll see what I can do. Dan Hardy and Bobby Doyle are still here. They work as observers, so you'll likely fly with one of them in the backseat tomorrow."

Hoot threw his bags on the cot. "How are you doing, old friend?"

"I'm staying busy, keeping my emotions and bad thoughts at bay," Wade said. "He's my son, and I'm concerned. I'll let it all out later. He's one of the most competent woodsmen that I've ever known. He's better than me, for sure. If there's someone suited to survive a situation like this, it's Boone. He's well-equipped. I inventoried the equipment I know he had, and it's substantial. He has a great chance of surviving, assuming he's alive and not badly injured. How are the girls?"

"They're dealing with it the same as all the other difficult circumstances they've faced," Hoot said. "Abby and Rachel will be here tomorrow afternoon. Abby is stoic about the whole thing, but Rachel's spun up. We'll have to work on her. She loves her daddy, and she's scared. Abby has faced circumstances like this, but Rachel hasn't. She was too young to remember the last time something like this happened to the family."

The two men joined Chappie and Bart at the command post for the evening briefing, where Trooper Larsen explained the days search route and results and then briefed the following day's flight assignments, assigned courses for each crew, and flight times.

"Today, we covered the route that Jimmy and Boone flew or were scheduled to fly," he said. "Tomorrow, we begin a grid search pattern of the area marked on the map. We connected the dots between Eagle Airport and the caches Jimmy serviced on Friday and back to Eagle. The area within that boundary is the search area. Each crew can look at your assigned route and flight times, posted on the chalkboard."

The CAP meteorological officer briefed the weather, confirming that it would be the last day of air searches for ninety-six hours. Low ceilings, wind, rain, and snow mix would prevent aerial search until Saturday.

"Weather briefing is tomorrow morning at 0600," Larsen said. "Any questions?"

The crews of each aircraft linked up, planned the next day's flight, and made final coordination. Maintenance crews topped off fuel and checked maintenance issues on all aircraft. The Chapman Aviation fliers migrated to the Chapman hangar and prepared aircraft and equipment for the next day's search.

Hoot rearranged his gear and organized his flight bag with headphones, kneeboard, notebooks, maps, checklists, and an E6B manual flight computer. He checked the aviator's survival vest that he'd taken to wearing when he flew in the backcountry. He pulled the handheld radio from its pouch, turned it on, conducted a radio check with the tower, checked the spare battery, and returned it to his vest. He pulled the Air Force survival knife attached to the front of the vest, stroked the edge on a sharpening stone a few times, oiled the blade, and replaced it in the sheath. Finally, he pulled the Colt 1911 pistol from its brown leather tanker holster. Cleared the pistol, wiped it down, oiled it, inserted a magazine, and placed it back in the holster. Then he checked the two spare magazines in the canvas pouch attached to the chest strap. He laid out his green Nomex flight suit, aviator sunglasses, and leather flight jacket. He was back in the fight.

CHAPTER TWENTY-FIVE
0745 Hours Local-Monday 28 September 1987
Boone's Camp-Day 4

First morning light filtered through the east-facing door of Boone's shelter. He slept well but was hungry and thirsty. He hadn't hydrated as much as he should have the previous day. Task one for the day was processing water. The morning was clear and cool with high-altitude, thin clouds, an indicator of the approaching storm. Luther called the wispy clouds "mare's tails." Boone grabbed his fly rod and shotgun, walked to the stream, and fished until he caught two trout. He filled his stainless-steel water bottle, pot, and cup, walked back to the shelter, and placed all on the fire to boil. He cooked the two small trout, ate, and drank the rest of the water. He filled his containers once more and boiled the water for later.

Other priorities stopped him from building signals the previous day. So, signals were next. They were looking for him from the air and would be grounded in the next twenty-four hours. He grabbed his shotgun, axe, and bow saw. Boone moved north to the tree line along a large open area fifty yards north of his shelter. He cut nine small saplings and made three tripods. He lashed a horizontal platform two feet from the top of each tripod. He placed the tripods in a triangle one hundred feet apart, thirty yards from the tree line. He covered the top of each platform with green spruce boughs and put a large fire lay, a tinder bundle with small sticks on each platform. He built a torch from a pine branch and boughs. If he heard an aircraft, he would light the torch and run to each tripod, lighting the fire on each platform. The fire would burn up through the green boughs, producing a lot of white smoke. Any aviator would recognize the pattern of three as the international distress signal.

With the signals in place, he focused on the last few tasks before the storm. He built a small smoking rack of saplings, returned to the river, caught twelve small trout, cleaned them, and placed them on the smoking rack. He started a small fire and fed it with alder branches, the bark peeled away. He covered the rack with his poncho and smoked trout all afternoon. He found branches he could use for snowshoes, cut them, and peeled off their bark. He planned to build the snowshoes after the storm hit, when he was trapped in the shelter.

As the sun reached its zenith, he lay on his back in the shelter and looked for open gaps in the roof. Finding a few, he added more foliage. He spent the afternoon drinking water, eating fresh fish, and preparing more firewood. The wind and clouds increased steadily throughout the day. By mid-afternoon, Boone detected a noticeable drop in the temperature and knew the storm was close. He was as ready as he could be. He could easily hunker down for four days. The search would continue Saturday, and they'd find him, Sunday at the latest.

The sun slipped below the horizon in the southwest shortly after 1900. Snow began to fall four minutes later.

***

The cloud ceiling and temperatures dropped, aircraft reported their completed search routes and flew off station. The State Police and CAP aircraft returned to Anchorage and Fairbanks. Chappie kept two Super Cubs at Eagle. He and Hoot could fly those in the event the weather broke early. He sent Bart and his other pilots back to Fairbanks with the Otter and Caribou. All aviation assets would return on Saturday morning to continue the search.

The snow accumulated on the tarmac when Chappie, Wade, and Hoot entered the Chapman Aviation hangar office. Abby was on the phone with her mother and mother-in-law, giving them an update on the day's search. Rachel was standing in front of the map, trying to get inside her father's head. She turned when the three men walked into the office.

"What do we do now?" Rachel asked.

"Honey, we do the only thing we can," Wade said. "We wait

151

for the weather to clear and then get back at it."

"That's not good enough," Rachel said. "Daddy's out there somewhere waiting for us to get him. What if he's injured? We have to do something. We can't just sit here. We can search with snow machines or dog sleds. There's snow on the ground now. Let's use that to our advantage."

Hoot took his granddaughter by the hand and led her to the hangar. They sat next to one another. He put his arm around her shoulder.

"Rachel, I can't imagine what you're going through right now," Hoot said. "But you have to reach down deep and find your strength. More importantly, some patience. A ground search would only put people's lives in danger with almost zero percent chance of success. First off, we don't know where to start looking. The search area is almost three million acres. Second, a person on the ground couldn't see twenty feet in front of them or hear any further. Your dad doesn't want people taking those risks for no return. He had three full days to get ready for this storm. If I know him as well as I think I do, some time on Saturday he figured out he would have to dig in. I'm sure that's what he did. He knew we were looking for him, but he knew he had to be ready to survive the storm. He built a shelter and a fire and caught fish or shot birds for food. He's fine wherever he is."

"I can't sit here. I'm going out of my mind."

Smiling at his young granddaughter, Hoot said, "I know, but you need to be strong. Think about this: Your mom is worried about a husband, your grandparents are worried about a son—me and your grandma a son-in-law. Be strong to help them get through this. We'll find him. He'll be fine. He's probably enjoying himself."

Rachel laughed and wiped a tear from her face. "He probably is. He's so aggravating like that."

"Yes, he is," Hoot said.

"Grandpa, how's everyone staying so calm in this? Mom and Grandma haven't fallen apart once. You and Grandpa Wade are dealing with it. Why am I falling apart?"

"Experience, dear," Hoot said. "We've all had a lifetime of dealing with stress and tragedy. You'll get there. Just being a member of this family seems to be a good place to learn how to deal with emergencies or contingencies, as Wade likes to say.

"We've all experienced combat from two perspectives. Me, Wade, Bobby, Dan, Chappie, Bart, and your dad all have too much experience in war zones all over the world. We've seen things go sideways in spectacular fashion, and we had to deal with it. Our friends were in danger, captured, wounded, or killed, and we had to maintain some control and work on the problem. That's one perspective. Your mother and grandmothers have had to live knowing the people they loved most were experiencing those things and were in harm's way. On top of that, they were managing the tragedy back home when another soldier's wife tried to put her life back together when her husband didn't come home. That's another perspective. You live long enough around soldiers, and you'll learn to deal with contingencies."

"Well, it sucks," Rachel said.

"Yes, it does, honey. It sucks." Hoot pulled her closer. They prayed together.

CHAPTER TWENTY-SIX
1142 Hours Local-Tuesday 29 September 1987
Boone's Camp-Day 5

High winds drifted the snow overnight but died down at sunrise. Now, the snow was knee-deep. Boone used a spruce bough to sweep the snow off the shelter every couple of hours, making sure not to remove it all. The snow was an excellent insulator, but it was also heavy, and he couldn't afford to let the weight destroy the shelter. He brought in more firewood and walked to the river for water. He knew it would be the last time for a few days. The snow was too deep to walk in without burning excess calories. After this trip, he planned to melt snow for water, a long, laborious task. But he had the time.

He ate smoked trout, drank half a bottle of water, and then started on snowshoes. He peeled the bark and squared four birch staves, five feet long. He wouldn't take the time to attempt bending the staves. He would make an Algonquin-style shoe by putting the staves side-by-side, tightly lashing the ends together, and slowly inserting progressively longer cross pieces to get the desired width. He worked on the staves all afternoon and into the early evening, interrupting his work only to sweep snow from the top of his shelter and add wood to the fire. So far, his shelter worked well.

He alternated between his hunting knife, Buckaroo knife, and Swiss Army knife. He used the larger knife to peel bark and chop the staves into their general shape. Then Boone turned to the smaller, more precise Buckaroo knife to smooth out and refine the shape. He used the tools on the Swiss Army knife and Leatherman tool to drill holes for the lashing and webbing. The work was slow, but what else was there to do? After several days of heavy snow he would need them to walk. Boone had plenty of experience walking in snowshoes, but this

154

was his first time building a pair. He needed to get it right. If they didn't find him when the storm was over, he began to consider the possibility of walking out. He would need good snowshoes.

As he worked on the snowshoes, he thought about the rescue operation going on right now. They would start by going to the cache sites, the hunt area, and the routes between them. They probably grid-searched the area between those points on Sunday and Monday. They would check other nearby airports and airfields to see if Jimmy had landed. They've already checked popular bush plane landing areas that Chappie used regularly. It's possible they'd already found Jimmy but had no time to pick up Boone before the weather hit. When it cleared, they'd rescue him. His dad was right, the plan was short on contingencies. Boone should've listened to him.

Then Boone began to plan his longer-term future. *How long do I wait here?* Conventional wisdom says to stay put and not attempt self-rescue. A stationary target is easier to find than a moving one. If he got impatient and started walking, he could walk into an area they'd already searched multiple times. Therefore, the rescuers would have no logical reason to return again, diminishing his chances for rescue. Moving also increases the risk of mechanical injury or drowning. There was no telling how many rivers and streams he would have to cross between his shelter and any road or village. Drowning during river crossings was a common way to die in Alaska. And if drowning didn't do it, hypothermia could.

There was also the risk of the elements as the weather turned colder and snow became permanent. He had to have shelter. His only options for shelter on the move would be his poncho, which wasn't a good alternative in snow and freezing temperatures, a snow shelter of some type, like a snow cave, or shelter in the cavity of snow formed at the base of a large spruce tree with low hanging limbs, or a debris shelter. It took a half day to build his first one, and with days growing shorter, that would only leave a few hours of walking before he had to stop, build a shelter, and collect firewood for a long arctic night. Available time and arctic conditions would keep the distance traveled each day to a minimum, just a few miles.

He decided that when the weather cleared, he would build a

155

more substantial shelter, hunt for food, and prepare to remain in place for a few weeks. It was too soon in the search for him to start a self-rescue and walk out. One of the key factors to the decision point of self-rescue was to know that the search was suspended. He knew it was too soon for that. Boone would stay put, but improve his situation.

CHAPTER TWENTY-SEVEN
0750 Hours Local-Saturday 3 October 1987
SAR Command Post-Eagle, Alaska-Day 9

The previously dark and closed-in world was suddenly bright and it hurt her eyes. Rachel pulled on her sunglasses and walked across the tarmac to the Command Post for the morning briefing. The low ceiling lifted overnight. When she came out at 0230, the sky was clear and cold, and the wind had died. The snow had stopped falling the previous afternoon, leaving almost twenty-four inches of new snow on the ground. According to yesterday's weather briefing, aircraft would have four to five solid days to search before the next weather system.

The small room was filled with now-familiar faces, including several family members and longtime friends of the family. Bill Larsen reviewed some final coordination points with Captain Brown, Chappie, and Bart. Her mother sat in the back row of folding chairs, making notes in a small notebook. Wade and Hoot flanked her like two protective gargoyles. Rachel sat down in the chair immediately behind her mother and put her arms around her neck. The four exchanged greetings and small talk as Bill Larsen stepped to the front of the room and began the morning briefing.

"Good morning, everyone. As you can see, we have good weather this morning, and since that's been the topic of conversation for the past several days, we'll start with a weather briefing."

He turned the briefing over to the CAP meteorological officer. Rachel wasn't listening to the droning talk that applied only to the fliers in the room, altitude density, and so on. She did pay attention to the forecast.

"We have four to five days of operational weather. Skies will be clear today and tomorrow with light winds. Winds will increase to

15 knots out of the southwest on 5-6 October but won't prevent flights. Daytime temps will increase over the next several days to the mid-40s, with lows at night in the mid-20s, causing the freeze-melt cycle common this time of year. You can expect rain and snow mix on 5 October with no additional accumulation and ceilings over one thousand feet. The weather supports flights for the next four days minimum. The next weather system is due in mid-day on 7 October. Winds are increasing to 30 knots, low ceilings, rain turning to snow with an additional eight inches accumulation over forty-eight hours."

Larsen continued the briefing with crew assignments, flight corridors, special searches, flight times, and rotations.

"As we get into this freeze-thaw cycle daily," he said, "remember to pay close attention to thawed areas. Snow accumulated on a metal airplane will melt quicker than snow on vegetation. Use the snow cover to your advantage. Last thing—you'll notice that we're down several aircraft. Two active emergency beacons pinging west of Fairbanks take priority over a search with no active beacon. We still have three Chapman Aviation aircraft, two CAP aircraft available, plenty to accomplish our mission."

Larsen discussed a few other minor details and concluded the briefing. Pilots and observers, including her grandfathers, sat with maps, charts, and flight computers, calculating the details of the day's mission. The crews collected their gear and headed for their aircraft. Her two grandfathers, approached Abby, quietly talked for a minute, and then they approached Rachel.

"We talked to your mom, not to ask her permission," Hoot said. "You're a grown woman and don't need her permission, but just as a courtesy. Do you want to fly backseat with me today as my observer?"

Turning to Wade, she asked, "What about you, Grandpa? He's your son. Are you going to be stuck on the ground?"

"Nope," Wade said. "I'm going out with Bart and Dan in the Beaver as an extra set of eyes. This way, we have one more pair of sharp eyes in the air, and you're not on the ground pacing holes in the tarmac."

Rachel smiled, almost jumping up and down in anticipation.

"Run back to the hangar and get some cold weather gear," Hoot said. "I'll meet you at the plane and brief you on safety procedures and our search area."

In ten minutes, Rachel was standing beside the Super Cub with her grandfather, wearing her cold weather gear, which consisted of a pair of Carhartt coveralls, fleece-lined denim jacket, wool watch cap, gloves, and a pair of Sorel rubberized shoe pacs she'd purchased in Fairbanks the day she arrived. She looked more like a ranch hand than a flight crew member on a Search and Rescue team, but she was ecstatic to be going along. Rachel was part of the mission, not a bench warmer.

Hoot started the briefing as he had hundreds of times in a career that had spanned dozens of aircraft and over ten thousand flight hours, World War II, and the Korean War with the Air Force and most of the inter-mountain states of the West and Alaska, as a Forest Service pilot. He covered their route, altitude, speed, and heading. He'd handle emergencics, including downed aircraft procedures and survival protocols, internal communications with other aircraft, and the command post. She marveled at the difference between Hoot Clark, the pilot in a serious contingency, and Hoot Clark, her grandpa. She recognized the same man, but there was something about his demeanor now that he had a mission. She couldn't help but think. *He must've been something when he was young*. When she imagined him as a young man full of this intensity that she now witnessed, it made her smile.

"What's so funny?" Hoot asked.

"Nothing Grandpa. I love you."

"I love you too, but you better keep your head in the game."

"Yes, sir," she saluted, and gave him a smile.

"Carry on," Hoot said as he helped her in the backseat of the Piper.

Five aircraft were now looking for Boone Taggart in a cloudless, bright blue sky. Six of the ten searchers were either related to him or close friends. They had flesh in the game.

***

159

Boone stepped out of the darkness of the shelter and stood in the sun without moving. His eyes were still closed against the bright reflection off the snow. He found his flight glasses in his coat pocket. The glasses made the light tolerable, but he noted that he would need to fashion some side pieces to protect his vision.

He used one of his newly fashioned snowshoes to carefully shovel the snow from the shelter entrance. He finished them the previous night, using most of the parachute suspension line cordage for webbing. It was worth the expenditure of a valuable resource. Snowshoes are a requirement. He knelt and lashed them onto his boots. *These boots won't be enough if this goes into deep winter.*

Boone walked out to his signal tripods in the clearing north of the shelter to test his snowshoes. It was less than two hundred yards round trip. It was a good test. He inspected them on return to camp. The webbing needed tightening. The nylon parachute cord stretched badly. Other than that, they worked well. *A backup pair wouldn't be a bad idea. Stay busy with useful work.*

He inspected the shelter, which held up great, better than he'd hoped. He was warm and dry throughout the four days of snow. It required his full attention to keep enough snow off the shelter not to collapse it, but enough in place to provide some insulation. This snow was wet and heavy, not the light, fluffy snow that would come to stay in a few more weeks.

Boone ate the last smoked trout and drank a full bottle of water before filling the bottle and cup with snow and setting them on the fire. He spent most of the day processing firewood from the deadfalls around him. It was incredible how much wood it took to keep a fire going around the clock. He fished and smoked his catch, adding eight smoked trout to his larder. While he worked that day, he continued to analyze his plan. *What next?*

He was at the end of his knowledge about the weather. He knew the previous storm was coming but now didn't know what each day brought. He was confident that rescuers would find him in the next few days, but he planned for the possibility they would fail.

"I'm going to build a cabin," he said out loud. "And hunt for meat, trap for fur."

I'll dig in for the long haul. If they find me fine, but I'm prepared if they don't. As he worked in the shelter through the previous four nights and read the books Rachel gave him, he thought back to survival school and the instruction of Master Sergeant Sobolewski. He trained them to always improve their situation.

"You're never finished," the old sergeant would say in his thick Polish accent. "You never sit down and wait to be rescued. Always improve your situation. Survival is a mental exercise. If you can keep your wits and think your way out, you'll survive. You must keep your mind and body busy with productive work, so work slowly and deliberately. If you spend your first night on the ground under the stars, spend the second night in a debris hut, then build a lean-to, then a cabin, and if we find you in six months, you better have a two-bedroom house with a garden planted and indoor plumbing."

Got it, Sarge. Tomorrow, I build on.

***

The Chapman Aviation crew and the Taggart-Clark family contingent sat around the tables in the Chapman hangar, eating Abby's delicious cooking. As they enjoyed apple cobbler and coffee, Wade and Hoot walked in to brief them on the next day's plan.

"We talked with Bill Larsen and Captain Brown," Wade said. "All agreed that we've searched the area well enough to expand and try another approach—we've grid-searched the primary area several times. Tomorrow, we'll send a crew to each cache site and start flying an expanding grid from those sites. We know they resupplied the caches, so they must've taken off from one of them and then crashed or set down."

"We're going to put the Chapman crews on the caches," Hoot said. "We only have three crews, so we'll start with three caches in the morning. Then everyone will rotate to the west, with the westernmost crew rotating to the easternmost cache in the afternoon. This will put multiple sets of eyes on each location. The CAP crews will continue a grid search in the northern sector."

"Hoot and Rachel will start at cache one in the southeast of the

161

sector. Bart, Dan, and I will start at cache two, and Chappie and Bob will cover down on cache three. Fly a twenty-mile expanding grid around each cache site. Any questions?" Wade said.

"What if we don't find him tomorrow?" Rachel said.

"Let's take one day at a time," Hoot said.

"This search tomorrow will put eyes on areas outside the grid search for the first time, so be alert," Wade said.

"We're going to find him, honey," Abby said. She put her arms around Rachel.

The crews dispersed and prepared their gear for the next day.

CHAPTER TWENTY-EIGHT
0750 Hours Local-Sunday 4 October 1987
Day 10

Boone spent the previous evening reading Louis L'Amour's *The Last of the Breed* by firelight. While he read, he used a smooth river stone to hone the edge of his ax. He started working on the cabin as soon as it was light enough to see. He needed three or four dozen logs between eight and twelve inches in diameter. Any bigger, and he would struggle to move them by hand. He also needed several smaller poles for rafters and purlins. His plan for the cabin was small and simple, four walls about six feet tall, twelve feet by twelve feet, an A-frame roof made of poles, spruce boughs, and birch bark covering the openings where the roof poles came together. There'd be no windows but a single door and a small rudimentary fireplace and chimney.

He had an ax, bow saw, and knife for tools and no building materials except what he found in the forest. The chimney would be small, combining stone and sticks covered in mud. His Scots Irish ancestors who settled the southern Appalachian highlands in the nineteenth century used a similar design, some still standing, two hundred years on. He calculated that building the cabin would take him ten days to two weeks. *They'll find me by then. This will keep my mind and body busy, and if, for some reason, they don't find me, I'll be more comfortable. Always improve your situation.*

If his isolation went on much longer, there were other requirements that he would need to fulfill. He needed skins for better clothing and meat for food. He knew if they didn't find him in the two weeks it would take to build the cabin, he was probably on his own. He'd have to decide to hunker down for the winter or quickly walk out before full winter set in. He'd build the cabin first. He knew he was running out of time if he had to stay, but he still had confidence that his family and friends would find him.

Boone selected a level, well-drained site for the cabin protected by a thick stand of trees and the ridge to his west, as well as an overwatch view of the river valley to the east. He took the logs from a stand of trees south of the cabin site. Using his saw to make the horizontal bottom cut, he notched the face cut with his ax and made the back cut with the saw. He cut timber consistently for two days, taking regular breaks, working slowly and diligently without stressing his body too much or sweating profusely.

As he dropped each tree, he bucked it to the proper length and formed multiple piles. The first, logs for the walls, second was what was left of the tree that would be used as rafters, purlins, or bough coverings. He spent the third and fourth days transporting logs and stone to the building site.

On the fifth day, a beautiful, perfect Alaskan late fall day, Boone pushed back the remaining snow, laid stones at the corners, placing the largest logs on stones that would form the front and back walls of his cabin. Then carved simple saddle notches to lay the first logs of the side walls. All without knowing how long, if at all, he would live in this cabin.

***

Hoot and Rachel landed at cache site number one to see if Jimmy and Boone had possibly returned to the cache for supplies, but it was untouched. They took off from the sandbar landing strip and, shortly after 0900, began flying an expanding square search with the cache at the center.

They were flying north across a small river valley, two miles east of the cache, when Rachel saw a glint of reflected sunlight out the right window, two o'clock off the nose of the plane. She raised her binoculars, scanned the area of the reflection, and confirmed a lake. *We're looking for a floatplane. It's obvious for it to be at a lake.* She keyed the intercom.

"Grandpa, I saw a glint of reflected light at a lake one mile at two o'clock off the nose."

"Roger." Hoot marked his current position on the map attached to his kneeboard. He banked the plane, saw the lake, and turned to a direct heading. They were over the lake in seconds. Hoot dropped to one hundred feet and put the lake off the left wing in a sharp circle. As they continued the bank on the north side of the lake, Rachel looked across the water to the south side, and there, partly covered by water at the end of a small bay under some overhanging trees, she saw what was left of a DHC-2 Beaver in the Chapman Aviation blue and yellow paint scheme.

"Grandpa, there it is. I see it."

"Where?" Hoot said.

"There at the south end of the lake just under the trees," Rachel said. "It's partly submerged, but the cockpit is out of the water against the shoreline."

Hoot leveled the plane and searched for the crash site. He saw it exactly where she described it.

"Good work, honey. Hang on."

Hoot turned the aircraft sharply to the right and flew perpendicular to the crash at just fifty feet. He slowed the Cub to just above stall speed, thirty yards behind the crash. They both confirmed this was the Chapman Aviation Beaver they were looking for. Hoot added power and began to gain altitude. He circled the lake on the map and handed it over his shoulder to Rachel.

"Figure out the coordinates of that lake. I'm going to get some altitude and call it in. Good work, Rachel."

At five thousand feet, Hoot keyed the radio. "Eagle Tower, this is November 2472 Delta reporting a crash site of a Chapman Aviation DHC-2 Beaver at the following coordinates, six-three degrees, three-nine minutes, two zero seconds North, one four one degrees, three three minutes, four zero seconds West. The crash rests partially submerged on the south end of an unnamed lake approximately five miles northeast of Chapman Aviation cache number one. Please pass to the SAR Command post. I'll transmit the same on the SAR frequency and remain on station until other SAR aircraft arrive. How copy over?"

165

"November 2472 Delta, good copy, over."
"72 Delta Out."

CHAPTER TWENTY-NINE
1215 Hours Local-Sunday 4 October 1987
Ninety-seven miles southeast of Boone's camp-Day 10

Hoot transmitted the report on the SAR frequency, and within minutes two Chapman aircraft were overhead. Hoot and Rachel had landed in a clearing just east of the crash site. Hoot grabbed the handheld from the cockpit, left Rachel with the other to monitor, secured the advanced medical kit from the plane, and started to the site. He heard Rachel right behind him.

"Stop and go back to the plane," he said.

"I want to go," Rachel said.

"Absolutely not. I know what airplane crashes do to the human body, and if your father's over there, I won't have that as your last image of him. Go back now. That's an order."

Rachel stood trembling as her grandfather moved through the trees to the crash site. She slowly turned and walked the few steps back to the Piper Super Cub and waited for the most important message of her life. In minutes, she would know if she'd lost her father.

Orbiting overhead at three thousand feet, Chappie called Hoot on the Chapman internal frequency. "Hoot, this is Chappie, over."

"Go," Hoot said. He moved quickly, and the crash site came into view.

"We'll stay on station to pass radio traffic to Eagle and the Command Post," Wade said. "Bart's coordinating with our ground crew to prep the survival packs for a drop from the Caribou. He's returning to Eagle to drop survival packs or refuel and rotate here on station. The Command Post is in contact with the Alaska Air National Guard Rescue Wing for rotary wing assets to assist. How copy, over?"

"Copy, I'm at the crash site," Hoot said. "Stand by."

Rachel closed her eyes and prayed as hard as she ever had. *Lord, please let him be alive. I need him.*

The silence on the radio seemed to last forever, and then Hoot's voice broke the emptiness. "Chappie this if Hoot, over."

"Go."

"Jimmy didn't make it. No sign of Boone or his gear," Hoot said. "How copy over?"

He's alive. Rachel thought. *Thank you, Lord.* Then, a sudden, terrible, overwhelming feeling of guilt and remorse as she realized her family could rejoice as Jimmy's family began their final mourning.

***

The State Police and Alaska Air National Guard took over the scene at the crash site, extracted Jimmy's body, and secured the site for the National Transportation Safety Board investigators. The Chapman crew met with Trooper Larsen at the Chapman Hangar in Eagle to formulate the next phase of the search.

"Chappie, what're your thoughts?" Larsen asked.

"What I saw and what Hoot described," Chappie said, "it's most likely that the kid hit an underwater obstacle as his floats came up on plane, just as he was fast enough to fly. Instead of sitting the plane back in the water, he likely pulled up, stalled, and cartwheeled. The tail breaking off put the ELT underwater, which explains why there was never an active emergency beacon. With a violent crash, it's hard to imagine Boone isn't injured, but it's also clear that he's not injured badly enough to be close to the crash site."

"I think it's likely Boone survived, is probably injured, although how bad is impossible to know," Wade said. "Jimmy's side of the cockpit was pancaked against a tree, but the co-pilot seat was intact. Boone saw that Jimmy was dead. Knowing the weather was coming in on them, he grabbed his gear and started the twenty-five-mile walk to the Taylor Highway. He's got to be healthy enough to carry his gear, so he may have made it to the highway before the snowstorm. We just haven't connected yet."

"There's another possibility," Hoot said. He looked around to

168

ensure that Rachel and Abigail couldn't hear his next statement. "Boone and his gear could've been thrown from the plane when it tore apart and sank."

"He could've drowned," Wade said.

"It may not be likely," Hoot said. "Why would he have been sitting in the back by himself instead of in the co-pilot's seat? But the aircraft breaking apart could explain why his gear isn't there. It sunk with the rest of the fuselage."

"So even if he didn't drown, Boone could be injured, and he started walking but had no gear to take," Wade said.

"Alright, let's start tomorrow with an aerial search, the three Chapman aircraft of a ten-mile-wide box from the crash site to Taylor Highway," Larsen said. "I'll have ground crews drive Taylor Highway, and we'll put one CAP aircraft on each side of the road for its entire length. I can get a dive team, too, to confirm what's in, or not inside the fuselage. Any questions or additions?"

"What about dogs?" Bobby said.

"I'm working with HQs to see if we can get a dog handler team up here, but this much snow creates a problem for them," Larsen said.

"The area you're talking about was searched multiple times in the past week," Rachel said. "Why didn't we find him? Why didn't he signal an aircraft?"

"Any number of reasons," Hoot said. "It's tough finding a single individual from the air. The only signal device we know he has is a signal mirror, and we might've missed him. You're not looking for an individual when you're looking for a fuselage. You're predisposed to see what you're looking for."

"We still have two days before the weather puts us out of business for a while," Larsen said. "Let's be in the air over the new search area first thing in the morning."

As the crews prepared for the following day's search, Boone Taggart worked on a small cabin ninety miles west of the new search area.

Trooper Bill Larsen and Captain Diana Brown sat on the sofa at the back of the briefing area with a map and overlay of the search area spread out on the coffee table in front of them. Both were dreading the conversation they were about to have with Boone Taggart's family and closest friends. Abby, Rachel, Wade, Hoot, Bobby, Dan, and the Chapman Aviation crew entered the command post and walked to the back of the room, taking seats around the table. The fliers and military personnel in the group knew what was happening because they'd experienced this many times. Abby and Rachel knew what was happening more profoundly and intuitively. They all prepared themselves for the discussion.

Trooper Larsen addressed Abigail directly.

"Mrs. Taggart, here's a graphic depiction of the grids we've flown over the search area."

Abby could see that the overlay was almost blacked out with grid lines. They'd thoroughly searched the entire area. And more.

"After we found the crash site, we searched the area between the lake and Taylor Highway from the air and with ground teams," Larsen said. "We searched Taylor Highway via ground vehicle, air, and on foot within a mile of the road, in the section Boone would've walked from the crash. The divers confirmed that your husband's gear wasn't in the back of the fuselage, and nothing was found in the lake. Today is the twenty-first day of the search, and we're officially suspending the operation until we have more information to act on. I'm sorry, ma'am."

"So, you think he's dead?" Rachel said.

"Miss Taggart, I don't know what happened to your father," Larsen said. "He may be alive, but I don't know where to look for him. From what these men have told me about him, he has a more likely chance to survive than any of us. My problem is that we can't search all of Alaska, and nothing points us to another search area."

Trooper Larsen and Captain Brown shook hands, offered their condolences to the group, and left the room. Wade led the group back to the Chapman Hangar. He and Hoot stayed close to Abby and Rachel, discussing alternatives and possibilities. The remainder of the team began to pack their gear for the Otter flight back to Fairbanks the following morning. Abby, holding her daughter's hand, asked her father and father-in-law, two men with depths of experience in tragedy, the question on her mind.

"What do you think we should do now?"

Chappie, Hoot, and Wade had a conversation earlier, knowing the search would eventually be suspended. They voiced possible scenarios and decided that Hoot and Wade, being family, should discuss them with Abby and Rachel.

"Larsen is certainly right about one thing," Hoot said. "We don't know where to look next, and Alaska is too big to keep making the circle bigger. There are a few scenarios I can think of, but I'm not sure which one is right."

"Go on," Abby said.

"An airplane crash is about as violent a thing as possible," Hoot said. "Looking at the condition of that airplane, it's hard to imagine Boone wasn't injured in the crash. If it were a brain injury, which is likely, it would be even worse. He could've grabbed his gear from nothing more than a soldier's muscle memory, wandered into the woods, and passed out."

"Another scenario," Wade said. "Is that he survived the crash intact or with minor injuries, started the walkout, and encountered another calamity—hypothermia, bear attack, or even drowning. There are several rivers between the crash site and Taylor Highway."

Rachel stood up and began to pace as she pushed back against her grandfathers' analysis.

"Let me play devil's advocate for a minute," Rachel said. "Dad

171

trained us kids to stay put if we were hurt or lost, saying he would get us. Why would he leave the aircraft? He knows that we'd be looking for him and an airplane is easier to see than an individual. Why would he walk away from the crash?"

"Rachel, your dad doesn't idle well," Hoot said. "He knew it was only twenty-five miles to Taylor Highway and had walked that far by himself many times in life. He also knew there was weather coming in and he could walk to the highway before the weather hit with time to spare. Your scenario assumes he was uninjured in the crash, which is highly unlikely."

"Is it possible that Jimmy dropped him off somewhere else and then crashed, and we were looking in the wrong place all along?" Rachel said.

"It's possible, honey," Wade said. "But there's no evidence that your father wasn't in the crash other than the absence of him and his gear. He could've simply grabbed his kit, walked out into the woods in any direction, and laid down."

"And died," Rachel said. "That's what you mean, isn't it?"

"Honey, we don't know that, but it's possible," Wade said. "He's my only son, and I don't like thinking about that either, but it may be exactly what happened."

"Let's all think about this overnight and have another discussion when we get back to Fairbanks before we make any decisions," Abby said.

With tears streaming down her face, Rachel hugged Hoot and then Wade.

"I'm sorry I snapped at you, Grandpa. I know this is hard on you, too."

"Don't worry about it, baby girl. These are hard times."

CHAPTER THIRTY-ONE
1125 Hours Local-Sunday 18 October 1987
Fairbanks International Airport-Day 24

Bart flew the Taggart and Clark Family, plus friends, back to Fairbanks in the Otter, followed by Chappie in a Super Cub. They deplaned and stacked gear in the Chapman Hangar and sat down to have their final discussion and support Abby's decision. Dan and Bobby had approached Abby in Eagle before they departed. They agreed with Chappie, Hoot, and Wade. Boone likely left the crash site and succumbed to injuries or another accident. Dan added that, even if Rachel's hunch that Jimmy may have put Boone down somewhere else was right, they didn't know where to start looking. Bobby thought it unlikely that Boone would've made that choice without notifying someone where he was.

Abby went around the group one last time and asked each man their view. Each gave it candidly, but each also said they would support whatever course of action she chose. They also agreed they would return immediately to the search if new evidence became available. Abby made the heart-wrenching decision.

"Well, that's it then," she said. "We suspend the search until we have more information."

They all stood in a circle holding hands. Wade said a short prayer. They hugged and said their goodbyes. Dan dropped Bobby at the main terminal and turned his truck south along the Parks Highway toward Fort Richardson. He'd already decided to drop his retirement papers when he got home. Tears welled in his eyes as he put more miles between him and his closest friend.

Wade, Hoot, and Abby loaded their gear into the Chapman Aviation Suburban for the short ride to the main terminal.

173

"You want me to load your gear, honey?" Wade asked Rachel.

"No, sir," Rachel said. "I'm staying here in Fairbanks, Grandpa. I'm not leaving Alaska without my father. He's still alive. I know it."

Rachel said the words with such resolve he knew there was no point in trying to persuade her, but he did know how to ensure she was protected. Abby wasn't so convinced. She and Rachel debated for ten minutes while Hoot and Wade developed a plan with Chappie and Bart. When Abby finally conceded, her father approached her.

"Abigail, Wade and I may have worked something out," Hoot said. "Chappie and Bart will offer Rachel a job and let her live in an apartment above Chappie's garage. They can watch out for her and keep us updated while she works through this."

"I don't suppose I have much of a choice," Abby said. "She's an adult who doesn't need my permission and is as stubborn as her father. At least she'll be close to the Chapmans. Thanks, Dad."

Abigail, Hoot, and Wade stood at the security checkpoint and said goodbye to Rachel, Chappie, and Bart. They were all accustomed to sad goodbyes since both families had committed large and intense periods of their lives in service to the country. The United States had never fought a war in which the Taggarts, Clarks, and Chapmans weren't directly engaged. They were all intimately familiar with this particular pain. Rachel and Abby held back tears as long as possible. Rachel smiled at her mother.

"Let's get this over with," she said.

Boone taught his children that "it's OK to cry at weddings, funerals, and airports." Now, the tears flowed as mother and daughter said goodbye. It was especially painful because so many unknowns still impacted their lives.

"Please don't do anything foolish," Abby said.

"I won't, I promise," Rachel said. "I just can't leave yet. He's still alive. Someone should be here when he walks out of the woods."

The four men shook hands as Abby and Rachel held one another in their final goodbye. Hoot and Wade stepped up to the security line as Abby said goodbye to Chappie and Bart.

"Please take good care of my girl," Abby said.

Chappie smiled and hugged her, "Like she was one of my own."

Abigail cleared the security checkpoint and met Wade and her father at the gate in time for the first boarding call for the flight to Denver via Seattle. They'd be home tonight and need to find a way to navigate the next phase of life. She'd have to guide her children through the loss of their father, maybe, and Wade and Rebecca through another tragic loss. She'd have to, at some point, accept that something unknown and terrible had befallen the love of her life.

***

Boone finished chinking the walls of his cabin with moss the previous afternoon. Almost fifty-six, four-inch diameter poles lay peeled next to the walls for the roof structure. He'd start in the morning. But today, he hunted—he was hunting illegally. He'd filled his caribou and bear tags, but these were extraordinary circumstances. He'd gladly pay the fine if the citing game warden would give him a ride back to Fairbanks. Boone was thankful for the fish the stream and river provided, but he was also tired of eating fish, and there were fewer ducks on the sloughs along the river. He'd killed a few ptarmigans near his shelter, which was a pleasant change of diet, but he wanted something more substantive, meat he could put up to last him weeks, not a day. He also needed fat and fur.

He sat on a windswept hilltop two miles northwest of the cabin and glassed the valley to his north. The caribou migration was over, but there were almost always stragglers. Bears, blacks, and grizzlies weren't in full hibernation yet, and there were always moose. The snow of the first storm had partially melted, but new snow was beginning to accumulate permanently on some of the highest hilltops. The day was overcast with only a light breeze. He guessed the wind chill was in the low twenties.

Using the old hunter's trick for a natural alarm clock, taught to him by his father, he drank a full bottle of water just before he went to sleep, requiring an early morning trip outside to relieve himself, a problem increasing as he aged. He arrived at his glassing site twenty

175

minutes before twilight and settled in for the morning. He visualized the hunt in his mind. The previous day, he built a small cache twenty feet high in a stand of birch trees, one hundred yards from his cabin. If he got a caribou or a black bear, he'd transport the meat and hide back to camp in two trips. It was only four miles round trip, and there still wasn't deep snow. A warm spell after the big snowstorm reduced the depth of snow by several inches. So, he could travel well, although the days were growing noticeably shorter. There was almost four hours less daylight than when he arrived in September. It was dark by 1830 now. If he got an animal later in the day, he'd cache half of it a distance from the gut pile, carry the other half home tonight, and collect the rest in the morning.

As the day brightened, he moved closer to the end of the ridge, allowing a wider view of the east-west running valley. Within five minutes, he noticed movement six hundred yards to his left. He watched the area through his binoculars, and the first sight of the caribou was the tips of antlers over low brush. Boone closed the distance by three hundred yards and anchored the bull with a single shot from the Winchester Model 70. In an hour, he had the animal quartered with half the meat and hide packed in his rucksack. He shouldered the weight and started the two-mile walk back to camp.

He spent the rest of the day and part of the next carrying and processing meat. He ate much of the back straps and smoked a good supply. He stored all the meat in the cache downwind of his shelter. He soaked the hide in water and worked it overnight. He scraped the hair off, removed all the fat from the hide, and stretched it. He needed rawhide to attach roof rafters to his cabin's ridge pole and replace the parachute cord webbing of his snowshoes. One caribou hide would provide much of that.

Boone completed his cabin over the next several days. He christened it Taggart's Station, a nod to the frontier posts along the southern Appalachian chain of mountains. It was a tribute to his family's frontier heritage. He collected firewood in the form of standing dead logs, cut in eight-to-ten-foot sections, and prepared for another hunt.

On his first night in the cabin, he sat beside the fire with his notebook and began his planning. He started his notebook on the second day of the hunting trip. This was the twenty-fifth day since Jimmy dropped him off at the lake. Whatever circumstances transpired—he knew Jimmy failed to tell anyone where he was. Maybe they hadn't even found Jimmy. Airplanes disappear all the time in Alaska. Boone had to own responsibility for a rookie move. He trusted Jimmy to notify someone where he was.

I just should've stayed in the plane.

"But you didn't—move on," he said out loud.

Boone calculated that by now, if the search wasn't suspended pending new information to narrow the search area, it would certainly be suspended within two weeks. They couldn't search forever. They would've thoroughly checked the area of the caches, hunting camp, and in between, but there was no reason to search much beyond. He was far outside the search area. They might not be coming after him. He was beginning to think he was on his own. He'd probably have to self-rescue. The question was, stay the winter and walk or paddle out in the spring, or walk out over the next few weeks?

He referenced the rudimentary map that he'd drawn on day one, based on his general knowledge of the terrain. If he calculated properly, he was about seventy to eighty miles west of Eagle and the Taylor Highway, about the same distance north of the Alaska Highway, about one-hundred-twenty miles from Fairbanks, but only about fifty to sixty miles south of the Yukon River. The easiest course of action was to walk to the Yukon River and wait for someone to come down it so he could signal them for help. He could cover the ground in three to five days.

But there was a problem with the Yukon River course of action. In days, winter would be here to stay. The ponds were already frozen, the river was on its way, and the snow line was rapidly creeping down the hillsides. He'd arrive at the Yukon in the transition between river and ice highway, and he wasn't even sure if anyone would be traveling that far east once the river froze. He wouldn't have shelter on the Yukon, either. The transition period between autumn and winter was difficult to travel. He'd be better off waiting until full winter, spending the next few weeks preparing, putting in meat, making better shoes and winter clothes, building a sled, maybe skis or at least another pair of snowshoes, and then walking to the Yukon River or Highway Six over to Circle.

The following morning, he walked to a glassing point on a hilltop two miles from his cabin. Along the way, he made his decision. He would prep for a couple of weeks and walk to Highway Six and then to the little village of Circle, along the Yukon River. In the time he needed to prepare for a self-rescue, not more than two weeks, he would know the search was suspended. He also had a cabin to fall back on during long periods of bad weather.

His decision wouldn't last long. *No plan survives first contact with the enemy.* Murphy was skulking through the hills six miles west of Taggart's Station.

Ol' Ephraim

"I find that the curiossity of our party is pretty well satisfyed with rispect to this anamal [grizzly]..."
Captain Meriwether Lewis
Missouri River, Montana 6 May 1805

CHAPTER THIRTY-TWO
1045 Hours Local-Tuesday 20 October 1987
Taggart's Station-Day 26

The previous day, Boone killed two more caribou that wandered near camp. Now he had more meat and was working the hides into a pair of mukluks, native winter footwear used for centuries. He needed four more hides to make an anorak to go over his wool Filson. He also needed a bear for fat and fur. With a few more resources, he'd be set to walk out. He worked on a second pair of snowshoes and had the makings for a pull-behind sled to carry meat and, hopefully, a bearskin blanket. He snared two beavers in the river giving him fur for mittens. Now, he sat on a knob, glassing the south-facing slopes still warm in the sun. They held the last food for the few bears not yet in their dens.

He caught a flash of jet-black movement against the patchy snow to his left, but then it was gone. He continued to glass through his binoculars and saw the fat black bear moving quickly, with a purpose, out of the alders along the creek to his front. The bear kept looking over its shoulder and moving almost at a trot. *What're you running from?* The bear moved in such a manner that Boone looked back to the left to see if something was chasing the bear. But saw nothing. *This is no time to overthink the situation. You needed meat, fat, and fur.*

The bear was on a course that would cross within two hundred yards of Boone's position. He set up for the shot and waited for the bear to cross the closest point. When the bear reached the point Boone selected, he made a "meuw" noise. The bear stopped instinctively and looked over its right shoulder. When the bear stopped, Boone pressed the trigger, and the bear dropped in its tracks. He cycled the action of the Model 70 and waited, watching the downed bear through his binoculars. In the twenty minutes that he waited, he continued to scan back to the left to see if something was indeed chasing the bear. Again, he saw nothing. Convinced the bear was dead, he walked to the carcass and touched the bear's rump with the rifle muzzle. No life left in him. Boone set to work skinning and butchering.

In just over an hour, Boone had the main cuts of the bear laying on the hide. He packed his ruck with as much meat as he could carry, strapped the hide to the outside of his ruck, and cached the remaining meat in a birch tree a hundred yards from the gut pile. He shouldered the ruck, picked up his rifle, and walked.

The creek where the bear had emerged flowed east, intersecting Charley River four miles downstream. The cabin was another two and a half miles along the river. It was farther but much easier travel, more level, than the hills if he took a straight line, but something was bothering that bear. He kept looking back down the valley. There might be a grizzly in the creek drainage.

Boone decided to split the difference. He followed the creek but, on the hillside. He stayed above the thick willows and aspens along the creek and Charley River. He checked his rifle to ensure a round was chambered, then pulled his Ruger and checked all six chambers. *Worried, Boone?* He could almost hear Dan's sarcasm, *"Why worry, you're only walking through grizzly country with raw meat on your back...alone."* He started to move as the gray sky spit snowflakes.

When Boone walked into the cabin's yard, he dropped his rucksack, drank water, cut more firewood for the pile, added to his supply in the cabin, and then put more water on the fire to boil. His life had slowed to mundane, predictable, but enjoyable daily tasks—process water by boiling, cut, split, and carry wood, and cook or smoke meat, process hides into usable items, fish, trap, and hunt...stay on the hunt.

His body had leaned in the weeks since the hunting party landed. Gone was the extraneous fat of a typical American diet, even for a better-than-average fit man. He now slept like the dead, and all through the night, unlike his restless sleep back in the modern world. It was the sleep of the exhausted, but in a good way. He'd

181

accomplished something real, tangible, and certain during the day.

He knew the pace of life would slow soon because of the weather. He almost had his little insular civilization built. He had shelter, the hides would provide the additional clothing he needed, and he had plenty of meat cached and smoked. *How long are you going to wait?* He kept asking himself.

He spent the rest of the evening processing meat one hundred yards from his cabin. He smoked or jerked much of the meat, but it was cold enough now that he could put the meat directly in his cache without the risk of spoiling. After eating a large caribou roast, Boone spent the rest of the night scraping the bear hide to tan. He hated polluters, but, in this case, the trash he occasionally found in the bush was a lifesaver. Three days previous, he walked through an abandoned camp along the river. From the looks of things, it was probably abandoned just before he arrived in the valley.

Sorting through the remaining trash, he found an old tin coffee can with a lid, a blue tarp, two tin cans of pineapples, a canvas meat bag, and some spent cartridges. The cans of pineapple weren't rusted or compromised in any way, so he opened one and devoured it on the spot. An act he regretted ten minutes later after experiencing the effects of a large can of tropical fruit in sugar syrup on the gastrointestinal system of a man on an exclusively carnivore diet for the previous month. He made it to the tree line but just barely. He decided to hold on to the other can for later. He spent much of that night rendering bear fat. He would need the fat to cook. Lard was a great dietary supplement to stay warm when the arctic winter arrived in full. By the end of the evening, he had a tin coffee can partially filled with the world's most delicious lard.

The following day, Boone retrieved the rest of the bear meat and the skull. He spent several days tanning hides and fashioning clothing—he hadn't tanned a hide in years. The last time was when he was seventeen and then, under Luther's supervision. He knew of several methods to process animal hides into some form of leather. He turned some into rawhide simply by scraping the hair and fat from the hide, letting it dry and become very hard. When he needed the rawhide, he made it pliable by cutting it to the appropriate size and soaking it in water. He used rawhide for repairs, cordage, and boot soles. He'd replaced the nylon 550 cord in his snowshoes with caribou rawhide, and it worked much better, drawing the wood joints together.

Another method was brain tanning. He'd already brain-tanned several caribou hides, some with hair on and the others with hair off. In this process, Boone used the animals' brains, mixed with some water, and worked the paste into the hide to give it a soft, supple finish for clothing. Fortunately, every animal has enough brain matter to tan its hide. Brain tanning the two hides reminded Boone of one of Luther's favorite insults if he questioned someone's intelligence: "He doesn't have enough brains to tan his own hide," he would say.

In the absence of brains, hides can be tanned with hardwood ash. The final step was to smoke the hide to give it color and some water resistance.

After several days of work, Boone had a new pair of Caribou shoe pacs warmer than his insulated Danner hunting boots. They provided additional leg protection, coming almost to his knee, a bear skin blanket to supplement his sleeping bag, a caribou anorak with a beaver fur cape and hood, and a pair of beaver mittens. He was prepared for colder temperatures and snow.

Boone could move now if he wanted, but he would give the SAR crews ten more days. He spent the time fine tuning his kit for his trip, including eating. Luther told him stories of his people's feasts after a buffalo hunt. "Eat well when you can," he'd say.

Boone was eating five to seven pounds of meat a day. He wouldn't be hungry on his walk.

Abigail stepped from the guest house porch and saw Wade's truck in its usual parking spot. The tractor was parked under the equipment shed, and the four-wheeler was sitting in front of the garage. She walked through the stable end of the barn to the corral, where Wade's palomino gelding stood unsaddled drinking water. The morning chores were finished, hay was in feed bins, and stock tanks were full and ice-free.

She left the barn, walked across the yard, and knocked on the side door at the kitchen, but there was no answer. She opened the door and walked through the living room into Wade's den, where he sat in his leather reading chair in front of the fireplace with a book and a coffee mug. Abby recognized the thousand-yard stare. She'd seen it in Boone too often and remembered it in her father's eyes at times, but had rarely noticed it in Wade, although she knew he'd experienced the vacuum often. War had left its mark on all the men in her life.

"Wade?"

He looked up and motioned her to take a seat next to him.

"Coffee?" he asked.

"No thanks."

"Whiskey?" he smiled.

"It's not even eight in the morning," she said. *He's the source of Boone's sarcasm.*

"I didn't get to talk to you yesterday at supper. How are you?" she said.

"I'm fine. How are you?" Wade said.

"I'm fine" is the male euphemism for I don't want to discuss

184

it." She said, winking at him.

"You're probably right, honey, but I'm fine," he laughed.

"It's going to take us all a while to adjust, right?" Abby asked.

"Abigail, none of us are ever going to adjust to this. We're just going to have to keep living," after a pause, he continued. "But I've been thinking about going forward and what's next. I want to help you finish the new house. We can't all sit here and mourn. We have to press on. And before you think I'm trying to get you and Caroline out of the guest house, I'm not. We love having you two here, but you need your own place. A home you can build. What do you think?"

"I'd like that, thank you."

More than a month had passed since any human being had seen Boone. Abigail felt guilty for thinking about such things, but she couldn't hold it inside any longer. She wasn't one to rely too heavily on hope. She was far more pragmatic. She didn't feel Boone alive like Rachel felt. She was afraid she was a widow but stumbled upon expressing it to anyone. Her mother detected Abigail's anxiety, and they talked, but she was more practical like her father. She couldn't imagine a scenario ending in Boone being alive and healthy.

Rebecca walked into the study. Abby moved to a spot on the hearth and gave her chair to her mother-in-law.

"Nonsense, dear. Keep your seat," Rebecca said in protest, but Abby sat still.

"What're you two discussing?" Rebecca asked.

"Fixing up Abigail's new house."

"And what else?" Rebecca asked, looking at Abby.

Rebecca noticed the pause in the conversation and a shift in Abby's demeanor. She understood what was in her heart.

"Abby, say what you need to say, dear. We'll listen," Rebecca said.

"I hate myself for feeling this way, but I'm afraid he's gone forever."

Abby began to sob when her thoughts became words. Wade stepped to her side and put his hand on her shoulder. She composed herself after several minutes of weeping. Wade handed her his handkerchief and sat down next to her.

"I fear the same, Abigail," Wade said. "I keep trying to think of some way this ends with Boone's survival, but I can't figure it out. I think we would know it by now if he was alive. I keep trying to think what we might've done differently, where we should've searched outside the area, but I don't know what or where. I pray we're wrong but we must deal with reality and keep moving forward. It's just terrible living without answers. We'll have to do the best we can."

The following morning, Abby stood at the kitchen sink watching snow fall on the Bighorns. She poured a third cup of cold coffee down the drain. Roan called the previous night and confessed that he'd lost faith that Boone was still alive. If he was, he would've already walked out, a scenario Abby tended to agree with. Caroline didn't know what to believe. She just knew her dad wasn't there. Rachel was the one she worried about. She refused to consider anything other than Boone walking out of the woods with a smile on his face. In her mind, there was no other possibility.

Abby hadn't seen her husband in fifty-one days, and he was listed as missing for twenty-seven days. She tried to logically analyze the possible scenarios so many of the people close to her suggested, but none of them ended well. Most of the searchers thought Boone survived the crash to have died in another accident. The two most likely causes of death were an animal attack or drowning in a river crossing. Wade and her father thought the most plausible scenario was that Boone was so injured in the crash that he'd grabbed his gear, walked into the wilderness, and died of his wounds. At least, she felt that's what they thought. They'd mentioned the possibility in Eagle but hadn't said they believed it as fact. Both were pragmatic men and were conditioned to death and tragedy. Hope wasn't a course of action. Her father had told her so many times. They were dealing with realities.

Only Rachel suggested a scenario in which Boone was alive. What if Jimmy had dropped him off somewhere before the crash? But, if that had happened, and he was healthy, why hadn't he walked out? He worked hard to mitigate risk. She didn't think he would get out of the plane at a location unknown to anyone except Jimmy. He was a risk-taker, but he wasn't reckless. Would he have trusted Jimmy to get

186

word back to Eagle about his location? If he had, why didn't Jimmy follow up? If Boone was alive, even somewhere they hadn't searched, why had he not chosen to walk out? He was a healthy man, in excellent shape, with all the wilderness skills to affect his rescue. The possibilities bounced through her head and did nothing more than confuse her. She didn't know what to believe or what to do next.

Abby knew one thing—they weren't together, remodeling their new house, starting their new post-retirement life. It wasn't supposed to be like this. He was retired—he'd made it. He survived the most dangerous situations possible.

As he loved to say, "I grew old in a profession where men die young."

He was settling down. He survived it all only to be killed on something as routine as a hunting trip. It was so unfair. Maybe she did believe what her father and Wade felt. Maybe he was gone. The tears came again, not just for the loss but for the guilt of thinking he was dead and for the uncertainty she knew she would always feel as she moved on with her life.

Rachel had spent the previous days settling into her new life. She talked to her academic adviser, explained her sudden absence from school, and said she wouldn't be back this academic year. Her advisor was sympathetic and agreed to take care of any administrative requirements so Rachel could return to school in the future without any problems. She extended her condolences and wished her the best in finding her father.

Rachel comfortably nestled into the Chapman homestead. Chappie and his "war bride," Elizabeth, settled just outside of Eielson Air Force Base, where they were stationed twice in Chappie's Air Force career. The first time was immediately following the war and Bart was born there shortly after they arrived. They put Rachel in the apartment over the two-car garage. It gave her privacy and independence without the burden of rent and utilities. The arrangement also allowed them to keep their promise to the Taggart and Clark families that they would keep an eye on her. They were thankful it would now be occupied by youth from a family they had such a long and powerful connection with.

After getting comfortable in her new home, Bart dropped her off at the storage area adjacent to the Chapman Hangar, where Boone's truck was parked. He handed her the keys to the truck, helped her get the trailer parked at his dad's house, and got the truck serviced and winterized. She finished all the administrative requirements of moving, driver's license, change of address, and the other details of life. Now, she was ready for her first day as the new and first Administrative Assistant, Dispatcher, and Logistics Coordinator for

Chapman Aviation.

She knew and deeply appreciated what the Chapmans were doing for her. Chappie and Bart had run this business for years and didn't need an assistant, but they were willing to create a job for her. She loved the insulated world of the military and the extended family that was integral to the experience. She had people worldwide, men and women whom her parents and grandparents had served with. People they'd created deep bonds with who would care for her, even if they'd never met her. They knew this was Hoot Clark, Wade Taggart, or Boone and Abigail Taggart's girl, which made her part of the brotherhood.

Chappie and Bart were busy over the previous few days as well. They rearranged office space to provide Rachel a workspace and discussed her duties. As the weather had all Chapman Aviation aircraft grounded for the next forty-eight hours, they were catching up on maintenance and administrative work—it was a great opportunity to introduce the new hire. When she walked through the office door from the hangar, they both greeted her. Chappie reached her first, hugged her.

"Do you need anything? Are you getting settled in?"

"Yes, sir. I have a new driver's license and a new checking account, and I have my truck registered and groceries in the refrigerator. I don't need a thing, thank you. I'm ready to work."

"Great," Wade said. "I'm going to start the orientation this morning. I'll introduce you to the people we regularly do business with. We'll meet for lunch and review your duties and responsibilities. Then Bart will take over this afternoon and introduce you to everyone we work with at the airport, including all the other Chapman employees. When the weather clears, you'll fly with Bart and me to the other Chapman facilities around the interior, and we'll introduce you to everyone at each of those sites. You'll be an old hand in a week and probably running the outfit in a month."

Rachel was overwhelmed by the Chapman's kindness. She knew her dad was close to Bart, and both of her grandfathers were close to Chappie, but she didn't know the exact circumstances that brought them all together. Roan had filled in some of the gaps when he shared with her the connection between Boone and Yeti, but whatever the exact circumstances, she was thankful to be a part of this.

"I can't thank you all enough," she said. "I don't know what I'd do if you weren't here for me."

"You're welcome, Rachel. Consider yourself part of the family now," Chappie said, hugging her.

"Don't be too happy," Bart said. "He'll get it all back in overtime. He's a taskmaster."

The three spent the next two days going over daily operations, roles and responsibilities of each employee, key people in town and at the airport, and Chapman facilities throughout the state. Bart gave her a lesson in aerial navigation on the large sectional maps posted on the office wall. Chappie explained the codes used for operations that tracked the movement of all Chapman aircraft. They finished the two-day orientation with a discussion on emergency procedures. When the weather cleared, she flew with Bart to Circle and Eagle and back to Fairbanks, meeting the Chapman employees and key people on each airfield. On the return flight to Fairbanks, she looked out of the left-side cockpit window, said a prayer for her father, and made a decision.

CHAPTER THIRTY-FIVE
1735 Hours Local-Saturday 24 October 1987
Chapman Homestead-Outside North Pole, Alaska-Day 30

With Rachel as the newest addition, the entire Chapman family gathered in Chappie and Elizabeth's cabin for Saturday night supper, a long-standing family tradition. When they weren't spread out all over the world, the Chapmans shared Saturday supper. Their cabin was quintessential Alaska, but the interior was a mix of Alaska and England. Chappie's den looked like what was left after a hunting lodge, library, and officer's club exploded. There were animal and fish mounts, guns, Native American artifacts, military memorabilia, and books everywhere. It had an organized cluttered look, but it made sense and fit the man now occupying it with his only son and grandson. Like most aviators, it wasn't long until both were "flying" with their hands.

The rest of the house looked like an English cottage. Chappie stayed out of Elizabeth's interior decorating. He had his den and the hangar, and she ruled the house. It was, after all, the least he could do after dragging her away from her ancestral home, roaming the world to dozens of postings and landing in North Pole, Alaska. He owed her.

Elizabeth put Rachel and her daughter-in-law, Susan, to work on the final details at the dining room table while she supervised her granddaughter finishing a cake for dessert. After only the first week, it felt like home for Rachel.

After dessert, the children were in the den reading as the adults enjoyed coffee at the dining room table.

"Are there any family rules about discussing work during family time?" Rachel said.

"Work is always an open topic of discussion, dear," Elizabeth

191

said, with her wonderful British accent. Chappie blew her a kiss.

"No restrictions, honey," Chappie said. "What's on your mind?"

"I have some money saved from graduation gifts, calf and horse sales, and I'm going to take flying lessons to get my pilot's license," Rachel said.

The four adult Chapmans exchanged glances with one another.

"Did I say something wrong?" she asked.

"No, you didn't," Susan said, smiling. She pushed her glasses atop her blond hair. "It's just that anyone who spends more than a day with this family wants to be Chuck Yeager."

"Have you talked to your mother about this?" Chappie said.

"No sir, but respectfully, I don't need her permission."

"Fair enough."

"Is this about finding your dad?" Bart asked.

"Maybe a little, but I grew up listening to Grandpa Hoot and you," she said, pointing to Chappie, "talk about flying, and it intrigues me. I might want to pursue it as a career."

"I can make a recommendation for your ground school," Chappie said. "And we're both Certified Flight Instructors. We can help you get your hours. If you'll pay for the fuel, I'll let you use the Cessna at work."

Rachel looked at Bart, and he nodded.

"Thank you all so much. I can never repay you."

"You don't have to repay us, Rachel. You're one of us," Elizabeth said.

Later that evening, Rachel called her mother and told her. Abby had concluded trying to talk Rachel out of something she wanted to do was as fruitless as trying to persuade Boone. She was relieved it was Bart and Chappie training her. Neither was reckless, and they were the best, professional aviators she knew, short of her father. He would be ecstatic when he got the news that Rachel would fly.

"Please be careful. I can't take more tragedy," Abby said.

"I will, Mom, I promise."

She'd do nothing but work and take flying lessons. If she had her license by spring, and saved enough money from work, added to what she saved for school, she could put a down payment on a bare bones airplane of her own. Rachel could start the search for her dad again by summer.

CHAPTER THIRTY-SIX

Boone left the cabin as soon as it was light enough to see. After several days of deliberation and rehearsal, he decided against pulling the sled. He packed twenty-five pounds of dried meat and the rest of the gear he would need into his rucksack and cached everything else near the cabin, including some meat he couldn't carry. He left his wading boots and a couple of smaller items in the cache, wrapped his Model 70 Winchester in a tarp, and left it in the rafters of the cabin. He'd come back for it next week after he was rescued.

He was ready to go. He'd prepared well, and would be reunited with his family and friends in seven days. He looked at the cabin and considered how much he enjoyed life in this valley. It was simple, close to the land, and satisfying. He'd stay if he could bring his family to him, but they were suffering severely, and he knew it. He had to fix this.

He carried another load of firewood into the cabin to make life easier for another traveler who might need shelter. He sat on a stump, secured his snowshoes to the caribou shoe pacs, shouldered his rucksack, and grabbed the shotgun. He checked his compass, took a three-hundred-degree magnetic heading, and started walking.

Boone walked up the valley seven miles northwest of his cabin, crossed a small stream, and saw several fresh sets of grizzly tracks. He was sure they were working the south-facing slopes for a final few calories and coming to this stream to drink, but within days every bear in the country should be holed up in their dens. Then, he wouldn't need to worry about an encounter. Half a mile from the stream, he stopped to drink water and eat jerky. He planned to walk for four more hours before he stopped and built a debris shelter. He was having a great time. He shouldered his rucksack, checked his gear, and then moved into the spruce trees.

Thirty feet into the trees, he was about to step across a small creek and announce his presence when he discovered what had been worrying the black bear whose skin he now carried on his back. He heard it, then felt it before he saw it and, more impressive, smelled it— a large boar grizzly had been napping in a small open area ten yards left of Boone's path. He heard a rush of leaves, broken branches, and a horrifying woofing noise as the boar made impact.

It felt what he imagined being hit by a speeding train was like. The initial strike sandwiched him between the bear and a large spruce tree, knocking the wind out of him, cutting a large gash across the front of his scalp, and lacerating his face and neck. By the time he hit the ground, the vision in his right eye was obscured by blood. The bear pinned him to the ground beneath the weight of his pack. He could smell the musky fragrance of the forest floor mixed with the pungency of the bear, an odor that reminded him of fish in the bottom of a trash can on a hot afternoon. It was an overwhelming smell that almost had a feel or taste. He fought his gag reflex.

His shotgun was gone, and so were his snowshoes. He did what he was trained to do during a grizzly attack. In a single motion, he pulled his knees underneath him to his chest, wrapped his fingers behind his neck, and put his chin on his chest. He closed his eyes and prayed the bear was only startled and would go away after realizing Boone wasn't a threat. More intensely, he prayed it wasn't a sow with cubs or defending a kill. So far, he wasn't seriously injured.

The bear savaged Boone's rucksack, shaking Boone like a doll. If the pack stayed intact, his back was protected, and if he could stay in the fetal position, the soft portions of his torso were protected, but the attack grew more violent. The bear continued to ravage the pack, trying, it seemed, to separate man from his protective shell. When the bear shook its head, Boone's entire body convulsed. The bear lifted the pack, along with the one-hundred-eighty-pound man attached to it shook and dropped it. Boone adjusted his position and grunted when he hit the ground. The sound and movement caused the bear to initiate the attack with even more enthusiasm. It seemed as if the attack had gone on for ten minutes. In reality, it was less than ten seconds.

Boone landed on his side as the bear attacked the pack again, but this time its nose slipped past the pack and pushed between Boone's left arm and chest. The bear pulled back short and bit into his upper left arm. Boone heard and felt the snap of bone. He screamed in pain and in shock but held his position. The bear descended on the pack again, growling, biting, and clawing at the canvas. The left shoulder strap snapped, and the bear had the pack. Boone's back was now exposed. Before he could react, the bear had Boone's left shoulder in his mouth. He screamed again as the bear pulled his head straight up and back, throwing Boone backward, landing ten feet away. Instinctively, Boone regained the fetal position, took one deep breath, and held it. He glanced to see the bear getting ready to strike again.

How can something so big move that fast and agile?

The bear stopped with his front paws on Boone's hips. It was terrifying, the tips of the six-inch claws digging into the flesh of his lower back. Worse was the bear's breath on the back of his neck, sniffing to see if this thing was dead or alive. It took every shred of discipline and control to remain silent. Motionless. As much as he wanted to survive the encounter, he decided he would go on the offensive if the bear attacked again. He couldn't sustain many more attacks. He could feel the weight of his revolver. Boone was still in the fight.

The bear seemed confused by the separation of the pack from the human. It turned back to the pack lying in the creek bed, thirty feet away.

Maybe it's over.

The bear attacked the pack again with more rigor than before. Boone opened his eyes but didn't make eye contact with the bruin. His grandfather had always said not to make eye contact with bulls "They can feel you looking at them," he told young Boone as they worked the cattle sorting pens at the ranch. It seemed like good advice now. But did the bear know Boone was looking at him or had he moved or made a noise? The bear dropped the pack and rushed out of the creek.

Boone lay on his right side, facing the charging bear. He

196

worked his right hand under himself and rested it on the leather holster pulled in front of him. His left arm was almost useless now. It wasn't pain. It was a stinging sensation and the tightness of swelling. When the bear got hold of him this time, he knew it would kill him. He made his decision. In one motion, he rolled to his back, cleared the revolver from the holster, cocked the hammer, put the front sight post just above the bear's nose, and pulled the trigger. He repeated the process twice.

The first round hit the bear's left eye and caused him to turn slightly to the left and snap at the air, but he instantly turned back on Boone with his mouth wide open. The second round hit the bear in the back of the mouth. It stopped momentarily and wrenched its neck, but the attack resumed as quickly as it had paused. He wasn't sure where the third round hit or, worse, if it had.

Bracing for another impact, Boone pulled the revolver to his chest, covered it with both hands, and pulled his legs to his chest, but it was too late. The now wounded bruin clamped its mouth on Boone's right knee and spun him one hundred and eighty degrees without letting go. Boone was on his back, the bear biting into his right leg. He cocked the revolver and extended his good arm, almost resting the gun's muzzle on the bear's head. Face to face with the animal that would, in the next second, either be dead or kill him, he pulled the trigger. The massive head dropped between his knees. Boone pushed away, stood, and put the last two rounds into the bear. He didn't want to fight this animal again.

The bear twitched half a dozen times but stopped breathing. Silence returned to the woods. The attack hadn't lasted more than thirty seconds, but he felt as if it were days later. He'd never experienced anything so violent. The smell of blood, gunsmoke, and rotten fish filled the air. He immediately felt the first effects of the adrenaline rush as he started to gag and wretch. He was struggling to stand and shaking uncontrollably. Steam from Boone's body and the bear's mixed in the cold early winter air as he struggled to reload the revolver.

After four attempts to reload he succeeded, holstered the revolver and drank a quart of water. Shock was moments away if he failed to act. He turned to evaluating his wounds. He was sure his left arm was broken between the shoulder and elbow. There was no bone through the skin, but it was swelling badly to the point that skin was stretched enough to hurt. There were several deep puncture wounds on his arm and his shoulder. His shoulder hurt, but it still worked. He didn't think it was broken. His scalp was badly cut from forward of his right eye, across his forehead, to just past his left ear. He had several deep cuts across his lower back and hips and multiple cuts and bruises over the rest of his body. The most life-threatening problem was the loss of mobility caused by the damage to his right leg. He took several deep breaths and let them out slowly. His heart rate was coming back down, but he continued to shake uncontrollably.

Triage the situation, Boone.

He limped to his rucksack, sat down, and pulled out the medical kit. Thankfully, it was robust. A lifetime in military service, almost every day of twenty-four years spent with light infantry, airborne, or Special Forces units, gave him plenty of contacts that could get him supplies otherwise difficult to come by, including advanced trauma medical supplies. Bobby maintained his contacts from his Special Forces career and had given each one in the hunting party a robust trauma kit which included antibiotics and painkillers. It was a godsend now.

Mitigate the risk that will kill you first—bleeding and then infection.

A bear's mouth is almost the worst petri dish in nature. Boone had plenty of experience with traumatic injuries, but this was different because he was the victim. There was no medic, no dustoff, and no Combat Support Hospital waiting to receive him. He was on his own.

"Get to work."

He shuffled around on one leg enough to collect wood, started a fire, and put water on to boil.

Just like the Westerns.

He laid the contents of the trauma kit on what was left of his shirt and set aside what he thought he would need: four triangular bandages, one full tube of antiseptic cream, plenty of gauze, a suture kit, a vial of antibiotics, a hypodermic needle, the bottle of antibiotics in pill form, pain killers, and a long pair of hemostat forceps. He found the unopened bottle of whiskey, opened it, and poured enough in the bottom of a canteen cup to soak gauze patches and strips.

This is going to hurt.

Stripped to the waist, with his pants around his ankles, he washed his hands as best he could in the almost-boiling water and poured a little whiskey over his fingers. He didn't want to add to the infection. He took a healthy drink of the whiskey and swallowed. Setting the bottle aside, he probed the wounds with his fingers. He could easily see the wounds on his chest, leg, and arm, but he would need to repair the back of his shoulder and hips by feel. He started there.

Boone probed the wounds on his back with his fingers and found three large punctures and several smaller ones. He pushed on his shoulder blade, collarbone, and shoulder socket. Everything seemed intact. He worked on the puncture wounds the entire circumference of the bicep and triceps. The swelling was getting worse, and he thought he could feel the spot where his arm was broken. The skin was tight and warm to the touch.

He reached around his waist with his right arm and found five cuts, about three inches long and not too deep, at his belt line. Then he turned to the left side of his chest. There were several deep puncture wounds caused by the bear's top canines, lesser ones behind those. The worst was the tear under his left pectoral muscle, a flap of skin maybe six inches long. It was deep.

He mentally reviewed his medical training. The best he'd ever experienced was with the two A Detachment medics during his first tour in the Central Highlands of Vietnam. The team commander at the time required everyone to receive advanced medical training by the two team medics. They were almost as good as doctors. They could perform emergency trauma medicine, light dental work, deliver babies, and even had some veterinary medicine experience. Boone was amazed by their capabilities.

He prepared the suture kit. He hadn't done this since he helped work on a Montagnard family in 1964.

How many years ago was that?

I don't know, it's math.

199

A lifetime ago.
Stay focused.

He cleaned the outside of the wound as best he could with gauze, used the forceps to dip a gauze square into the whiskey, took a deep breath, and exhaled, steadying himself.

Oh Lord, this is going to hurt like homemade sin.

Boone put the whiskey-soaked gauze into the wound and worked it back and forth to clean the inside of the wound. He'd never experienced a burning sensation so intense. It felt like his entire chest cavity was on fire. He kept at it. Once finished, he used another gauze pad soaked in antiseptic cream and liberally applied it to the inside of the wound. His hands were shaking, he was breathing hard and sweating profusely, but he had that much finished.

He took another long pull of whiskey, paused a moment, and then began to stitch the skin together with the suture. It took several stitches to close the wound. Boone applied more antiseptic cream along the stitches and covered the wound with gauze. He cleaned and applied antiseptic cream to the other wounds on his chest. The forceps added six inches of reach to get to the wounds on his back, but all he could do was clean them and put antiseptic in the wounds. He couldn't stitch or bandage wounds on his back with only one functional arm.

The gash on his head, neck, and face were next. Using his signal mirror to see, he closed all but one deep cut with butterfly bandages. The cut needed three stitches. He cleaned and bandaged the wounds on his leg, pulled up his pants, and splinted the leg with tree branches. Finally, he immobilized his left arm to his chest with a sling and bandage.

The medical procedures took over an hour, and he was completely exhausted. He took one more pull of whiskey, a couple of painkillers, and a shot of antibiotics. He rewarded himself with a dip of rationed snuff and a cup of hot, strong, coffee. He stopped shaking as the warmth of the whiskey, coffee, and fire seeped deeper into his body.

What now?

Boone couldn't make it seven miles back to the cabin tonight. He could fashion a crutch, but it would probably take two or more days to get back to the cabin. He would have to move far enough away from the bear carcass to be safe from other scavengers, but he would head back to the cabin in the morning. His plan to walk out was over. His window to leave was now closed. He was here for months, and the seven miles between him and the cabin was a battle.

Solve one problem at a time, Boone.

He found a nearby branch, cut it to length, leaned on it, and walked to the bear. He pulled his hunting knife and took the skin from the back and sides of the bear hide—the blanket. He would need it later.

CHAPTER THIRTY-SEVEN
0730 Hours Local-Sunday 1 November 1987
Day 38

In the late summer of 1823, the Ashley-Henry fur trapping expedition abandoned the Missouri River route to the Rocky Mountain fur streams to open alternate overland routes. The violence with the Arikara closed the Missouri River passage to the trapping grounds in the Rockies. The brigade divided into two groups. The first, led by Jedediah Smith, followed the White and Cheyenne Rivers, while the other group, led by Andrew Henry, followed an overland route to Fort Henry at the mouth of the Yellowstone River.

In late August or early September, Hugh Glass, a leading hunter for the Henry branch of the expedition, was mauled by a sow grizzly along the Grand River in what's now central South Dakota. Two of his fellow trappers were financially persuaded to stay with him until he died and then give him a proper Christian burial. The two trappers stayed with Glass for several days, but when the old mountain man refused to die, and hostile tribes began to appear close to their camp, they decided to abandon Glass and return to the main trapping party.

Hugh Glass didn't die—at least not from the grizzly attack. He dragged and limped across two hundred and fifty miles of prairie, limping into Fort Kiowa at the confluence of the Grand and Missouri Rivers in mid-October. It seems that revenge was the motivating fire that kept Hugh Glass alive.

Boone Taggart lay beneath spruce boughs as the new day's light filtered through the foliage and thought about Hugh Glass. He'd heard the story many times in his youth from his father and grandfather. He heard a similar version from Luther, who reminded

202

him that Glass got help from a band of Lakota, but he never in his wildest imagination considered he would one day be in almost exactly the same situation.

What's the fire that keeps you alive?

He immediately answered his own question.

He woke several times through the night to take painkillers and drink water. Each time he lay down, he could feel the pull of self-pity and the suffocating feeling of impending panic, but he fought them off throughout the night. Twelve hours before, he was planning his post-rescue life. The seven-mile hike from the cabin to where he was attacked was filled by planning his trip home. Thirty seconds before the attack, he was going through the logistics of driving back to Wyoming, oil changes, topping off fuel, and checking tires.

He thought about the relief his family and friends would soon experience, the creature comforts he would enjoy, and at least once during the day, a counter-intuitive thought crossed his mind: there was a part of him that was enjoying this experience and would miss it. That's what he was thinking when the brown freight train pancaked him into a spruce tree. Since that moment, his world was small, and his immediate future was questionable.

His mental state was different just a few hours later, wrestling for sleep and fighting the fear, pain, and panic.

The middle of the night is the worst.

It'll be better in the light of day.

Don't panic.

Panic kills.

Put your emotions in a box.

Solve your problems one at a time.

If Glass did it so could he, if he made the proper choice. Now, in the morning light, the decision he rolled in his mind was one Glass didn't have to make. He'd had only one survival option: getting to a fort and provisions. Boone had two options before him. He could continue the seventy miles to the highway and end this experience, or he could cover the seven miles back to the cabin, heal, and walk out later.

Boone built up his fire, chewed on some jerky, and drank

water. The decision to travel seven miles or seventy became clearer when he started to move. It took him almost an hour to stand. When he took his first steps, he fell. His right leg supported no weight. He could hardly move his knee, and his leg, as was his left arm, was badly swollen from mid-thigh to his ankle. He looked at his face in his signal mirror, and the view revealed what he felt. His head throbbed and was swollen, shutting his right eye.

The previous night, he traveled only two hundred yards from the bear carcass, and it exhausted him. This morning, his adrenaline was gone, and soreness, pain, swelling, and stiffness were the new order of the day. Everything hurt, but he couldn't waste time. He must decide. He figured it would take him several weeks, maybe a month, to travel the seventy miles to the highway, maybe two days to return to the cabin. He wouldn't walk in either case, at least not for a while. He would have to drag himself. Days were getting shorter, temperatures were dropping, and snow was increasing, making travel more difficult. Dragging himself through seventy miles of snow seemed impossible. He'd freeze to death. It would be bad enough getting back to the cabin. He estimated his healing time at six weeks to two months or maybe more if he could keep infection at bay, which would mean a mid-winter, not autumn, transit across the tundra or another heart-wrenching decision to wait until spring and float out.

One decision at a time.

Boone stared up at the steel-gray sky and spoke out loud. "I'm going back to the cabin and heal."

CHAPTER THIRTY-EIGHT
1830 Hours Local-Saturday 7 November 1987
Chapman Homestead-North Pole, Alaska-Day 44

Gravel, ice, and snow crunched beneath the tires of Boone's 1986 Dodge pickup when Rachel turned off the main road. She parked in her spot beside the garage apartment that was now home, and ran to the house just as the family was taking their seats around the dining room table.

"You were almost late, girl," Chappie said.

"I know, sorry."

Slipping out of her Sorel pac boots, she hung up her Carhartt jacket.

"I finished my exam today instead of waiting until Monday," she said. "I passed."

Everyone clapped and cheered as she took her place at the table.

"Good job," Bart said. "Ground school is done. Are we going to start flying now?"

"Yes, sir. If you have the time," Rachel said.

"Here's what I was thinking," Bart said. "I know you want to work this hard so we can fly in the morning and the afternoon. If I can't instruct, Dad can take you up. You can knock out your hours and start racking up ratings. We can get you through your private and commercial after you get enough hours, instrument, multi-engine ratings, high-performance, complex, and tailwheel endorsements, and then all the bush pilot techniques not in the books. This summer we'll work on your float rating. By this time next year, you should be an old hand."

"I won't let this get in the way of my office work," Rachel said.

205

"I can work between flights and before and after the sun is up as the days get shorter."

"School starts on Monday," Chappie said.

"Good," Rachel said, smiling.

After supper, the family took their desserts and coffee and migrated to their favorite corners of the house. The guys ended up in Chappie's den, and the girls around the dining room table. Chappie stepped into the kitchen, rinsed his plate, put it in the sink, and filled his coffee mug. Elizabeth stepped beside him and worked on a cup of tea.

"Tonight, was the first time Rachel has been happy since she came to Alaska looking for her father," Elizabeth said.

"Yes, ma'am, you're right," Chappie said. "I don't think she's over his loss, but she's moving forward."

"Look again, Love," Elizabeth said. "She doesn't think her father is dead. In her mind, she's happy because she's actively involved in his rescue. That young woman believes that her father is alive, and she's determined to find him, but that's not all. She's on her journey. She's looking for something other than her father. She's changing."

"You think?" Chappie said.

Elizabeth looked at him sadly, "If only you could feel the subtleties in the human soul you do in a machine."

Chappie smiled and then more seriously, said, "I just hope she doesn't get hurt more than she already is."

"What if she's right? What if Boone is still alive?" Elizabeth asked.

"I hope she is, but I doubt it, and I don't want to think what it would do to everyone who gave up," Chappie said.

Three weeks later, on a beautiful Alaska winter day, Rachel Taggart taxied the Cessna 150 to a stop in front of the Chapman Aviation Hangar at Fairbanks International Airport and shut down the engine. When she stepped from the cockpit, she was ear-to-ear smiles, jumping up and down, laughing hysterically. Chappie and Bart hadn't experienced this kind of happiness in a long time, but both could remember when they felt the same joy. She soloed. She happily submitted to having the tail cut off her new shirt, the long-standing tradition for students who soloed. She was joining the ranks of aviators.

While Rachel, Bart, and Chappie celebrated her milestone, one hundred twenty miles east, Boone Taggart was engaged in a desperate struggle.

CHAPTER THIRTY-NINE
1210 Hours Local-Sunday 29 November 1987
Day 66

The journey back to the cabin was hellish. It was a seven-mile walk, or more often a crawl, accomplished in fifty-foot increments. He couldn't carry his rucksack, so he strapped his shotgun to the outside, attached a fifty-foot length of caribou rawhide, and dragged it. He took the exact route back to the cabin as he had walking out. Which meant, the few inches of permanent snow were packed down. When he could walk, he kept a snowshoe on his left foot, but his right leg was dragged behind. He couldn't put any weight on it, and his knee barely moved. The pain and stiffness caused him to swing the splinted right leg forward just enough to hold himself on a hefty walking stick in his right hand and then move his good leg. He fell what seemed a hundred times before his body got the knack of moving in this new and foreign way. Within minutes, new problems emerged, and muscles not usually used in walking began to cramp and spasm. He stopped, rested, massaged, and then moved again.

Boone's method was to hobble the length of the rawhide tug, stop, turn around, pull his rucksack to him, move another fifty feet, and pull the rucksack again, repeat, repeat. Within the first few hours, he broke the code about moving on level ground but eventually came to the first downhill section of the trail. To his amazement, he found the first thing that was easy—easy being relative to difficult.

On downhill stretches, he lay on his back and scooted through the snow headfirst. He could make pretty good time sliding downhill. Conversely, uphill sections of the trail were next to impossible. He determined it was easier to crawl, several times, lying on his belly, pushing with his good leg, and pulling with his opposing good arm.

208

He also discovered that it was even easier to walk uphill backward. He tried that technique until he couldn't take the pain it created in his neck, and this technique wouldn't allow for a snowshoe.

Each night, he sheltered under the low-hanging boughs of spruce trees. The cavity below the limbs was almost devoid of snow. He built a long fire, put the bear hide blanket down, and crawled in his sleeping bag as best he could. He ate jerky and drank as much water as he could. He knew he was using an extraordinary number of calories and was dehydrated the entire time.

Boone was close to breaking on the afternoon of the fourth day, crawling, sliding, and hobbling. He fell hard trying to maneuver across a small stream, landing on the far side of the creek. He could feel several of his injuries begin to bleed again, and the pain in his leg was incredible. He was sure he blacked out for a few minutes or, for all he knew, a few days. He hurt so bad it made him angry, and he began to feel the emotions rising and two conversations playing out in his head. Fortunately, he had some experience with the two voices.

They were the voices of his internal conversation. One seeks comfort and offers solutions through excuses, rationalization, and victimhood. It was the voice leading to submission, quitting, and ultimate failure. It whispered when he experienced adversity and challenges. He'd heard the voice in Basic Training, Airborne School, Ranger School, and the Q Course. He heard it in Laos and Vietnam multiple times and now, faced it again.

The other voice was tempered and trained through past adversity and discipline. This voice said he could do it. He wouldn't only survive but thrive and master his environment. He would meet the challenge and be victorious. This was the voice reminding him how many times he'd been here or in worse circumstances. The voice reminded him it can always get worse, so keep it in perspective. The voice reminded him, if Hugh Glass could do it so could Boone Taggart.

As he lay face down in the snow, starting to feel sorry for himself, he felt panic rise in his chest, tears forming in the corners of his eyes, and he made his choice. Push.

Listen to the voice of victory.

Never surrender.

Keep going.

Get hold of yourself.

Throwing a fit won't help.

You'll be mad and still in the same situation.

Break it down into small tasks.

He returned to his training at Camp Mackall as a young Green Beret.

C'mon Boone, you know what to do.

Master Sergeant Sobolewski trained us to survive, not fall apart.

Boone looked up the trail to the top of the ridge, and as he pushed with his good arm, he felt a rock about the size of a baseball under the snow. He quickly dug it up, held it momentarily, and threw it up the trail.

Crawl to the rock, Boone.

He started moving. He broke the remainder of the journey into crawling or hobbling the distance he could throw the rock.

As he crawled, his mind was a jumbled, disorganized mess of disparate thoughts. But a memory began to take clear form in his mind. The Sunday before Boone had left for the hunting trip, the preacher talked about overcoming adversity. His point intrigued Boone at the time and now it really meant something. God didn't necessarily protect us from adversity, but He did guide us or help us navigate the challenges. On the sixth day after the attack, as Boone stumbled down the ridge with the cabin in sight, he took stock of his situation and said a prayer of gratitude. He had the training, equipment, and, most importantly, medical supplies. The cabin was built, and his wounds showed no sign of infection. This whole thing could've been far worse.

Enjoying the cabin's warmth, he was convinced he'd made the right decision to return. A seventy-mile crawl/walk combination would've taken him months, and true winter would've caught him in the open. The first full day back at the cabin, he ate, drank water, tended to his wounds, and enjoyed the warmth of the fire.

Four weeks after the attack, he was healing. He succeeded in keeping infection at bay. The puncture wounds healed well, although he had the beginnings of some terrible scars. His arm was doing well, also. He was ready to start "physical therapy." He took his arm out of the sling and lightly exercised to improve his strength and range of motion. It was his right leg that created his greatest problem. A mobile one-armed hunter was far more capable than a hobbling-on-a-crutch hunter with two good arms, and Boone was the latter. It was difficult to move through the snow on crutches. It was nearly impossible on snowshoes.

He could hobble to get firewood, snow for water, and food in his cache, but he was running low on meat. He had to hunt, trap, or fish for food and process more firewood. He was thankful he'd put away ample supplies before the attack, but he was running out of everything, and then he would have to move again. Having those supplies available allowed him to heal, but time was upon him.

His mental state was another challenge. Up to the point of the bear attack, this was all a grand adventure. He was healthy, had plenty of gear and the knowledge to use it and thrive in this environment. Once he concluded the search was suspended, he knew he could walk out when he was prepared with enough food. He knew his family was worried, but in his mind, their anxiety would end in a matter of days. Old Ephraim ended it all when he almost tore off Boone's right leg.

Now, his rescue went from weeks to months, if at all. He played the scene out many times in his head. It was day thirty-seven when he left the cabin to walk out. He expected to be back in Fairbanks and this over on day forty-five or forty-six. It would be just one more adventure in the Taggart Family pantheon of epics. They wouldn't have had time to process the possibility he was gone for good.

Now, his friends and family would begin to conclude it was over, he was dead.

What implications does that carry with it?

Can Abby have me declared dead?

How long does someone have to be missing to be declared dead?

Would she remarry?

That peckerwood at the home supply store flirted with her every time they stopped for supplies. He's just the kind of guy that

211

would want me dead.

What if she spends the insurance money, and then I turn up?

"Alright, that's enough," Boone yelled out loud.

This doesn't get me anywhere.

Work the problem.

Keep your mind in the middle.

The one thought haunting him throughout the experience was his family grieving his death, and he was ashamed because of the pain it caused. Pain, he brought on them by his failure.

Three weeks later, Boone's self-imposed physical therapy had paid off. He removed the splint and sling from his left arm and had close to full range of motion. Although he felt muscle atrophy, he could improve his strength in time. His leg finally started to heal. It was easier to walk to the stream a hundred yards from the cabin. He'd learned to use the snowshoe on his good leg to press the snow in front of his bad one to stabilize his walking. But it was obvious, walking was going to be a challenge for a long time. He was almost out of food. Hunting consumed his thoughts.

CHAPTER FORTY
2030 Hours Local-Thursday 24 December 1987
Chapman Homestead-North Pole, Alaska-Day 91

Rachel sat leaning against the stone fireplace hearth, holding a mug of cocoa, running her fingers across the coarse hair of the brown bear rug on the floor. She listened to the stories that made up the Chapman Family's oral history. Like her family, the Chapmans were more an ancient tribe than a family. The consistent themes of the story were separation, sacrifice, and hardship, oddly looked at in hindsight with nostalgia. Chappie's time in Europe and Burma during the war, Elizabeth's experience during the Battle of Britain, Bart's tours in Southeast Asia, loss of friends, and the challenges of the Alaskan wilderness. This family had lived large, and they reveled in recounting their history. Rachel couldn't stop smiling because it was so familiar. She grew up hearing similar stories, in some cases they included the people sitting in the den. Now, with her first Christmas away from home, she was building her own story and adding to the tribe's lore.

Chappie stood center stage in the living room, regaling his grandchildren with a story of flying Christmas presents to children in post-war Europe. Elizabeth delivered cups of eggnog. She began organizing the family for gift opening, which quickly diverted the children's attention from grandpa to their grandmother. Bart donned his Santa Claus hat and began to pass out gifts at his mother's instructions.

"I'll finish the story later," Chappie said as he patted Elizabeth on the butt.

"Sorry, love, I want to see what you got me this year," she said.

Bart passed out gifts, and in a mad minute of paper tearing, screams of childish delight, smiles, tears, and hugs, the wait was over,

213

and the presents revealed. Rachel relished the moment and felt a deep wave of gratitude for this second family that took her in when she needed them. She'd vowed, at least to herself, she wouldn't leave Alaska until she knew her father's fate and knew she would be unimaginably lonely fulfilling the vow if not for the Chapmans.

"Bart, there's one more package," Chappie said as he pointed to the tree. On hands and knees, Bart crawled beneath the tree and retrieved the final gift, reading the tag and handing the box to Rachel.

"You didn't have to buy me gifts," Rachel said, tearing into the wrapping paper like a kid.

"It's from all of us," Chappie said.

Rachel tore the box open to reveal the soft, broken-in leather of an Air Force flight jacket. Her name was embossed in gold lettering on the left side. She paused to look at it momentarily before lifting it from the box. She grew up seeing Grandpa Clark in his, and Chappie and Bart wore theirs daily. This was more than a Christmas gift. It was an initiation into the community of flyers.

"Every pilot worth their salt should have a flight jacket," Bart said as he hugged her.

"Thank you all so much," Rachel said. She pulled the jacket on, a perfect fit, and zipped it up.

"It only has your name on it now," Chappie said. "You'll add the wings, squadron patches, and so on. It'll eventually take on your personality."

"I will, I promise. Thank you again," Rachel said. She hugged each member of the family.

Bart and Susan organized their children to get home for bed and another round of gifts in the morning. Chappie put his favorite Dean Martin Christmas album on the stereo, leaned back in his recliner, and snored within a minute. Elizabeth looked at Rachel, laughed, and shook her head.

When the crooner sang the first notes of *Silent Night*, Rachel stepped out on the deck adjacent to the living room and closed the door. Standing against the rail, she looked up at the northern lights and cried. Snow crunched beneath light steps. Elizabeth put her arm around Rachel's shoulder.

"They're quite magnificent, aren't they?" Elizabeth said, looking at the lights in the Arctic sky.

"Yes, ma'am, they are."

"What're you thinking about, dear?" Elizabeth said.

"Tradition." Rachel leaned her head on the shoulder of her surrogate grandmother.

The family's matriarchs were determined to lean on long-standing Christmas traditions to bring stability back to their world. Abby said she didn't want to celebrate this year and mentioned to Roan maybe he could spend the holidays with a buddy closer to Fort Campbell or his girlfriend's family. Alice and Rebecca were having none of it. It was to be a traditional Clark-Taggart Family Christmas. Now with the family around the harvest table in Rebecca's dining room, Abby was grateful she'd listened to them. After Wade said grace, they ate, talked, enjoyed one another's company, and shared their common family stories. Boone was at the center of many of this year's remembrances.

"Did Dad ever tell you the Silent Night story?" Roan said.

"No, he didn't," Rebecca said.

"I know the story," Abby smiled at the memory.

"Tell it, son," Hoot said.

"He told me this story when I was probably in high school," Roan said. "And I've never thought about it again until I flew home the other day. On Dad's first tour in Vietnam, and his first Christmas away from home, a Catholic chaplain flew into their camp in the Central Highlands and held a midnight Mass. Not being Catholic, Dad took radio watch in the Command Bunker so his buddies could attend. He was alone in the bunker, so he tuned a transistor radio to Armed Forces Network, sat on a stool at the bunker's door, watched the stars, and waited for his buddies to return. At midnight, *Silent Night* came over the radio, and Dad sat on that stool looking up at the stars and cried. He'd probably kill me if he knew I told you all the story."

215

"No, he wouldn't," Abby said. "I'll add to the story. I don't think he would mind at all. It shows a side of your father you didn't see often. Every Christmas Eve at midnight since that year, he went outside and listened to or sang *Silent Night*. It was his favorite Christmas tradition."

They sat in silence for a moment, and then Abby began to sing, *"Silent night, holy night…"*

The family joined in the song.

2030 Hours Local-Thursday 24 December 1987
Taggart's Station

Earlier in the day, Boone replaced his crutches with walking sticks. He was moving better now but still with difficulty. He could stand long enough to cut firewood and was walking short distances. He hunted rabbits and ptarmigan close to camp and trapped beavers under the ice of a nearby pond. He saw plenty of moose sign and an occasional caribou track. Meat was running low again. He had to hunt.

He sat next to the fire and prepared his last cup of coffee. He saved the last of the coffee, whiskey, and Copenhagen for a Christmas Eve celebration. While the water warmed, he pulled the brown bear hide onto his lap and started the work which consumed his thoughts for several weeks. Early in his isolation, he was so busy performing the tasks for physical survival he gave little thought to reflecting on the past or planning for the future. He was spending more time in the cabin as the temperatures dropped, and as snow increased, his mind drifted back to earlier winters and settled on December nineteen fifty-eight.

He closed his eyes and remembered sitting beside Luther in the warmth of his lodge, drinking hot cocoa and watching him work. Luther experienced so much injustice, racism, and unfairness in his life. He had no opportunity to live the free life his people experienced in his grandfather's generation. But there was no outward bitterness or resentment. He simply lived his life. He found peace. *How does a man who experienced so much bad not become bitter?* Luther was generally a happy and content man. *How did he do that?* His history wasn't a

216

source of turmoil. It was his comfort, a source of solace. He saw himself as part of the circle, a part of the bigger history of his people.

Boone began at the center of the grizzly hide and worked his way out in a circle.

Where do I start, and what do I include?

He mixed the last of his coffee, held the warm metal cup in his hands, savored the warm liquid and thought. Then he set the cup aside, having decided where it all started, and drew a picture of a bear, a boy, and an Ogallala warrior.

Drawing the image created other ideas in his mind: his marriage to Abby, the year that he became a Green Beret, Luther's death, each tour in Vietnam, each friend he lost, the birth of each of his children, his sister's murder, the fall of Saigon, and the Susitna River trip with Dan, his retirement, Roan joining the Army, the hunting trip that brought him to this valley and the bear attack. At some point in the future, he would record his rescue, being reunited with his friends and family, grandchildren, and many other happy and tragic events. It would be his tribe's history in pictures, his first Winter Count.

He lay the hide aside and considered the story to this point. Luther was right. It goes in cycles. He poured the last shot of whiskey and packed the final dip of snuff in his lip. He smiled and then chuckled.

Abigail will be pleased to find out I finally quit this nasty habit.

He looked at his Rolex, 2355 hours. Five *more minutes,* he thought. He struggled to stay awake. This was a long-standing tradition. He looked at his watch, 2400 hours, and started to sing.

"Silent Night, Holy Night..."

217

Resurrection

"I walk in the shoes of the men of today. I fly their planes, I eat their food, but my heart is in the wilderness with feathers in my hair."
Louis L'Amour—Last of the Breed

CHAPTER FORTY-ONE
0900 Hours Local-Sunday 17 April 1988
Taggart Ranch-Sheridan County, Wyoming-Day 206

Abby stood at the kitchen sink of her recently remodeled stone farmhouse, watching Wade put Caroline and her new cow pony through the paces in the round pen. The Taggart grandparents became increasingly protective and indulgent since Boone disappeared. One of the results of their overindulgence was prancing around the pen in the form of a gelding named Little Sorrel—a Christmas gift from Grandma and Grandpa Taggart, but not the only horse in the remuda. Not to be outdone, the Clark side of the family added a four-year-old bay mare named Dollar to the mix. Other animals were added to the ranch as Caroline assembled a small flock of Targhee sheep, a three-cow herd of Texas Longhorns, and two Scottish Highland heifers, all masked as 4-H projects. The responsibility of a small-scale rancher helped to occupy Caroline's thoughts and time as she adjusted to her loss. The exposure to life close to the land fit her well. She showed an innate talent for ranching, land stewardship, and animal husbandry.

Her daughter's newfound place also focused Abby's thoughts from the loss of the love of her life to the joy of a blossoming young girl and the love of parents and parents-in-law. Abby was grateful. Everyone faces tragedy in life, but the blessed have people around them to hold them up through their misfortunes. Once the rescue party returned from Alaska, the Taggart and Clark patriarchs and matriarchs took up a new mission—pull the family through another catastrophe. Decades of combined service exposed both lines of the family to deep tragedy. They'd all lost friends and family, and they'd helped dozens of others through the process of loss. Now it was their turn, and as was their character, Wade Taggart and Hoot Clark had to act, they had to fix. So, they fell in on Abby and the children and pulled them through.

Abby's thoughts were broken by her mother-in-law's voice.

"Where do you want these, dear?" she asked, holding a box marked 'linens and towels.'

"Just drop them in the hallway, Mom. I'll put them on the shelf in the hall closet later."

"This is the last box," Rebecca said. "You're officially moved in."

"Thankfully."

"This place sure did turn out nice. I didn't think it would ever look this good after being gutted and sitting empty as long as it did, but it looks great."

"It sure does," Abby said. "I really appreciate you and Wade letting us stay in the guest house for so long, but it's wonderful to have a permanent place of our own. Lord willing, we won't have to move in three to four years."

The sound of gravel crunching beneath tires drifted through the open kitchen window. It was a glorious, bright spring day. Abby enjoyed the breeze through the house and the sun's warmth. The season was beginning to change.

She approached the window and saw her parents, Hoot and Alice Clark, parked at the round pen, watching Caroline and Wade work Little Sorrel. She and Rebecca walked outside to meet them.

"She's turned into quite a cowgirl," Hoot said. His pride was obvious when he kissed his daughter.

"Yes, she is, and apparently, she knows it because she has developed the typical Taggart-Clark self-confidence," Abby said.

"Don't worry," Alice said. "She has time to develop some humility. Right now, she needs the confidence."

"You're right."

"Have you heard from Roan and Rachel lately?"

"I talked to Roan last night," Abby said. "He's doing great, loving life, getting ready to be promoted. He should be home on leave in August. I talked to Rachel last week. She's working on her hours to get her Commercial Rating and start flying for money. She said she doesn't do anything but work, fly, sleep, and eat."

"That should keep her out of trouble," Hoot said.

"It should, but she's different now," Abby said. "She's so serious. She seems," Abby paused, "old."

"The circumstances made her that way, Abby. It's just life," Hoot said. "Being thrown into difficulty at her age tends to shorten one's youth. It happened to me and your mom, also Wade, and Rebecca, because of depression and war, and to you and Boone because of war. That's life."

"I wanted her to enjoy her young years," Abby said. "She's just eighteen, and she acts like she's fifty. I talked to Elizabeth Chapman, and she said Rachel doesn't go out, she's not dating, no social life. Just flying and work, that's it."

"Honey, sometimes people find themselves, their calling, in adversity and sorrow," Alice said. "Look at Caroline there. She's flourishing—she found something she loves, and maybe that's the case with Rachel. Maybe she's mature beyond her years, but it will serve her well. The opposite would be tragic. Rachel's on a journey to become the woman she wants to be. It's tough, but you must allow her to take the journey."

"I know. I'm just worried about them," Abby said.

"You're their mother," Alice and Rebecca said in unison.

Caroline led Little Sorrel through the round pen gate and into the barn where she curried him, put feed and hay in the feeder, and then turned him out in the outer corral. She sat on the top fence rail and watched him until he finished eating and trotted into the pasture, jumping, and twisting in the new grass. When she finished her chores in the barn, she joined the rest of the family in the kitchen. She hung her jacket on the hook in the entryway and pulled off her muddy boots and addressed her mother.

"Mom, we need to decide on a brand for this outfit," Caroline said.

Abigail smiled hearing her father-in-law's voice from a twelve-year-old girl's mouth. "Alright, what're your thoughts on the topic?"

"How about 5T?" Caroline said. "Get it? The five Taggart's."

"I get it, honey. I think that's a great idea."

221

"I know a blacksmith who can make you a brand," Wade said. "I'll talk to him tomorrow."

"Well, that's settled, it's the 5T," Abby said.

The previous day was the first full day Abigail Taggart didn't shed tears since Wade called with the tragic news the previous September. She was fighting hard to keep them at bay. She had to keep moving forward.

1015 Hours Local-Sunday 17 April 1988
Fairbanks International Airport, Alaska

Bart "Yeti" Chapman filled two coffee mugs and sat at the table across from a concentrating Rachel Taggart. He slid the white China mug emblazoned with Master Parachutist wings on one side and "Captain Boone Taggart" on the other.

"I found this in some of your dad's stuff in the office," he said. "I figured he would want you to have it."

Rachel looked at the mug and smiled. "I remember this. Uncle Dan gave it to him when we were stationed up here," she said. "He wouldn't mind if I borrowed it for a while. I used to use it when I was still at home. Thanks, Yeti. I appreciate this."

Bart didn't miss her point about using the mug on loan. He'd thought about saying something to her for a while and couldn't bring himself to crush her hopes. But it was a hard winter in the interior, and he'd lost faith that Boone was still alive.

"Rachel, I've put off saying something to you, but…" She cut him off.

"Don't, Bart," Rachel said. "I'm not giving up. Not yet. I'm not naive. I know there's a possibility he's been dead for months, but I'm not giving up yet. I'll know when. I appreciate your concern and can't thank you enough for all the Chapmans have done for me. I'll never forget it."

"Truth be told, you gave more than you got in return," Bart said. "We're glad to have you here. What're you working on?"

"Logbooks, ratings, and endorsements. I was working on a plan before I came to talk to you and Chappie," she said.

222

"Shoot. What do you have so far?"

"I'm finished with my instrument rating, tail wheel, and complex endorsements," she said. "I don't have enough hours yet to get my Commercial Rating, but I want to start on my floatplane ticket in the next few weeks. I should have enough hours to work on my commercial by mid-summer, and I also want to work on my multi-engine rating this summer. Thoughts?"

"My thoughts are I've never seen anyone dig into flying like you have and accomplish so much so fast. Well, except me, of course," he said, smiling. "It sounds good to me. We'll have a floatplane here in the next couple of weeks, so we'll work on that endorsement. Keep putting in the hours, and we can work your Commercial and multi-engine tickets over the summer, but it may take longer. Things are about to get busy around here with the weather improving."

"Good deal," Rachel said, packing her gear.

"Now work. After you get the daily operations going here, I need you to fly out to Eagle with some new parts and return the old ones, please. You don't mind flying, do you?" he chuckled.

"No sir, I'll get right on that," She said, heading to the office.

*****

Boone pulled the beaver fur collar up to shield the back of his neck from the north wind blowing across the snow fields. He glassed the hillsides of the valley that had been home for over two hundred days. The bears were beginning to come out of dens and move around, and he needed meat, fat, and more fur. Spring had come to the Arctic, and with it, the miseries of breakup, the thaw-freeze cycle, overflow streams, soft ice on the lakes, and the first mosquitoes. With the aggravations though came warmer temperatures and longer days. It was time to move.

The winter brought ancient challenges and ancient solutions as well. His main efforts were focused on fire, water, food, and shelter. His entire life conformed to the pace of hundreds of generations before him—cutting wood for fire, improving shelter to have a place to live, hunting and fishing to feed himself, finding water to drink, and

223

recording his tribe's history. This ancient daily life was completely different from his modern daily life—paying bills, making phone calls, watching TV, and a hundred other meaningless tasks. If it wasn't for his intense love for his family he could stay, but staying would be selfish.

Boone spent a good deal of time during the previous winter considering how he could replicate this once his family knew he was safe and alive.

I wonder if they've had a funeral.

He'd always lived close to the land, closer to nature than most of his peers. Not everyone who soldiered was an outdoorsman or a gun guy, but he was, and he gravitated to others who were. Like everyone else, he was wrapped up in all the trappings of modern life, but the convenience and innovations left him empty. He ached to think about what his family was experiencing. He couldn't have survived on the other side of this situation if the roles were reversed.

But a great blessing had come with the tragedy. He found peace again in the wide-open wilderness. He slept better, his mind was clear, there were no nightmares, and the forced sobriety proved invaluable. For the first time in decades, he was at peace. Like his father told him, quiet was easy, creating peace is more difficult. He'd created peace in this frozen, lonely valley but it was incomplete. Were it not for the absence of his family…but he missed them terribly.

It's all quite confusing.

He'd given little thought to the logistics of rescue until the last two weeks, but now he was working on projects which would get him back to his family. He'd spent the previous two weeks cutting trees to construct a raft. By mid-winter, he decided a raft was the most plausible course of action for success. His leg had healed, but he still had limited range of motion in his knee. Thus, a seventy-mile walk would take him weeks at the rate he could walk, while a float would be a matter of days down the Charley River into the Yukon. Both rivers were highways for pilots, and he might be found by a passing aircraft or a boat. If he wasn't found, he could float to Circle, Fort Yukon, or the Dalton Highway bridge and catch a ride back to Fairbanks. If all went well, he could be in Fairbanks a few days after launching.

Four hundred yards away, he saw movement. It was time to hunt.

CHAPTER FORTY-TWO
1400 Hours Local-Sunday 1 May 1988
Chapman Aviation Hangar-Eagle, Alaska-Day 220

Rachel smiled from ear to ear when she stepped out of the cockpit of her red and white Piper Super Cub and saw Chappie walking to meet her. With a combination of saved money on her part, "grants" from both grandfathers, and grace from a seller Chappie had a long history with. Rachel was a new aircraft owner. The airplane came on the market suddenly. She hadn't thought ownership possible then, but "strike while the iron is hot," Grandpa Wade said, so she did. It was cheap because it was trashed when she bought it. This airplane was a barn find. Bart and Chappie helped her put it back together and upgrade what needed fixing by loaning the time of their mechanics after hours and getting the bird airworthy and certified.

"Beautiful bird," Chappie said. "What're you going to call her?"

"I'll call her *Revenant* since we brought her back from the dead."

"Good name."

Chappie helped her tie the Piper down on the tarmac and put his arm around her as they walked to the hangar office. Rachel had become part of his family over the past several months, and now, he couldn't imagine their life without her.

Rachel stowed her gear in the back room, stepped into the hangar, inspected, and weighed the half dozen boxes she would carry back to Fairbanks the following morning. Satisfied with their condition and knowing the weight of each, she pulled them to her plane on a flat cart and loaded them, making sure they were secured correctly.

Chappie stepped down from the de Havilland DHC-7 Caribou the mechanics were working on.

"Can I buy you supper tonight, Rachel?"

"You mean, can you warm me a can of beans on the hot plate in the office?"

"I might be able to do a little better than that," Chappie said. "How about it?"

"Absolutely."

Chappie's Eagle Airport operation dispatcher stepped out of the office and waved Rachel over. "Hey, Rachel, Rick's in the office. He needs to talk to you."

Rachel stepped into the office. "What's up?"

"A few days ago, I went through Jimmy Regan's personal effects in his desk and found something that might help the search for your dad. It's probably nothing, and I almost didn't say anything. I don't want you hurt if it doesn't pan out."

"What is it?" she said.

"I found a business card from a fly shop in Fairbanks," he said. "Jimmy did some guiding for the guy a few years ago. When I saw the card, I remembered how much your dad talked about landing a trophy grayling. I thought the guy at the fly shop might know some of the places Jimmy took clients for big grayling. It's probably nothing, but there it is."

He handed her the business card.

Midnight Sun Fly Shop
Fairbanks, Alaska
Michael Hanson, Owner

"Thanks, Rick. I appreciate this. It might help. I'll let you know."

She threw her arms around his neck, thanked him again, and left the office. Trotting into the hangar, she yelled at Chappie.

"Hey Chappie, I need to take a rain check for supper. I've got to get back to Fairbanks tonight to check on something. See you in a few days."

227

She waved as she left the hangar without slowing down. Chappie waved to her backside as she left. She pre-flighted her Piper, took off, and headed west to Fairbanks.

0912 Hours Local-Tuesday 3 May 1988
Taggart's Station-Day 222

"It floats."

He constructed the raft to sit well above the water so the deck would only be awash due to waves or faster currents. Six large driftwood logs formed the lowest level of the raft, the flotation. Perpendicular to those were lashed six more smaller logs. Across the second layer of logs was a layer of small poles lashed side by side to form the deck.

A sweep on the bow and stern was positioned so he could stand in the middle and use both simultaneously. He saw this configuration on a drift boat in Idaho years ago, and it worked well. He lashed his gear to the deck, his rucksack wrapped in the waterproof material from his chest waders, a tarp wrapped with thirty pounds of dried and smoked meat, his bearskin bedroll, and Winchester Model 70 rifle. He packed specific survival gear in his vest pockets, fire-making kit, fishing kit, a pound or so of jerky, and wore his gun belt with his Ruger Super Blackhawk, spare ammo, and hunting knife. Finally, he slung his Remington 870 shotgun over his back. He didn't want to be left with nothing if he went into the water and lost the raft and his gear. He wasn't worried about the raft sinking—he was confident sinking the beast was impossible, but it could break apart, and he didn't want to be stranded again without gear.

He used a diamond willow walking stick to help stabilize his walk up the hill to his cabin. He stepped into the small structure that was his island since September and felt the coals of the fire to ensure they were completely cold. He took the small notebook from his vest, pulled a page out, placed it on the log beside the fireplace, left, and closed the door. He stood in front of the cabin and took one more look.

It would be best if you were ecstatic right now, Boone.

But he would miss this place. He walked back to the raft,

228

pushed the walking staff beneath the tie downs, untied the rawhide bowline, stepped aboard, and pulled the sweeps, launching the raft into the current. Once in the middle of the stream, he watched the cabin as the raft drifted around the first bend in the river. Boone was going back to the world.

CHAPTER FORTY-THREE
0910 Hours Local-Tuesday 3 May 1988
Midnight Sun Fly Shop-Fairbanks, Alaska-Day 222

The bell rang when she opened the door of the shop. The place had the feel of an old country general store. It reminded her of the place where her grandparents took her in western North Carolina. It was part of the ancestral returns to southern Appalachia her family still observed, a method to keep peace with the family for being the clan nomads.

"Hello, I'm Mike, the owner. How can I help you?"

The thirty-ish man was tall and athletic with blond hair and beard. He had a youthful gait, but his speech and eyes suggested someone with a lot of experience for his age, an old soul. He was dressed more like a logger than a fishing guide—faded blue Carhartt loggers, green and black plaid flannel, red suspenders, White's Smokejumper boots, and a green and white Orvis cap.

"Hi, Mike. I'm Rachel Taggart, and I don't need any fishing gear."

"I hate to hear that," he chuckled.

"I don't mean that," she said. "I'm sure I will later in the summer, but I'm looking for information."

"Sure," Mike said. "How can I help?"

"Last fall, my father went missing around Eagle. We found the plane he was in, unfortunately the pilot, Jimmy Regan, didn't make it but my father wasn't in the plane when we got there. The search was suspended after a few weeks. Yesterday, one of the guys at Chapman Aviation found one of your business cards on Jimmy's desk. I thought there might be some connection with your shop, and maybe you could help me."

"I heard about Jimmy's crash," he said. "That was terrible. He was a wonderful person. He guided me a few times, and I flew into a lot of really great places with him. We made some good memories together. I hate he's gone, but I'm unsure how to help."

"The guy who gave me your business card said on the morning Jimmy went to pick up my dad, he said something about finding him a trophy grayling. Maybe you might know some of the lakes or streams in the area where Jimmy fished."

Her voice cracked as she talked.

"Did you say your last name was Taggart?" he said. "What was your father's name?"

"Boone Taggart, and he's still alive," Rachel said, her voice steady again.

"I'm sorry, Rachel. I didn't mean to imply he was gone. I can point out some of the lakes in the area where Jimmy might've dropped him, but I'm warning you, there's a bunch of them."

"It's alright," she said. "It would narrow the search. That's been the problem so far. Too big an area."

"You got a map?" He asked.

"Yeah, hang on, let me get one from the truck."

She returned with an aviation sectional of eastern Alaska and spread it on the glass-top counter. Mike taped a clear acetate document cover over the map and used a red marker to circle twenty-one lakes that might hold the kind of fish Boone was looking for.

"There you go. I hope that helps."

"This is great," Rachel said, smiling. "This is the most information I've had since the search was suspended. I'll let you know how it turns out."

"Rachel. I hope you find your dad. He's a good man." Mike said, pointing to a black and white framed photo on the wall behind the counter.

A photo of a group of young men in green fatigues, wearing maroon berets, smiling into the camera. Penciled at the bottom of the photo was "C/4-23 Infantry, Malamute Drop Zone, October 1975." Standing in the front row, center with his arm around a younger Michael Hanson, was her father smiling at her. Tears ran down her cheek. Mike put his arm around her shoulder.

"I remember that day," she said. "It was the family day jump. We all came out to the Drop Zone, watched the company jump, and then had lunch. I remember, and you were there."

"I signed into the unit two days after your dad took command," Mike said. "He was the best soldier I ever served with, and if anyone can walk out of the wilderness, it's him. He taught me so much about leadership and soldiering. He finished my education as a man. There's just no better. When you find him, bring him by. I'd love to thank him for everything he did for me."

Rachel hugged him, wiped the tears from her eyes, and found more resolve than she had for months. "I will. Thank you so much, Mike."

1210 Hours Local-Tuesday 3 May 1988
Fairbanks International Airport, Alaska

The three flyers stood before the aviation sectional on the hangar's wall. Chappie and Bart were concentrating on the acetate overlay taped to the map, listening to Rachel.

"I'll admit it was always an outside chance," Rachel said. "But there's at least the possibility Jimmy dropped Dad at one of these locations to catch the grayling he wanted so badly while Jimmy serviced the cache sites. He got busy, forgot to transmit Dad's location, or maybe had radio trouble. Therefore, Dad's location was lost when Jimmy was killed. There was no reason to look in these places then, but now we've narrowed the search."

"There are several lakes ninety miles from where we were searching," Chappie said.

"But some are close to the search area. We didn't have any reason to go there and then, we found the crash site," Rachel said. "which focused the search in the east of the sector."

"It's worth trying," Chappie said. "Let's get back after it tomorrow. It may be a Chapman only operation. I don't know if it's enough evidence for the SAR community to re-launch a mission."

"I'll start making some arrangements," Bart said. "We'll launch from here this afternoon and stage out of Eagle. We can start

232

looking at each one of these lakes."

"Can I borrow the phone to call home, please? Both of my grandfathers will want to be in on this," Rachel said.

CHAPTER FORTY-FOUR
0600 Hours Local-Thursday 5 May 1988
Chapman Aviation Hangar-Eagle, Alaska-Day 224

Rachel was correct. Wade and Hoot wanted in on the search. Wade, Hoot, and Abby took red-eye flights out of Denver the same day and were now huddled around the map-covered table in the Chapman hangar, collaborating on the day's search. Chappie was correct. Due to a lack of evidence, resources, and existing operations, the SAR community was sitting this one out. The Chapman Aviation family would have to figure it out alone. Rachel, Bart, and Chappie had searched three lakes the previous day and found no additional evidence. They could expand now with one more pilot.

Chappie started the briefing. "We'll conduct an aerial search of these lakes, but we also need to land and look for evidence if Boone was there. Hoot will be in a Super Cub, Rachel and Wade in her aircraft, and Bart and I'll be in the Beaver on floats. Call us if you get to a lake and don't have a place to put it down, and we'll land on the lake and search. We'll each look at three areas and then back here. We'll be close enough to talk, so if you see something, holler. There's plenty of help. Check the weather and let's taxi in fifteen. Any questions?"

Chappie pulled Wade and Hoot off to the side privately, away from Abby and Rachel. "I don't want to be seen as insensitive or morbid, but with the warming weather, keep your eyes open for flocks of ravens or other predators. Understand what I'm trying to say?" The two experienced men nodded their heads.

The pilots secured their gear and turned for the flight line when Abby stopped them. "Wait. Come here. All of you," she said.

They gathered around her.

"Please be careful," Abby said "Don't take too much risk. Rachel, I'm looking at you. I can't take another loss. I'm used up. Let's say a little prayer before you go."

They stood in a circle, joined hands, and bowed. Hoot prayed.

"I love you all," Abby said as they left.

***

Boone beached the raft, secured the bowline to a large stump, collected his gear, and started camp. He was exhausted. He estimated he'd traveled thirty river miles, but it wasn't easy. The spring melt clogged the river with trees and stumps. It felt like he'd cut a hundred cords of wood just clearing enough debris to pass downstream. Too many times, he grounded on a sandbar and wrestled the raft for hours to break it free. It was a heavier craft than he anticipated. Until he moved it by hand, he didn't realize how heavy it was. The raft was solid but also unwieldy. It wasn't as nimble as a canoe, and there were many obstacles he couldn't avoid, but he was making progress. He guessed he was likely one-third of the way to the Charley and Yukon confluence. Depending on the conditions, three or four days to the Yukon.

He boiled water, threw debris over a drift log for shelter, and ate caribou jerky. He was too tired to fish today, and he hurt all over. Standing on the raft all day, and constantly shifting his weight, racked him with pain. But he was moving. He drank water, pulled the bearskin blanket over him, and instantly fell asleep.

CHAPTER FORTY-FIVE
1400 Hours-Sunday 8 May 1988
Chapman Aviation Hangar-Eagle, Alaska-Day 227

"All right. Listen up," Chappie said, as he started the morning briefing. "Today, we look at the last six lakes. We keep the same flight assignments. Here are the locations I want each of you to search."

He pointed to the map and waited for each pilot to confirm.

"If we have nothing at the end of today, we'll have a meeting tonight to discuss our next step, but let's not get ahead of ourselves. Search these areas closely. Don't miss anything. The weather that grounded us this morning has cleared to the east, so we should be good to go the rest of the day and for the next two to three days. Questions?"

In ten minutes, all three aircraft were airborne and heading west.

***

Rachel put the lake off the left wingtip and circled, looking for anything evident from the air.

"I don't see anything from up here, Rach. Let's find a sandbar we can put down on and walk back, take a look," Wade said.

"Copy," Rachel said, over the intercom.

She flew over the riverbed at two hundred feet, found a suitable sandbar, circled and landed. She positioned the Piper for takeoff on the downwind side and tied down to logs and rocks. Wade shouldered his rucksack and pulled his Marlin Model 1895 lever gun from behind the seat. They waded across the stream and started up the hill to the lake, four hundred yards east. When they arrived at the lake, Wade stood at the water's edge and looked around.

Rachel watched him. *He's trying to figure something out.*

"What're you doing, grandpa?" she said.

"I'm trying to recreate what he would've done when he arrived. That'll narrow down where to look for signs."

"Do you think you can track him?" she said.

"Probably not. Tracks would've long ago faded, but there might be other signs around."

Rachel began to look, too, although she didn't know what she was looking for.

Walking the water's edge for ten minutes, Wade stopped. "Right here."

He reached down and picked up the purple egg-sucking leech fly. "I tied this fly," he said. "This is the lake where Jimmy dropped him."

"Are you sure you tied that fly? Aren't these pretty popular? Anyone could've tied it."

"I tied that fly, little girl."

He took a strip of orange engineer tape from his vest and tied it to a bush where he found the fly. "OK, Luther. Where'd my boy go from here," he whispered to himself.

Wade moved fifty yards to the northeast on high ground and looked around. Rachel watched in fascination.

"Rachel, there's some trees three hundred yards or so north of here. I'll bet dollars to donuts it's where Boone spent his first night."

"What makes you think so?" she said.

"It's the closest cover, got him out of the weather, near water to drink and fish to eat. He wouldn't have stayed out in the open. Come on."

He started moving north at a brisk pace. Rachel was having trouble keeping up. She'd never seen him so focused.

He must've been a badass when he was young. If it wasn't for the seriousness of the situation, she would swear he was having the time of his life. When he stepped into the wood line, Wade stopped and looked around again. "There," he said, pointing.

"There, what? Where?" Rachel said.

"Right there," Wade said, moving deeper into the trees. "He

237

burned a long fire right here to stay warm. It was turning cold by the time we were pulling out. This fire lay is great for keeping you warm overnight. Look at this. See how the limbs are cut from these two trees up to about head height? And then they're stacked under one tree, not both. Somebody cut them and stacked them. Now, look at the pine boughs stacked between these two trees. You can barely see them now, but those were put there on purpose as a mattress, and I bet..." He paused and looked at the two trees closer. "Yep, look here. The rope burns on the tree about waist high. He slept under a poncho right here between these two trees."

"Are you sure, grandpa?"

"Really?" Wade said. "Now, you're losing faith. You're the reason we're standing here, girl. I'm pretty sure your dad would've fished until he knew Jimmy wasn't coming back that day, camped here, and waited the next day. But he wouldn't have stayed here knowing a storm was coming. He would've needed better shelter. Let's get back in the air and call it in. We can fly over this area and look more closely, and the other guys can come help."

In thirty minutes, Wade and Rachel were back in the air. The other two crews were inbound to help as they circled the area.

Rachel flew increasingly larger concentric circles at three hundred feet. "Grandpa. Take a look at what looks like a brush pile on the left wingtip."

"Whatever that is, it didn't happen by accident," Wade said. "A human put it together. Find us a place back on the river to land."

In ten minutes, they were on the ground.

Wade wouldn't wait. He moved up the hill, while Hoot landed on the same sandbar, met Rachel, and followed. Bart and Chappie circled overhead. Wade was three hundred yards ahead of Rachel and Hoot when he arrived at the shelter. It was a solid debris shelter but old, months old. It hadn't been used in a while. There was a fish-smoking rack a few yards from the shelter. It was confirmation Boone had lived there.

"Right there," Wade said. "That's Boone," pointing to the fire pit. "It's not a circle like most people build. It's a "C" shape with one open side and the back taller than the sides. It drafts better. Luther taught him on a canoe trip in Canada."

He looked around, saw an open area fifty yards north, and started moving again. "They'll be a signal of some kind in the field," Wade said.

They stepped into the field and saw the three tripods.

"How did you know that?" Rachel said.

"Your dad was trained to do that," Hoot said. "He was here."

"He sure was," Wade said. "But he didn't spend the whole winter here. This hasn't been lived in for months."

"Honey, your daddy didn't die in a plane crash last fall," Hoot said. "He was here fishing. Jimmy must've set him down here to find his fish, forgot to call it in, or had radio trouble and couldn't call it in before he crashed."

"We probably should head back to Eagle, refuel, and re-provision for a ground search starting tomorrow morning," Wade said. "What do you think?"

"I concur," Hoot said.

CHAPTER FORTY-SIX
0800 Hours Local-Monday 9 May 1988
Confluence of the Charley and Yukon Rivers-Day 228

Boone topped off his water bottle, packed his gear on the raft, and stepped to the edge of the Yukon River. "My Lord, that sucker's running fast."

Not only was the river running fast, but entire uprooted trees were floating past him. It was an intimidating sight, and for a moment, Boone thought of staying put, setting up signals, and waiting for a plane or boat to come by. Too many people got killed trying to get home, but he had no idea when someone would come along. He had to move. To take his chances on the river. After all, his family already thought he was dead.

Who Dares Wins!

He slung the shotgun over his back and pulled the raft into the current. With a little luck, he would be in Circle tomorrow, maybe even tonight.

***

Rachel, Hoot, and Wade stood at the debris shelter, ready to start a ground search.

"Here are my thoughts," Wade said. "Check my math. Boone would've stayed put for a long time on the assumption Jimmy called in his location. Even when he figured out maybe Jimmy didn't call it in, he would've stayed because it's easier to find a stationary target than a moving one. He knew we were looking for him."

"But we were looking in the wrong place almost a hundred miles away," Rachel said.

"Rach, we were going on the best information we had at the time," Hoot said. "That's all we could do. Don't beat yourself up."

"But he knew he needed a better shelter to last longer than a few days," Wade said. "This shelter got him through the first storm, and if he built a better shelter, it would be close. He would want to be near where he was dropped off, believing we would eventually look here. There's another shelter close."

Bart and Chappie were overhead, flying in increasingly larger circles. The radio squawked as Wade started moving southwest through the trees to where he thought Boone might've built.

"Wade, this is Chappie, over."

"Go, Chappie."

"We found a cabin. It's really small, but we're circling the site now. Start heading our way. Over."

"Roger. I got you. Moving."

"Let's go," Wade said, taking off through the trees.

Ten minutes later, the three stepped into the clearing facing the cabin. Wade and Hoot smiled. Rachel began to cry.

"C'mon girl," Wade said.

With his rifle in front of him, Wade dropped his rucksack, opened the door, and stepped inside. Hoot and Rachel followed.

"This was lived in until recently," Hoot said.

Rachel saw the letter on the log next to the fireplace and picked it up. She dropped to her knees and began to sob, handing the paper to Wade.

To whoever finds this, Greetings,

My name is Boone Taggart, Lieutenant Colonel United States Army (Retired). I was stranded here in September 1987 and have lived in this cabin since. I'm not sure what happened that landed me here this long. Jimmy Regan of Chapman Aviation dropped me here to catch a trophy grayling but never returned. By the way, I caught the grayling but had to eat it. A series of weather events kept me here through October, and when I attempted to walk out in November, I was attacked by a grizzly and severely injured. The bear suffered a far worse fate. I healed over the next several months and have begun my journey to Fairbanks. I built a raft and launched it, heading for the

Yukon River. If you find this, please get in touch with my family in Sheridan County, Wyoming. Thank you, and God bless.

Signed,

> *Boone Taggart*
> *LTC, Infantry*
> *Dated 3 May 1988*

"My Lord, that was just a few days ago," Hoot said.

"That's classic Boone," Wade said.

Wade and Hoot hugged, wiped tears from their eyes, and consoled Rachel.

"C'mon, darling. Let's go find your daddy," Wade said.

As they walked back to the sandbar landing strip, Wade radioed Chappie and briefed him on the next phase of the operation. "Chappie, you, and Bart return to Eagle, pick up Abigail, and meet us in Fairbanks. We're going to fly the river until we find Boone. How copy?"

***

Rachel and Wade were in the lead aircraft, followed by Hoot in another Piper. They followed the Charley River low, one aircraft on each side of the river, flying just above stall speed. At the confluence of the Yukon, they turned west and flew the banks of the river at the same speed and altitude.

CHAPTER FORTY-SEVEN
1150 Hours Local-Monday 9 May 1988
Yukon River-Day 228

Boone pulled the sweeps for everything he was worth and wondered if he wouldn't sleep on the shores of the Bering Strait tonight. He'd dodged several enormous sweeps and sawyers along the banks and worked the raft farther into the main channel. He was almost too busy operating the raft to notice a nearby boat or plane. Had he heard something? He jarred himself out of the concentration it took operating his boat and listened. Just the sound of the river. He pulled at the sweeps again.

No, there it was again.

He dropped the sweeps, turned, and looked behind him as two Piper Super Cubs flew toward him on each side of the river.

CHAPTER FORTY-EIGHT
1150 Hours Local-Monday 9 May 1988
Yukon River-Day 228

"Grandpa!" Rachel said as she depressed the push-to-talk button.

"What?"

"There in the middle of the river. A raft," she screamed.

Wade keyed the radio.

"Hoot, increase your altitude 500 feet and hold in a circle. We may have something here. We're going to check it out."

"Copy," Hoot responded. He saw Rachel turn much too steeply as he added power and altitude.

"Rachel, you're too steep and too slow. Settle down and fly the airplane," he shouted into the microphone.

"I'm with him. Quit trying to hug your daddy and fly the bird." Wade yelled without the assistance of the intercom.

"Copy," Rachel said. She added power, leveled off, and took a deep breath. She turned right in a coordinated turn and flew back down the river at one hundred feet with the raft off the left wing.

"OK, Grandpa, I'm flying the airplane. You confirm it's him."

"Copy."

Wade pulled his binoculars to his eyes, trained them on the raft, and focused on the image of a man standing in the middle of the raft, pulling on both sweeps and grinning. His bearded son looked like he'd just stepped from a Rocky Mountain stream in 1823, but it was him. He was alive. He keyed the push-to-talk button on the radio.

"We found him. It's Boone. I say again. It's Boone."

Rachel couldn't help herself. As she added power and altitude, she glanced out the left window and looked at her father, waving at her and smiling for the first time in over two hundred days.

244

CHAPTER FORTY-NINE
1158 Hours Local-Monday 9 May 1988
Yukon River-Day 228

Boone recognized the yellow and blue paint scheme of Chapman Aviation, but what got his attention was the nearly fatal maneuver of the red and white Piper as it turned to intercept his position. It almost fell out of the sky from two hundred feet as it aggressively banked right over the river and then recovered.

I hope I don't have to go home with the rookie flying that airplane.

As the plane regained control and banked in a more coordinated fashion, he continued pulling on the sweeps, dropping one momentarily to wave. He could see the pilot and could've sworn he saw a brunette ponytail coming out the back of the pilot's ball cap, and he was reasonably sure the backseater was his dad.

That'd be just like him. Boone thought.

The red and white Piper turned one hundred and eighty degrees, flew directly over the raft, and rocked its wings.

They see me.

Both planes lined up on a sandbar one half mile downstream and landed. He began pulling on the sweeps to ground the raft on the same sandbar.

CHAPTER FIFTY
1206 Hours Local-Monday 9 May 1988
Yukon River-Day 228

At the end of the landing run, Rachel applied power and hard left rudder pedal, turning the Piper out of the way of Hoot's approach, one minute behind her. She chopped the power, removed her safety harness, and jumped from the cockpit at a dead run. Wade stepped from the rear seat and joined Hoot as he parked the second Piper.

Boone pulled hard on the sweeps, using the mass of the raft and the current to push the bow onto the beach of an eddy just a few feet out of the river's main current. He retrieved the diamond willow walking stick and stepped onto the beach as Rachel jumped into his arms, nearly upsetting his balance. At first, they said nothing. They simply held one another and cried.

"I knew you weren't dead," Rachel whispered. "I just knew it. I never gave up."

"No, I'm not honey. I love you."

"I love you too, Daddy."

Wade and Hoot made their way across the beach, unable to contain their joy and relief. The two old warriors laughed through tears. Wade was the first to his son. He hugged him and held on.

"You gave us quite a scare, son," Wade whispered as he hugged him.

"I know, Dad. I'm sorry," Boone said. "I should've never gotten out of the plane in the first place. I'm sorry for what I put everyone through."

"Don't ever blame yourself," Wade said. "It just happened. That's the way life is sometimes. What's important is you're safe." He stood back from his son, holding him by the shoulders, and looked into his eyes.

"I love you, boy," Wade said, his voice trembling.

"I love you, Dad. Thanks for coming and getting me."

"Welcome home, son," Hoot said, hugging his son-in-law.

"Thanks, Hoot. It's good to be back," Boone said. "Y'all wouldn't happen to have any coffee, would you?"

"Stand by. I've got some in the plane," Hoot said, turning to retrieve his flight bag.

Rachel and Boone sat on the raft's edge and held one another. She wept. Months of anxiety and fear poured down her face in release. Boone held her in his arms and didn't say anything. He held her, relishing the moment he'd dreamed of so many times. Wade stood beside them, with his hand on Boone's shoulder, looking down at his son and granddaughter. He was filled with joy, pride, and gratitude. He offered a prayer of thanksgiving.

Hoot returned with his flight bag and handed Boone a Stanley thermos of coffee. Boone opened it, poured the hot coffee into the cup, and drank.

"Oh man, that's so good. The nectar of heaven," Boone laughed. "I don't suppose anybody has a tin of snuff?"

Without letting go of her father, Rachel reached into her jacket pocket and handed him a tin of Copenhagen.

"That's my girl," Boone smiled and then added, "Don't tell your momma."

"I doubt she'll mind under the circumstances," Rachel said.

Boone packed his lip with the snuff, closed his eyes, and smiled. "It sure is good to see y'all."

"You wouldn't happen to have a bar of soap in your bag, would you Hoot?" Wade asked, laughing.

"You saying I stink?"

"Yes," Rachel said.

"It has been a while."

"Well, tell us the story, son," Wade said.

"Dad, you wouldn't believe me if I told you."

Hoot set his camera on a rock cairn and set the timer. The photo trapped the moment in time, the four of them standing in front of the

248

Revenant, smiling at the camera. It was over.

CHAPTER FIFTY-ONE
1530 Hours Local-Monday 9 May 1988
Fairbanks International Airport, Alaska-Day 228

They all stood at a distance, Rachel included, as Boone and Abigail held their embrace, standing in the middle of the hangar. They held one another for several minutes in silence.

"Boone, I'm sorry," Abby said, through her tears.

"Honey, you didn't do anything wrong."

"Yes, I did. I gave up. I gave up, went home, and moved on with my life."

"What else were you supposed to do? Don't be so hard on yourself."

"I was supposed to do what Rachel did," Abby said, sobbing. "She never doubted. She never quit. She never gave up. She stayed here and worked on your rescue. She's the reason we found you. I'm ashamed. I should've believed her, stayed, and helped."

"Stop it," he whispered. "I don't want to hear another word about this. Rachel could afford to be stubborn. She didn't have a family to care for, a house to finish, parents to help, or a ranch to run. No evidence would've led you to stay and keep searching. Honey, you did the right thing. I'm the one who should apologize. I knew better than to put myself in this situation. My decision led to all the anxiety and fear everyone had to deal with. I should've never gotten out of the plane. I'm the one to blame, not you."

"Let's put it behind us and go home," Abby said. "We've endured too much of this in our lives. How about some peace now?"

"Okay," Boone said. "I agree. Let's go home."

"How about a shower first?"

"Fair enough," he said. "You want to join me?" He winked.

"You think sex is the solution to everything, don't you?" Abby threw her arms around her husband's waist.

Epilogue

"A private who loses a rifle suffers far greater consequences than a general who loses a war."

Lieutenant Colonel Paul Yingling
Armed Forces Journal, 2007

CHAPTER FIFTY-TWO
1500 Hours Local-Monday 27 May 1988
Base Hospital, Elmendorf AFB, Alaska

Two weeks in the base hospital left Boone weak enough he was breathing hard when Rachel opened the truck door. He handed her his crutches, pulled himself into the seat, and closed the door. As Abby opened the driver's side door, she noticed the full breath he drew in. "Are you alright?" she asked.

"Yeah, I'm OK," Boone said. "It's amazing how out of shape you get when you lie in a hospital bed for two weeks. I need to get back in shape when I ditch the crutches."

It was the first time Boone had returned to Fort Richardson since his Alaska tour in the mid-1970s. There were a few changes, but some things remained the same. Much to Rachel's delight, Abby drove them past their former quarters, the building where Boone's company lived, and where he worked during his tour as company commander. As they passed, a group of soldiers stood in formation between the building of the barracks where, twelve years earlier, Boone stood before the men of Charlie Airborne.

"Hold up a second honey," he said.

Abby stopped the truck in the alley behind the row of buildings.

"I want to see something," Boone said.

He rolled down the window, listened, and watched the activity in the company area. The voices were the same. The faces and activities were the same, and the equipment hadn't changed much either. There was something comforting about the consistency over time.

"I wonder if you could transport yourself back to a frontier post a hundred years ago and discover that the voices, faces, and activity were the same," he said. "Soldiers don't seem to change much, do they?"

"Not in my experience," Abby said. "I know four generations of soldiers or airmen, and you're all cut from the same cloth."

Abby stopped the truck in front of the Brigade Headquarters three minutes later.

"I'll be waiting here in one hour," Boone said.

"Alright, we'll be here."

Boone put his crutches under his arm and made his way to the front door as gracefully as possible. The Staff Duty orderly left his desk and opened the door.

"Can I help you, sir?" The young soldier asked.

"Lieutenant Colonel Taggart to see Colonel Hardy, please. I have an appointment."

"Please have a seat, sir. I'll inform the Staff Duty NCO that you've arrived," The private turned into the foyer office.

Thirty seconds later, an African-American Sergeant First Class in starched fatigues, spit-shined boots, and freshly cut high and tight haircut stepped into the foyer. The NCO was the size of an NFL linebacker and bore all the indicators of an experienced combat soldier. Sewn to the left side breast of his Battle Dress uniform was the badge of a Master Parachutist, Air Assault badge, Pathfinder badge, and, on top of all three, a Combat Infantryman's Badge. On his right sleeve was the patch of the unit he'd served a combat tour in Vietnam, the Screaming Eagles, "Old Abe" of the 101st Airborne Division. He'd been around.

"Good afternoon, Colonel. Please come with me, sir. The Commander's expecting you."

Boone wrestled with his crutches and started down the hall.

"Those things are a pain in the ass, aren't they, sir?" the sergeant said. He slowed his pace, not to put pressure on Boone's gait.

"Yes, they are."

"I spent a while on them just before I got here last summer from Bragg. I broke my ankle on my last jump before I left the unit. Stupid rookie mistake. I got cocky." The sergeant said.

254

"Been there," Boone laughed.

"You're the man that got attacked by the bear and wintered over in the bush, aren't you, sir?"

"Check," Boone said. "Also, a rookie mistake—I got cocky. I failed to follow instructions, and it bit me in the ass."

"Been there too, sir. I thought I recognized you from some pictures in the old man's office."

"Yeah, we've shared a lot of real estate," Boone said.

"Me too, sir. I was a private in 2-502 Infantry in '70 when the boss was the Operations Officer."

"Well, you and I've shared some real estate, too. I saw Colonel Hardy several times during that tour."

When they arrived in the outer office, Colonel Daniel Hardy, Brigade Commander, emerged from his office.

"Sergeant Jenkins, why would you bring this homeless cripple into my headquarters?" Dan laughed.

"Felt sorry for him, sir. He looked lost," Sergeant Jenkins said. "It's an honor to meet you, sir. Godspeed." He shook Boone's hand and left the office.

Dan turned to the young administrative specialist at the desk beside his office.

"Sergeant Godkin, don't disturb us unless someone with stars on his collar shows up. Understood?"

"Yes, sir."

"After you, my friend," Dan said, gesturing for Boone to enter his office.

Dan followed him and closed the door. While Boone got situated in a leather chair with his leg on an ottoman, Dan poured coffee into two mugs and handed one to Boone.

"Take it with you when you're done. Consider it an early Christmas gift," he said.

The white China mug had Master Parachutist wings on the front with "LTC Taggart" in gold lettering below the wings. "Thanks, buddy. I appreciate the update. Rachel absconded with my other one," Boone said.

"Look on the back."

Boone turned the mug around. A picture of a snarling grizzly bear was embossed in the center and beneath it in gold lettering, "The Bear Slayer."

Boone laughed. "Thanks. I'm glad you find joy in my pain."

"Better you than me, man. How are you doing? You look better than when I last saw you in the hospital."

"I'm good for now," Boone said. "The docs say I have a couple more surgeries to go on the leg and lots of physical therapy, but otherwise, I'm healthy. It'll take me a while to recover from a two-week stay in the hospital, though."

"Yeah, hospitals are good places to go to die. By the way, you need a haircut and shave Ranger."

"Nope," Boone said. "This is the new look. I'm tired of the funny looks people give me and I'm tired of explaining the scars."

"You're pulling a Jed Smith, aren't you?" Dan said, referring to the nineteenth-century mountain man.

"I figure I'm in good company," Boone said, smiling.

Dan put his coffee mug on the table between them, leaned forward in his chair, and looked Boone straight in the eyes. "Buddy, I'm sorry I left you out there. So is Bobby. We should've kept looking. We shouldn't have quit searching."

"Stop," Boone said, holding up his hand. "No one did anything wrong here except me. I made the mistake that started all this. I don't know why Jimmy didn't call it in, but I'm sure it's a simple explanation, but I shouldn't have let him drop me off. I should've stayed with him and come home, but I didn't, and here we are. This is all my responsibility. What you went through, what Abby and the kids, my folks, Chappie, Bart, everyone. This is my fault, not yours or anyone else's. I'd have done the same thing as you did based on the same information."

"No, you wouldn't have but thanks," Dan said. "As happy as I was to know that you survived, I was a little nervous about seeing you for the first time. I was ashamed."

"No reason," Boone said. "I never had those thoughts. I still don't. I felt bad about what I put everyone at home through. But since I spent the past two weeks laying on my back having nurses and the kids, my folks, and Abby wait on my every need, I've thought about this a lot and decided there are good things to come out of this mess."

Both men paused, sipping their coffee, until Dan couldn't take it anymore. *He's the best friend I have. I can ask him.*

"So, what did you learn out there, brother?" Dan said.

"I made my peace, Dan. I made my peace with the war and with retirement. I had plenty of time to think about this. I didn't just put it on the back burner until I was rescued. I decided to use my time in the wilderness to resolve it in my mind for good, and I did. My life got stripped down to the basic necessities of survival. I spent all my time cutting firewood to stay warm, hauling water to drink, trapping fur to clothe myself, and hunting and fishing to feed myself. For the first time in my life, I lived like humans before the modern age. I discovered I loved it. If my family were with me, I'd still be there.

"I suppose it was the contentment and the simplicity of the work. I could think about all of the things I was so confused about. There were no ankle-biter stressors or modern, up-in-your-face problems that didn't mean anything in the long run. I was able to think clearly, and I made my peace. I decided it's not our fault the politicians, bureaucrats, and generals screwed the war up. Our country called, and we answered the call.

"We did some good in a terrible set of circumstances. We conducted ourselves honorably on the battlefield, and that's not nothing. Others will have to answer for their conduct in Congress and the Pentagon. My career didn't end the way I wanted, but I served and did my job well. I trained and influenced another generation of young leaders, which is important. I also decided life isn't over because I hung up the uniform. I'm a blessed man and maybe my best work and biggest contributions are still in the future. I made my peace."

"I'm glad for you, brother," Dan said. "I made my peace, too. As I drove home after the search was suspended, I decided to retire and devote more time at home. I don't regret that decision, either. I dropped my retirement papers when I got back. I'm due to change command and retire in October. Consider yourself invited to the ceremony."

"Don't you think you were on track to make general officer?"

"Maybe, but I don't care," Dan said. "I don't want that. I want to finish where I started, with troops. Brigadier Generals are a dime a dozen at the Pentagon, and that's where I'd go. I'm just not interested. I don't like what seems to happen to too many men who make it to the general officer ranks. Maybe it was their real character all along, and it just comes out in spades when they pin on those stars. I agree with you. We were called, and we answered the call. We did well where others didn't. I can live with that."

"Me too," Boone said.

CHAPTER FIFTY-THREE
2030 Hours Local-Monday 8 August 1988
Taggart Ranch-Sheridan County, Wyoming

One clear indicator proved Abby hadn't given him up for dead. She finished and decorated the entire house except for his study. She'd wanted him to finish this room. The decision wasn't lost on Boone. She wanted it to be a space reflecting him, his personality, his life of service, and his interests. It was where his memories surrounded him.

Between the surgery to repair his knee and leg, physical therapy, visits to his therapist, and the inevitable press interest, he hadn't had time to complete the study until the previous two weeks. He arranged the furniture to see the Bighorns from his desk. He placed the leather couch and reading chairs in front of the fireplace, filled bookshelves, placed animal mounts on the stone wall of the fireplace, and filled the wooden paneled walls with pictures, unit flags, and other mementos of his life. He reserved the wall space behind his desk for two centerpiece items—a brindle cowhide of Luther's Winter Count and, immediately below that, the grizzly hide of the Winter Count of his life he painted in the Alaskan wilderness.

The room finished to his satisfaction. He sat on the couch, picked up his book, *The Haunted Mesa* by Louis L'Amour, and began to read.

"Whatcha reading?" Rachel asked as she sat beside him.

"New book by Louis L'Amour," he said.

"Can I read it when you're done?"

"Sure," Boone said. "I owe you a few books. I'd have lost my mind last winter if it wasn't for your gift."

"How many times did you read those two books?"

"Not sure. Enough to almost quote them."

"I thought about you every time I picked up a book. About how much you'd miss your library," Rachel said.

"That's what I missed the most, after my family. Missing books got to me more than tobacco and coffee," he said, laughing.

Abby and Roan watched Boone and Rachel through the French doors from the kitchen.

"She's a lot like him, isn't she?" Roan said, more as a statement than a question.

"She is, but you're your father's son, my boy. There's no denying it," Abby said.

"I gave up last fall, mom. I'm so thankful he's alive and healthy, but I was certain he was dead. I should've been there with Rachel. She never lost faith. I gave up and moved on."

"Your dad has had this conversation with several of us, me, your grandparents, Chappie, and Bart," Abby said. "There was no reason and no means to keep looking for him. We all made decisions based on the information available to us at the time. It's all we could do. It's no one's fault, although your dad believes it's his fault. He's beating himself up pretty well for leaving the plane instead of flying back to Eagle. I gave up and moved on, too, honey."

"Rachel didn't," he said.

Abby thought she detected pride in his voice, not resentment or jealousy. "No, she didn't."

"I wonder why?" Roan asked.

"Rachel has always felt things more intuitively than most," Abby said. "Sometimes it's a good thing, sometimes it's not, but it's how she seems to operate. It might be she didn't know your father was alive, but she refused to admit he was gone, and this time she happened to be right. I don't know."

"Her detective work paid off, though. She found him," Roan said.

"But he was already on the move when she found him," Abby said. "If she hadn't done the detective work, he would've floated into town later the same afternoon."

Roan glanced through the glass at his dad and sisters. Rachel leaned over and kissed Boone on the cheek and laughed. Roan smiled.

"Roan, your dad is exceedingly proud of you. He's never thought Rachel rescued him and you didn't, so put it out of your mind." Abby put her arm over his shoulder and kissed her son's cheek.

***

"I have to go back to Fairbanks, Dad," Rachel said.

"I figured you'd be heading back soon," Boone said. "What're your plans?"

"I'm not sure at the moment. Last fall, I figured I'd go back to school after this was all resolved, but now I don't want to go to school. I love flying, so I'll keep working for Chappie for now. I'll see where it takes me."

"I think you're onto something, Rach. It's a great coup when you figure out how to do something you love when you're young. Grab it and run with it, honey. Mom and I are proud of you."

"I'm going to miss you all, Dad," she said.

"I'll miss you too, honey, but this is life," Boone said. "It's your turn. Mom and I have had ours. Go out and tackle the world. We're always here to help."

Caroline lay on the cowhide rug in front of the fireplace and opened a book. Abigail handed Boone a glass of sweet tea and sat beside him on the couch. Roan sat in a reading chair. It was the first time they'd all been in the same room since before Boone's disappearance. It was also when Boone Taggart understood this episode was complete.

CHAPTER FIFTY-FOUR
1400 Hours Local-Thursday 5 July 1990
Alaskan Interior

Warrant Officer One Rachel Taggart, United States Army, sat in the right seat of the de Havilland DHC-2 Beaver next to her former flight instructor and friend, Bart "Yeti" Chapman. She turned onto the downwind leg to the lake where the family would spend the next ten days, camping and fishing. It had been over a year since she'd landed a floatplane, but it all came back immediately. Yeti smiled as she transitioned from brand new Army helicopter pilot back to Alaskan bush pilot.

When the pontoons touched the water's surface, Rachel cut the throttle, and the big plane sank deeper. She taxied to the small beach on the south end of the wilderness lake, cut the engine, and drifted onto the sand. Bart exited his door, tied the bowline to a log, and directed the unloading of two inflatable rafts, camping and fishing gear, and the inevitable survival gear. Boone Taggart was almost pathological about it after his last Alaskan experience.

Twenty minutes later, Boone stepped onto the pontoon and stood beside the open cockpit door. Bart sat in the cockpit, finishing the departure checklist.

"Meet us in Circle, in ten days," Boone said to Bart. "We'll fish here for a few days and start floating out."

"Got it. Same rules as before: if you need something, put out a panel, and I'll call you on your handheld radio. You're only a few miles south of my route from Fairbanks. I can dogleg it into Eagle."

"Thanks, brother."

"You bet. You guys, be safe. Let history not repeat itself, please. Okay?"

262

"I promise," Boone said.

***

Roan and Rachel pitched the canvas-wall tents, Abby set up the field kitchen, while Boone and Caroline cut and collected firewood and water. Their home for the week was finished in a little over an hour. Boone inflated one of the rafts, and Roan and Rachel hit the lake for evening fishing. Boone and Caroline walked to the hill above camp to glass for wildlife and Abby enjoyed all the activities while she finished supper. They were together, and they were safe.

Roan and Rachel were competing as always, but Roan had developed newfound respect for his little sister in the previous few years. He was trying to teach her to fish. She was objecting based on the fact she'd already caught more and bigger fish. She reminded him that she outranked him, and he reminded her that she was an officer, which made it sound like an insult the way he said it. Abby couldn't help but laugh.

She'd reached a point in the spring of 1988 when she didn't cry for her husband. She thought he was dead, and then, following his rescue, she went through months of daily tears for the husband who miraculously floated out of the wilderness. Tears of joy mixed with guilt because she'd given up hope he was alive, and she'd have to learn to live without him. Abby had quickly adjusted to having him home again.

With him home, safe, and retired, her thoughts shifted to her two oldest. Roan, a Special Forces sergeant, a younger version of his father, and Rachel, an Army helicopter pilot. She'd just signed into the 101st Airborne Division at Fort Campbell, Kentucky, an assignment she asked for so she could be close to her big brother, assigned to 5th Special Forces Group, also at Campbell.

Abby worried as all parents do, but her children stayed in the family business. There was a time, as Boone approached retirement, she thought her worries would end, but then Roan followed his father's profession and now Rachel. Her time flying in Alaska, and the combined exposure to so many military and aviation professionals,

263

proved to be a consuming call for her, too. She was accepted into the Army's Warrant Officer Flight Training Program, where she, not surprisingly to her parents, finished as an honor graduate in both the Warrant Officer Candidate Course and her flight school class. Now, a UH-60 Blackhawk pilot for the premier Air Assault division in the world, she was having the time of her life. Abigail took her mother's advice and spent more time praying.

At least there wasn't a war.

The following day broke clear, cool, and calm. Rain passed through the night before but blew out, the sun was bright, and the wind had laid down. It was a perfect Alaskan summer morning. Boone started the fire and set the percolator on the grate. While he waited for coffee to brew, he peeked into the kids' tent and noticed Roan was already up and out of the tent. Caroline was trapped at the bottom of her sleeping bag, and Rachel was mouth wide open, snoring like her mother. He stepped from beneath the canvas rainfly which formed the kitchen and walked toward the lake. He didn't see Roan. As his concern started to rise, he heard a splash at a smaller lake two hundred yards down the valley and saw his son fighting a nice-sized trout.

Roan expertly worked the fish to within reach of where he stood waist-deep in the water and, in a single elegant swing, netted the large trout. Boone watched him for several minutes, proud of his mastery of the environment. He was at home in the backcountry. Boone was thankful for the wilderness rite of passage he'd experienced in his youth and replicated it for his children. The only difference was Luther was gone, and now the ritual included girls. Rachel and Caroline had to pass through the crucible as well. Wade took all his grandchildren on their coming-of-age expeditions in the Bighorn Mountains.

Roan waded smoothly back to the shore, almost without leaving a ripple in the water. He dispatched the fish at the water's edge and had it cleaned in under a minute. He returned to camp, pausing to cut a cedar branch to cook the fish.

"How long have you been spying on me?" he asked his father.

"Long enough to know you're a fine angler, son."

"Even a blind hog finds corn every now and then, Dad."

264

"We both know you're not a blind hog when it comes to fishing."

"Not according to Rachel," Roan laughed.

Rachel stepped through the opening of the tent she shared with her siblings. "That's right," she said. "You just got lucky this morning. I could catch a minnow like that with my eyes closed. You should be ashamed bringing that little thing up here. There's a reason you got up early to fish. You couldn't stand the competition."

She stood with her hands on her hips, glaring at her brother through one open eye.

"You should've been up earlier anyway," Roan said. "You aviators are all the same. Crew rest. You need twenty hours of sleep a day to function."

"Do we have to start in at this hour?" Abby shouted from inside her tent.

"Mom's right. Let's get the morning chores done and breakfast on," Boone said.

Boone and Abby enjoyed another cup of coffee as their children finished morning dishes and prepared for the day's fishing. When they'd finished the chores, Roan helped Caroline tie extra flies while Rachel packed a lunch and loaded the raft. The three Taggarts planned to spend the morning fishing for grayling and land-locked silver salmon and then hiking to the river to hunt for caribou sheds.

"Rachel told me this is *the* lake," Abby said.

"Yep. It's *the* lake," he said, looking down at his coffee mug.

"Why'd you want to come back here?" she said. "Any specific reason?"

Boone pushed salt and pepper hair back out of his eyes.

"If you're asking if I came up here for closure or some kind of New Age philosophical crap like that, the answer is no," he said, pulling his hair into a ponytail and tying it with a small leather string.

She still marveled at how differently he looked with longer hair and a beard. It wasn't the act of post-military defiance from shaving and short hair that many of his friends had experienced. His longer hair and beard covered scars from the bear attack. In classic Boone Taggart fashion, he admitted getting the idea from Jedediah Smith, the famous mountain man. A grizzly attacked him in the summer of 1823, and he wore long hair and a beard to cover the scars.

"You don't have to be snarky," she said, smiling. "I was just wondering why you wanted to return to this spot."

"I still want the grayling."

He filled their mugs as their children laughed and yelled at one another, trying to launch the raft.

"Do you want to see where I lived that winter?"

"It's close?"

"About three-quarters of a mile that way," he said, pointing west across the river.

"Yes, I'd like to see that," she said. "It might help me."

Later in the afternoon, the Taggart Family hiked to the trees where Boone spent his first night, the debris shelter where he stayed during the first storm, and finally to the cabin where he healed through the winter. Roan inspected the cabin and the surrounding area. From Boone's perspective, his son was inspecting his work. Abigail and Caroline walked around the cabin and stepped inside. Boone thought they were trying to imagine him in the setting three years earlier. Rachel had been here before. Boone stayed close to her as she seemed to relive the emotions of the day that she, Wade, and Hoot found the cabin.

For Boone, returning to the valley was bittersweet. The recovery from the bear attack was painful and stressful. He'd worried about infection and immobility, but neither manifested themselves. He missed his family terribly while exiled in this frozen valley, but part of him thrived here as if he belonged or maybe even had been here before. Although the last thought confused him.

He had a deep appreciation for what happened during the long winter sequestered in this frozen valley. He'd put the war to rest. He replayed the discussion with Dan along the Susitna River dozens of times. Dan was right, he usually was. They brought leadership during very difficult circumstances. The war would've been even more difficult for their soldiers had a careerist led them instead of these two warriors and others like them. They didn't get everything right, but they loved their soldiers and sought to stand as a filter between them and the insanity of irrevocably broken policies and strategy. They served honorably in a nearly impossible situation.

The Winter Count helped assuage his grief, frustration, and anger. He said goodbye to the past. He buried his ghosts. He made peace with a tragic past. Recounting his own history helped him see his life was blessed by people he loved their love in return, and by a purpose for his life. It showed the two great substances of life: relationships and meaningful purpose—a mission. He had both indelibly etched on the grizzly hide. The Winter Count also demonstrated what Luther taught him—life moves in a circle. Death and birth, failure and accomplishment, war and peace, beginnings and endings, a time for every purpose under heaven.

The wilderness was therapeutic. It nearly killed him on more than one occasion during his time in the valley, but it also healed him. He hadn't had alcohol since his Christmas Eve celebration in the cabin. He came to admit he'd used whiskey as medication to deal with his demons for far too long. Long enough it had become detrimental, not only to him but the people he loved. His drinking was starting to affect other aspects of his life. Months in the wilds of Alaska proved it was a problem but also gave him the clarity to recognize he no longer needed it. His mind was clear, and his heart was finally at peace. His dad was right—it wasn't easy, but it was worth it. He was a different man when he floated away from Taggart's Station, a better man. For that he would be eternally grateful.

Roan broke the silence. He slapped his dad on the shoulder. "Nice job, pop."

"Glad it meets your approval, junior," Boone said, smiling.

"Where'd the bear get you?" Roan said.

"Seven miles north of here. And I don't want to go back and visit."

"Neither do we," Abby said, wrapping her arms around his waist.

***

Boone sat on the hill above camp with his binoculars, glassing the

267

valleys and hills that were his home for months. This was familiar terrain but so different in the summer's warmth and green compared to winter's frozen darkness. It was breathtaking in all seasons, and he loved this place. A small caribou herd wandered on the hills across the valley to his north.

"See anything?" Roan asked. He and Rachel sat down on each side of their father.

"Small herd of caribou over there," he said. "And I thought I saw a black bear in that thicket by the river, but he never came out."

The three sat in silence for several minutes, and then Boone spoke. "I want to talk to you two about something."

His serious tone obvious, Rachel said, "Go ahead Daddy. We'll listen."

"You both decided to join the family business. I've given you some advice along the way, just the basics, but now I want to share some more important thoughts. You'll have to make a choice one day. You're going to come to a crossroads at some point in your career. One way makes you somebody, and the other allows you to do something. Down one road is your career and what you can make of an opportunity. On that road, you start worrying about assignments and awards, the best places to serve, and working for people or in units that will positively influence your career. You worry about the bullets on your efficiency reports, you worry about checking the career blocks, you'll compromise your personal principles and relationships, but you'll get promoted, your superiors will say good things about you, and your subordinates will likely hate you. Still, you'll be a member of the club.

"This path is for the careerist, and they're legion. There are careerists in the NCO Corps," he said, looking at Roan, "but it's worse among the officers," he said to Rachel. "These are the people who're in it for the accolades, what the Army can do for them. Be a Sam Damon. Don't be a Courtney Massengale. It's an empty path to nowhere.

"I'm advising you to take the other path. The choice to do something instead of being someone, make an impact, and do something for your soldiers, the Army, and the country. I'm not saying be a contrarian for the sake of being contrary. Be humble and stoic, keep your own counsel and keep your ego in check not as an act or a tactic, but organically. Develop these as a habit. Train your soldiers as hard and as well as you can.

War is unbelievably difficult. Poorly trained soldiers don't rise to the occasion—they fall back on their highest level of training. So, train them hard and hold them to the standard. They may not love you, but they'll respect you. If they ask questions, answer them honestly. They aren't children. They're grown men and women who're as smart and dedicated as you. You've been selected to lead them. If you lead, they'll follow.

"I caught a case of the sniffles once about an assignment I didn't want, so I whined to someone who I thought could get me a better assignment. He gave me some great advice, 'Wherever you're planted, bloom,' and he was right, it turned out to be the assignment I had the most impact on the Army. The best career advice is to quit trying to manage your career and perform well in every task you're given. See to your character, and your career and reputation will take care of itself. Be a solid performer in everything, never shirk a task, give everything your all, and don't seek attention. Give that to your soldiers."

"Uncle Dan told you that, didn't he?" Rachel said, smiling.

"Those files are still classified," Boone said, chuckling. Then he turned serious again.

"There's one more thing I want to share with you. If history is any indicator, the two of you will fight another war, at least if you decide to stay in for a career. When it happens, take care of the people around you. I hate to steal any idealism you have, but the politicians, bureaucrats, and too many generals will be wrong about too much. The national security apparatus has been wrong about almost everything since the end of World War II.

The politicians will use rhetoric to get what they want, and the generals will ask for more troops, money, and time, and then they won't listen to the people on the ground. We're soldiers, and we don't always get to pick the wars we fight. It's not an excuse to do anything immoral but a reminder that the people at the top look at it through a different lens than we do, including the green suiters at the top, not just politicians. When it happens to you, take care of your soldiers, do your duty, and lead them through the situation as best you can. You can do a lot of good in a bad situation. You can make a positive impact on people's lives. Any questions?"

"No, sir," they said in unison.

"Alright then," Boone said. "I'm walking down to the creek there and cutting some diamond willows for a new walking stick. Tell Mom I'll be back for supper."

As Boone walked down the slope toward the willows, his children sat next to one another, watching him. Their father had given them advice throughout their lives, but this was deeper and reflected some of his pain. He was passing the torch. He admitted, as much as he made life look fun all the time, he was troubled by the past, but he reconciled it, too. It was the first time they experienced him as more than Dad. They watched as he walked into the willows along the creek, stood, and started toward camp. They walked back to camp, not just brother and sister, but fellow warriors. The legacy of warriors.

***

Boone ambled through the stand of willows along the creek, looking for two or three good diamond willows, straight and thick enough but not too big and with good distinctive diamond knots. After a few minutes without success, he saw some possibilities on the far side of the creek and stepped into knee-deep, cold water. Halfway across the stream, something to his right, caught his attention. He turned, and a large grizzly boar stood mid-stream forty feet away. The bear just watched for a moment. Boone stopped and squared his body to the bear, snapped the safety strap of the holster. He pulled the Ruger Super Blackhawk and cocked the single-action hammer. He held the revolver at his side.

In one smooth motion, the grizzly stood on his hind legs to his full height, sniffed the air, and then returned to all fours. The bear and the man stood in the water regarding one another without a sound for a full minute. The bear turned right and crossed the creek into the willows. Boone turned right and went back the way he came. Once in the willows, he holstered the revolver and walked up the ridge toward camp. As he gained elevation, he turned and looked behind him. On the opposing ridge, the grizzly sat on his back haunches, watching Boone walk up the hill. Boone turned to face the bear. The bear turned and walked up the ridge. Boone watched him until he crossed over the top and was gone.

***

Boone woke up long before the rest of the family, dressed, grabbed his fishing gear, and launched the raft. He rowed to the middle of the lake and dropped the raft's field expedient anchor—a bag filled with rocks. He connected on his fourth cast with a brand-new purple egg-sucking leach fly, tied by his father. He set the hook, and the rod doubled. He palmed the bottom of the reel as the fish made its first run, slicing through the water. He worked the fish from entangling with the anchor line. Successfully, he brought it back toward the opposite end of the raft and, for the first time, it broke water. He saw the giant dorsal fin, a grayling. And it was a whopper.

Don't mount it yet, Boone. He continued to work the reel.

"Get him, Daddy," Caroline screamed from the lake shore.

Boone glanced up quickly to see his family gathering around the second raft.

"Bring a camera," he yelled.

For the next several minutes, Boone fought the beautiful iridescent fish as his family paddled the raft to his side. Landing the fish, Boone removed the hook and held the fish in front of him.

"It's the biggest grayling I've ever seen, Daddy," Rachel said.

"Good job, pop," Roan said.

"You finally have a grayling to mount in your study," Caroline said.

"Take a picture, please," Boone asked Abby.

Smiling, Boone gently held the fish in front of him, and Abby snapped several pictures. Another moment of their history frozen in place and time.

271

"He's beautiful, honey," Abby said. "We can get him mounted in Fairbanks before we drive home."

"Nope. Not this one. A picture is enough."

Boone placed the grayling gently in the clear water and moved it back and forth, pushing the oxygenated water through the gills until it slapped its tail and disappeared under the raft.

"I'm proud of you," Abby said. She leaned forward and kissed her husband.

CHAPTER FIFTY-FIVE
1748 Hours Local-Thursday 2 August 1990
Officer's Club, Elmendorf Air Force Base, Alaska

Colonel Daniel Beckwourth Hardy, United States Army, retired, was settled into his second career, although it was directly connected to the first. When he retired in October 1988, he and his bride decided to remain in Alaska. This was their home. He loved Alaska and never wanted to leave, although they took one vacation each January to Hawaii to thaw out for a couple of weeks. A former boss reached out to Dan in the last months he was on active duty and offered him a job as the Director of the Emergency Operation Center (EOC) for Alaska Command. He was a GS-15 Department of Air Force civilian, and the money was good, considering he also received his retirement and a VA disability pension. Linda made good money as a professor, plus he relished his role of dad to two wonderful daughters. Life was good.

The job as EOC Director was relatively straightforward. He and his staff orchestrated the chaos of emerging threats and situations impacting the command until the Commanding General's staff took over the operation. The EOC handled everything from Russian bomber violation of airspace to civilian complaints of low-flying aircraft, a problem he often reminded the complainant was "the sound of freedom." Dan's thirty years of military experience prepared him well for this job and still allowed for a better family environment than he had on active duty. Plus, he had plenty of time to continue his outdoor pursuits.

The operations tempo in Alaska Command wasn't as fast paced as he was accustomed to while on active duty, and for that, he was thankful. Alaska Command was considered a military backwater as the Soviet Union went through its death throes. Many soldiers and

273

airmen stationed in the Great Land were here because they wanted to be assigned to the "Hunting and Fishing Brigade," as it became known. Dan was happy with the slower pace—he'd run for three decades, his hair on fire, and it was time to live a little more. It was a welcomed change of pace, but the pace had increased the previous afternoon.

Just after lunch, while Dan was trying to get out of the office early, the young Air Force major serving as the day shift Watch Officer brought Dan a copy of a classified message from their higher headquarters J2 Intelligence section. Dan started to read the message as the CNN Headline News anchor read an almost identical report on the large monitors at the front of the EOC.

How do they do that? Dan thought. The message and the CNN report outlined the initial Iraqi invasion of Kuwait.

Now, the evening after the invasion, Dan walked into the Officer's Club to keep an appointment with an old friend. The club consisted of several bars and dining rooms. Dan headed for an informal, quiet one where the old farts hung out. There was a quiet jukebox with some Motown oldies selections, and you could get one of the best cheeseburgers on base. He stepped past a couple of Air Force colonels in their Mess Dress, attending a formal affair, and made his way to the bar. He saw Boone sitting with his back to the wall, watching the news reports on the TV behind the bar.

Boone saw Dan working his way through the evening crowd. He was still confident and athletic in his mid-fifties but looked so out of place in khaki pants, a long-sleeved button-down shirt, and a blue blazer. Boone couldn't let the opportunity pass.

"You look like a college professor, Poindexter," Boone said, as the two friends embraced in a bear hug.

"And you look homeless."

"I love the beard," Boone said, reaching up and tugging on Dan's now three-year-old beard.

"Thanks, man. I haven't shaved since the morning of my retirement ceremony."

The two sat at the table and caught up for several minutes. Boone recounted his family's recent fishing trip, a Chapman update, the usual children update, ranch life in Wyoming, and the latest on his parents. Dan caught Boone up on Linda and his girls, eight and six, and his job. As they swapped stories about their families and new lives, a young, attractive, well-dressed waitress walked past them, delivered an order, turned, and stopped at their table.

"Good evening, gentlemen. What can I get you all?" she asked in a distinctive southern drawl.

"We'll both have cheeseburgers, fries, and sweet tea and give the check to the cowboy," Dan said, pointing at Boone, laughing.

Smiling, the waitress looked at Boone and asked, "Is that right, sir? Are you picking up the tab tonight?"

"I guess I am," Boone said. "Where's that accent from?"

"East Tennessee. My husband is on an AWACS crew, and I work at the club. We met in high school, and I followed him up here after basic and tech school. We love it up here but faced wrath from our families for leaving the mountains and wandering the earth."

"My wife's people are from East Tennessee," Boone said, "I thought I recognized the accent. Her folks faced the same wrath when they left, but it's been a great adventure, you two hang in there and enjoy the ride."

"Well, it's a small world, meeting someone in the Officer's Club in Alaska from the same place back home," she said. "I'll take your advice. Thanks. I'll have those burgers out in a minute."

"Put bacon on mine, please," Boone said.

"You bet."

"Do you even possess the capacity to not flirt with beautiful women?" Dan asked, once she was out of earshot.

"That wasn't flirting. I was being a gentleman. That's the way we do it where I'm from. Besides, I only have eyes for one woman, and as soon as she finishes at the commissary, she's meeting us here."

"You guys heading back soon?" Dan asked.

"Yeah, in a couple of days. The camper needed to be restocked." After a moment, Boone said. "Is this thing going anywhere?" Pointing to the television reports from Kuwait.

"Can't say for sure, but if I was making an educated guess, yeah, it's going somewhere," Dan said. "I doubt we're just going to sit it out. We've become more interested in the Middle East over the past few years and this is a big move on Iraq's part. The odd thing is we armed them to fight the Iranians."

"Enemy of my enemy is my friend," Boone said absently, as he continued watching the scenes from Kuwait City.

"That policy gets us in trouble a lot," Dan said.

The two were quiet, watching TV as the young waitress returned with their orders.

"You've still got skin in the game," Dan said.

It wasn't academic for Boone, and this time, as the country was poised to go to war, it wasn't him in harm's way but two of his children. He was on the other side of the equation. It's easy to be down range. It's infinitely more difficult being at home waiting, inactive.

"Yep," Boone said. "And I think it'll all turn out the same for them as it did for us. It won't be exact, but it'll happen again, eventually. The men and women in the field will be ignored by the so-called national security experts and politicians. I talked to Roan and Rachel while we were camping. I gave them the same speech you gave me one time. I told them to do their best, train their soldiers, and try to do good in bad circumstances. I think it's the best any of us can do. It doesn't seem to change at the top. Different people, same rhetoric. Fifteen years ago, you and I sat on a sandbar beside the Susitna River with a bottle of whiskey and had this same discussion, word for word, only about another war. Do we ever learn our lessons?"

Dan thought quietly and then pointed to the TV as Pentagon and State Department officials, flanked by general officers, held a press conference. The words couldn't be made out over the background conversations in the bar and the sound of Louis Armstrong's *What a Wonderful World,* coming from the jukebox. But Dan, Boone, and every other experienced soldier in the bar knew what they were saying. It was the same script for a different war.

"We do," Dan said. "But they don't," he pointed at the screen, "and they never will."

CHAPTER FIFTY-SIX
1830 Hours Local-Thursday 21 March 1991
Camp Eagle II-Saudia Arabia

Captain David Farmer lay on his cot reading a letter from his grandfather which included two stories from his time assigned to the same unit during World War II. Farmer was always proud of his grandfather's service and was particularly proud when he was attached to 3-502 Infantry, 101st Airborne Division. In fact, Farmer's was a long tradition in the division—as his father was a Screaming Eagle in Vietnam. The senior Farmer jumped into Normandy and Belgium and then survived the winter of 1944-45 at Bastogne. Now his grandson had just completed his first combat experience, but he didn't feel the same pride for his actions as his grandfather did. Desert Storm wasn't much of a war, compared to his grandfather's or his father's.

Farmer had never considered a life outside of uniform. He couldn't remember a time when he didn't have complete confidence the profession of arms was his calling. As the division deployed to Saudia Arabia in August 1990, he was nervous but excited. He was walking within the legacy of generations of soldiers before him, but he was also scared. He was concerned that he would fail his friends, subordinates, and unit. What if he turned out to be a coward under fire or couldn't do his job properly? A sincere discussion with his Battalion Executive Officer a month into the deployment fixed the problem. He leveled out and performed superbly. He was more confident than ever that this was his calling, but it wasn't without reservations, particularly after his first war experience.

The United States had grown more deeply involved in the Middle East since the late 1970s and while Desert Storm certainly was a quick tactical victory, he was less sure of the strategic implications.

Listening to the handful of older, more experienced officers he trusted, particularly the Vietnam veterans, it sounded like they would be back in the desert to fight again. This might be his generation's war. But for now, the unit was recovering and preparing for their movement back to Fort Campbell.

As he finished the letter from his very proud grandfather, the mail clerk entered the tent,

"Hey, sir. I found another letter for you in the mail room. Sorry we didn't get it to you at mail call."

"No problem," Farmer said. "Thanks for bringing it by."

The young soldier handed Farmer the letter and he turned it to see the Sheridan County, Wyoming return address. He immediately knew the author of the letter. Farmer began to read the letter that included a schematic of the overall battle plan in the writer's hand and pre-dated December 1990.

"Operational art," Farmer said quietly, remembering the many lectures of his Professor of Military Science. He knew how we would fight this campaign, but it was the final paragraphs that caught his attention.

Just over three years ago, you and I crossed at opposite ends of military service. On the same day that I commissioned you, you participated in my retirement ceremony. If you recall, the Brigade Commander asked me to relate my best day in uniform, and I did—at least it was the happiest.

Later that day, you asked me a more poignant question. You asked me about my worst day in uniform. It was an honest question, and you deserve to hear the answer. I couldn't answer your question then, or maybe I wouldn't. I've had a lot of time to think about my years in service, and I'm ready to answer your question. My worst day in uniform was 21 November 1970 in Saigon, South Vietnam.

Very Respectfully

Boone Taggart
LTC, Infantry

Author's Note

In August 2021 I, like many Americans, watched heart-broken, the disastrous withdrawal of American Forces from Afghanistan. It was reminiscent of another withdrawal which played out on television in 1975. I remember watching it at the age of eleven. In the wake of the withdrawal, I set out on a detailed study of the long chain of events which led to the moment. War, particularly counterinsurgency, is extraordinarily complex, and it's fair to conclude we won't get it right every time, but I wanted to know if there were historical analogs which could have guided us in our involvement in Iraq and Afghanistan. As I began to read and study, it was clear that most of the foreign policy mistakes of the previous fifty years were too often repeated within the highest levels of the national security, intelligence, and military establishments. The lessons of our recent history were there for the learning, and we failed.

As part of my study, I came to grips with some key and disturbing facts about the officer corps of which I was a member. First, our historical understanding as a whole is wanting. I can't attribute this memory to a specific source, but it was said of most Army officers of the late twentieth century, that the collective knowledge of the American Civil War far surpassed what anyone knew about counterinsurgency. I found that to be true. We must be specialists of all forms of warfare but particularly the failures of previous efforts. Our historical understanding must be guided by a detailed understanding of conflict through our enemies' eyes. We have, too often, made the mistake of seeing war through a post-Second World War American lens. The American officer corps must be lethal specialists in all forms of warfare.

Secondly, the highest levels of our national security and intelligence establishment continue to be strategic amateurs. At the tactical level, the force is as flexible, adept, and lethal as it always is, at least when allowed. But at the highest level we were inadequate throughout our involvement in Southwest Asia. The force adapted quickly at the tactical level, but the tactics never nested within a cogent strategy, because there wasn't one. I also had to conclude that it wasn't the first time we made this mistake. The same can be said of our involvement in Vietnam.

Finally, I concluded that careerism is a cancer within the officer corps, and it starts at the source of commissioning. Too many young lieutenants are trained, whether directly or by implication, to manage their image and career rather than to be the best and most lethal soldiers and combat leaders possible. Gone are the days when an officer who wasn't the best choice for an assignment could be sent where he or she might thrive without a service-ending stain on their record. Gone are the days when warriors naturally ascended the ranks to command positions in times of war. We have, for too long, attempted to turn out "cookie-cutter" soldiers and it hasn't worked. There are too many politicians in uniform. Our republic deserves better. The soldiers we lead deserve better. We must bring back a culture of a warrior ethos across the American military structure.

It wasn't long after the country was engaged in Afghanistan and Iraq, that comparisons to Vietnam began to surface. The word "quagmire" was ubiquitous in the media. Unfortunately, it proved more accurate than most were willing to admit. On more than one occasion, during my tour in Afghanistan in 2009-2010, I was counseled by higher ranking officers not to make historical comparisons to Vietnam or the Soviet or British experience in Afghanistan and yet, a greater understanding of both by senior military officers, national security "experts" and politicians could have avoided the suffering of coalition members and the Afghan people, if applied. Once again, we were more concerned with managing images than winning wars.

One of my goals in this novel was to explore my own service in our national efforts in the Global War on Terror in the context of a

281

similar situation: Vietnam. If only the decision makers had applied so many of the lessons, we learned from our involvement in Southeast Asia…but they didn't. It was a lost opportunity.

If you're interested in a deeper study of American involvement in Vietnam and the lessons we could've learned, I recommend the following: *About Face: The Odessey of an American Warrior* by Colonel David H. Hackworth; *A Bright Shining Lie: John Paul Vann and America in Vietnam* by Neil Sheehan; *Dereliction of Duty: Lyndon Johnson, Robert McNamara, The Joint Chiefs of Staff, and the Lies That Led to Vietnam* by H.R. McMaster; *The Best and the Brightest* by David Halberstam; *The Pentagon Papers: The Secret History of the Vietnam War* by Neil Sheehan, Hedrick Smith, E.W. Kenworthy and Fox Butterfield; *Vietnam: A History – The First Complete Account of Vietnam at War* by Stanley Karnow; *Our Vietnam: The War 1954- 1975* by A.J. Langguth. Another critical read for all Americans is *The Afghanistan Papers* by Craig Whitlock and *The Generals: American Military Command from World War II to Today* by Thomas E. Ricks.

I wrestle with the idea of historical cycles. Mark Twain is credited with the observation that history doesn't repeat itself, but it does rhyme. I think he used the illustration of a kaleidoscope. Sometimes familiar patterns line up similar to the past. It seems there are general patterns more than cycles. If a historical pattern exists it the fulfillment of Hegel's observation, "We learn from history that we do not learn from history." We can learn something about ourselves from a candid and diligent study of history, our own as well as others. There was a short period in the early 1990's when military leaders tempered by their Vietnam experience attempted to influence the national security dynamic of military intervention with ideas such as the Powell Doctrine. The men who experienced Vietnam as lieutenants, captains, and majors were general officers at the end of the century. They learned and applied many of the proper lessons from the nation's experience in Southeast Asia, but it was short-lived.

The generation of national security leaders and military officers that designed and implemented the American effort in Iraq and Afghanistan, were coming of age as the American experience in Vietnam fell apart. They hadn't experienced it on a personal level.

They vowed it would never happen again because we learned our lessons. But we didn't. Giving the enemy sanctuaries, not holding high level commanders accountable for failure, lack of development of cogent and overarching strategies with properly nested tactics, inaccurate assessments of the situation, failure to see the war from our enemies' perspective, and the hubris of nation-building were failures we made in Vietnam and made them again in Southwest Asia. Perhaps the mission in the Graveyard of Empires was a bridge too far but it appears we didn't even try to learn the lessons of those who went before. And we're making the same mistakes again. We must do better for future generations.

"Those who cannot remember the past are condemned to repeat it."
George Santayana

Acknowledgements

The description of the fall of Saigon in chapter one was drawn from Stanley Karnow's account in *Vietnam: A History – The First Complete Account of Vietnam at War*. It's an intriguing and well documented account of the final day of American involvement in the war. He highlights the actions of Colonel Bui Tin, a newspaper reporter for the People's Army of Vietnam, but also the ranking officer in the Presidential Compound on that fateful day. He received the surrender from President Minh.

In 1992, the same Colonel Bui Tin testified before the Senate Subcommittee on POW/MIA Affairs. At the conclusion of his testimony, Senator John McCain, a former naval aviator and POW held in the Hanoi Hilton for over five years, left his seat, and embraced the colonel. Later in the hearing, McCain severely berated Dolores Alfond, the spokesperson of the National Alliance of Families of POW/MIA. Mrs. Alfond was the sister of Captain Victor Apodaca, USAF. Captain Apodaca was shot down over North Vietnam on 8 June 1967 and is listed as Missing in Action. It seems everything about the war was upside down.

A special word of thanks to **Colonel Carl Hicks, US Army (Ret.)**. Not only did Colonel Hicks advise me on the aviation sections of the book but was also influential in my development as a soldier, officer, and a man. He guided me through a difficult time in my life and I'll always be indebted to him. He's a steady, calm, and constant combat leader. Thank you, sir. **Technical Sergeant Chrisopher Hubbard US Air Force (Ret.)** advised me on the survival portions of the novel. Thank you for your insight and encouragement. **Colonel Gary Bridges, US Army (Ret.)** gave me the first encouragement to write but more importantly, stalwart leadership for a young, sometimes misguided Lieutenant. Thank you, sir.

I'm forever thankful for my trusted readers, who gave me such important and insightful feedback on my first draft. **Lieutenant Colonel Mark Caruso, US Army (Ret.)** is closer than a brother to me. We met when I was seventeen and have shared a bond of brotherhood since. We've shared adversity and triumph. Thanks for everything, Mark. **Major David Wims, US Air Force (Ret.)** and I are connected by more than common service to the Republic. As he shared with me, we both have one foot in the present and one foot firmly planted in the American Frontier past. Thanks, Dave. Finally, **Molly Sayre, my youngest daughter**. Your insights were invaluable and the note you left me on the final page of the manuscript changed my life forever. I love you.

Thank you, **Jocelyn Ludlow**, for your insights, encouragement, and counsel. It was invaluable and I deeply appreciated it.

Thank you, **Meredith Blevins**, for your hard work editing this manuscript. I can't thank you enough for your experience, encouragement, and wisdom advising me in this project. Thank you so much.

I owe a great debt of gratitude to my parents, **Jerry and Lavon Sayre**. You set me on this path through encouragement and by buying me books when you really couldn't afford them. When I was in the third-grade dad gave me a book he read as a child, *Cowboys and Cattle Trails*, and it set all of this into motion. Thank you both, I love you.

My **children and grandchildren** are the joy of my life. I love you all and you're a continual source of pride, happiness, and inspiration.

Sharon, the love of my life. Thank you for the forty years of dedicated love, loyalty, and companionship. It's been quite a party. Thank you for the encouragement and the support for this project. I love you with all my heart.

Glossary of Terms

12 gauge: Gauge is the American term while "bore" is the British term for the unit of measurement of the inside diameter of the barrel of a shotgun. It's the number of balls created from one pound of lead, if those balls were the same size as the barrel, i.e., a 12 gauge is the diameter of 12 balls from one pound of lead. The larger the number of gauge, the smaller the size of the bore. The 12-gauge shotgun is probably the most prevalent shotgun gauge in the world. The right combination of choke and shot size allows a 12 gauge to be used against game from squirrels to grizzly bears. In conjunction with sabot slugs or similar cartridges, the 12 gauge is an excellent size for bear defense.

.300 Magnum: is a .30 caliber rifle cartridge (7.62x67) introduced by the Winchester Company in 1963. It's an extremely versatile and powerful cartridge that's popular among big game hunters, especially in Alaska.

.30-06: is another .30 caliber rifle cartridge (7.62x63) formerly known as the .30 Gov't '06, introduced in 1906. A favorite hunting cartridge in Alaska for smaller game, i.e., Caribou and throughout the lower 48 states.

.30-30: The .30-30 Winchester (or .30 Winchester Center Fire or WCF) was first introduced in the Winchester Company's Model 1895. It's probably the most popular deer rifle cartridge in the United States and is commonly known as the cartridge that has killed more whitetail deer than any other cartridge. It often serves as a young man's first deer rifle cartridge.

.44 Magnum: The .44 Remington Magnum is a .44 caliber (10.9x33) cartridge used in both handguns and rifles. The cartridge was developed by Elmer Keith in the mid-1950s. Smith and Wesson produced the first handgun chambered for .44 Magnum in the Model 29. It's a favorite handgun for bear defense.

.45-70: Known as the .45-70 Government or .45-70 Springfield, this rifle cartridge was originally chambered in .45 caliber sitting on 70 grains of black powder and developed, predominantly, for government service. It was developed at Springfield's Army Armory for use in the Springfield Model 1873. It's a superb choice for a bear defense rifle as well as a hunting rifle for large game such as moose and T-Rex.

.270: A rifle cartridge developed by the Winchester Repeating Arms Company in 1923. It's an excellent choice for smaller bodied big game such as Caribou, Whitetail and Mule deer.

550 cord: A lightweight nylon kernmantle cordage. It's ubiquitous in the US military. Known as 550 cord due to the tensile strength, it's known by its civilian nomenclature as para-cord. It's the cordage used as suspension lines on all US military parachutes.

A-1 Skyraider: A US ground attack aircraft developed and built by the Douglas Aircraft Corporation. It flew in service with the Navy and Air Force from 1946 to the early 1980s. A Wright R-3350-26WA Duplex-Cyclone 18-cylinder air cooled radial engine produced 2,700 hp. It's long range (1,316 miles) gave it an excellent loiter time and in conjunction with its payload capacity (over 7,000 pounds) and versatile weapons payload, it was a favorite close air support aircraft during the Vietnam War. It was the aircraft chosen to escort rescue helicopters during search and rescue missions throughout Southeast Asia. In this configuration it was known by the callsign Sandy. The A-1 was also known as the Spad.

A-7 Corsair II: A carrier-capable subsonic light attack aircraft developed and built by the Vought Aircraft Company. Developed in the late 1950s it first flew in 1965 and was introduced into the Southeast Asia theater of operations as a close air support aircraft for both the Air Force and the Navy.

Above Ground Level (AGL): The altitude of an aircraft above the terrain as opposed to sea level altitude.

A-Detachment: The A- Detachment is the smallest organizational element of the US Army's Special Forces or "Green Berets." Comprised of twelve highly trained specialist charged with a wide range of missions, including but not limited to counterinsurgency, foreign internal defense, unconventional warfare, and counterterrorism. During the Vietnam era, teams consisted of a Captain (Detachment Commander), a senior First Lieutenant (Detachment Executive Office or XO), two operations and intelligence NCO's (one serves as the "Team Sergeant"), two weapons specialists, two demolition or engineer specialists, two medics, and two communications specialists.

Army of the Republic of Vietnam (ARVN): The Army of South Vietnam, allied to the American forces.

Airborne Warning and Control System (AWACS): The E-3 Sentry is an airborne warning and control system with an integrated command and control battle management staff as well as surveillance, target detection, and tracking capabilities. The E-3 is a modified Boeing 707. Flown by the US Air Force, it's part of the Strategic capability of the US Air Force.

Cessna 150: The Cessna Aircraft Company developed the Cessna 150 in the mid and late 1950s. It's a two seat, tricycle gear general purpose, general use aviation aircraft. Many private pilots learned to fly in the 150.

Cessna 182: Developed in the late 1950s, the Cessna 182 Skylane is a four-seat, single-engine light general aviation aircraft produced by Cessna Aircraft Company.

Civil Air Patrol (CAP): The official auxiliary of the United States Air Force. The Civil Air Patrol is charged with a three-fold mission: a national Cadet Program, Aerospace education for the general public and search and rescue within the continental United States.

Civil Twilight: The period before sunrise and after sunset when the sun is approximately six degrees below the horizon.

Close Air Support (CAS): Aerial warfare actions, generally air-to-ground by military aircraft.

Colt 1911: Designated as the Colt 1911 or Colt Government it's a single-action, recoil-operated, semi-automatic pistol, chambered in .45 ACP. Developed by John Browning and used throughout the US military for decades. It was retired from regular service in the late 1980s but brought back into service by US Special Operations Forces in the Global War on Terror.

Departure Estimated Return from Overseas (DEROS): The date upon which a military member departs from an overseas assignment.

Data On Previous Engagement (DOPE): It's the gathering and collection of information of previous engagements or shots based on range firing, training, or other engagements. It's the data to input to the scope based on range to target, wind, and other considerations to make an accurate shot.

DHC-2: The De Haviland Canada DHC-2 is known as the Beaver. It's a single-engine, propeller-driven, high-wing, short takeoff and landing (STOL) aircraft manufactured by the de Haviland Canada Corporation. It's one of the best bush planes in existence. It's a common sight in the Alaskan bush.

DHC-3: The De Haviland Canada DHC-3 is known as the Otter. It's a larger, more capable version of the DHC-2 Beaver. It's a single-engine, propeller-driven, high-wing, short takeoff and landing (STOL) aircraft manufactured by the de Haviland Canada Corporation. It's one of the best bush planes in existence. It's a common sight in the Alaskan bush.

DHC-4: The De Haviland Canada DHC-4 is known as the Caribou. It's a twin-engine, propeller-driven, high-wing, short takeoff and landing (STOL) cargo aircraft.

Dustoff: The slang term for a Medical Evacuation (MEDEVAC) helicopter.

Emergency Locator Transmitter (ELT): An electronic device, installed in aircraft to "ping" a signal on 121.5 mhz frequency in the event of a crash.

Emergency Operations Center (EOC): A command-and-control element within major US military commands and bases. Staffed with a wide array of specialists, an EOC generally controls the initial actions of an emerging military crisis.

Escape and Evasion (E&E): A common term describing the military actions taken to escape from enemy captivity or evade it prior to capture. In modern military nomenclature the acronym is expanded to Survival, Evasion, Resistance, and Escape or SERE.

Flight Base Operator (FBO): An organization granted the right to provide aeronautical services at a fixed based airport.

Forward Air Controller (FAC): Guidance to close air support aircraft intended to control the right aircraft with the right ordnance on the proper target. FAC's were generally US military pilots in light aircraft who directed CAS against enemy targets.

HH-3: The Sikorsky HH-3 helicopter, known as the Jolly Green Giant, performed Combat Search and Rescue (CSAR) in Southeast Asia.

HH-53: The Sikorsky HH-53 Super Jolly Green Giant was introduced to the Southeast Asia theater of operations in 1968 as a replacement for the older and less capable HH-3.

Marlin Model 1895: The Marlin Firearms Corporation lever-action rifle produced in the late 19th century and chambered in a variety of calibers.

Murphy's Laws of Combat: Often known as simply "Murphy." The origin of this idea is highly contested but one popular origin story is connected to Captain Ed Murphy, a development engineer from Wright Field Aircraft Laboratory. It was said that "if there's any way to do it wrong, he will." And thus began the legend. There are hundreds of Murphy's Laws, and the list is continually growing. I've attached a few in the Appendix at the end of the book.

Montagnard's: The indigenous people of the Central Highlands of Vietnam. The French term describes "mountain dwellers" and is a carryover from the period of French colonialism. They were heavily recruited as allies to the US and South Vietnamese forces, although they were often marginalized due to their ethnicity by the Vietnamese. US Special Forces teams worked heavily with the Montagnard's and came to have a deep respect for their capabilities as soldiers.

North Vietnamese Army (NVA): A US and South Vietnamese term for the People's Army of Vietnam (PAVN).

O-1 Bird Dog: The military application of the Cessna 170. It's a light liaison and observation aircraft. Armed with marking rockets in wing pods, the O-1 was used throughout Southeast Asia as a forward air controller aircraft.

Officers Candidate School (OCS): One of a few commissioning sources of US military officers. OCS is offered to eligible enlisted personnel, and the curriculum prepares them for commissioning and service within the Officer Corps.

Permanent Change of Station (PCS): The event that occurs for military personnel and families every 36-48 months. PCS is the process of changing duty stations.

Piper Super Cub: A two-seat, single-engine high-wing monoplane introduced by the Piper Aircraft Corporation in the late 1940s. The PA-18 traces its lineage to the J-3 Cub. It's a mainstay aircraft in the Alaskan bush.

Poncho Liner: A lightweight, quilted, nylon blanket carried by military personnel. Also known as the "woobie", it's one piece of kit that the US military got right.

Post Exchange (PX): The general store on most Army posts. PXs often deploy to combat zones to provide personnel with basic comfort items.

Professor of Military Science (PMS): The senior military officer in a ROTC detachment. The PMS is generally a Lieutenant Colonel responsible for the training and education of officer candidates.

Remington Model 870: A pump-action shotgun manufactured by the Remington Arms Company. Equipped with a tubular magazine and side ejection port, the 870 is one of the most popular and rugged shotguns in production.

Reserve Officer's Training Corps (ROTC): One of a few commissioning sources of US military officers. ROTC detachments are assigned to many public and private universities throughout the United States. The ROTC program produces the majority of commissioned officers in the US military.

Ruger M77: A bolt action rifle developed and produced by Sturm, Ruger & Co. Designed in the late 1960s, it's chambered in a variety of calibers and models. It remains one of the most popular hunting rifles in Alaska.

Ruger Super Blackhawk: It's a six-shot, single-action revolver produced by Sturm, Ruger & Co. Produced from 1955 to present. The "Super" is a sub-model of the Blackhawk chambered in .44 magnum. It's a favorite bear protection gun in Alaska.

S-3 (Operations): Military staff are divided into functional areas and given designations. "S" designations are given to staffs at Battalion and Brigade level, "G" designations denote Division, Corps and Army level, and "J" is the Joint designation. The assigned number denotes the functional area: 1 = personnel and administration, 2 = intelligence, 3= operations, 4 = logistics. Examples: An Infantry battalion operations officer is the S-3, his section is known as the S3 section or "shop"; A Division level logistics officer is designated the G-4; A Joint Command intelligence officer is designated the J-2, and so on.

Smith and Wesson Model 29: A six-shot, double-action revolver produced by the Smith & Wesson Company. Developed in the 1950s it's manufactured in a variety of barrel lengths and finishes and two calibers (.44 Special and .44 Magnum).

T-54: A series of Soviet produced main battle tanks designed in the 1940s and fielded throughout the Soviet Army in the 1950s. As the Soviet Union improved their main battle tank design and production, it was widely exported to Soviet satellite nations in the 1960s and 70s.

Unites States Geological Service (USGS): Assigned within the Department of Interior, the USGS is the US government agency responsible for mapping and cartography.

Will Comply (WILCO): A radio communications proword. It means the recipient of the message clearly understands the message and will comply with the directives of the sender.

Winchester Model 1886: A lever-action repeating rifle designed by John Browning to handle more powerful cartridges, including the .45-70 Government.

Winchester Model 70: A bolt-action hunting rifle manufactured in a variety of barrel lengths and chambered in dozens of calibers. It's one of the best American hunting rifles in production.

Appendix

Here are some basic survival principles to consider when going into the woods. The first is the military acronym from FM 21-76 and taught for years within the military SERE community.

Size up the situation:
Consider your surroundings, weather, your physical condition (be honest – men are notorious liars in this regard, regularly overestimating their capacity). What equipment do you have, what about skills, knowledge, and mindset? Did you leave an emergency plan with someone? STOP (Stop-Think-Observe-Plan—only a soldier would put an acronym inside an acronym.)

Undue haste makes waste:
Reduce your false starts, apply a little planning before you execute, get it right the first time as much as possible, physically slow down. This can help to reduce the possibility of a mechanical injury.

Remember where you are:
Use your "mental map" if you don't have a real one. How did you get where you are? Can you confidently get back on track?

Vanquish fear and panic:
Fear is normal but must be controlled. Panic kills – so don't. Training and experience develop confidence and thereby reduce panic and fear. Remember that it can always get worse, trust me, it's true. Use your logic – not your emotions. Put your emotions in a box.

Improvise:
Think unconventionally. Inventory available resources. Consider alternatives for requirements.

Value living:
Find a reason to survive family, faith, unfinished business, meanness,

stubbornness, revenge, it doesn't make any difference but not having a reason to survive is a self-fulfilling prophecy.

<u>Act like the natives:</u>
Learn the skills of the people indigenous to your region. They had figured it out a long time ago. It wasn't a survival situation for them, it was just Tuesday. Study the local environment.

<u>Learn basic skills:</u>
Get some basic training and remember that these are perishable skills and must be regularly practiced and rehearsed.

Other survival principles:
- A person's capacity in the outdoors, specifically in a wilderness area, is a question of mindset. Thriving in an austere environment is a thinking person's endeavor. Mindset and knowledge are more critical than gear and gadgets; that isn't to say that gear isn't important, but mindset and knowledge outweigh gear. Mindset isn't just a switch to be flipped but a muscle to be exercised. Training, skill, experience, and the mastery of one's equipment can lead to a more properly aligned mindset.
- In an emergency of any type, wilderness or otherwise, mitigate the risk that will kill you first. Ask yourself: What'll kill me next? Most people have heard of the rule of threes. This is a good framework to begin to prioritize your lines of effort and priority of work. They can provide guidelines for one to think through a crisis.
  - **Three minutes without air** – this is just a reminder that you must address the elephant in the room. If you dump a canoe in whitewater, you'll drown before you get a chance to build a shelter, start a fire, establish signals, and set snares. Get out of the water first! It may be fire, the presence of an apex predator, a sinking boat, or any number of other threats; get yourself secure before you work on other priorities.
  - **Three hours without shelter** – this is the reminder to maintain a proper core body temperature. There are

three primary considerations that fall within this reminder: proper clothing, fire, and shelter. Proper clothing is the first line of defense. Don't go into the wood line unprepared for the vicissitudes of life in the open. Dress properly. Be prepared to start and maintain a fire in the conditions you'll face in your area of operations. Be able to build a shelter or carry one with you. This depends on the environment that you're operating in, but you must be able to get out of the elements. Most people who die in an outdoor situation die from exposure. Read here, hypo- or hyperthermia. They fail to maintain a proper core body temperature.

- o Three days without water – like the previous principle this is a reminder that rests on a sliding scale. If you're lost in the Arizona desert near Yuma in August, you DO NOT have three days to maintain your water intake. You have to do it sooner. Don't think that because it's cold outside you don't need to hydrate – you do. Water is life.
- o Three weeks without food – Most of us can't wrap our minds around surviving three weeks without food and we shouldn't put off caloric intake that long. This is just a reminder that it's probably not your first priority.
- When you're going outdoors, carry the proper gear that you need to thrive in your environment.
- Always leave an emergency plan with a responsible adult.

Murphy's Laws of Combat
(Just a few)

1. Friendly fire – isn't.
2. Recoilless rifles – aren't.
3. Suppressive fires – won't.
4. You aren't superman; paratroopers, Marines and fighter pilots take note.
5. A sucking chest wound is nature's way of telling you to slow down.
6. If it's stupid but works, it isn't stupid.
7. Try to look unimportant; the enemy may be low on ammo and not want to waste a bullet on you.
8. If at first you don't succeed, call in an airstrike.
9. If you're forward of your position, your artillery will fall short.
10. Never share a foxhole with anyone braver than you.
11. Never forget that your weapon was made by the lowest bidder.
12. If the attack is going really well, it's an ambush.
13. No plan ever survives first contact with the enemy.
14. The easy way is always mined.
15. Teamwork is essential; it gives the enemy other people to shoot at.
16. There's no such thing as the perfect plan.
17. There's no such thing as an atheist in a foxhole.
18. Five second fuses burn in three seconds.
19. Never draw fire; it irritates everyone around you.
20. Incoming fire has the right of way.
21. If the enemy is in range, so are you.
22. The important things are always simple; the simple things are always hard.

23. The only thing more accurate than incoming enemy fire is incoming friendly fire.
24. No combat ready unit has ever passed inspection.
25. No inspection ready unit has ever passed combat.
26. Tracers work both ways.

About the Author

Jerry A. Sayre is a retired soldier. He served in the United States Army for twenty-one years. He's also a retired minister. He's the father of four children and has twelve grandchildren.

He and Sharon, his wife of forty-one years, divide their time between a small farm in East Tennessee and their travel trailer, where they're spending their retirement seeing the country, chasing the history of the American West, and enjoying adventures in the wide open. He's a lifelong woodsman and still hunts, fishes, hikes, and canoes at every opportunity. Jerry continues to teach wilderness skills courses.

Made in United States
North Haven, CT
02 July 2025

70316135R00166